MURDER
IS
MY BUSINESS

MURDER IS MY BUSINESS

EDITED BY
MICKEY SPILLANE
AND MAX ALLAN COLLINS

A DUTTON BOOK

DUTTON
Published by the Penguin Group
Penguin Books USA Inc., 375 Hudson Street,
New York, New York 10014, U.S.A.
Penguin Books Ltd, 27 Wrights Lane,
London W8 5TZ, England
Penguin Books Australia Ltd, Ringwood,
Victoria, Australia
Penguin Books Canada Ltd, 10 Alcorn Avenue,
Toronto, Ontario, Canada M4V 3B2
Penguin Books (N.Z.) Ltd, 182–190 Wairau Road,
Auckland 10, New Zealand

Penguin Books Ltd, Registered Offices:
Harmondsworth, Middlesex, England

First published by Dutton, an imprint of Dutton Signet,
a division of Penguin Books USA Inc.
Distributed in Canada by McClelland & Stewart Inc.

First Printing, December, 1994
10 9 8 7 6 5 4 3 2 1

 REGISTERED TRADEMARK—MARCA REGISTRADA

Library of Congress Cataloging-in-Publication Data

Murder is my business / edited by Mickey Spillane and Max Allan
Collins.
p.   cm.
ISBN 0-525-93901-6
1. Detective and mystery stories, American.   I. Spillane, Mickey.
II. Collins, Max Allan.
PS648.D4M873   1994
813'.087208—dc20   94-19774
                                                         CIP

Printed in the United States of America
Set in Janson Text
Designed by Leonard Telesca

CONTENTS

·····································

INTRODUCTION
MURDER WAS HIS BUSINESS
* *
BY MAX ALLAN COLLINS

The name Mickey Spillane has become synonymous with the business of murder—fictional murder, of the best-selling variety.

While his hardcover debut, *I, the Jury* (1947), raised some critical eyebrows, it didn't set the publishing world on fire; however, the later Signet paperback edition exploded, and in the early 1950s, the six Spillane novels that followed were so popular that the first publisher of paperback originals, Gold Medal Books, was formed to provide an eager reading public with more Spillane-style fare.

Readers (to their pleasure) and critics (to their dismay) agreed that Spillane's success was due in no small part to his frank, even shocking (by early fifties standards) depictions of sex and violence. Even the acknowledged masters of hard-boiled crime fiction who preceded Spillane—Dashiell Hammett, James M. Cain, and Raymond Chandler—paled next to the literary mayhem perpetrated by the brash World War II vet Frank Morrison Spillane.

But more astute readers and critics (particularly today) acknowledge that Spillane's heady sex-and-violence cocktail was only part of his postwar appeal. A great natural storyteller and a true poet of violence, the Mick spoke to an audience that had been traumatized by a horrendous world war. Like the cheap crime films that have become canonized as film noir, the novels of Mickey Spillane—and those of a handful of his early fifties peers, including Charles Williams, Jim Thompson, and David Goodis—endure as both great yarns and vivid snapshots of an era.

While Mickey remains known primarily for his best-selling novels, his roots were in shorter fiction. As a young man he learned his craft by studying the pages of the (now) classic pulp magazine *Black Mask*, in particular the works of the man who created the private eye story, Carroll John Daly. Daly's hard-hitting, trigger-happy PI Race Williams might be Mike Hammer's father; they have much in common, although Race is rather afraid of girls . . . never a problem for Mike Hammer.

As early as high school, and through his several years of college, Spillane wrote pseudonymous tales for pulp magazines and the slicks as well. His by-line first turns up on comic book work; he was a prolific contributor to such legendary titles as *Sub-Mariner*, *Captain Marvel*, and *Batman*. Primarily, though, he worked for Marvel, where one of his chief duties was writing short stories, text pieces, that were necessary in order for the comic books to squeeze by the postal code.

Among these text-page stories, published immediately before and shortly after Spillane's World War II duty, are numerous crime tales, including private eye stories. And it was his creation of a comic book private eye character, Mike Danger, that led to a prose version ("Hammer" substituting for "Danger") when the comic book market went soft.

But Spillane's interest in, and allegiance to, the shorter fiction form have remained a constant in his career. During the fifties and early sixties, when he temporarily abandoned the novel field, Mickey was a regular contributor of short fiction to men's magazines, including *Cavalier* and *Male*. And he was frequently seen in the pages of the early fifties successor to *Black Mask*, *Manhunt*.

In fact, that late, lamented digest-size crime pulp was launched with the serialized publication of a new Spillane novel. Mickey was the hottest writer in the country at that moment, and his participation guaranteed the new magazine instant success.

But both *Black Mask* and *Manhunt* are long gone, and a sad fact of life for both writers and readers of tough mystery fiction is that there are very few places where a hard-boiled crime story can be sold or told. Chatting about this with Martin Greenberg, the "king" of the anthology field, and with Mickey Spillane himself led to the notion behind this book (and several more that will follow, all bearing the Spillane imprimatur).

We decided to invite some of today's top writers of crime and mystery fiction, as well as a handful of talented newcomers, to contribute to a series of anthologies, each of which will have a specific theme. This is the first of those anthologies, and its theme is murder for hire: contract killers, their victims, and their employers.

In these pages you will encounter the hit man, at times as the virtual "hero" of the tale. These include Barry N. Malzberg's chilling portrait of political assassination "Improvident Excess"; Edward Wellen's darkly comic "A Nice Save," providing a quick view of a hit man's worldview; and Lawrence Block's stunning novella "Keller on Horseback," an understated look at the life's work of a melancholy, good-natured, very professional killer. My series character, Quarry, veteran of five novels, makes a rare short story appearance in "Guest Services"; Quarry has retired from the killing business but, as you will see, occasionally keeps his hand in.

There are heroes here, too, and not antiheroes either. Some of them are also veterans of popular novel series, among them Andrew Greeley's Father Blackie Ryan, in the fast, clever "The Bishop and the Hit Man"; Wayne D. Dundee's midwestern private detective Joe Hannibal, in the wild, Spillane-tough "Hitback"; and Warren Murphy's Trace, in "Without a Trace," a light slice of PI wry.

Darker views of professional murder are presented in Teri White's "Runner and the Deathbringer," an oddly touching tale about two lost souls in a vaguely futuristic world of street gangs and political assassins; Carolyn Wheat's gritty, twisting "Undercover"; and Stephen Mertz's "The King of Horror," a devastating portrait of a once-talented hack writer's descent into self-delusion. Typical of Ed Gorman, a master short story writer, "Surrogate" provides both compassion and coldness, poetry and brutality in its look at the tragic consequences of young crime.

But there is humor here, too: John Lutz, another master of the short form, serves up his comic tale "With Anchovies," while policeman-novelist Paul Bishop keeps us smiling and titillated with his surprising tale of a sexy female hit man, "The Man Who Shot Trinity Valance."

Two young writers are making their national fiction debuts here: Lynn F. Myers, Jr., a scholar of the tough detective story (as his regular column in *Mystery Scene Magazine* reveals), delivers a hard-edged, lightning-fast period crime tale that is perhaps the most overtly Spillane-influenced in this book; and Daniel Helpingstine, whose award-winning stories at the Mississippi Valley Writers Conference attracted my attention, delivers a dual character study with many suspenseful moments.

The final yarn in this book isn't a short story; it's a full-length novel. *Everybody's Watching Me* is vintage Spillane—Spillane at the peak of his popularity, Spillane at the top of his form. One of his later novels (which I will not mention, because doing so might spoil a reader's fun) was somewhat influenced by this earlier tale, and perhaps that's why Mickey waited so long before allowing it to be collected.

The novel was written for *Collier's*; but that famed slick magazine went out of business before the serial could be published, and *Manhunt* became the beneficiary.

There could be no better way to round out this fine collection of murder for hire stories than to present a full-length hard-as-nails 1953 Mickey Spillane novel.

Like the other writers in this collection, I'm proud to have a story in a book that bears the name of this living legend of the mystery field. My only fear is what Mickey will say and do to me when he reads the preceding sentence.

THE BISHOP AND THE HIT MAN

A BLACKIE RYAN STORY

ANDREW GREELEY

"I've put down thirty-two men, Father," he told me. "I could give you all their names . . ."

"That won't be necessary," I assured him.

I have often argued that if the rule of celibacy is to be lifted partially for Catholic priests but only for a certain period each week, Sunday night would be the appropriate time. In a dark and lonely rectory, quiet for the only night of the week, the priest who mans the fort feels that he is isolated from the human condition. This is especially true if the rectory is a monumental monstrosity like that of Holy Name Cathedral, a place which at the best of times is filled with silent emanations from the past and an occasional spirit of a departed bishop—or even Cardinal—is said to walk the corridors.

I've never seen one such, however, being the most empirical and pragmatic of men.

It is perhaps an appropriate time and place to open the door at 720 North Wabash in the so-called Windy City (Richard M. Daley, mayor, and Michael Jordan, owner) and encounter a self-professed hit man.

"I don't know," he continued. "Some of them probably deserved it. But I never asked about that. Like in any line of work, you do what you're told and don't ask questions. It's my line of work, Father."

"Indeed."

He talked like a character in one of the many films about the Outfit (as we call it in Chicago). However he did not look like Robert De Niro or any of the other stars who appear in such violent films. He was trim, of medium height, and dressed in a conservative three-piece charcoal gray suit (with a faint hint of a line in its weave). His thin brown hair receded only marginally from an utterly unremarkable face, and his skin was pale and bland. Only his hard blue eyes, innocent of emotion or mercy, suggested that he might be a psychopath.

"See this." He opened his expensive attaché case and revealed what looked like a toy weapon. "This is a twenty-five-millimeter automatic. Small, isn't it? Looks like a toy, huh? I don't carve any notches in, but I've put down ten men with it."

"Remarkable."

Who would put out a contract on an inoffensive little priest? I wondered.

"It's not loaded." He fitted an instrument which, from frequent attendance at the cinema, I identified as a silencer. "Some night soon I'm going to walk up behind Mr. Richard Powers as he's taking his walk down East Lake Shore Drive, confident that nothing can happen in that busy and affluent street, yell, 'Hey, Dick,' and put a bullet right between his eyes. No noise, no blood, no mess, and he's facing God."

"Astonishing."

He unfastened the silencer and put the gun away. My guardian angel and I began to breathe again.

"This is all under the seal of confession, isn't it?"

"As you wished."

When I had ushered him into the "counseling room" on the first floor of the Cathedral rectory and hung up his saturated raincoat, he told me that he wanted to go to confession, a wish expressed less frequently now than it used to be because Catholics are freer from compulsions about minor matters ("I missed Mass on Sunday, but I was sick") than they used to be.

Multiple homicide was not, however, a minor matter.

"I'm the best there is in the country," my guest insisted. "No one is as neat or as professional as I am. Not a single arrest. The cops don't know who I am. Or where I live. Even my clients don't know who I am. All the contact is indirect. My family and my neighbors think I have a small business, which I do as a cover. But this is my real line of work."

"Ah."

"I'm known only by my nickname—the Pro. Neat, isn't it?"

"Indeed."

"I don't do too many jobs anymore, Father. One, two a year, and that's all. I get two hundred big ones for each job, half on agreement, half on fulfillment. They don't want to pay that kind of money, they don't ask for the Pro, huh? A man needs that kind of money these days to put his kids through college, know what I mean?"

"A major expense."

"All my kids are in Catholic schools, Father. A boy in college, two high school kids, and one little doll that just made her First Communion. I'm raising them all to be good Catholics, Father."

"Admirable."

"I pray to God every night that they'll never find out what their daddy really does for a living."

Dickie Powers is not one of my favorite people. He is, not to put too fine an edge on things, to the right of Neil of the Nine Hostages, both politically and ecclesiastically. He presumes that because he's a highly successful developer (though he owns a lot of vacant land in our current recessionary times), he would more ably run the Archdiocese of Chicago than Sean Cardinal Cronin, presently, by the Grace of God and the impatient toleration of the Apostolic See, Archbishop of Chicago. Milord Cronin has a long record of more than holding his own against rich and conservative Catholics. However, Dick Powers also thinks that he knows more about how the Cathedral parish ought to be run—down to such tiny details as the Sunday Mass schedule—than the inoffensive and ineffectual little priest who actually does run it. And proposes to continue to run it. Democratically, of course.

His basic strategy for dealing with the problems the Church faces today is to purify it of all who may disagree with certain of its teachings.

"Throw out everyone who won't accept the birth control teaching! Get rid of them all! They're all going to hell anyway! We don't need them and don't want them!"

My problem with such a strategy is not merely that it would empty the Cathedral and that there would be no income to pay the heat and light bills and keep the schools (of which we have two) open. My problem is that even if we tried it, the laity would not leave. Despite Dickie Powers, we no longer have an Inquisition available to turn the recalcitrant over to the secular arm for suitable disposal.

I would not go so far as one of my young colleagues who, with lamentable lack of charity, remarked at the table the other night, "Dickie Powers is one of the great assholes of the Western world."

I did not dispute the point, however.

"I don't know what this Powers guy did to offend my clients . . . you can guess who they are, Father. Probably welched on a deal. My clients don't like welchers. A deal is a deal, and if they let one guy get away welching, then everyone would, isn't that so?"

"Arguably."

Recently Dickie had done something extraordinary which could have increased the number of people who disliked him. He had taken unto himself a new wife, twenty-five years younger than his fifty-five years, his first wife having finally escaped him to her eternal reward—helped by acute cirrhosis of the liver, in turn the result of, among other things, chronic alcoholism.

"Being married to Dickie," Milord Cronin had remarked, again with scandalous lack of charity, "would drive anyone to drink."

I may have added, "And a new wife would drive to the creature those who have expectations of inheritance at the time of his departure for whatever reward God may be planning for him."

To make matters worse for his allies on the Catholic right, Regina, Dickie's intended young woman (as far as I can see quiet, presentable, and intelligent and perhaps capable of taming Dickie), not only was not of the household of the faith but had been married before—at twenty for a brief period.

"I don't believe in those annulment things," Dickie had bellowed at me. "So don't pull that stuff. Her first husband was a bastard. I want a church wedding just like my first marriage."

Dickie was a big, strong, well-preserved man, handsome in a rugged way with a square blunt face (usually red with anger) and thick iron gray hair. His bride-to-be watched him intently, not with fear but with admiration.

I explained that there would be certain difficulties since both his bride-to-be and her first husband were baptized Christians. There were some steps we might take—

"I don't want to take any steps," he had shouted. "I have been a good Catholic all my life, and I demand to be married in this Church, by Father Martin, two weeks from today."

I don't make the current marriage rules for the Catholic Church, and I don't necessarily like them. But no way I was going to apply them to everyone else but Dickie Powers, a loudmouth shanty Irishman if I ever met one.

Nor, as far as I could see, would Father Martin, the head of a right-wing "secular institute," dare to violate publicly the Vatican's rules on such matters.

During the shouting match in my office (well, he was shouting anyway), I felt sorry for Regina, who knew nothing of our Church, was not seeing us at our best, and seemed astonished by the anger of her groom. I felt less sympathy with the Powers offspring, who had been brought along to the rectory for reasons that escaped me. Rick and Melissa—the sole issues of the marriage—smirked through the whole session, delighted at the spoke I had thrown into the wheel of their father's marriage bandwagon and triumphant over their prospective stepmother, to whom they blatantly refused to speak.

Both children were economically useless. Rick, an overweight, long-haired snob, who wanted passionately to produce "important" films, ran an "off-Loop" theater group which performed, with notable lack of critical or financial success, obscure modern plays, sometimes made more obscure because they were done in the original language—like Hungarian. Melissa, a brittle blonde, owned a boutique on Oak Street which sold, or rather did not sell, women's apparel that has been described to me by my nieces as "like totally *funky*, you know."

In that context the adjective was not spoken in admiration.

While he disapproved of the occupations of both his children and of their swinging-singles lifestyles, Dickie resolutely funded their efforts and kept from them not only starvation but the necessity of purchasing cheap liquor.

So Dickie and Regina were married in a civil ceremony by an elderly judge who was a friend of his. Most of the invited guests stayed away from the wedding, less for religious reasons than because they didn't like Dickie.

In addition to the union workers, who hated Dickie for hiring scabs, and the other developers, who resented his bidding tactics, and, according to my strange penitent, the Boys Out on the West Side, there were other actors who would benefit from his death before he changed his will to favor the new wife: Rick, Melissa, and Father Martin's happy little band of brothers, who were now, in alleged obedience to St. Paul and in imitation of the Amish, ostentatiously shunning their greatest benefactor.

"I've got cold feet for the first time in my life, Father," the hit man continued, his face narrowing into an anxious frown. "This is a tricky one. He'll probably have his own bodyguards, and there'll be cops, too. I've handled tough ones before, but this will be one of the toughest. What if they get me? What if I don't make it home?"

"Your children will know you are a criminal?"

"Nah. No one will link the hit man with me. I mean, they'll find out my real identity from my prints. But back home I'm someone else and no one has my prints." Tears appeared in his eyes. "As far as the wife and kids are concerned, I'll vanish from the face of the earth."

"Ah."

"No, what I'm scared about is God." He rubbed his hands together nervously. "God is pretty mad at me these days. He's not gonna like to see me when I show up. I don't figure I can cop a plea with him. It'll be curtains for me."

"You fear eternal damnation?"

"What else will I get? And no time off for good behavior either. I mean, I never really thought about dying before. I figured that I'd get a chance on my deathbed, and that way I'd make it. But what if I'm killed while I'm trying to hit someone else? Then it's the pit of hell for me, isn't it?"

I personally hold with the late Cardinal von Baltassar that salvation for everyone is not inconsistent with the Catholic tradition —and himself a favorite of the Pope at that. But I was not about to explain that position just at the moment.

"God's love is without limit," I said, "its fullness beyond our wildest imagination. One always gets second chances, opportunities to turn away from what separates us from God and to begin our life again."

"Yeah, Father"—he shook his head sadly—"but not professional killers."

"Yes, even mass murderers. Compared with some political leaders I might mention, you're small time."

"You mean, I might still make it?"

"Precisely."

"But what if I'm killed during the hit?"

"Cancel the hit, return the down payment, live off the income from your other business."

"My clients wouldn't like it, Father."

"I thought they couldn't find you."

"I'm a pro, Father. I do my work. I keep my promises. Besides, I need the money. I've got family expenses. I can't give it back. It costs a hell of a lot of money to put four kids through college."

"Nonetheless, you know you should get out of your line of work."

"I know that, Father. I know it. This will be the last one, I promise. Can you give me absolution now?"

"How can I invoke God's love to reconcile you with God's people when you tell me that you are going forth to kill someone?"

"Maybe he deserves to die."

"We all do, but in God's time."

"Yeah . . . but a job is a job. I'm a professional, Father. That's why they call me the Pro."

"You believe that God will accept that argument?"

Tears were pouring down his face. "Gee, how could He? I'm caught. Damned no matter what I do . . . You sure you can't give me absolution so I could receive Holy Communion tomorrow?"

I gave up on the new-fashioned theology of reconciliation and stated my position in old-Church terms: "I can't absolve you unless you have a firm purpose of amendment."

"Yeah, I have that, too."

"Not if you intend to kill someone."

"I don't want to kill him. I *have* to kill him. Damn it, Father, don't you understand that?"

"I'm afraid I don't. There is no excuse for murder, and you know that well."

"Yeah, Father, I guess I do."

He continued to weep. "Jeez, what would my ma say if she knew up in heaven?"

"Pretty much what I'm saying. Take this chance to change your life."

"It's too late." He stood up. "I'm damned already. Thanks for listening, Father. I gotta be going. Pray for me."

He extended his hand and shook mine firmly.

"Come back again if you want to," I said lamely.

What the hell do you say in such circumstances?

"You're sure this is under the seal of confession? You can't tell anyone?"

"Not a soul."

"Good-bye, Father," he said to me at the door. "You've been a big help. Remember to pray for me."

"I will certainly do that. Remember, it's never too late to begin again."

"Not for me," he said, and disappeared into the rain and the darkness.

I returned to my room, glanced briefly at the posters of the three Johns of my young adulthood—Pope, President, and quarterback of the Baltimore Colts—poured myself a generous amount of Jameson's twelve-year special reserve to calm my nerves, and sat back on my easy chair to think.

I thought for a long time.

The doorbell rang again. The hit man again.

"Nah, Father." He stood in the rain, water pouring off his anguished face. "Forget about that seal of confession thing. You can tell them that there's a contract out on Richard Powers and there's a professional hit man in town to do the job. Maybe that will help me with God."

Before I had time to challenge his absurd reasoning, he had faded back into the watery darkness.

Upon return to my study, I found that the poltergeist that shares my quarters, had, as is his custom when I leave for a few minutes, finished my drink. I was constrained to fill my Waterford tumbler again.

Once more I thought for a long time.

Then I dialed Captain John Culhane of the Chicago Police Department, commander of Area Six Detectives, a smart and honest cop, at his private home phone.

"Culhane."

"Father Ryan, John."

"Yeah, what's up, Bishop?"

"Have there been any threats against the life of a certain Richard Patrick Powers lately?"

"How lately?"

"Recent weeks."

"Only four or five, the usual number. Lot of people hate tricky Dickie."

"So I've been led to believe. Any rumors of his being in trouble with the Boys Out on the West Side?"

"He's been in trouble with them for years. They're scared of him."

"Another threat was called to my attention tonight, purporting to be serious."

"Yeah, well, he's got his own bodyguards. Doesn't want us around because he says we're all crooks. I'll tell him about it and offer some police protection. I suspect he'll laugh in my face. Should I say the Outfit is involved?"

"You might mention that."

My obligations fulfilled, I retired for the night and slept peacefully.

After the morning Eucharist (what we now call the mass when we remember to do so) and breakfast, I made a phone call to an acquaintance who is what is known as a "friend of friends." I wanted some information on two questions. He was able to answer them both, as I thought he would, without consulting those friends.

John Culhane called me later in the morning, just as I returned from the grammar school and the eighth graders whom I enjoy greatly. But then I'm not their parent.

"Like I said, Bishop, Dickie Powers laughed in my face. Then, get this, he called back to apologize because his new wife made him. So it ends up with him saying thanks but no, thanks. She may be his salvation."

"Arguably. God usually knows what She is doing."

Two weeks passed, and there was no hit on Dickie Powers.

Then one evening, after I had listened to a husband and wife who once had been deeply in love spew hate at each other, John Culhane was on the phone.

"It went down tonight, Bishop. Dickie Powers. Classic mob hit. Dickie's walking down East Lake Shore Drive with his wife at night, his bodyguards a few yards behind him. A man with a turned-up coat collar comes out from beneath one of those canopies in front of the buildings on the street, calls, 'Dick,' softly, and puts him down with a twenty-two with a silencer. He jumps into a car that pulls up and is gone before the bodyguards see Dickie slump to the ground."

"Dead?"

"No, the hit man blows it. A bullet in the lung, but he's going to make it, I think. He's on his way to Northwestern."

"Lung?"

"Yeah, I know. They usually go for the head. Maybe this guy was going for the heart."

"Or can't shoot straight. I'm on my way to the hospital."

The Hit Man Who Couldn't Shoot Straight, not bad as a title for a film.

In the emergency room Dickie Powers was conscious when I administered the Sacrament of the Sick to him. His wife, her face stained with tears, clung to his hand and answered "amen" with him to the prayers, though there was some confusion with the doxology at the end of the Lord's Prayer.

"Thanks for coming, Father Blackie. I'm through being a bastard. It'll be tough, but I'm going to change my life."

"He means it," Regina said firmly. "He really does."

"I'll try," he whispered, "but you gotta help me."

"Count on that," she said firmly. "And thank you, Bishop. Perhaps I could come over to talk to you in a couple of days."

"Surely." I smiled benignly, figuring that once again Herself had called me in to straighten out the minor messes after She had accomplished Her major goals.

Maybe, just maybe it was not too late for Dickie Powers to undergo a metanoia.

John Culhane, trim and fit, as always, silver blue eyes twinkling behind his glasses, met me in the corridor.

"What do you think, Bishop?"

"If I were in your position, Commander, I would arrest Rick Powers immediately and charge him with the attempted murder of his father. I believe that lacking willpower to match his cleverness, he will break down and confess at once."

So it went down.

"You had it right, Bishop," he told me while I demolished my pancakes and bacon at the cathedral breakfast table the next morning. "He broke down immediately. Not much guts there."

"Very little, I fear."

"How did you know?"

"I had a visit a couple of Sunday nights ago from a purported professional hit man, who said he was known as the Pro. He told me under the seal of confession that he had killed thirty-two men and that there was a contract to make Dickie Powers number thirty-three. He went through considerable and, on the whole, credible agonizing about the state of his soul, his relationship with God, and his eternal fate, then departed, having argued that his need for money and his obligation to honor his contract forced him to continue with the hit.

"I was intrigued that he would tell me the name of the intended victim. There seemed to be no need to do that. Then he came back a half hour later and released me from the seal on the grounds that maybe God would be more sympathetic with him if he gave Powers a fighting chance by letting him know there was a mob hit man in town.

"That was clearly nonsense. In his first manifestation the hit man did not want to die because of his wife and family. In the second he was putting his life at enhanced risk for no obvious purpose. The devout Catholic he pretended to be would know that from God's point of view, murder is murder whether you put yourself at risk or not.

"The next morning I called a certain source and asked him two questions. He gave me the answers I expected.

"Patently I had been played for the fool by a very clever actor. I was supposed to put out the word that there was a contract on Dickie. Then, when a few weeks had passed and the hit finally went down in Outfit fashion, we were all supposed to figure the hit was a fulfillment of the contract. Rick hired a good actor—probably from out of town—who carried off the scenario to fit his script.

"The scheme was clearly designed to divert suspicion from him. I doubt that it would have worked in any case. But he failed to carry out his part of the scenario when his hand wavered at the end and he didn't kill his father. Hit men may have occasional guilt feelings, but they shoot straight.

"Which turns out to be fortunate for the hit man who couldn't shoot straight. The charge against him will only be attempted murder. When he comes out of prison, I presume he will continue to aspire to make films. Perhaps he will make one about life in prison.

Perhaps then his creativity at plot construction may be of some use to him."

"He wanted the money so he could be a film producer," John told me. "He even had a script for a film. He had almost talked his father into financing it. When the old man met Regina, he changed his mind. With Regina in charge, Rick saw his hopes go up in smoke."

"The actor recited his lines well, but finally the script was inadequate and the direction less than convincing," I said, trying to sound like my good friend Roger Ebert. "One and a half stars."

"What were the two questions you asked your source?" The commander rose to leave.

"The first was whether there was a hit man named the Pro. My source, who would know, said he had never heard of him. The second was whether two hundred big ones were out of line for a hit. He whistled and said he had never heard of anything like that. If Rick Powers's script when he emerges from jail is truly about prison life, presumably he will have, courtesy of the state of Illinois, done better research than he did for this script."

THE MAN WHO SHOT TRINITY VALANCE

PAUL BISHOP

Trinity Valance was a master assassin, one of the best in the game. The word on the street, for those who concerned themselves with such things, was that her prowess was second only to that of the enigma known as Simon.

Ever since the thrilling rush of completing her first crude hit, Trinity knew that she had found her true calling. She adopted the cover name of Starlight, and as her reputation grew, it rapidly became clear that killing was something at which she excelled. But for Trinity excelling wasn't good enough. She had to be the best.

To this end, Simon became an obsession with her.

Twice the two assassins had crossed swords while competing for the same open contract. And twice Simon had snatched the kill from directly in front of Trinity's proverbial gunsights. Even in her anger Trinity sensed that Simon had been playing cat and mouse with her, showing his disdain for her techniques of killing from a distance—through the use of booby traps—while he killed up close and personally—personally enough to feel his victim's fading heartbeat.

But while Simon's figurative laughter taunted Trinity, his true identity eluded her.

Trinity took pride in achieving letter-perfect executions with a trademark touch of flair or panache. She had developed a delicious knack for choosing an intriguing location, or a difficult time when the victim was surrounded by a crowd, or a situation where both the trigger and the mark would be on the move when the hit went down, or anything else that would add to the challenge and heighten the rush.

However, even though she planned each of her hits down to the finest detail, Trinity still felt that Simon was always a step ahead of her, mocking her, constantly letting her know that she wasn't quite good enough to be the best, to be considered numero uno.

As Trinity soaked in the bathtub, hot water channeled a thin, sensual canal between the swells of full breasts turned lobster red by the heat. Tendrils of blond hair, having rebelled at being confined in a bun on the top of her head, hung limply with the steam rising off the water.

Running a soft sponge down her body, she glanced up at the eight-by-ten glossy taped to the fogged bathroom mirror. Tonight, she thought, tonight the kill would be different. Tonight she would be inside the kill zone, and all of her senses would be alive with the thrill.

But the biggest rush of all tonight would come in her snatching the mantle of superiority from Simon's goading shoulders.

Trinity had accepted this new assignment immediately upon the successful completion of her last score. Normally she would have taken a break before making her next move, but this time she had been instantly infatuated by the face of her target. It was as if there already existed a link between the executioner and her intended victim, a link that ran beyond mere fate and into the sensual.

The features in the photo were hollowed almost to the point of being considered gaunt. The sharp cheekbones and neatly clipped beard served only to emphasize the pointed chin and cadaverous cheeks. The eyes, however, that peered out from below heavy brows seemed to hold a Santa Claus twinkle that was immediately betrayed by the cruel line of the lips. Trinity considered that the sparkle in the eyes was really nothing more than a trick of the photographer's flash, whereas the draw of the lips perhaps exposed a true glimpse of the inner man.

Whenever she looked up at the photo, Trinity felt the butterflies of anticipation change their direction of flight as they fluttered through her stomach. For the first time a contract was becoming very personal, touching her for some reason at the core of her sexuality. She longed for the kill, lusted for the sexual release of it, and knew that this time she needed to be close enough to touch, smell, and taste the target, to feel the tingle in her loins when she pulled the trigger.

In the bath her fingers were drawn inexorably downward across her abdomen as she closed her eyes and opened her mind to the fantasy.

Professor Royce Kilpatrick rested his large-boned hands on the padded steering wheel as he guided the snowy white Lincoln Town Car through the heat of the desert that was Las Vegas. He had always admired his hands, and he stared at them now as he drove, drawing comfort from their perfection. The tendons and veins that ran across their backs looked almost sculpted, and his long fingers had character etched into each individual knuckle and smoothly polished fingernail.

He knew that in the Old West hands like his would have been referred to as gambler's hands: hands best suited to dealing or double dealing cards, shuffling, cutting, nimbly and invisibly snatching cards from the bottom, middle, or top of the deck, hands that could make you rich or make you dead, with either option being better than poor. Royce cherished that image because he was by nature a gambler and cards were his natural vice.

He took one of his long-fingered hands off the steering wheel to smooth his beard across hollowed cheeks. His job as a professor of English at the University of Nevada Las Vegas didn't pay nearly enough to cover the style of living that he strove to maintain. Items like the leased Town Car he was driving and the expensive but out-of-date clothes covering his body did not come cheaply, and they were well beyond his professor's salary. Still, there were other ways to make money.

Recently, however, his losses had been higher at the gambling tables than usual. His touch for the cards seemed to have deserted him. He knew it would only be a little while before he managed to get back on track again, but until then he knew he had to keep hustling, not just with cards but with the dice, the sports books, the ponies, or even how hot the temperature would be the next day. Experience had taught him that if he could just get enough balls up in the air, something would come through. He secretly loved the rush he got from it all. Anything that smacked of a game of chance pumped his blood like a fire hose turned on full blast.

He'd been in gambling trouble like this once before—way in over his head, watching out for leg breakers at every turn, living life on the cutting edge of the envelope—but that time he'd scammed his way to safety by riding a fixed horse race that gave the bookies a bath and had given him enough ready cash to pay off his markers, renew his lifestyle, and begin to work his way back into the hole again.

Royce had been one of the small fish in that scam, a bottom feeder who sucked up a diamond by pure luck, and as such he'd been ignored by the heavy mob that were sent after the players who pulled the coup. Royce figured it was because he was a sharp operator. The fact was that the big boys knew he'd be back. There was no way somebody like Royce stayed away. And there was no way he'd get away again.

If he'd been honest with himself, delving beyond the arrogant facade of education that he used to keep his students in line, Royce would have realized that this latest streak of bad luck was taking him down a long tunnel where the light at the end was nothing more than an onrushing train.

Every once in a while a worry would sneak into his conscious mind, but it was more a worry about finding a casino that would still let him play than about the markers that were piling up like a child's block tower. If the thought of how much he owed ever battled through his defenses long enough to be recognized, he shoved it casually aside. The big boys didn't kill anyone over being in debt. They wouldn't kill the golden goose. If he were dead, how the hell would they ever get their money? How the hell would he ever get even again?

Nah, the big boys wouldn't kill you for just being in debt.

Would they?

The first time Royce saw the intriguing blonde in the hot red convertible was in his rearview mirror as she roared up behind his cruising Town Car entering the outskirts of Las Vegas. The red convertible pulled to the left and blasted past in a flash of color. All Royce could see of the blonde was a mass of flying hair and a glimpse of a red choker around a long, elegant neck. Watching her, Royce felt primal male instincts move within him, as if he were an old lion intrigued by a lioness from another pride.

Off the highway and driving along the Strip heading for downtown, he saw the blonde again. There were faster ways to get to the downtown area of Vegas, but Royce enjoyed driving along the Strip with its crush of tourists and its flashing lights coming to life in the early-evening dusk. The Strip never failed to energize him, to build up his anticipation for the evening ahead, an effect like that of a lover's foreplay.

Stopped behind the limit line at a traffic light, Royce heard an engine revving quietly next to him. Looking over, he was surprised to see the blonde in the red convertible who had blown past him as they came into town.

In profile, without her hair blowing in the wind, he could see that she was cast from the mold of the classic beauties. This time he could see that the bloodred choker matched the color of both her lipstick and her perfect fingernails, which tapped a beat across the convertible's black steering wheel. Even in the deepening dusk it was easy to see that the color perfectly offset the blonde's pale, flawless skin.

As if she knew Royce was staring at her, the blonde turned her eyes toward him, smiled briefly in acknowledgment of her own beauty, and then left him standing flatly at the light as she accelerated away. A horn sounding from behind him brought Royce back to reality, and he fumbled to pull away from the light himself.

The evening did not start out well for Royce. The first two casinos he entered had security moving immediately. Royce knew all about the overhead cameras and other techniques used by the casinos to keep undesirables at a distance and to make sure that the majority of the chips stayed on the right side of the table.

In the Empress Royce was frozen out immediately at the cashier's window when he tried to exchange a chunk of ready cash he'd picked up earlier in the day from a hot tip on a horse in the fourth at Hollywood Park. He had a cash-and-carry deal with the bookie he'd used for the bet, and it was one of the few resources he hadn't tapped out.

Now, at the Empress cashier's window, he was approached by the floor manager, who told him he would have to make a payment on his credit line before he would be allowed to play further. The cash burning a hole in Royce's pocket wouldn't go very far if he tried paying off debts at this point. He had to parlay it, make it into a sizable chunk before he paid off on past miscalculations. And to do that, he had to get on to the tables.

At the Golden Nugget Royce got as far as sitting down at the blackjack table before trouble brewed. He was three hands into the shoe—two wins and a loss—when he saw Benny Harrington moving toward him. Royce felt a stab of panic lance through his chest. If ex-Mr. Universe Benny Harrington was around, then his twin brother, Billy Harrington, also an ex-Mr. Universe, couldn't be far behind.

Benny and Billy were a tag team of leg breakers. They enjoyed their work. For them a gambler past his credit limit was a rawhide chew bone to be abused by two bull mastiffs in a tug-of-war. Royce scooped his chips from the table and fled. It wasn't cool, but it was smart.

There was something more to the unpleasant start to the evening, however. Ever since the blonde had roared away from him at the traffic light on the Strip, Royce had found thoughts of her popping in and out of his mind. Royce never had much trouble seducing women, as several of the female staff and female student body at the university could attest; it was just that sex never did as much for him as gambling. For some reason, though, the brief glimpses he'd had of the blonde in the red convertible had set his hormones racing. As a result, the unrequited sexual lust was taking the luster off the usually arousing prospect of the slap of the cards.

Royce managed to get into a poker game in the Pacifica, but he soon ran through the majority of his collateral and was forced to withdraw when no credit was forthcoming.

Making his way back to the center of the Strip, he entered the Citadel casino. He hadn't been in the Citadel for a while and hoped that he might find a friendlier reception there. He decided to try his luck and approached the cashier's window to see about extending his credit line.

"No problem," said the clerk, after consulting her computer screen.

Surprised, Royce quickly drew out a thousand dollars in chips before the clerk changed her mind or realized the computer had made a mistake. With a bounce in his step and an immediately growing confidence, he made his way to the playing floor.

And then he saw her.

A brief flash of bloodred around a long, pale neck.

He brought his attention back to the craps table and saw the blonde from the red convertible as she placed a stack of chips on the green baize. The shooter fired out the dice to the admiration of the small crowd, which "ooohed" and "ahhhed" over the result. The blonde was cool as the stickman pushed a stack of chips in her direction.

Royce felt a stirring as he took in the blonde's complete package: white sequined dress over red seamed hose and bloodred high heels. She was broader through the shoulders than most women, as if she had been a competitive swimmer at some time, but slim and flat through the hips. She was tall, just below six feet, and her legs seemed to go on forever.

As he watched the blonde, Royce's pulse rate increased in anticipation. Never one to turn down a long-odds proposition, he made his way over to the table and into an open position next to the blonde. She looked at him and smiled. It wasn't a dazzler, full of perfectly capped teeth and Pepsodent, but it was more of a seduction, a mocking acceptance of Royce's motives for standing where he did.

"Hello," he said, in response to her look.

The blonde nodded casually and returned her attention to the table. She took several chips from the stack in front of her and placed them on the baize. Without hesitating, Royce placed his chips next to hers.

Even before the shooter rolled the dice, Royce felt his luck click back into place. It was almost a physical sensation, a trilling of the nerve endings. The dice tumbled and bounced, but Royce didn't even bother to watch them. He knew he was going to turn up a winner. And indeed, he did.

Double sixes, boxcars, showed their faces when the dice came to rest, and there were Royce's chips sitting sweetly on the number 12 next to the blonde's.

As their winnings were pushed across the table, the blonde looked at Royce again. "It appears as if I'm good luck for you," she said.

"It certainly does," he replied.

The blonde extended her right hand. "Trinity Valance," she said, introducing herself.

Royce took her hand. Like the blonde's disposition, it was cool and dry, her fingers lingering in his grasp for the extra second that determines the difference between friendly and sensuous. "Royce Kilpatrick," he said.

"And a fine Irish name it is, too," said Trinity. Her voice was throaty with promise, the sound of silk sliding down a willing thigh.

Royce laughed. "And your name?" he asked. "Any relation to Liberty Valance?"

"Let's put it this way," Trinity said, her heart pounding at being this close to her quarry. "The name of John Wayne is never mentioned at any of my family reunions." She smiled, and this time it was a dazzler.

This is it. The thought raced silently through Royce's mind and rapidly became a belief. Lucky streak city.

The rest of the evening and night passed in a whirlwind. There was no game that could not be bowed before the combination of Royce's skill and Trinity's luck. They laughed, touched, and gathered in their chips: intimate strangers riding a bullet train from which there was no getting off.

Trinity was thrilling to the sensations of being so close to a man she was about to kill. She had known of Royce's gambling problems and had arranged on her own account for the extension of credit to him at the Citadel. She was extremely pleased with the way she had picked Royce up while leaving him with the feeling that he was the one doing the picking.

The cat and mouse overtones of the whole hit appealed to her, making her feel vibrant and sexy. For her, death had become so close to sex in so many ways that she understood why the French referred to orgasm as "the little death."

From the gaming tables Trinity deftly moved Royce away and into a darkened lounge in one corner of the vast casino. It was just after midnight, and the room was populated by couples swaying to a live samba beat across the dance floor.

Royce knew he was being led but was loving every second of it. Under normal conditions he would have stayed at the tables as long as he was winning, a slave to the drug of gambling that always promised the next score would be the big one, the one that would give you enough "screw you" money to walk away for good. But nobody ever did, because there was not enough "screw you" money in the world to keep a true addict away from the rush of the risk.

Royce also knew, however, that the current circumstances weren't normal. Trinity Valance was a wild card that could make every hand a winner, and her spell was stronger than that of any game of chance. Somehow she had turned up in the hand he'd been dealt, and Royce could do nothing but play her out.

Moving into his arms, Trinity guided Royce out onto the dance floor. The beat had become slow and sultry, the lighting a subdued hue of blue tinged with red edges. The combo on the small stage was unknowingly caught up in Trinity's seduction.

As she leaned against the wiry muscles of the body next to her, Trinity's breath took on a ragged edge, and she truly realized for the first time why Simon had always laughed at her. He had always known the intensity of life that came from making death personal, the power of being right there next to the target and knowing that you could snatch his very breath away any second you desired.

Trinity leaned hard into Royce, her lips next to his ear. She nipped his earlobe hard with her small white teeth, and when he didn't pull away, she whispered, "I have a room upstairs."

He squeezed her tightly, and by mutual consent they moved off the dance floor, out of the lounge, and toward the elevators. Alone, inside the small boxlike projectile, Trinity wrapped herself around Royce. Their mouths met, lips full and open, tongues intertwining and darting away as if they were birds executing a mating ritual. Royce's hands moved up to cup Trinity's braless breasts. Her nipples were already as hard as nailheads, and she moaned through their kiss.

They broke their clinch as the elevator doors opened and moved with the speed of desire down the long corridor to Trinity's room. She fumbled to unlock the door as Royce ran his hands all over her from behind, biting at her neck and eliciting a jealous "Disgusting!" from a pair of passing matrons.

The couple tumbled into the room and fell onto the deep pile carpet. They pulled at each other's clothing, animal passion taking over from human compassion. Naked, except for the bloodred choker around Trinity's neck, they made a halfhearted move for the sheets and comfort of the turned-down bed but didn't make it. Still on the floor, they embraced—killer and quarry—their metaphysical beings separated only by the physical barriers of skin, bone, blood, and muscle.

Bloodred nails scrabbled against taut back muscles. Long fingers entwined in masses of blond hair. Pelvic movements sought each other and joined in a ritual as old as animalkind.

The heat and the passion burned brightly from one completion to the next, and the next, until Royce lay exhausted, his eyes closed as he savored the last lingering sensations of his giving. Beside him, Trinity breathed deeply, trembling on the edge of consciousness.

In time Royce drew himself up, and Trinity heard him enter the bathroom and close the door. There was the rush of water as the shower came to life. Deep within her, Trinity felt the quiver of the final orgasm that she had been holding back, nurturing, denying herself the pleasure of its release until the right moment.

Pulling her legs underneath her, Trinity stood up and moved in naked beauty to the bed. Leaning over, she pulled open the night side table and withdrew her gun. She checked the load for the hundredth time and turned toward the bathroom.

In a soft voice she crooned the perverted mantra from which she took her work name. "Star light. Star bright. First star I see tonight. I wish I may, I wish I might, kill myself a man tonight."

Silently she twisted the bathroom door handle and pushed it inward, to be met by clouds of steam. Blood was screaming through her veins, bringing her closer and closer to the ultimate climax with every passing millisecond, the gun in her feminine right hand becoming the ultimate extension of male sexuality.

Simon. Simon. Simon was right. Every fiber of her being trembled.

She moved forward, slid open the opaque shower door with a violent shove, and thrust her gun hand into the billowing steam.

For a moment her orgasm froze as she stared into the empty stall, and then she felt the ice-cold ring of a gun muzzle as it pressed into the back of her pale, swanlike neck. Above the noise of the running water, she heard the gentle laughter that had haunted her dreams.

Royce's voice seemed to reach her from a long way off. "Simon says, you lose."

Her orgasm and the assassin's gun at her neck both shattered time and existence together.

The following Monday morning Trinity Valance ducked out of her humanities class at the University of Nevada Las Vegas and made her way quickly across the campus quad to a scheduled meeting with Professor Royce Kilpatrick. At the Student Union she stepped through the open double doors and saw him waiting for her in front of a large portable bulletin board. Standing next to him was a petite blonde who was scribbling violently in a shorthand notebook.

"Trinity! Over here," Royce called out, waving when he spotted her. When she was close enough, he drew her to him with an arm around her shoulders and introduced her to the smaller blonde. "This is Lynn Berkster," he said. "She's a reporter for the local rag." The two women nodded at each other in the assessing way that instant rivals have. "It seems," Royce continued, oblivious of the antagonism, "that the university's staff have been causing the usual ruckus over our annual Killer tournament. Lynn has come out to cover the action. I was just showing her the obituary board."

Royce, alias Simon, took his arm away from Trinity's shoulders and turned to examine the board behind them. "You see, Lynn," he said in his best professor's mode. Trinity could see, however, that the reporter wasn't impressed; that raised Lynn several notches in Trinity's estimation. "Trinity is proof that women can be very good at this game. This was her first tournament, and she took second place. I was really amazed."

Trinity cringed. Amazed, was he? She was going to amaze him all right. The fact that he had beaten her was bad enough, but his chauvinistic, condescending attitude was far too much of a goad to swallow. She refused to be considered second best.

The bulletin board held twenty eight-by-ten glossies. Royce's picture, a duplicate of the one that had been taped to Trinity's bathroom mirror, was at the top with Trinity's right below it. All the photos except Royce's had the word "deceased" stamped in red across the subject's features.

"Killer is simply a role-playing game acted out on a life-size scale." Royce continued his lecture. "It's harmless. A modern version of cowboys and Indians, or James Bond versus the bad guys, for adults using confetti bombs, or starter pistols, or other harmless devices. Each player chooses a secret identity and is then given an

assignment to assassinate another one of the group who is also trying to assassinate another player. Once a hit has been successful,
the killed player turns his assignment over to the player who
bumped him off. In this way the tournament is a virtually self-
destructing circle, leaving only one player to be the top assassin at
the end of play. Participants know only the code names of the other
players but not their true identities. Trinity is in one of my lecture
classes on campus—and doing very well, I might say—but neither
of us knew the other was involved in the role playing when the
tournament started. Part of the role-playing game, however, is using your own devious methods to discover the true identities of the
other players, as I did with Trinity. That way you can bump them
off before they can get a crack at you."

Oh, you smug bastard, Trinity steamed silently. Her stomach
churned as she thought about what a fool she'd been. She'd thought
she was leading her target along when all the time the target was
leading her, smirking at her, laughing up his sleeve at her.

Royce had learned her true identity and then played with her,
watching as she prepared to "assassinate" two of her Killer targets
and then beating her to the punch by "assassinating" them himself.
She was embarrassed by the memory of how she'd been manipu-
lated, and humiliated by the way she'd fallen for Royce, allowing
her to learn of his real-life gambling problems in order to lure her
into his web.

Damn! She was angry.

"Players also don't know how close to the top of the obituary
board they are getting." Royce continued his explanation. "That
side of things is run by a gamemaster who oversees all the action
and is the final judge when rulings are needed. In order to keep
players from learning their competitors' identities too easily, the
gamemaster keeps the obituary board a secret until the end of the
tournament.

"This year I took the code name Simon and came out numero
uno. Trinity, here"—Royce patted his rival—"was known as Starlight. She did a fine job but wasn't quite good enough to beat the
best." He laughed softly, and fingers of anger and humiliation again

wrapped themselves around Trinity's spine at the familiar, taunting sound.

Berkster looked up from her notebook long enough to pose a question. "The university staff is worried not only about a game which could be construed as morally repulsive but also about a player who might blur the line between fantasy and reality. How do you feel about that proposition?"

Royce laughed softly again. "Come on. We're all adults here just having a little fun. There are worrywarts everywhere who still think rock 'n' roll will destroy the world, that children's cartoons will pervert the masses, and that superhero comic books will corrupt the next generation. All of them are full of hot air.

"Playing Killer no more distorts the line of reality than playing Battleship or reenacting historical battles with tin soldiers. Or live ones in dress-up, for that matter. I'll tell you what, why don't you come along to the celebration beer bust tonight and talk to some of the other players? You'll see that Killer is no more harmful than swallowing goldfish, cramming students into a phone booth, or any other college fad."

"That's what they said about college hazing," the reporter replied. "But I'll come and talk to the others." She stuffed her notebook away.

"Good," said Royce. "We'll see you there." He put his arm around Trinity, but it was obvious his sexual antenna was pointing in another direction.

"Oh, just one thing," Trinity said, breaking away from Royce. "You might need this for protection." From her purse she withdrew the starter pistol she'd used in the Citadel's hotel room and tossed it to the reporter with a grin.

Smiling, she moved back into the curve of Royce's arm. The purse that she'd slung back over her shoulder was only slightly lighter. It was still comfortably weighted by the bulk of the brand-new fully loaded .38 Smith & Wesson nestled inside.

For Trinity reality and fantasy did blur on occasion, and soon she would show everyone who was really the best. Numero uno. Number one with a bullet.

WITH ANCHOVIES

JOHN LUTZ

This guy, Joey Longo, laid a deluxe pizza box on the table and slipped into the booth to sit down across from Hamish. He drummed his thick fingers on the low, flat box and said, "Lemme get right to the point."

Hamish, who was on his second lite beer and had thought he'd finally get to eat when the pizza was placed on the table, said, "Please do." The spicy aroma rising from the box was making him even hungrier.

Except for one thing. Anchovies. He was certain he smelled anchovies, and if they were on the pizza he was sure he'd ordered with pepperoni and cheese only, he wouldn't be able to eat supper for a long time. Anchovies were for Hamish something of an allergy. He responded to them the way some people responded to penicillin or bee venom. He was almost swelling up and itching now, just catching a whiff of the unfortunate little fish.

Longo introduced himself despite the plastic name tag on his white chef's uniform, then glanced around as if to make sure there was no one else in Longo's Pizzeria, so they could talk privately. He was a medium-height, muscular guy with wavy black hair and a dark dusting of beard. Women might find him attractive despite the fact that he had a pattern of moles with hair growing out of them on one side of his nose.

When Hamish extended his hand and said, "Ralph Hamish," Longo ignored the hand and said, "I know who and what you are, Hamish."

"What I am is a customer," Hamish said, getting irritated. "And what I smell is anchovies. I'm sure I told the waitress no—"

"This isn't your pizza," Longo said, smiling with what seemed to be strained tolerance. "Yours ain't quite ready. This pizza"—he drummed the box with his fingertips again—"is for a job I want to hire you to do."

It took a second for Hamish to recover from his surprise. "I came in here for supper, not a job."

"Don't waste my time with pride, Hamish. You came in here because of the coupon in this morning's paper and because you can't afford to eat at a higher-price restaurant. I've checked into you very carefully, my friend, and you ain't got a pot to plant petunias in. And that's why I figured you gotta be interested in this job. In fact, there's no way a loser like you's gonna turn down this little piece of action, hey? So, you hired?"

"No. Still hungry, though."

Longo smiled. The warts looked particularly nasty when he did that. "What I want you to do will take less than an hour, my friend, and the pay is excellent."

Hamish considered the stack of unpaid bills on his desk. Then there was the collection agency that was making his life hell. Then there was the mounting sum he was discovering his medical insurance didn't cover after his prostate operation. Then there was his former wife . . . well, there was more. "So what is the pay?" he asked.

"It's worth fifty to me. You do it, then you get the money."

"When and how do I get paid?"

"Don't worry, I'll get it to you."

"It's not a bad hourly wage," Hamish admitted.

Longo grinned. "Not for a guy like you. Middle age, losing your hair, getting a fat gut and a thin bank account to take you into your old age. You're a private dick, Hamish, and that's a sleazy profession, hey? You guys'll do anything even when you're not desperate. And you're desperate, my friend."

Who did this guy think he was? "You aren't paying so much I'll endure insults," Hamish said. He started to slide from the booth.

"Okay, okay," Longo told him, smiling hard. "So I was too rough on you, and I apologize. But on the other hand, you shouldn't be too proud, Hamish. Too much false pride is how you got where you are, hey?"

Hamish couldn't deny it. "Hey," he said. He settled back down in the booth. "So what's the job?"

"I want you to deliver this," Longo said, pressing his palm lightly on the pizza box.

"There's gotta be more to it than that."

"There is. When the guy opens the door to reach for the pizza, instead of handing it to him, you give it to him right smack in the face."

"A joke, huh?"

"You might say that. He's home alone, so he'll open the door."

"What's he look like?"

"Guy in his sixties, gray hair, kinda short and wiry."

"Like he just got a haircut?"

"I mean the *guy* is short and wiry."

"He a good sport?"

"What the hell's that matter? You just do your job—splat! in the face—then you collect your pay, and that'll be that, hey?"

"Not quite," Hamish said.

"Oh?"

"We got a deal only if you throw in a free pizza. And one without anchovies."

"You serious?"

"Everything *but* anchovies," Hamish said. Despite what Longo might think, he had his pride.

"You got a deal," Longo said. He fished a stubby yellow pencil from a shirt pocket and scribbled an address on a napkin. Then he stood up from the booth and grinned down at Hamish. "Deliver the pizza your special way anytime within the next hour."

"Soon as I'm finished with my supper," Hamish said.

Longo laughed. "Sure. I'll send the waitress right out with it."

"Wanna take this pizza back and keep it warm till I go?"

Longo laughed even harder. "Sure, why not, hey?" He swaggered back toward the kitchen, carrying the flat pizza delivery box. "You guys are something," he called back over his shoulder.

"Us guys like to eat when we're hungry," Hamish said. But even as he spoke, the waitress appeared with his pizza and a third bottle of lite beer on a tray. She was smiling at him a little nervously, maybe treating him with new respect because he was a fellow employee.

The address Longo had given him belonged to a sprawling English Tudor house in Ladue. There was a gate with an intercom. Hamish parked his rusty ten-year-old Plymouth and climbed out. He pressed the button on the intercom box, and a voice said, "Yeah?"

"Pizza," Hamish said.

"This a quiz?"

"I'm delivering a pizza," Hamish told the box.

"I didn't order no goddamn pizza."

Hamish didn't think this guy sounded like a good sport, but he forged ahead. "It's from Longo's Pizzeria."

"Huh? You sure?"

"Yep. I was told to deliver it here to this address. No mistake about it."

After a pause the voice in the box said, "Drive on in."

The tall chain-link gates glided open as Hamish got back in the Plymouth. The pizza's anchovy smell had tainted the air inside the car, making his entire body itch slightly. Well, he'd drive home with the windows open, as soon as he was finished here.

He steered the Plymouth up a long blacktop driveway lined with identical small pine trees, then parked in the shade of a portico. He got the flat white box from the backseat, removed the pizza and hefted it until he felt comfortable holding it in his right hand, then went to a door that looked as if it belonged on a castle. With his left hand he worked a big brass knocker in the shape of a lion's head.

Hamish widened his stance and drew back his right arm, balancing the pizza. He was ready.

There was a faint sound from inside the house; then the big, heavy door swung open.

A small man, probably in his late sixties, stood there looking curious. He had gray hair and a wiry build and the face of a wary accountant. Hamish recognized his target with the instantaneousness and intelligence of a smart bomb. He struck with the pizza.

The little guy opened his mouth, starting to say something, but *splat!*—too late.

There the guy stood, cheese and tomato sauce stuck to his face and running down his white shirt. Anchovies dotting the mess like nasty little sequins. Surprised, all right.

Hamish realized he'd better not take too much time admiring his work. He turned away from the astounded man, got in his car, and was just closing the door when he heard the man yell, "I'll kill you, you bastard!"

Whoa! Longo had this guy wrong. He was no sport. He was furious, wiping the colorful goo from his face, stepping toward the car and waving his fist like some character in a cartoon before the feature film.

Hamish was glad he'd left the engine running. He slammed the gearshift lever into drive and tromped the accelerator. Fortunately the driveway made a circle up near the house. He jockeyed the old Plymouth in a tight turn, then sped down the driveway toward the street.

As the car jounced over the curb and he made a screeching left turn, he glanced in the rearview mirror and saw the tall gates gliding shut behind him.

His heart was beating hard, and his stomach was grinding.

Then, half a mile from the house, he cranked down all the windows and sat in the rush of wind, giggling, then laughing so hard he had trouble steering. It hadn't worked out exactly as Longo had told him, but by now the old guy was probably in the shower and had calmed down and was thinking the whole thing was kind of funny at that. Maybe he'd done something similar to Longo and Longo owed him one. Maybe they were even now, or the old guy would get Longo back. Order a bunch of pizzas to be delivered to some nonexistent address. That kind of thing.

Anyway, Hamish thought, parking in front of his apartment, it was an easy fifty dollars, and he no longer itched.

It wasn't until the next morning that he noticed the bullet hole in the car's trunk.

That gave him pause for thought. He drove immediately to the Fifth District station house to see his friend Police Lieutenant Will Malloy.

Malloy, a tall man who was a spiffy dresser and had known Hamish since childhood, sat patiently and listened, then adjusted his cuff links and said, "You are in so deep that whales have never been there, Ralph."

Hamish stared at him. Malloy actually appeared modestly worried, and that in turn worried Hamish. Not much bothered Malloy as long as he could wear his expensive civilian shirts on duty.

"The old guy you hit in the face with the pizza is Paul Marin."

The name was remotely familiar to Hamish, but he couldn't remember from where.

Malloy was gazing at him with disbelief. "You really don't get it, do you?"

"That's why I'm here," Hamish said.

"Marin doesn't get much publicity because he doesn't want it, but he controls all organized crime in the city," Malloy said.

Now Hamish did have a vague recollection of seeing the name in the papers, on TV news during some story about . . . *half a dozen bodies fished from the river.* Ho, boy! "You mean he's kind of like the Godfather?"

"Very much like."

Hamish swallowed. It might have been heard out in the hall.

"Joey Longo is Marin's archrival, Ralph. You misunderstood him. He hired you to hit Marin all right. But not with a pizza."

Hamish sat motionless for a long time, listening to the sounds of the station house sifting into the office, the distant chatter of a police radio, voices from the booking area, laughter from the squad room. "Maybe if I went back and explained everything to Marin."

Malloy leaned forward and locked gazes with him. "Ralph, you hit the kingpin of organized crime in the face with a pizza. Marin can't let that pass. He won't be satisfied until . . . well, just until."

"What would you do if you were me?" Hamish asked.

Malloy stared into space and touched his tie knot lightly, absently checking to make sure it was tight and neat. "You got a passport?"

"No. What about if you have me locked up for a while, for safekeeping?"

"Ha! You think you're in danger on the outside, Ralph, think about a prison. Any con in there would be set for life if he did the guy hit the Godfather with a pizza. Protective custody's outa the question. Inside, you're good as dead. Who you gotta watch out for on the outside—besides Joey Longo, of course—are Marin's two sons."

Exactly like the Godfather in the movie, Hamish thought. "I guess one son's gentle and sensitive and the other's a hotheaded killer," he said.

"No," Malloy told him, "they're both cold-blooded killers."

Hamish got up from his chair and started for the door.

"Where you going, Ralph?"

"To hide out in some other city. Maybe—"

"Don't tell me where," Malloy interrupted. "I mean, in case I'm, uh, asked persuasively, it'd be better if I didn't know your whereabouts."

"You're a friend," Hamish said, going out the door.

Behind him Malloy said, "Please forget that for a while."

Hamish's phone was ringing when he opened the door to his office. He lifted the receiver tentatively and identified himself.

"You made a fool outa me," Longo's voice said, in a tone as flat and cold as yesterday's pizza. "People don't do that and live, my friend. I trusted you, hey? I thought we was chums with a business arrangement, even paid you the money before I knew the job was done."

"I never got any money."

"Look on your desk."

Hamish leafed through his unopened mail, and there it was, an envelope containing fifty thousand-dollar bills. He dropped it as if it were hot. "I'll give the money back. Really."

"I don't want the money. What I'm gonna do is make you earn it the hard way. Gonna hang you by your bozongos with piano wire and listen to you beg—"

Hamish slammed down the receiver. His stomach was bucking, and he was trembling. He'd been paid not fifty dollars but fifty thousand, and these were hard people he'd gotten mixed up with. Piano wire! His hand floated to his neck, then dropped lower. Bozongos! He shivered and started getting everything out of his desk drawers he might want to take with him to . . . oh, say, Cincinnati. He might be safe in a city he couldn't spell.

"Don't be in a rush," a voice said.

Hamish jumped, whirled, and stood motionless, listening to his heart.

Two men stood just inside the door. One was tall and dark, with reptilian eyes and a cruel slash of a mouth. The other looked exactly like him only squashed down to slightly over five feet tall. They were wearing identical black suits, white shirts, red ties with tiny, tiny knots, lots of glittery gold jewelry, and the expressions of sadists contemplating a party.

"I'm Jack Marin," the tall one said. "This is my brother, Curtis. Everybody calls him Crush. Maybe that's because he couldn't pronounce his name when he was two . . . I'm not sure."

Crush smiled. "I think it's for some other reason."

From beneath their suit coats both men drew steel blue semi-automatics with silencers attached. Jack said, "Bet you can guess why we're here."

"Paul Marin is your father?" Hamish said.

"Unfortunately for you," Crush said, "that's true. He's a man would kill either one of us if we hit him in the face with a pizza. I mean, he put me in the hospital for a week when I was sixteen 'cause I put a dent in the car. You can imagine what he wants done with you."

"He'd rather not imagine," Jack said. He leveled his gun and casually blasted Hamish's telephone. The shattering plastic made more noise than the shot.

"That thing under warranty or anything?" Crush asked.

Hamish shook his head no.

"My brother had some trouble with federal people tapping his phone," Crush explained. " 'Cause of that, he doesn't like phones, so whenever he gets a chance, he drills one. I guess that's better'n where his next shot might go, huh?"

Hamish didn't know what to say, so he said nothing. Merely trembled.

"We talked to Pop," Jack said. "He agreed to give you the chance to go on living, but only under a certain condition."

"Like . . . maimed?"

"No, no, nothing like that. A business condition. A job. For you to stay alive, Joey Longo has to be dead within twenty-four hours."

It took Hamish a few seconds to realize what they were saying. Demanding. They were telling him he had to hit Longo—and not with a pizza.

"It's your only chance," Crush said, "so there shouldn't be much hesitation. You turn us down, or you don't get the job done, and we come see you and kill you slow."

"I hope you do the hit on Longo," Jack said. "Crush has got this thing he likes to do with a pair of pliers, and I don't want to have to see that again."

Both men nodded, unsmiling. Crush winked at Hamish. Then they silently slipped out the door.

Somehow they made no noise descending the creaking stairs, but Hamish heard the street door open and close.

Hamish looked at the ceiling and said, "For God's sake, now what?"

Twenty-four hours.

Pliers.

Piano wire.

Hamish sat paralyzed with terror until almost noon, when the phone rattled beside him, startling him.

It wasn't a death rattle, the damaged instrument was actually ringing. Or trying to ring.

He lifted the receiver and pressed it to his ear. Said hello.

"Hamish, this is Longo. I been thinking things over. You got twenty-four hours to do what you was hired to do, or you're gonna be the next guy to get it in the face, anchovies and all. You understand? Hey?"

"Hey," Hamish said, and hung up. The receiver split into two sections, buzzed loudly, then was silent.

Hamish looked out the window, thinking, Cincinnati.

He was packing his least threadbare clothes that evening when he saw it on local TV news: A crowd of shocked onlookers. Police cars and ambulances. Yellow crime scene ribbons. A pretty blond anchorwoman said, "Two local crime kingpins were killed just hours ago."

The handsome anchorman next to her said, "Paul Marin was shot and killed at his home around noon today."

"And Joseph 'Joey' Longo, another infamous hoodlum—"

"—was strangled a few hours later," the anchorman finished for her. "Police have no leads—"

"—nor are they releasing any details of the crimes," said the anchorwoman.

"—either to the press—"

"—or to the public—"

"—regarding either death."

"Speaking of dead, Bob, the wind has sure died down out there. What's our weather got in store for us?"

Hamish switched off the TV. He was interested in the weather only in Cincinnati, where he would sit down and try to figure all this out.

Under the name of his old algebra teacher in high school, Hamish reserved a seat on the next flight to Cincinnati. He was preparing to carry his packed suitcases down to the car when there was a soft knock on the door.

He went to the door but didn't open it. Instead he stood listening, marveling that his knees were actually knocking. He hadn't thought such a thing was possible.

"Mr. Hamish?" The voice from the hall was soft, respectful. "Mr. Hamish?"

Hamish opened the door an inch and peered out.

He wished he hadn't.

Four men were standing in the hall. They were all huge and looked like gorillas who'd been shaved and sent to a skillful tailor.

"We wanna talk, is all, sir," said the one with greased back hair and a wilted carnation in his lapel.

Somewhat stunned, Hamish stepped back, and they filed into the apartment.

They introduced themselves. They had names like Knuckles, Meathook, Big Lou, Bigger Lou. Bigger Lou, with the wilted carnation and crude-oiled hair, seemed to be the spokesman.

He said, "We can't work for Jack Marin."

Hamish, feeling trapped in a kind of dark Damon Runyon piece, said, "What's that mean?"

"It means now that you've hit the old man and Joey Longo, we got problems. It's no secret how loyal me and Big Lou was to the old man, and Knuckles and Meathook was close to Joey, in a business sense."

Hamish understood. "So the Marin brothers don't trust you."

"Which means they'll hit us," Bigger Lou said. "It's just a matter of time, like with you."

Hamish's stomach plunged. "Me?"

"Sure. You don't think they'll let a loose end like you walk around forever, do you? Not to mention, if you got the bozongos to hit people like Joey and the old man, you might get ideas about running the show yourself."

More understanding pushed its way through Hamish's fear. "Now wait a minute!"

When he raised his voice, all three huge men backed away. He scratched beneath his arm. Even Bigger Lou turned pale.

Hamish said, "I think I understand. You want me to beat them to the punch, to take over the city's criminal operations before I'm killed."

"That's about the only choice you got," Bigger Lou said. "And we can make everything easier for you. As a kind of act of future loyalty on our part. All we ask is you do nothing while we make our moves. After we do away with the competition, you're in charge and you get your cut of all the action." He beamed. "Whaddya say, boss?"

Hamish stared at them. All four men were grinning as if the primate cage had been left unlocked.

Hamish finally fully grasped his position. Jack and Crush had murdered their father and then Joey Longo, using Hamish as the patsy. Hamish had a powerful motive for both murders: his survival. A few words in the right ears, and word had gotten around. Hamish the hit man was the most feared individual in the city. And he was trapped. If he claimed his innocence, he wouldn't be believed. And the Marins would never change their story. If the brothers exposed him as a phony and not a hit man, they'd be nailed for the murders either by the police or by elements who were loyal to Paul Marin or Joey Longo. The police wouldn't be able to prove anything, but they probably thought he was the killer, too.

Hamish didn't want to be a kingpin of crime, but there he was. Almost.

"Just don't say no, Mr. Hamish," Bigger Lou pleaded. "That's all we ask. All we need."

Hamish walked to the window and stood staring out at the starkly shadowed buildings across the street. A row of pigeons on a ledge seemed to stare back at him, as if they and Hamish had something in common.

After a few minutes Meathook rasped, "He ain't gonna say no, I think."

Bigger Lou said, "Fine, boss. That's plenty good enough for us."

When Hamish turned around, he found himself alone.

The gang war was brutal and far-reaching. Within a week the death toll had reached a dozen. A few of the casualties' names were familiar. Hamish had run into the soldiers and hangers-on of the organization or heard or read about them in the news. He couldn't tell by reading the Cincinnati newspapers who was winning.

Then he read that Crush Marin had been found dead in a culvert with a meat hook in his throat. That ruined Hamish's breakfast.

It also suggested he might be able to return home. The war was winding down. He'd soon be the king of the underworld.

He should stay in Cincinnati and be king of nothing, he knew. But there was something in him, perhaps something perverse, that made him call the airport and book a flight for that afternoon. Not using his real name, of course. The warring factions might be watching the airlines; people like that, they had connections. John Bigg, he told the reservationist on the phone. Mr. Bigg.

This king-of-the-underworld idea was growing on him.

The first thing he noticed when he walked into his office was the new phone. Probably a gift, he figured, a gesture of respect from his men. The second thing he noticed was the envelope containing the fifty thousand dollars. He picked it up, stared at it for a while, then stuffed it toward the back of a file cabinet door.

Then he sat down behind his desk, clasped his hands behind his head, leaned back, and wished he had a cigar. Cuban and hand-rolled. The king of the underworld deserved no less.

The phone rang. Sort of chimed, actually. A chime of respect.

Hamish picked up the clean white receiver, noticing it was heavy. An expensive phone. He said hello.

"This is Jack Marin, Hamish."

"Shtill alive, hey?" Hamish said. He was imagining the cigar in his mouth, even though he didn't have it yet.

"You won't feel so tough by the time I hang up, you phony gonzolla."

Hamish wondered what that meant. Had he been called a Venetian boat?

"Your boys got me backed in a corner," Marin said. "I'm jittery even going out and starting my car, afraid I'll get blown up the way you're gonna."

"Me?" Hamish stared at the phone. The heavy receiver. Was it possible the thing was packed with explosives? That it could somehow be detonated through the phone lines by Marin? Surely not!

"Your life won't last long after I pass the word you didn't hit my old man and Joey Longo."

"If you do that," Hamish reminded him, "*your* life won't last long."

"Not if I tell everybody it was Crush did the hits," Jack said smugly.

"You'd blame your own brother for that?"

"I killed my own father, jerkhead, so why don't you think I'd hang the rap on my brother? Besides, he's dead, so what the hell's he gonna care?"

Those were both pretty good points, Hamish had to admit to himself.

"So long, Hamish," Jack said with a nasty little chuckle. "Either here or in Cincinnati, where you thought you were hiding out, you're a dead man that just needs a place to lie down. Or maybe you should try some other city. You don't think Bigger Lou can track you down within hours, you're dead wrong." He laughed. "It don't matter if he can spell the place or not, he's got ways to find you wherever you go."

Click. Buzz.

The connection was broken.

Hamish slowly replaced the receiver. He was scared. No longer Mr. Bigg. Mr. Frightened-out-of-His-Wits now.

Grateful he hadn't unpacked, he drove to his apartment and tossed his suitcases into the trunk of the Plymouth. Then he got in the car and drove south. He didn't even bother considering a destination. He simply drove. Distance was what he craved. Distance between himself and immediate danger.

But not for a second did he forget the more distant danger. Organized crime was called that for a reason. He knew Jack Marin was right: Bigger Lou would find him wherever he went.

And if Bigger Lou didn't, Jack Marin would.

Hamish didn't get a chance to run far. The next morning, as he unfolded a newspaper in his cheap motel room, he read that Jack Marin had been arrested and charged with the murders of his father and Joey Longo.

Hamish phoned Malloy and asked him what it was all about.

"It's all about you, Ralph," Malloy said. "The case against Jack Marin is based on the wiretap recording of his phone conversation with you."

"Me?" Then Hamish remembered the new phone in his office, replacing the one Jack Marin had shot. "So it was the law that replaced my phone," he said, "not my men."

"I don't know anything about that," Malloy said. "I figured it was the guy who tipped us to put a tap on it."

Hamish sat down on the edge of the mattress. "What guy was that?"

"One Louis Willard Davidson."

"Big Lou?"

"Nope. Bigger Lou. The war's over, Ralph. There's a cease-fire, and it's Bigger Lou who's left standing, now that Jack Marin's up on a murder charge."

"Then it's safe for me to come back?"

"I'd say so. Bigger Lou's lost some respect for you as a tough guy, but he no doubt regards you as a friend. Insofar as guys like Bigger Lou have friends."

Hamish wasted no time. He was tired of hotels and motels, of fear and greasy restaurant food. Especially fast food. He didn't want to eat any of it ever again.

He did make an exception when the pizza, which he hadn't ordered, was delivered to him his first night back home.

The box was lettered "Bigger Lou's Pizzeria."

The pizza was the deluxe with everything on it.

Except anchovies.

GUEST SERVICES
A QUARRY STORY
· ·

MAX ALLAN COLLINS

An American flag flapped lazily on its silver pole against a sky so
washed out a blue the handful of clouds was barely discernible. The
red, white, and blue of it were garishly out of place against the
brilliant greens and muted blues of the Minnesota landscape, pines
shimmering vividly in late-morning sunlight, the surface of gray-
blue Sylvan Lake glistening with sun, rippling with gentle waves.
The rails of the grayish brown deck beyond my quarters were like
halfhearted prison bars that I peeked through, as I did my morning
sit-ups on the other side of the triple glass doors of my well-
appointed guest suite.

I was not a guest of Sylvan Lodge, however; I ran the place.
Once upon a time I had owned a resort in Wisconsin not unlike
this—not near the acreage, of course, and not near the occupancy,
but I had *owned* the place, whereas here I was just the manager.

Not that I had anything to complain about. I was lucky to have
the job. When I ran into Gary Petersen in Milwaukee, where he
was attending a convention and I was making a one-night stopover
to remove some emergency funds from several bank deposit boxes,
I was at the loosest of loose ends. The name I'd lived under for
over a decade was unusable; my past had caught up with me, back

at the other place, and I'd lost everything in a near instant: my business yanked from under me, my wife (who'd had not a clue to my prior existence) murdered in her sleep.

Gary, however, had recognized me in the hotel bar and used a name I hadn't used since the early seventies: my real name.

"Jack!" he said; only that wasn't the name he used. For the purposes of this narrative, however, we'll say my real name is Jack Keller.

"Gary," I said, surprised by the warmth creeping into my voice. "You son of a bitch . . . you're still alive."

Gary was a huge man, six-six, weighing in at somewhere between three hundred pounds and a ton; his face was masked in a bristly brown beard, his skull exposed by hair loss, his dark eyes bright, his smile friendly, in a goofy, almost childlike way.

"Thanks to you, asshole," he said.

We'd been in Vietnam together.

"What the hell have you been doing all these years, Jack?"

"Mostly killing people."

He boomed a laugh. "Yeah, right!"

"Don't believe me then." I was, incidentally, pretty drunk. I don't drink often, but I'd been through the mill lately.

"Are you crying, Jack?"

"Fuck, no," I said. But I was.

Gary slipped his arm around my shoulder; it was like getting cuddled by God. "Bro, what's the deal? What shit have you been through?"

"They killed my wife," I said, and cried drunkenly into his shoulder.

"Jesus, Jack, who . . . ?"

"Fucking assholes . . . fucking assholes . . ."

We went to his suite. He was supposed to play poker with some buddies, but he called it off.

I was very drunk and very morose, and Gary was, at one time anyway, my closest friend, and during the most desperate of days.

I told him everything. I told him how after I got back from Nam, I found my wife—my first wife—shacked up with some guy, some fucking auto mechanic, who was working under a car when I found him and kicked the jack out. The jury let me off, but I was finished in my hometown, and I drifted until the Broker found me. The Broker, who gave me the name Quarry, was the conduit through whom the murder for hire contracts came, and what? Ten years later the Broker was dead, by my hand, and I was out of the killing business and took my savings and went to Paradise Lake in Wisconsin, where eventually I met a pleasant, attractive, not terribly bright woman and she and I were in the lodge business until the past came looking for me, and suddenly she was dead, and I was without a life or even an identity. I had managed to kill the fuckers responsible for my wife's killing, but otherwise I had nothing. Nothing left but some money stashed away that I was now retrieving.

I told Gary all this, through the night, in considerably more detail though probably even less coherently, although coherently enough that when I woke up the next morning, where Gary had laid me out on the extra bed, I knew I'd told him too much.

He was asleep, too. Like me, he was in the same clothes we'd worn to that bar. Like me, he smelled of booze; only he also reeked of cigarette smoke. I did a little, too, but it was Gary's smoke; I never picked up the habit. Bad for you.

He looked like a big dead animal, except for his barrellike chest heaving with breath. I looked at this man. Like me, he was somewhere between forty and fifty now, not the kids we'd been before the war made us worse than just men.

I still had liquor in me, but I was sober now. Too deadly fucking sober. I studied my best-friend-of-long-ago and wondered if I had to kill him.

I was standing over him, staring down at him, mulling that over, when his eyes opened suddenly, like a timer turning on the lights in a house to fend off burglars.

He smiled a little; then it faded. His eyes narrowed, and he said, "Morning, Jack."

"Morning, Gary."

"You've got that look."

"What look is that?"

"The cold one. The one I first saw a long time ago."

I swallowed and looked away from him. Sat on the edge of the bed across from him and rubbed my eyes with the heels of my hands.

He sat across from me with his big hands on his big knees and said, "How the hell d'you manage it?"

"What?"

"Hauling my fat ass into that medevac."

I grunted a laugh. "The same way a little mother lifts a Buick off her baby."

"In my case you lifted the Buick onto the baby. Let me buy you breakfast."

"Okay."

In the hotel coffee shop he said, "Funny . . . what you told me last night . . . about the business you used to be in?"

I sipped my coffee; I didn't look at him, didn't show him my eyes. "Yeah?"

"I'm in the same game."

Now I looked at him; I winced with disbelief. "What—"

He corrected my initial thought. "The tourist game, I mean. I run a lodge near Brainerd."

"No kidding."

"That's what this convention is. Northern Resort Owners Association."

"I heard of it," I said, nodding. "Never bothered to join myself."

"I'm a past president. Anyway, I run a place called Sylvan Lodge. My third and current and I swear to God everlasting wife, Ruth Ann, inherited it from her late parents, rest their hardworking souls."

None of this came as a surprise to me. Grizzly bear Gary had always drawn women like a great big magnet—usually good-looking little women who wanted a father figure, Papa Bear variety. Even in Bangkok on R&R, Gary never had to pay for pussy, as we used to phrase it delicately.

"I'm happy for you. I always figured you'd manage to marry for money."

"My ass! I really love Ruth Ann. You should see the knockers on the child."

"A touching testimonial if ever I heard one. Listen . . . about that bullshit I was spouting last night—"

His dark eyes became slits; the smile in his brushy face disappeared. "We'll never speak of that again. Understood? Never."

He reached out and squeezed my forearm.

I sighed in relief and smiled tightly and nodded, relieved. Killing Gary would have been no fun at all.

He continued, though. "My sorry fat ass wouldn't even be on this planet if it weren't for you. I owe you big time."

"Bullshit," I said, but not very convincingly.

"I've had a good life, at least the last ten years or so, since I met Ruthie. You've been swimming in Shit River long enough. Let me help you."

"Gary, I—"

"Actually I want you to help me."

"Help *you*?"

Gary's business was such a thriving one that he had recently invested in a second lodge, one across the way from his Gull Lake resort. He couldn't run both places himself, at least not "without running my fat ass off." He offered me the job of managing Sylvan.

"We'll start you at fifty K, with free housing. You can make a tidy buck with no overhead to speak of, and you can tap into at least one of your marketable skills and at the same time be out of the way. Keep as low a profile as you like. You don't even have to deal with the tourists, to speak of; we have a social director for that. You just keep the boat afloat. Okay?"

"Okay," I said, and we shook hands. Goddamn, I was glad I hadn't killed him. . . .

Now, a little more than six months into the job and a month into the first summer season, I was settled in and damn near happy. My quarters, despite the rustic trappings of the cabinlike exterior, were modern: pine paneling skirting the room with pale yellow pastel walls rising to a high pointed ceiling. It was just one room with bath and kitchenette, but it was a big room, facing the lake, which was a mere hundred yards from the deck that was my back porch. Couch, cable TV, plenty of closet space, a comfortable wall bed. I didn't need anything more.

During off-season I could move into more spacious digs if I liked, but I didn't figure I'd bother. Just a short jog across the way was an indoor swimming pool with hot tub and sauna, plus a tennis court; a golf course, shared with Gary's other lodge, was nearby. My duties were constant but mostly consisted of delegating authority, and the gay chef of our gourmet restaurant made sure I ate well and free, and I'd been banging Nikki, the college girl who had the social director position for the summer, so my staff relations were solid.

I took a shower after my push-ups and got into the usual gray Sylvan lodge T-shirt, black shorts, and gray-and-black Reeboks to take a stroll around the grounds and check up on the staff. I was sitting on the couch tying my tennies, with a good view of the patch of green and slice of sand below my deck, when I heard an unpleasant, gravelly male voice tearing somebody a new asshole.

"Why the fuck *didn't* you rent the boat in advance, Mindy?"

"I'm sorry, Dick."

"Jesus fucking Christ, woman, you think I want to come to a goddamn lake without a goddamn boat?"

His voice carried into my living room with utter clarity, borne by the wind coming across the lake.

I looked up. He was big—not as big as my friend Gary, but big enough. He wore green-and-red plaid shorts and a lime green golf shirt and a straw porkpie hat with a wide leather band; he was as white as the underbelly of a crocodile, except for his face, which was a bloodshot red. Even at this distance I could see the white tufts of eyebrows over narrow-set eyes and a bulbous nose.

He was probably fifty, or maybe more; his wife was an attractive blonde, much younger, possibly thirty-five. She wore a denim shorts outfit that revealed an almost plump but considerably shapely figure, nicely top-heavy. Her hair was too platinum for her age and too big for her face, a huge hair-sprayed construction with a childishly incongruous pink bow in it.

Her pretty face, even from where I sat on my couch, was tired-looking, puffy. But she'd been beautiful once. An actress or a dancer or something. And even now, even with the too-big, too-platinum hair, she made a man's head turn. Except maybe for my chef.

"But I thought you'd use your brother's boat—"

"He's in fucking Europe, woman!"

"I know . . . but you said we were going to use Jim's boat—"

"Well, that fell through! He loaned his place *and* his boat to some fucker from Duluth he wanted to impress! Putting business before his own goddamn brother—"

"But I didn't know that—"

He grabbed her arm, hard. "You should've made it your business *to* know! *You* were supposed to make the vacation arrangements; God knows you have little enough to do otherwise. I have a fucking living to make for us. You should've got off your fat ass and—"

"Let's talk to Guest Services," his wife said, desperately. "Maybe they can help us rent a boat somewhere in the area."

"Excuse me!" I called from the deck.

Still holding on to the woman's arm, the aptly named Dick scowled my way. "What do you want? Who the hell are you?"

I was leaning over the rail. "I'm the manager here. Jack Keller. Can I be of any help?"

He let go of her arm, and the plump, pretty blonde moved toward me, looking up at me with a look that strained to be pleasant. "I called both numbers your brochure lists and wasn't able to rent a boat—"

"It's a busy time," I said. "Let me look into it for you."

"We're only going to be here a week," Dick said. "I hate to waste a goddamn day!"

She touched his arm, gently. "We wanted to golf while we're here . . . we did bring the clubs . . . we could do that today. . . ."

He brushed her hand away as if it were a bug. "Probably have to call ahead for that, too."

"I'll call over for you," I said. "You are?"

"The Waltons," he said.

"Excuse me?"

"We're the fucking Waltons! Dick and Mindy."

The Waltons. Okay . . .

"Dick, I'll make the call. After lunch, around one-thirty a suitable tee time?"

"Good," Dick said, pacified. "Thanks for your help."

"That's what I'm here for," I said.

"Thank you," Mindy said, and smiled at me, and looped her arm in his, and he allowed her to, as he walked her over to the restaurant.

I called over to the golf course and got the Waltons a tee time and called Gary over at Gull Lake Lodge to see about a boat.

"They should've called ahead," Gary said. "Why do you want to help these people? Friends of yours?"

"Hardly. The husband's an obnoxious cocksucker who'll browbeat his wife into a nervous breakdown if I don't bail her out."

"Oh. The Waltons."

"Addams Family is more like it. So you know them?"

"They were at Sylvan the last two seasons. Dick Walton is a real pain in the ass and an ugly drunk."

"Maybe we don't want his business."

"Trouble is, he's as rich as he is obnoxious. He's from Minneapolis—runs used-car lots all over the Cities. Big fucking ego—does his own commercials. 'Big Deals with Big Dick' is his motto."

"Catchy."

"It's been popular with Twin Cities school kids for a couple decades. He's worth several mil. And he brings his sales staff up for conferences in the off-season."

"So we cater to him."

"Yeah. Within reason. If he starts busting up the bar or something, cut him off and toss his ass out. When he starts spoiling things for our other guests, then fuck him."

"I like your attitude, Gary. But what about a boat?"

"He can use mine for the week. It's down at dock nine."

"That's generous."

"Generous, my ass. Charge him double the going rate."

The restaurant at Sylvan's is four-star, and it's a real asset for the business, but it's the only thing Gary and I ever really disagreed about. Dinner was by reservation only, and those reservations filled up quick, and the prices were more New York than Midwest.

"The goddamn restaurant's a real calling card for us," Gary would say. "Brings in people staying at other lodges and gives 'em a look at ours."

"But we're not serving our own guests," I'd say. "We're a hotel at heart, Gary, and our clientele shouldn't have to mortgage the farm to buy supper, and they shouldn't get turned away 'cause they don't have reservations."

"I appreciate your dedication to the guests, Jack. But that restaurant brings in about a third of our income, so fuckin' forget it, okay?"

But of course, I didn't. We had this same argument at least twice a month.

That particular evening I was having the house specialty—pan-fried walleye—and enjoying the way the moon looked reflected on the silvery lake when I heard the gravel-edged sound of Dick Walton's voice, singing a familiar tune.

"You're a stupid cunt!" he was telling her.

They had a table in the corner, but the long, rather narrow dining room, with its windows on the lake, didn't allow anyone much privacy. Even approaching nine-thirty, the restaurant was full. Older couples, families, a honeymooning couple all turned their eyes to the asshole in the lime sport coat and green-and-white plaid pants who was verbally abusing the blond woman in the green-and-white floral sundress.

She was crying. Digging a Kleenex into eyes whose mascara was already smeared. When she got up from the table to rush out, she looked like an embarrassed, haunted raccoon.

He shouted something unintelligible at her, and sneered, and returned to his big fat rare steak.

The restaurant manager, a guy in his late twenties who probably figured his business degree would get him a better gig than this, came over to my table and leaned in. He was thin, sandy-haired, pockmarked; he wore a pale yellow sweater over a shirt and tie.

"Mr. Keller," he said, "what should I do about Mr. Walton?"

"Leave him alone, Rick. Without his wife to yell at, I doubt he'll make much more fuss."

"Should I cut him off with the bar?"

"No."

He gave me a doubtful expression, one eyebrow arching. "Personally I—"

"Just leave it alone. If he passes out, he won't bother his wife or anybody, and that would probably be ideal."

Rick sighed—he didn't like me much, knowing that I was lobbying to have his four-star restaurant turned into a cafeteria—but he nodded in acceptance of my ruling and padded off.

I finished my walleye, touched a napkin to my lips, and headed over to Walton's table.

"You got my message about the boat?" I asked.

His grin was tobacco-stained; the tufts of white eyebrow raised so high they might have been trying to crawl off his face. "Yeah! That was white of you, Jack! You're okay. Sit down, I'll buy you one."

I sat, where his wife had been (her own walleye practically untouched on the plate before me), but said, "I had enough for tonight. I know my limit."

"So do I, buddy boy." He pointed a steak knife at me and winked. "It's when the fuckin' *lights* go out."

I laughed. "Say, what was the little woman riding you about? If you don't mind my asking."

His face balled up like a fist. "Bitch. Lousy little cunt. She fucked up royal this afternoon."

"Oh?"

"Yeah, fuck her. We're playing with another couple—the Goldsteins, from Des Moines. He's a dentist. Those docs are loaded, you know. Particularly the Hebrew ones."

"Up the wazoo," I affirmed.

"Anyway, Mindy is a decent little golfer . . . usually. Shoots a nineteen handicap on the country club course back home, but this afternoon she didn't shoot for shit. I lost a hundred bucks because of her!"

"Well, hell, Dick, everybody has a bad afternoon once in a while."

His aftershave wafted across the table to tickle my nose: a grotesque parody of the pine scent that nature routinely provided us here.

"I think she did it just to *spite* me. I'd swear she muffed some of those shots just to get my fuckin' goat."

His speech was pretty slurred.

"That sounds like a woman," I said.

He looked at me with as steady a gaze as he could muster. "Jack, I like you."

"I like you, Dick. You're a real man's man."

I offered him my water glass for him to clink his tumbler of scotch on the rocks against.

"I'll have to sneak away from the little woman," he said, winking again, "so we can spend some *quality* time together."

"Let's do that," I said. "You going fishing tomorrow?"

He was lighting up an unfiltered cigarette; it took a lot of effort. "Yeah—me and that kike dentist. Wanna come along?"

"Got to work, Dick. Check in with me later, though. Maybe we can take in one of the casinos."

"One of the ones those Injuns run?"

Gambling having been ruled legal on reservation land, casinos run by Native Americans were a big tourist draw in our neck of the woods.

"That's right, Dick. A whole tribe of Tontos looking to fleece the Lone Ranger."

"Ha! How 'bout tomorrow night?"

"We'll see. If you're getting up early tomorrow morning, Dick, to fish, maybe you ought to hit the sack."

He guzzled at his drink. "I ought to hit that fuckin' cunt I'm married to, is what I oughta hit."

"Take it easy. It's a hell of a thing, but a man can get in trouble for hitting a woman these days."

"Hell of a thing, ain't it, Jack? Hell of a thing."

I walked out with him; he shambled along, slipping an arm around me, cigarette trailing ash.

"You're a hell of a guy," he told me, almost crying. "Hell of a guy."

"So are you, Dick," I said.

Outside the real pines were almost enough to cancel the room-freshener cologne he was wearing.

Almost.

I was sitting in the dark, in my underwear, sipping a Coke in the glow of the portable television, watching a Randolph Scott western from the 1950s. I kept the sound low because I had the doors to the deck pushed open to enjoy the lake breeze, and I didn't want my movie watching to disturb any of the guests who might be strolling along the beach, enjoying the night.

Something about the acoustics of the lake made her crying seem to echo, as if carried on the wind from a great distance, though she was at my feet, really—stumbling across the grass beneath my deck.

Underwear or not, I went out to check on her—because the crying sounded like more than just emotions; there was physical pain in it, too.

"Mrs. Walton," I called, recognizing her. She still wore the flowered sundress, the scoop top of it displaying the swell of her swell bosom. "Are you all right?"

She nodded, stumbling. "Just need a drink . . . need a drink . . ."

"The bar's closed. Why don't you step up here, and I'll get you a beer or something?"

"No, no . . ." She shook her head, and then I saw it: the puffiness of the left side of her face, eye swollen shut, the flesh already blackening.

I ran down the little wooden stairs; if somebody complained to the manager about the man running around in his underwear, well, fuck 'em: I was the manager. I took her by the arm and walked her up onto the deck and inside, where I deposited her on the couch in front of the TV, where Randolph Scott was shooting Lee Van Cleef.

"Just let me get dressed," I said, and I returned with pants on and a beer in hand, which I held out to her.

"It's all I have, I'm afraid," I said.

She took it and held it in her hands like something precious, sipped it like a child taking first communion.

I got her a washcloth with some ice in it.

"He's hit you before, hasn't he?" I said, sitting beside her.

She nodded; tears trickled from the good eye. Her pink-bowed platinum blond hair wasn't mussed: too heavily sprayed for that.

"How often?" I asked.

"All—all the time."

"Why don't you leave the son of a bitch?"

"He says—he says he'll kill me."

"Probably just talk. Turn him in for beating you. They go hard on guys who do that nowadays, and then it'll be harder for him to do it again."

"No . . . he would kill me. Or have somebody do it. He has . . . the kind of connections where you can get somebody killed if you want. And it'll just be written off as an accident. I bet you find that hard to believe, don't you?"

"Yeah." I sipped my Coke. "Sounds utterly fantastic."

"Well, it's true."

"Are you sure you're not staying 'cause of the prenup?"

She sighed, nodded slowly, the hand with the ice in the wash-cloth moving with her head. "There *is* a prenuptial agreement. I wouldn't get a thing. Well, ten thousand, I think."

"But you're not staying 'cause of the money."

"No! I don't care about the money . . . exactly. I've got family I take care of. A younger sister who's going to college. Mom's got heart trouble and no insurance."

"So it *is* about money."

The good eye winced. "No! No . . . it *was* about money. That's why I married Dick. I was—I was trash. A waitress. Topless dancer for a while. Anything to make a buck . . . but never hooking. Never!"

"Where did you meet Dick?"

"In a titty bar a friend of his used to run. I wasn't dancing then. I was a waitress. Tips in a topless place are always incredible."

"So I hear."

"This was, I don't know . . . over ten years ago."

"You been taking this shit all that time?"

"No. He was sweet at first. But he didn't drink as much in those days. The more he drank, the worse it got. He calls me stupid. He can't have kids; his sperm count is lower than he is. But he calls *me* 'barren' and hits me . . . says I'm fat. Do you think I'm fat?"

I'd been looking down the front of her sundress at the time and swallowed, and said, "Uh, no. I don't like these skinny girls they're pushing on us these days."

"Fake tits and boy's butts, all of them." Her lips were trembling; her voice sounded bitter. "He has a girlfriend; she works in a titty bar, too. A different joint—this is one that he's got money in. She's like that: skinny little thing and a plastic chest and a flat little ass."

"You should leave him. Forget his threats. Forget the money."

"I can't. I—I wish he were dead. Just fucking dead."

"Don't talk that way."

Her whole body was trembling; she hugged herself with one arm, as if very, very cold. "I need a miracle. I need a goddamn miracle."

"Well, here's a suggestion."

"Yes?"

"Say your prayers tonight. Maybe God'll straighten it all out."

"With a miracle?"

"Or something," I said.

"Hop in," he said.

He was behind the wheel of a red-bodied, white-topped Cadillac; his bloodshot face was split in a shit-eating grin as he leaned over to open the door on the rider's side. He was wearing a green-and-orange plaid sport coat—it was as if a Scotsman had puked on him—and orange trousers and lots of clunky gold jewelry.

I slipped inside the spacious car. "Didn't have any trouble getting away?"

"Naw! That little bitch doesn't dare give me any lip. I'd just knock some *more* sense in her! Anybody see you go?"

"No. I think we're all right."

I'd had him pick me up at the edge of the road, half a mile from the resort, in darkness; I said I was on call tonight and wasn't supposed to be away.

"You tell your wife where you were going and who with?"

"Hell, no! None of her goddamn business! I tell you, Jack, I should never have married that lowlife cunt. She's got a family like something out of *Deliverance*. Poor white trash, pure and simple. No fuckin' class at all."

"Why don't you dump her then?"

"I just might! You know what a prenuptial agreement is, don't you, Jack?"

"Got a vague idea."

"Well, my lawyer assures me I don't have to give her jack shit. She's out in the cold on her flabby ass, soon as I give the say-so."

"Why don't you then?"

"I might. I might . . . but it could be bad for business. I use her in some of my commercials, and she's kinda popular. Or anyway, her big ol' titties are, pardon my French."

"She helps you put up a good front."

"Ha! Yeah, that's a good one, Jack . . . that's a good one. . . ."

The drive to the casino was about an hour, winding through tall pines and little bump-in-the-road towns; the night was clear, the moon full again, the world bathed in an unreal, and lovely, silver. I studied the idyllic landscape, pretending to listen to Walton blather on about his accomplishments in the used-car game, cracking the window to let some fresh air cancel out his Pine Sol aftershave and cigarette smoke.

It was midweek, but the casino looked busy—just a sprawling one-story prefabricated building, looking about as exotic as a mobile home, but for the huge LAKEVIEW CASINO neon; the term "Lakeview" was cosmetic, as the nearest lake was a mile away. Some construction, some expansion were going on, and the front parking lot was a mess.

He pulled around back, as I instructed; a couple of uniformed security guards with guns—Indians, like most of the employees here—were stationed in front. None was in back. A man and a woman, both weaving with drink, were wandering out to their car as Walton found a place to park.

"No limit here, right?" he asked.

"Right. You bring a pretty good roll?"

"Couple grand. I got unlimited cash access on my gold card, too."

The car with the couple in it pulled out and drove unsurely around the building. Once their car lights were gone, it was as dark as the inside of a cow back there. I got out of the Cad.

"If you need a couple bucks, Jack, just ask."

He had his back to me as we walked toward the casino. When my arm slipped around him, it startled him, but he didn't have much time to react; the knife had pierced his windpipe by then.

When I withdrew the hunting knife, a scarlet geyser sprayed the night, but away from me. He fell like a pine tree, flopping forward, but the sound was just a little slap against the pavement. The knife made more noise as it clattered against the pavement; I kicked it under a nearby pickup. He gurgled awhile, but that stopped soon.

Yanking him by the ankles, I dragged him between his Caddy and the dumpster he'd parked next to; a slime trail of blood glistened in the moonlight, but otherwise he was out of sight. So was I. I bent over him, using the same flesh-colored rubber-gloved hand that had held the knife, and stripped him of his gaudy gold jewelry and lifted his fat wallet from his hip pocket, the sucker pocket the dips call it. I removed the wad of hundreds and tossed the wallet in the dumpster.

The jewelry was a bit of a problem: if somebody stopped me to talk to me about the dead man in the parking lot, I could be found with it on me. But a thief wouldn't leave it behind, so I had to take it, stuffing it in my jacket pockets. Tomorrow I would toss it in Sylvan Lake.

Right now, with my couple of thousand bucks, I walked around the front of the casino, said, "Nice night, fellas," to the Indian security guards, who grunted polite responses to the paleface.

Inside, the pinball machine–like sound of gambling fought with piped-in country western; the redskins seemed to favor cowboy music. I found Nikki where I knew she'd be: at the nickel poker machines. The slender girl had a bright-eyed, pixie face and a cap of brown curls.

"Jack! I'm doing *fantastic.* . . . I'm up four dollars!"

"Sounds like you're making a killing."

"How about you?"

"Same."

I had told Nikki I'd meet her here; we usually took separate cars when we went out since the manager and his social director weren't supposed to fraternize.

She moved up to the quarter poker machines, at my urging, and ended up winning about thirty bucks. Before long I was up two hundred bucks on blackjack. If somebody found the body while I was there, things could get interesting; I'd have to dump that jewelry somewhere.

But I didn't think anybody would be using that dumpster tonight, and I knew nobody would use the Caddy. Leaving too soon would be suspicious. So I stayed a couple hours.

"Jeez," I said as we were heading out finally, her arm in mine, my hand on my head, "I think I drank a little too much."

"That's not like you, Jack."

"I know. But you better drive me home."

"What about your car?"

My car was back at the resort, of course, parked where Nikki wouldn't see it when she went to her own cabin.

"I'll have Gary drive me up for it tomorrow."

"Okay," she said, and she steadied me as we walked back around to the parking lot in the rear.

It was still dark back there, and quiet. Very quiet. I could barely make out a dried dark streak on the pavement, over by the Caddy, but nothing glistened in the moonlight now.

First thing the next morning the police came around to see me; Gary was with them, a pair of uniformed state patrolmen. It seemed that around sunup one of our guests had been found dead in the parking lot at the Lakeview Casino. His wallet, emptied of money, had been found nearby.

"Mr. Walton wore a lot of jewelry," I said. "The gold kind?"

"Asking for trouble," said one of the cops, a kid in his mid-twenties.

Gary, wearing a gray jogging suit, wasn't saying anything; he was standing behind them like a mute grizzly, his eyes a little glazed.

"That casino's probably gonna get sued," the other, slightly older cop said. "Bad lighting in the parking lot back behind there. Just asking for it."

"Both Walton *and* that casino," the young one said.

I agreed with them, said sympathetic things, and pointed them to the cabin where they could find—and inform—the new widow.

Gary stayed behind.

"You know," he said quietly, scratching his beard, "I'm glad that bastard didn't get killed on our grounds. We might be the ones getting sued."

"Right. But that's not going to happen around here."

"Oh?"

"Don't worry, Gary." I put a hand on his shoulder, had to reach up to do it. "*We* have adequate lighting."

He looked at me kind of funny, with narrowed eyes. He seemed about to ask me something but thought better of it, waved limply, and wandered off.

I was doing my morning sit-ups when she walked up on my deck, looking dazed, her perfect, bulletproof platinum hair wearing the girlish pink bow, her voluptuous body tied into a dark pink dressing gown. She stood looking through the crosshatch of screen door, asking if she could come in.

"Of course," I said, sliding the door open, and took her to the couch where she'd sat two nights before.

"You heard about Dick?" she said, in a small voice. She seemed numb.

"Yes. I'm sorry."

"You—you won't say anything, will you?"

"About what?"

"Those . . . terrible things I said about him." Her eyes got very wide; she seemed frightened suddenly, but not of me. Exactly. "You don't think—you don't think *I* . . ."

"No. I don't think you did it, Mrs. Walton."

"Or—or hired somebody . . . I mean, I was saying some crazy things the other night."

"Forget it."

"And if the police knew about Dick hitting me—"

"Your face looks pretty good today. I don't think they'll pursue that angle."

She swallowed, stared into nothing. "I don't know what to do."

"Why don't you just lean back and wait to inherit Dick's estate? You can do those TV commercials solo now."

She turned to look at me, and the faintest suspicion seemed etched around her eyes. "You've been . . . very kind, Mr. Keller."

"Make it Jack."

"Is there anything I can do to . . . repay your kindnesses?"

"Well . . . you can keep coming to Sylvan Lodge despite the bad memories. We could sure use your business, for those sales conferences and all."

She touched my hand. "I can promise you that. Maybe we could . . . get to know each other better. Under better circumstances."

"That would be nice."

"Could I just . . . sit here for a while? I don't really want to go back to the cabin. It still—still smells of Dick. That awful cologne of his."

Here all you could smell was the lake and the pines, real pines; the soothing touch of a breeze rolled over us.

"Stay as long as you like," I said. "Here at Sylvan Lodge we strive to make our guests' stay as pleasant as possible."

THE MATCHSTICK AND THE RUBBER BAND

LYNN F. MYERS, JR.

Alex Ramey did not feel the rain that was pounding down on him. Repeated sips from a pocket flask of bourbon had numbed him from both the wet and the chill of the night. Besides, he had a job to do. He put the flask back in his pocket, then brushed his hand up the side of his massive body so that he could feel the familiar lines of the .45 automatic harnessed under his jacket. He tried to smoke a Piedmont, but the pack had gotten soggy. So he went back to the bottle for another nip. And waited.

Ferris Cummings pulled his new Packard into the darkness of the park and shut off the lights. He listened as the rain pounded his windshield in an intense moment of heightened fury. He debated whether or not to leave the warm confines of the vehicle. When he remembered he had an umbrella in the back, a smile formed on his thin lips, and he traced the line of his pencil mustache with a fingertip. Business was business, he thought. So what if he got a little cold and wet and ruined his new dinner clothes? With the money he was picking up tonight, the price of a new suit would be peanuts.

Cummings took a deep breath. He removed himself from the car and walked into the park.

A strong gust of wind took the umbrella out of Cummings's hands, and he cursed loudly. In a matter of moments he was soaked to the bone. He pushed his hands deep into his pockets and hunched his shoulders. Still no sign of anyone. Cummings's stomach knotted up. Maybe his demand had angered Purcell. But he shook off the thought. No. Dutch Purcell *needed* him. Cummings was a police commissioner with a lot of influence. It was primarily because of him that the department had been turning its head for so long, allowing Purcell to run his gambling houses and speakeasies in a city that was laughing at Prohibition.

Ramey's thick form stepped out from behind a clump of bushes and confronted Cummings.

"It's about time you showed." Cummings coughed. "I've been waiting for over twenty minutes."

"You got the time," Ramey said in his low, rumbling voice. "And I got something for you."

"Let's have it," Cummings said, licking his lips. "I'm late for a dinner engagement, and now I must change these wet clothes before I go."

Cummings pulled back a sodden sleeve to glance at his watch. When he looked back up, he saw the shape and dull glint of the .45 in Ramey's fist.

"Oh, my God," Cummings gasped.

The gun went off. Its report was lost in the wind and the splashing rain.

Ramey went to the fallen body, leaned over somewhat ponderously, and removed the watch. Worth a hundred bucks if it was worth a dime. A little bonus for the night's work. Ramey was more concerned about the trinket than he was about taking the man's pulse.

Ramey put the watch on and left the park, walking toward the boarding house. He thought about his warm room and a fresh bottle of blended whiskey.

There was a knock on the door of Ramey's room.

"Yeah?" he barked in response.

A voice came from the hall outside. "It's me—Pete Fletcher."

Ramey opened the door a careful crack and took a good look at Fletcher's familiar pockmarked face.

"I got your money," Fletcher said.

Ramey smiled. "Sure. Come on in."

Fletcher went in and stood, a puddle forming at his feet.

"Where have you been, Fletcher? You're as wet as a drowned rat."

Fletcher ignored the question. He said, "So how'd it go, Alex?"

"Slick," the big man answered. "Just like always. You seem to forget I've been doing this kind of work for twenty years. It always goes slick for me."

Fletcher nodded. "Right, Alex. Dutch just wanted me to make sure, that's all."

Ramey grunted and went back to putting on his shirt and fresh collar. "So where's my money?"

Fletcher reached inside his coat and withdrew some bills. "Two grand," he announced, handing them over.

Ramey didn't bother to count the money, simply shoved the wad into his pocket. Jutting his chin toward the piece of mirror on the wall, he splashed some toilet water on his freshly shaven face.

"Going to see the girls?" Fletcher asked.

"Yup. Rosa's place. After a killing is the best time."

"That's pretty expensive."

Ramey patted his pants pocket. "So?"

Fletcher turned and started for the door. Over his shoulder he said, "I heard they got a new tomato there. Just broke her in. Name's Maria, I think."

Ramey looked at him. "I didn't know you was still interested in stuff like that, Fletch . . . you taking that low slug and all."

"I used to be plenty interested, in the old days. You're just lucky, Alex. Lucky time hasn't affected you the same way the bullet did me."

The reference to his age chafed Ramey. He crowded Fletcher out the door and closed it hard after him.

"So I'm fifty," he said to no one then. He glared at himself in the piece of mirror. "The tomatoes like me because I'm a man—not for my money."

He pulled the bottle off the dresser and tipped it up for a long time before he was ready to leave the room.

Dutch Purcell was a small man with slick black hair and delicate hands. He'd been muscular once, but money had added fat rolls around his middle and dictated that other men do the rough stuff for him now. He rose from behind his huge ornate desk and came excitedly around its end to greet Fletcher when the pockmarked man entered the room.

"Ferris Cummings is still alive!" Purcell exclaimed.

"I know," Fletcher said calmly. "I just talked to the doctor at Parkview Hospital. Cummings is in critical condition. The bullet glanced off his rib cage."

"You were right about Ramey, Fletch. He *is* getting old. You'll have to do something about him."

Fletcher smiled.

"With him being a friend, I'll understand if you want to hire it out," Purcell said.

Fletcher shook his head. "No. I'll handle it myself. I won't even have to use a gun."

Purcell eyed him with piqued interest. "What did you have in mind?"

"Something from his past will catch up with him. I've had this ace for twenty years."

Fletcher went over to a red velvet couch, sat down, and paused for effect. The fat man motioned for him to continue.

"Ramey and I started in business together in 1906. We were Murphy men at that time—no scam too small. Well, Ramey liked his women even then, and once he asked me for fifty dollars because he'd gotten this girl in trouble.

"I gave him the dough, and the big dummy thought everything was fixed. The last thing a con man needs is a wife and kid, right? But I talked to the woman, told her if she kept the kid I'd make it worth her while, pay her plenty. The woman agreed.

"By 1908 Ramey was into tougher stuff. That was the year he

killed his first man. I followed him after that first hit. The lug went to a church and cried. Then he even took a cut of his pay and put flowers on the grave." Fletcher paused to give a brittle laugh. "That's when I knew my ace would pay off for me someday. Ramey has a sentimental streak a mile wide."

Purcell tapped his Cuban heel on the floor impatiently. "How about Ramey's kid?"

Fletcher's smile grew bigger. "It was a baby girl. Name of Maria. A couple years after she was born the mother up and died and I had the kid sent to a foster home—the same one I grew up in. I knew the kid would turn out rotten, just like I did. I waited. The kid turned out to be rotten all right, but she also turned out to be a real knockout. She's twenty now. Failed at every job she ever tried. So not so long ago I had a couple of your boys recruit her for Rosa Cantell's place.

"Tonight things are in motion. Ramey's drunk and feeling sorry for the poor bastard he thinks he killed. I made a point to tell him about the new girl at Rosa's, and he's there now, trying it out. He doesn't have the slightest idea who she really is."

Purcell mimicked Fletcher's smile. "You really are a rotten bastard."

Fletcher's expression went cold. "I've waited twenty years for this night. I did just as many hits as Ramey, but I never got the big reputation. Twenty years of being in Ramey's shadow will end tonight. When he gets back to his crummy little room, I'll be there to tell him what he just did with his own daughter. . . . You should be able to figure out what will happen. Ramey will do his own contract."

"But that still leaves our greedy little police commissioner," Purcell reminded him. "I want him done tonight. Finished. I'm going to give you a new recruit to help get the job done."

Fletcher opened his mouth to protest, but Purcell motioned him silent. "As long as I'm in charge, you'll do it my way. You know the kid—Jason Galloway, a redheaded punk with a lot of guts. Shot his way out of a bank heist that went sour a little while back. You'll like him, Fletch. Doesn't smoke, drink, or gamble."

"But why a new recruit? Why now?"

"It's just like you said, Fletch. You're as old as Ramey. Once you were just as wild. But the point is, you're just as old. Maybe you got ten good years left. Maybe not. An organization like mine thrives on new blood, and no matter how crafty you are, you'll still do what the hell I tell you. The Galloway kid is waiting for you in your car."

Fletcher did not speak, but the anger mottling his face said it for him.

"Name's Jason Galloway," the redheaded kid said to Fletcher when he climbed in on the passenger's side of the car. He offered his right hand, which Fletcher ignored.

"I remember you," Fletcher said. "You were running one of Purcell's speaks near the campus before the feds busted up the place."

The kid nodded, allowing some pride to show through on his face. "That's right."

"Drive," Fletcher said.

"Where to?"

"Parkview Hospital. If you wanted some excitement, kid, you're going to get a bellyful tonight."

"A killing?"

"And a police commissioner, at that." Fletcher eyed the redhead as he set the car in motion. "You sure you want to tag along?"

"I'm not afraid, if that's what you're thinking."

Jason braked the car for a red traffic light.

"Why does a kid like yourself want in on this kind of business?" Fletcher wanted to know.

The kid's eyes took on a faraway look for a second or two as he peered ahead through the windshield. Then he said, "There's something I want out of this line of work. Something to make up for the stuff I didn't have growing up. Stuff like a father, an education . . . a chance. For right now I want the money. Later I'll get . . ."

The kid groped for the right word. Fletcher tried to supply it for him. "Revenge?"

"That wasn't the word I was looking for. But maybe you're right. Yeah, revenge."

The light changed, and the car rolled ahead through the intersection.

"Kid," Fletcher said, "a man who sets out for revenge usually gets nailed."

"Not if he only goes for it once. I have just one job in mind. Just one. And I can hardly wait."

Fletcher didn't push for whom the kid had in mind. The hospital wasn't that far away, and he had other things to think about.

At 10:22 P.M. a nurse discovered Ferris Cummings dead in his hospital bed. She had no way of knowing initially that what looked like a heart attack was in truth the result of a massive dose of chloroform. After double-checking Cummings's vital signs, she hurried out into the hall and went looking for the new doctor, the tall one with the pockmarked face she had seen making rounds only a short time ago.

"That was pretty neat," Jason said to Fletcher, steering calmly through traffic as the pockmarked man wriggled out of the white starched smock in the car seat beside him.

Fletcher said nothing.

"That thing you did with the matchstick, though," Jason went on. "Purposely bending it in half and leaving it like you did. What was that all about?"

Fletcher smiled. So the kid *had* noticed.

"It's sort of a trademark of mine," Fletcher answered. "Like the distinctive signature in the corner of a painting."

Jason nodded thoughtfully. "I guess I'll have to come up with something, too."

"Yeah, you do that, kid," Fletcher said. "But before you worry too much about that, we got another stop to make."

Jason watched the confrontation between Ramey and Fletcher through binoculars from the window of a flophouse located directly across the street from Ramey's own drab quarters. Ramey seemed to take it all sitting down, his face buried in his huge hands. Fletcher walked to the window and smiled, bending a matchstick. Minutes later he left the room.

"What did you see, kid?" he asked immediately upon arriving back across the street.

Jason turned and looked at him. "Went just like you said it would. He put the gun to his head as soon as you were gone."

Fletcher said, "Did you see the look on his face—the defeat? That's when you know you've really made it as a professional, kid. Your heart skips a beat when you see that look."

Jason nodded. "I can almost feel it now."

Fletcher sat on the bed. "Twenty years to be the best there is."

"I still don't know how you knew it would work."

"All you have to do is shove their past in their face. That's why I'm the best. I buried my past then changed. No way I'll end up like Ramey."

"So now what?" Jason asked.

"Ramey's daughter. It's your turn, kid."

"Someone paying for it?"

"No."

"I thought you told me revenge is wrong."

"It is. This isn't revenge; it's wiping the slate the rest of the way clean. Ramey's daughter belongs in the past."

"And you must destroy the past?"

"She'll never expect it."

"Is that part of the game, too—when the victim doesn't expect it?"

"Maybe the biggest part of all. Anticipation feels almost as good as the actual killing."

Jason carefully wrapped the leather straps around the binoculars and laid them on the dresser. "I have my trademark all ready."

Fletcher smiled. "Yeah? Let's see it."

"In front of you, by the nightstand."

Fletcher looked down and saw a broken rubber band. "Hey, just as good as a used matchstick. A rubber band that didn't quite make it to the trash can. The cops probably won't even notice."

Fletcher looked up at the kid and froze.

"You like it?" Jason said above the gun that had appeared in his hand. "A thirty-eight special. Doesn't make a lot of noise."

"Nice," Fletcher said, his throat dry. "Now point that thing in some other direction. That's the trouble with you young punks— always playing when you should be thinking."

"I *am* thinking. I'm thinking about the look on your face. You look almost as pathetic as Ramey did."

"Put it away, kid."

"No. You taught me a lot in the last three hours, Fletcher. I'm ready now."

Fletcher was going to stand up but decided against it when the kid thumbed back the .38's hammer.

"Why?" Fletcher wanted to know. "Did Purcell get you to do this?"

Jason shook his head. "No. This is the one I told you about. The one for revenge. I'm from your past, Fletcher. Now I'm going to give you a lethal dose of your past, just like you taught me."

"What could you possibly have to do with my past?"

"Once there were two petty crooks who made it to the big time. One was old and sentimental, and he died. The other was old and conceited. Now it's his turn to die."

"You're just muttering, kid."

"No, I'm not. You only thought you buried your past."

"What?"

"You were just like Ramey yourself once. And once you made the same mistake he did. And you never knew either—until now."

The gun roared.

Fletcher tipped forward off the bed. "I don't g-get it."

The kid holstered the revolver and smiled at the dying man. There were only two words left to say, and he said them.

"Good-bye, Dad."

HITBACK

A JOE HANNIBAL STORY

•••••••••••••••••••••••••••••••••••••

WAYNE D. DUNDEE

Somebody had punched a hole in the sky, and all the rain in the heavens was leaking out, hammered to earth by thunder and lightning and hard gusts of wind. It was a great night to be indoors somewhere where it was warm and dry, maybe adding to the warmth with sips of smooth brandy, ideally cuddled up with someone who was soft and curvy in the right places and willing all over.

Dream on.

All I had was the booze. It wasn't brandy, just cheap bourbon in a dented flask. It was doing an okay job of stoking a warm glow inside me, but I was too tired to appreciate it. My eyes were rolling around in sand-lubricated sockets, and my stomach was sour and empty from too much hastily gobbled junk food too long ago.

I'd been crisscrossing the Midwest for the past four days, always just a half step behind a bail skip who carried the unfortunate handle of Oscar Weams. The chase had started in Rockford, Illinois, my home base, and had taken me as far west as Nebraska and as far south as Missouri, and now had come nearly full circle by bringing me here to Chicago's South Side. It was 2:00 A.M., and I was sitting in my car, fortressed against the blighted neighborhood, parked catty-cornered across the street from the brownstone apartment building where Oscar's sister lived. Cyrus Hazelford, the bondsman who'd hired me when Weams skipped on him, had received a tip that Oscar was expected to show up here sometime tonight. I'd had the place staked out since before midnight, and my patience was stretched about as thin as a pair of Roseanne's control-top panty hose.

The wind howled; the thunder grumbled and belched; the rain drummed a monotonous beat on the car hood. The only light that showed in any of the brownstone's windows was reflected lightning.

I took the unlit Pall Mall from between my lips—unlit because I didn't want to risk a cigarette glow in case Weams was somewhere nearby, also watching and waiting—crumbled it in my fist, and threw it down on the floor mat with the half dozen others that had already met the same fate. I raised both hands to my face, closed my eyes, massaged my temples with the heels of my palms.

I'd just lowered my hands and opened my eyes again when the first car came skidding around the corner. It was a boxy, battered taxicab going at a high rate of speed—way too fast to make the turn on rain-slick pavement. The nose made it around okay, but the rear end overshot and tried to pull the vehicle crossways in the street. The driver knew what he was doing, though, and fought the wheel expertly. The nose swerved back in line, and the rear end followed, fishtailing now, but in lesser and lesser arcs. The headlight beams flicked back and forth across my face like gauntlet slaps, their brightness stinging my eyes. The crazy fool might have made it then if his left front tire hadn't found a pothole, a big *mother* of a pothole. The tire blew. The car jerked around ninety degrees, flipped, and came hissing down the street on its top, throwing water out ahead like a snowplow at high tide.

The upside-down taxi was still in motion when the second car shot around the corner, also traveling too fast for conditions. It was bigger, longer, sleeker, but apparently had a less experienced driver. It went into a sidelong skid, trying to negotiate the turn, ricocheted off two parked cars in front of the brownstone, bounced back out into the street amid a spray of sparks, and came fishtailing wildly in pursuit.

The taxi ground to a halt, rocking gently on its partially flattened top. In the headlight beams of the chase car, I could see, amazingly, that there was activity inside the overturned vehicle. As the second car braked to a halt only a few feet short of the taxi, two people scrambled out through the shattered windows on my side. One was a broad and bulky male; the other slimmer and shapelier, obviously female. The bulky one made frantic gestures with his hands. As doors began popping open on the second car, the two separated and moved hurriedly in different directions. The female, bare legs and shoulders and a mane of pale hair flashing wetly in the lightning bursts, cut between two parked cars and made for the mouth of an alley. The bulky male came pounding on a course that seemed bound to take him right past where I sat.

When the taxi flipped, I had reached for the door handle as a reflexive first move toward getting out to be of assistance. In the wild seconds that followed, I had gotten no further than that. Now, not comprehending entirely what was going on but sensing very real danger, I continued to remain motionless. It seemed impossible, what with the darkness and the storm and all, that any of the participants out there could have an inkling of my existence. The street was lined with parked cars, all, they would reasonably assume, unoccupied.

Four tall shadows slid from the chase car. Two broke immediately after the fleeing girl; the remaining two hustled around the end of the wrecked taxi and came after its bulky driver. Instead of pursuing the plodding man, however, these new arrivals drew to a measured halt with feet planted wide, and each raised what appeared to be an oddly shaped handgun.

The sound of rapid-fire gunshots ripped the night, superseding the howl of the storm. The first bullets hit the driver just as he came even with the front of my car. I heard the meaty smacks of the slugs impacting, saw his body jerk and arch backward as his feet did a stutter step. He reeled and fell against my fender. More bullets riddled him, and the car lurched as one of the tires went. Errant rounds whanged off metal, and then the windshield dissolved into a visually impenetrable spiderweb of cracks.

I threw myself sideways in the seat.

Uzis, for Christ's sake! my mind screamed. They're blowing the poor bastard away with Uzi submachine guns!

I scrambled across the seat, clawing my .45 from the shoulder rig under my jacket. For the first time I can ever remember, the cold steel in my fist did not feel as completely reassuring as it always had in the past.

The wounded man staggered forward into sight again, falling once more against the car, his face pressing flat to the window of the driver's side door. His eyes, wide with pain and fear, tried to focus on me. He opened his mouth as if to speak. His breath made a small circle of fog on the glass. And then something went out of his eyes, and there were no more breaths and no more spots of fog. He began to slide down with a wet, squeaking noise.

I shouldered open the passenger's side door—which activated no dome light, something I'd rigged long before—and slipped out onto the curb, keeping low. Still no reason to think the shooters had spotted me, but I was betting at least one of them would come for a closer look to verify their kill. So I wasn't out of this yet, not by a damn sight. If I could stay out of view until they were gone, though, there remained a chance to walk away without my blood joining that of the cabbie's in the rain-doused gutter. I flattened myself against the side of the car, .45 raised and ready just in case, and listened intently.

It seemed like forever, with only the growl of thunder and the relentless tattoo of the rain filling my ears, before I heard the scrape of shoe leather on the other side of the car. Then the wind carried an exchange of muttered words, unintelligible, followed by snorts of snickering laughter.

I think I could have held off if the sonsofabitches hadn't done that. Hadn't laughed at the poor schmuck who'd slid down my window with his dead eyes pleading for me to do something to help him. Well, I hadn't been able to do anything for him. Not then. But that didn't mean I couldn't do something about his killers standing over there, laughing about it now.

Until that moment my only conscious thought had been to get

away from this scene of destruction and slaughter as fast and as far as possible. Suddenly I had different priorities.

I kicked to a standing position, whirled, leveled the .45 in a two-fisted grip across the top of the car. They sensed my movement before I could say anything. Their faces snapped in my direction, and their ugly weapons started to rise. No words were going to stop the intent of those deadly muzzles. At least, I remember thinking, I won't have to shoot them in the back the way they did the cabbie. I began squeezing the .45's trigger. The faces disappeared in red splashes, Uzis dropping from limp fingers as their bodies spun and jerked in epileptic dances before collapsing only inches from the seconds-old corpse of their victim.

The alley was long and narrow and dark, its walls as shiny black as patent leather. I felt like Jonah going down the throat of the whale. Rainwater gushed from broken downspouts, and a sewer rat the size of a Harley-Davidson waddled across in front of me.

I gripped the reloaded .45 in my right fist and one of the Uzis in my left. I'd confiscated the latter while taking time for a quick frisk of the two men I'd burned. During the frisk my mind had raced wildly, threatening to panic with thoughts that despite their actions, maybe the two were cops or some kind of government spooks. But their pockets yielded no identification, nothing. Not that this ruled out anything for certain, but it made me feel a hell of a lot better than uncovering a city shield or a ticket from uncle would have. As I straightened from the grisly task, I'd experienced another urge to run, just to get the hell away from that place and what I'd done. The storm had masked the gunfire, even if shots in such a neighborhood would have warranted any special attention in the first place. All I had to do was get me and my bullet-riddled heap out of there and there was nothing to tie me to any of it.

But inside me it was too late for running. In for a penny, in for a pound, as my grandmother used to say; I'd dealt myself into this—whatever it was—and now I had to see it through. Besides, somewhere out there a young woman was literally running for her life. My involvement—right here, right now—might be the only thing that stood between her staying alive or ending up another blood- and rain-soaked body lying in the street. Every indication was that the two men who'd come after the cabbie and the two who'd gone into this alley were a professional hit team. There were still a handful of pro hitters out there who preferred to work alone and do their jobs with one or two expertly placed shots from a small-caliber weapon like a .22, but by and large, they were becoming almost as extinct as dinosaurs. The paramilitary mind-set was in place. More power. Bigger-caliber guns, more rounds fired. Chop the victim into hamburger, make a statement. Whatever your philosophy on such matters, my reasoning that the cabbie was just unlucky enough to be providing a ride to the wrong fare and that the girl with the flashing bare legs and blond hair was the real target of these shooters meant she must be something more than an ill-mannered debutante who'd offended her hostess by using the wrong fork on her crab cakes. Regardless of what she was or might have done, however, for the time being I had jumped and landed on her side of the line in the dirt.

So into the mouth of the alley I went. For all I knew, into the belly of the beast . . .

The alley eventually came to a T, opening onto the high, windowless wall of a huge building that ran perpendicular to the ones I'd been passing between. A new alley, formed by the wall and the ends of the other buildings, ran for a short distance to my right before feeding into a well-lighted area that appeared to be some sort of parking lot; to the left, it ran for several hundred yards and faded into gloomy darkness. Foreboding as the latter was, it seemed the likelier route for someone trying to elude pursuers. That's the way I went.

It didn't take long for the gloom to swallow me. Soggy, unseen things squished underfoot, and only the occasional flashes of lightning that were able to penetrate into this man-made crevice lighted my way. I gripped the guns more tightly and reminded myself that I was supposed to be a hard-drinking, hard-slugging PI who ate trouble for breakfast and danger for lunch and shouldn't let a little darkness bother me. But the big, empty blackness gets to us all, doesn't it? It makes us feel tiny and insignificant and fuels our most primitive fears. I gripped the guns more tightly still and tried to imagine how deep the fear would run in an unarmed girl plunging into this blackness with a pair of killers on her heels.

I knew I was emerging from the alley when the strobelike bursts of lightning became more frequent. I found myself standing on the edge of a factory district, abandoned during one of the many economic slumps that had broken the back of this part of the city. All streetlamps had long ago been burned out or stoned out or in some other way destroyed. On nights when a storm wasn't raging, this was likely a shooting gallery for dopers or maybe a playground for gang bangers.

I paused for a minute, scanning the flickering scene that stretched before me. In one direction, sections of chain-link fence and buildings of various sizes and shapes seemed to choke off the street. The other way, the macadam, crosshatched by a mad tangle of railroad tracks, angled toward a multicolored glow of lights two or three blocks away. Would the fleeing girl opt to hide among the buildings somewhere or head for the lights? Toss a coin.

I sleeved rain from my face and decided that in her place, having just emerged from the smothering gloom of the alley, I'd go for the lights.

I began moving along the edge of the street.

After a couple of blocks I crossed cautiously to the other side. The factory buildings were giving way to a string of service shops and warehouses, also abandoned, their shattered windows staring out at me like empty eye sockets in a row of skulls.

The rain continued to slam down.

Halfway through the next block I turned down another alley, broad and heavily littered, running between two chunky buildings. At the other end, on the next street, patches of light beckoned. I was moving faster now, less cautiously, getting desperate for a sign of something, someone. Poke and hope time. Any route I chose at this point was strictly—hell, almost literally—a shot in the dark. The girl and her pursuers could have taken any one of a dozen different turns. She might have already escaped them or might already be dead. Just as I'd counted on the din of the storm to drown out the gunfire back at my car, it could have worked the other way around and I would have heard nothing.

At the far end of the alley, on the edge of its shadows, I paused. The glow of the streetlamps, even blurred by rain, seemed harsh, like walking into sunlight from a shuttered room. This new street was lined with bars, pawnshops, a drugstore, and a Salvation Army used-goods outlet. Even though they were closed at this hour and had metal grates fastened over their doors and windows, at least they were signs of life, of civilization—the first, it felt like, I'd seen in a long time.

And then I spotted the hunters.

One was a hundred or so yards off to my right, the other a slightly lesser distance to my left. They were on opposite sides of the street, moving slowly, eyes scanning windows, doorways. . . . They obviously had lost their quarry and were circling now, trying to pick up her spoor again.

I tightened against the alley wall and slid back into the shadows as far as I could. A battered garbage Dumpster blocked any further retreat along that path, and I was reluctant to swing out around it for fear of drawing attention with the movement. The two hitters appeared to be reconverging on a point in line with where I stood, giving the impression they had emerged from this same alley and then fanned out in an attempt to discover some sign of the girl.

The guns in my hands seemed suddenly to grow heavier, as if some force were purposely calling my attention to them. If the hunters did indeed come together in line with me—directly in my sights, in other words—what should I do? That they were subhuman pieces of crud who deserved to die, I had little doubt. But mowing somebody down in cold blood ain't exactly my style; the two back at the car had been as close to that as I ever wanted to come. And calling out, "Freeze!" or, "Hold it right there!" to a couple heavily armed pros is the kind of movie/TV dumbness that can get your head blown off in real life. So what then? Walk away from it after coming this far, assume the girl made good her escape, let somebody else deal with these assholes another day? I knew that wasn't the answer either.

Nuts.

As I stood there, rainwater pouring off me, wrestling with the demons of indecision, watching the hunters slowly but surely converging, I became aware of a soft, high-pitched sound from somewhere in back of me. A distant whistle or siren, I thought at first. No. A squeak, the groan of unoiled metal. Closer. Turning, I was somewhat startled to see the lid of the garbage Dumpster slowly rising. I froze against the wet bricks of the wall.

The lid continued to rise. Four inches . . . six . . . ten . . . a foot. I saw the glimmer of eyes—striking, even in the murkiness—and then could make out the pale oval of a face framed by an even paler spill of hair. The eyes flicked back and forth, intent, alert, scanning the street scene.

Holy shit, it was the girl! Hiding right there in the garbage.

Before I could say anything, she sensed me, and her gaze swung in my direction. Under different circumstances, her reaction might have been comical: the sudden widening of the eyes, the sharp intake of breath, the lid clanging shut as she jerked away and fell back inside the Dumpster with a hollow thump. As it was, of course, those sounds also fell on the ears of her pursuers, and there was nothing funny about the looks on their faces as they wheeled about, eyes blazing above the lethally protruding snouts of their weapons.

Indecision time was suddenly past. I knew that firing from where I stood now would amount to almost certain suicide. Too much distance still separated the two men in the street for me to cover them both effectively. Even if I got one with my first shot, that would still give the other plenty of time to spray the breadth of the alley with an Uzi burst before I could do anything to stop him. In addition to endangering myself, one or more slugs blasted randomly like that could easily penetrate the thin metal casing of the Dumpster and possibly injure the girl—the very thing I was trying to prevent.

So I spun and bolted back into the alley.

I reasoned that one figure fleeing through the rain-smudged night would look pretty much like another. Plus they would *expect* any fleeing figure to be the girl. What I wanted was to draw the action away from her.

The alley seemed to have tripled in length since I'd traveled it only minutes ago. I covered the distance this time running full out, my heart hammering, my lungs on fire, my back tingling in anticipation of a bullet's bite. As I exploded out the other end, I threw a glance over my shoulder. The hunters filled the passageway behind me, running shoulder to shoulder, pounding right on past the Dumpster.

Perfect.

I veered to the right. Ran a dozen more feet, skidded to a halt, turned, dropped to one knee, and raised both guns. When the pair emerged from the alley, expressions eager, eyes sweeping in search of their quarry, I opened fire. I sprayed a gut-level burst with the Uzi that stopped them short, then took more deliberate aim with the .45 and put them down with two head shots.

I remained kneeling for a long time. Thunder rolled across the sky, sounding like an echo of the gunfire. Smoke curled from the two weapons in my fists; steam rose off the two bodies lying in the rain.

Was what I'd just done any different from my going ahead and simply ambushing the two men the way I'd been contemplating? I tried to convince myself it was, that they had given chase, shown very serious aggression with their drawn guns, and I had merely retaliated. Yeah. Sure. If there'd been anything on my stomach, I think I might have puked.

I threw open the lid of the Dumpster, half expecting the girl to be gone, but she wasn't.

What I wasn't expecting at all was for her to come popping up like a jack-in-the-box and try to brain me with a broken-off chair leg. I twisted away and got an arm up in time to take the blow on the side of my biceps. It smarted like hell. When she went to swing again, I got hold of her wrist and twisted it back and down and forced her to drop the club. While I was doing that, she balled her other hand into a fist and hit me in the throat.

I wrenched the arm I had hold of some more, leveraging her

torso painfully over the lip of the Dumpster, forcing her to stop struggling.

"Jesus Christ, lady," I panted, "I'm on your side. Will you settle down, for crying out loud?"

I let go of her arm, and she jerked away hard, tipping back into the Dumpster. She grabbed the sides to keep from falling. Her eyes were narrowed into the distrustful glare of a trapped animal.

Even for all that, she was something to look at. A vision of startling contrast and striking beauty in spite of everything she'd been through. Her strapless, low-cut black evening gown accentuated elegant bare shoulders and full, mature breasts that were too fine to be depreciated by the streaks of grime and bits of refuse that clung to them. Her matted hair still shone like pale gold, and the face under the tangled pile was highlighted by features too bold to be ruined by a little dirt replacing the washed-away makeup. She was somewhat older than I'd judged from the initial glimpse I got of her running into that alley—middle thirties rather than middle twenties, maybe even nudging forty. But well preserved, nature's gifts augmented by conditioning and careful attention.

She said, "The men who were after me . . ."

"They've been dealt with," I told her.

"There were others, more than the two who chased me here."

"They've been dealt with also."

"You're not one of them?"

"Not hardly."

Her glare softened. "There was a cabdriver who helped me."

I shook my head. "Him I wasn't able to save."

"Who are you?" she wanted to know. "Why are *you* helping me?"

"That's a good question. Under the circumstances, though, don't you think I've earned the right to be the one asking you a thing or two? For openers, wouldn't you like to get out of there?"

I held out my hand. She regarded it for a moment as if it might be something less desirable than the pile of garbage she was in, then finally decided it wasn't and accepted it in a cool, firm grip. I hauled her up and out of the Dumpster.

She dropped lightly to the ground beside me. She stood only a few inches short of my six-one, but a lot of that was due to the pair of dramatic high heels she had on. It struck me as amazing she was able to walk in such things, let alone run the way she had. Above the heels, an expanse of shapely leg showed through the slitted skirt of the gown. She was dressed to kill—not be killed.

Lightning sparked in the sky, followed by a trembling roll of thunder. The girl—make that woman—cupped her palms around her upper arms and hugged herself, shivering.

"You must be freezing, dressed like that," I said somewhat inanely.

"Believe me, mister, that's the least of my worries."

I did the best I could, pulling off my soaked-through jacket and draping it over her shoulders. "Maybe this will help a little."

She touched my arm as I finished doing that. "I need to know who you are."

I looked down at her. "The name's Hannibal. Joe Hannibal. I'm a private detective. I was working stakeout on a completely unrelated thing when your taxi flipped in the street back there and the men with guns came out of the car that was chasing you. I saw them cut down the cabbie, and . . . well, I dealt myself in."

"The cabbie was very brave. He could have dumped me off at any point and let them have me. You must be very brave, too."

"Brave or crazy. The jury's still out on that one."

Her hand closed, clutching my sodden shirt and some of the skin and hair underneath. "We've got to get out of here."

"Take it easy, kid. They can't hurt you anymore now. What we've got to do is find the nearest phone and make a call."

"Not the police! You don't understand."

"What I understand," I said, "is that five men just died in the space of the past few minutes—all tied some way or other to you. Now, the lines between the good guys and the bad guys looked pretty clear to me or I wouldn't have tossed in the way I did. But the final say on the whole thing is going to have to come from the cops, and I can only hope to Christ they see it the same way."

"I'm not sure I can trust the authorities—not the ones in this town."

"It's a big town. We'll have to take our chances."

She shook her head, snapping rainwater from the sopping tendrils of hair hanging around her face. "You've got to listen to me! All of this—the men you killed, the reason they were after me— it's part of something much bigger than you realize. There are people back East, government people, who can square things. You have to let me contact them. Nobody in between."

"What? You're telling me you're some kind of spy or something?"

"Nothing like that. Big in a different way. Complicated. Complex."

"You'll have to do a better job of convincing me than that."

Her gaze went past my shoulder, slid a little one way and then the other. As if she were looking for a place to run. Her hand was still touching my arm. It occurred to me that maybe I ought to be the one keeping hold of her.

"There are dead men lying in the street," I said. "Three of them are within inches of a bullet-riddled car registered in my name. No way I can deny that. Sooner or later I'm going to have to answer to the cops, and I've been around enough to know that no matter how bad it is, it'll be a hell of a lot worse if I make them come looking for me."

"I told you, my contacts back East can square things."

"How? Why? You've got to give me more than that if you expect me to lay any more on the line than I already have for you."

The storm howled around the mouth of the alley. In the lightning flashes, we traded hard stares, each trying to measure how far the other could be trusted.

"All right," she said finally. "You're familiar with the government's witness protection program?"

"In a general way, yeah."

"Well, I'm on it. I was relocated here to the Chicago area six months ago, after my testimony was instrumental in putting away a very powerful East Coast mobster. Never mind names or what my exact association with that individual was. Moira Blaine is what I call myself nowadays. My looks have been altered. I was provided a complete new identity and a job at the cosmetics and perfume counter of a major downtown department store. Looking and smelling good were among the few suitable qualifications I had for the straight working world. I won't say it was an easy adjustment, but I was making it. Getting by. Tonight, for the first time since starting this new life. I'd even gone out on a date, finally accepting the invitation of John, one of our assistant managers. Dinner and dancing at one of the finest clubs; a very nice time."

Her face was expressionless, her voice without inflection as she talked. The words came steadily, neither hurried nor hesitant. Her eyes were no longer locked on mine, but they were still throwing that hard stare, mentally fast-forwarding, I guessed, through the same scenes she was so sparely describing.

"It was when we were leaving the club," she continued, "that my past caught up with me. John and I were getting into a cab— the one you eventually saw get wrecked. I was hurrying because of the rain, John was holding the door for me. I guess it was my quickened movement that threw the shooters off. The other car came sweeping down the street with guns blazing from both its passenger-side windows—like some black-and-white old gangster movie, for God's sake. I escaped everything but a little flying glass. Poor John wasn't so lucky. He took several bad hits and went down on the sidewalk. While the killer car was trying to turn around for another pass, the cabbie had enough presence of mind to punch it and get us the hell out of there." Her gaze returned to me. "You pretty much know the rest."

I said, "And you figure these hitters were sent by the guy you testified against?"

"Who else? There's no doubt he can order that kind of action, even from behind bars."

"A four-man hit team . . . He must hate you plenty."

"No argument there. Don't you see the rest of it, though? In order for him to direct a hit against me at all, there had to be some kind of leak in the protective blanket I'm supposed to be under. I know damn well *I* didn't do anything to crack my cover."

"So if we go to the cops with the leak still in place, then you remain in danger."

"That's what I've been trying to tell you."

"But then what makes you so sure you can trust your East Coast contact either?"

"Believe me, right now I'm not sure of anything. But I do know they had me in protective custody there for almost a year before the trial finally went down. Right in the middle of the man's power base, and nothing ever came close to this. Six months here: bullet city. So pardon me if my faith in the setup on this end is shaky. Besides, I've got to trust somebody. Like you said, neither of us is in a position where we can just walk away, try to deny any of this happened."

She seemed to have all the answers, this incongruously clad blonde whose beauty couldn't be spoiled by a raging storm or a narrow escape from a professional hit team or even a romp in a garbage pile. But which was the real reason I was feeling a crazy inclination to go along with what she wanted: because she had the answers she did, or because she looked the way she did?

We took the rental car the shooters had used, the sleek, black, hearselike Buick. My car with its blasted windshield and flattened front tire was effectively out of the running.

It was easy to think of hearses with the bodies still littering the street. The scene was eerie when returned to, rain- and wind-lashed, licked by tongues of lightning, undisturbed since I'd left it the handful of minutes ago that seemed like so much longer because so much had happened. The brownstone apartment building where Oscar Weams's sister lived hovered in the background like a distant memory.

Moira had convinced me that she didn't have the number of her East Coast contact committed to memory, that we needed to go to her Schaumberg apartment in order to get it. Once she made that call, she kept assuring me, machinery would be set in motion to throw a wrap around the night's bloody deeds efficiently and leave her in the least amount of danger and me in the least amount of trouble possible.

Reviewing the bodies strewn in my wake, so cold and still and unintimidating now, I was struck full force by the extremity and the irreversibleness of my involvement. I can't say that I felt remorse because I remained convinced the things I killed were pieces of crud not worth breathing up good air. But seeing them like that picked at my self-doubts like a fingernail picking at a scab. What gave me the right to make such life-and-death decisions? If I was wrong, then was I any different from the kind I'd felt so justified in blowing away?

"You know the way, you take the wheel," I told Moira as we piled into the Buick. I laid the Uzi on the seat between us and settled back against the pillowy contours of the backrest. Moira took time to fasten her seat belt. The sound of it snicking shut drew a wry smile out of me. Even though it is illegal to drive or ride in a car in Illinois without proper seat restraints, I've never bought in; I'm one of those hardheads who'd rather take the gamble on getting thrown clear over being crushed or pinned in flames. Personal philosophies aside, however, to worry about such minor points of legality and/or safety under present circumstances struck me as more than a little ludicrous.

Even though I'd been a Chicago cop in the distant past and even though I'd managed to find Weams's sister's address okay, the Windy City was no longer my turf, and I didn't know this part of it all that well. I was even less familiar with the suburb of Schaumberg, where we were headed. Besides, planting Moira behind the wheel gave me more control over her. If I were the one occupied driving the car, that would've left her a better chance to jump out and bolt at any corner or stoplight. I'd seen her run, remember, and I'd seen that rabbit look on her face back when she was having trouble selling me on the idea of not calling the cops right away. It wasn't that I didn't trust her exactly, but I had a hell of a lot riding on this mysterious lady with her talk of turncoat testimony and government contacts and vengeful crime bosses. If she suddenly took a powder on me, I'd be the one left holding a bag of shit deeper than I could walk out of on stilts.

The Buick glided ghostlike through deserted streets, fat tires hissing softly on the wet pavement. One anonymous burb blended into the next, all looking alike in the steady rain and the intermittent pops of lightning.

When I dug out a pack of cigarettes, Moira mooched one off me. After I'd lighted one and handed it to her, she took a long drag, then tipped her head back and exhaled, exposing the classic lines of her bare throat to the greenish glow of the dashboard lights.

"I haven't had one of these in over three years," she said. "God, it tastes wonderful!"

We didn't talk much other than that. We each had plenty to chew over in our minds. Me, I kept thinking that the more time passed and the farther we drove away from the scenes of the shootings, the farther I was sticking my neck out.

Eventually, as we threaded a path through an upper-middle-class–looking residential neighborhood, its streets and driveways dotted with numerous station wagons and family vans, Moira said, "Not much longer now. My apartment building is just around the next corner."

I started to relax. I wanted to believe that she was on the level, that I wasn't letting myself be set up for some kind of prize chump. I wanted to believe in that East Coast contact who could wave a magic wand and smooth over everything that had gone down tonight.

She turned down the next street. I leaned forward to stab out my cigarette in the dashboard ashtray.

"There the bastards are!" she said suddenly. In the same instant she punched the accelator and the big car surged forward in a mighty lunge of power. I was slammed back in the seat and plastered there like a jet pilot going for the sound barrier. The cigarette I'd never gotten squashed out sailed through the air, spraying a rooster tail of sparks.

I saw Moira give the steering wheel a hard yank to the left, then stiffen both arms, bracing herself tight in her restraint straps. The impact came a split second later, the bone-jarring, metal-twisting, glass-shattering complete halt to our vehicle's forward momentum.

I crashed against the dashboard, taking most of it on my shoulder and jaw, then pitched back, rapping the back of my head on the door handle.

I lay half on, half off the seat, stunned. It seemed as if I could hear individual bits of glass and metal tinkling to the ground in slow motion. I was aware of a sticky warmth running down inside my shirt collar.

And then, as if through the haze of a vague dream, I was aware of something else. Of Moira moving next to me. Unsnapping her seat belt. Of her slender hand curving expertly around the Uzi that remained on the seat, undisturbed somehow except for a dusting of glass shards. Lifting it, turning away. Floating out the door, shoulder muscles flexing under creamy skin, hair catching the glisten of fresh rain.

When she disappeared from sight, I tried to move, tried to sit up so I could see where she went. But nothing worked. My arms and legs were made of Jell-O. My mouth opened, but I didn't have enough breath in me to make a sound.

Other sounds came, though. Curses. A scream. And the chatter of the Uzi, as relentless as the thrumming rain.

Then silence. Only the storm.

I tried again to sit up. I'd just fallen back from the failed effort when the car door above my head opened. Rain splashed onto me.

I looked up and saw Moira standing over me. She held the Uzi with casual confidence. Droplets of rain fizzled on the heated barrel.

She knelt beside the car, dropping one knee to the pavement, lowering her face close to mine.

"Sorry for the bumpy ride, Joe Hannibal," she said. "You busted up bad, or just the wind knocked out of you?"

I shook my head, meaning I didn't know what all I had sustained. I managed to prop myself partway up on one elbow. I could see over the dash now, see, through the cracked and rain-streaked windshield, the parked car she had rammed—another rental Buick almost identical to the one we'd commandeered. Inside it I could see slumped silhouettes.

I scraped out some words. "A second hit team . . . waiting for you at your home."

She nodded. "I had a hunch there might be. The first team must have picked me up at the store. I worked late, then freshened and changed and left on my date straightaway from there. They waited until I was leaving the club—it was later, darker, fewer other people around—to make their try. But in case they failed for any reason, having a backup planted on my door would be a reasonable second measure."

"Backup," I said. "That's what you wanted me for. Your real reason for bringing me along."

She shrugged with one shoulder. "I had no way of knowing what kind of setup I'd walk into here. You proved yourself pretty handy with the first team, so . . ."

"So thanks a fucking bunch for clueing me in."

"I might have gotten around to that if I hadn't spotted this crew parked right out front in their rental car like sitting ducks. Stupid asses. Professionals they're supposed to be. Punks playing commando is more like it. They wouldn't know how to kill a mosquito with anything less than an assault rifle, and then they'd expect a mop-up squad even for that. Yet all of them together still forgot how hard this particular mosquito is capable of stinging back."

I looked at her. "Just how much of that kind of stinging have you done?"

"Everything I told you about me was true, except I never elaborated on exactly what my association had been with the man I ended up testifying against. I used to be a hitter for him, too, you see, until somebody else's screwup put me in a box where I had to deal to save my own ass. I was the best he had. I worked alone, and I worked quiet and clean—none of this blowing away half the landscape to get the job done."

I tipped my head in a creaky nod. "I guess that explains sending two full teams after you. Taking down the best is hard."

Moira brushed a spill of wet hair away from her face. "I damn near made it easy for them, playing my part so good in this 'new life' I was supposed to be leading. Allowing myself to be caught weaponless when they came out of the night . . . I'll tell you right now, I have absolutely no intention of staying under the government's umbrella. I'd already started to make some plans, skimmed some money from the store to seed a getaway stash, arranged yet another new identity. Tonight tears it the rest of the way. I'll be making the move quicker than I'd figured, but the leak is real, and next time I might not be so lucky. So I do it now. The stash and papers are hidden in the apartment; that's why I had to risk coming back here no matter what. I can have them and be gone in three minutes."

"Leaving me in the soup, is that it?"

"My East Coast fed is solid. He'll know how to deal with the locals, everybody else. I'll leave all the information you need in the apartment. When they find out everything you know about my identity and the leak in their program and the attempts on my life that caught innocents like John and the taxi driver, they'll be willing to sweep you as clean as a nun's nightie in return for your silence."

She reached out and pulled the .45 from my shoulder rig. "I'll leave this in the apartment, too. Wouldn't want you getting a notion to try to stop me."

She didn't know about the derringer in my boot. But it didn't matter; I was in no condition to try for it, even if I'd wanted to stop her that badly. My shoulder and jaw were throbbing; the gash on the back of my head was still dripping blood. The arm I was propped up on was starting to tremble from the effort. "Lady," I said, "I just saw a small army try to stop you. All I am is one tired and beat-up soldier."

Sirens could be heard in the distance, drawing closer. Lights had blinked on in several of the houses up and down the street. Some phone calls had evidently been made. This was a different kind of neighborhood from the one where the taxi had crashed and where the bodies were probably still lying unnoticed.

Moira stood up. "Apartment Six-B is where you'll want to take the blues when they start showing up. I'll be long gone, but the stuff you'll need to sell your story will be there waiting."

She turned partly away, then paused and looked back. "I'm grateful for everything you did, Hannibal. I don't know what else to say. Don't be too hard on yourself."

And then she was gone, and there was just me and the storm and the newest bunch of dead guys and the approaching sirens.

UNDERCOVER

....

CAROLYN WHEAT

You can get away with murder if you don't mind copping to something worse. I learned this life truth from Mr. Carlucci. I learned a lotta things from Mr. C. You might say he made me what I am today.

What I was was a cop. In 1952 I graduated the academy with a hundred other micks hungry for the street. Last year—can it really be 1967 already?—I got the three quarters and a bum knee. And nothing to do for the rest of my life but limp around like an old fart.

Chick Dunahee, outa the old one-nine, always starts in on how three quarters is one thing for a guy who's shot, but anything less is just goldbricking.

I say, you gonna grudge three quarters to a guy gave his whole life to the department? Who sat around shootin the shit after his tour was over on account of the precinct was more like a home than his home? Who spent more time in a black and white than he ever did in his own Chevy it took him seven years to pay for? It don't make no difference how the guy bought it, a shotgun blast or a lousy little fender bender put his knee out permanent.

That accident was the best damn thing ever happened to me is what I tell everybody. I slap the stupid bitchin knee and say, I got all the time in the world.

Yeah. Time. Time for a third cup of coffee at Klinger's deli, for a fourth beer down to Hanrahan's. Time to play another hand of gin with Harve Petrovich and Chick Dunahee.

Time. Time to sit on a park bench with all the other old farts who don't know what the hell became of their lives. Time to drink too much and time to think too much.

I miss the gun. I can't hardly believe it; I mean, I never fired the damn thing the whole time I was in uniform, except on the firin range, but the weight of it being gone is like having one less arm. Without the gun, I'm nothin. Worse than nothin.

I decide to look up Mr. Carlucci. Notice the "mister." You talk about a mutt, you don't call him mister. You call him Jones or hey, you or slimebucket, but you don't call him mister. He's just a mutt; he don't deserve no respect. But Mr. C, I don't care how much dope he deals, or how many hookers he's got on the street, or how many guys took a swim in the East River on account of him. He's a gentleman, Mr. C.

I used to stop by the restaurant when I was a rookie hoofing a beat. God, I loved the beat. I loved the feeling that the streets belonged to me, that I was there to take special care of my blocks, my people.

So one night I dropped into Carlucci's, just to see that everything's A-OK. What I seen was an underage busboy carrying a drink to a table. Now, it goes against my grain to hang up a nice place like that over a petty beef, so I call the maître d' over and mention it, casuallike, just so he knows for next time. But the guy's a wise-ass, one of your smooth types with patent leather hair. He starts givin me grief, daring me to write him up, tellin me his boss has a hook with the State Liquor Authority. I'm about ready to bust the place when I suddenly see the guy's face go gray. Next thing I know this tiny little man with silver white hair and sharp blue eyes is looking up at me. He don't look like no Italian, but he says he's Mr. Carlucci and what's the trouble here?

I tell him. I don't even look at Patent Leather Hair; it's like he's gone even though he's still there. Mr. C whispers a few words to the monkey suit, and he goes about his business.

Mr. Carlucci apologizes. Not like he's scared or nothin, more like he's pained that I should be treated bad in his place. Like he invited me to his house and somebody insulted me. Then he takes me over to his own personal table, the one with the red carnations in the middle. I sit down. It feels good to take a load off my feet. He snaps his fingers at a kid in a white coat, and next thing I know I'm sittin in front of the biggest plate of spaghetti bolognese you ever saw. A big glass of vino joins the pasta, and so does a basket of breadsticks, the kind with the little seeds all over.

Some cops always eat on the arm, never open their wallets the whole time they're on the job. Other cops are regular Mr. Cleans, never take so much as a cookie. Me, I was somewhere in the middle. I never took food from nobody I didn't think could afford it, and I never took from nobody I didn't respect.

To me, Mr. C was just trying to make up for the grief his maître d' give me. He was being a gentleman. So I reached for the cut-glass dish of fresh-grated Parmesan and ladled it on thick.

It got to where I stopped in once, twice a month. Not too often, not like I was takin advantage, but just enough to let Mr. C know how much I liked the food and appreciated the hospitality. In six months I put on ten pounds and hadda get new uniform pants. Nothin worse for a cop than a beat with good food.

Course, I heard the rumors. How Mr. C was a lot more than just a guy made great manicott'. But I never seen him bring that side of things into his restaurant.

About a year later I got transferred to the four-four. It was a real Bronx Zoo up there, let me tell you. And nothin to eat but cuchifritos and Shabazz bean pies. I lost the ten pounds, and then ten more.

I haven't gone there since I got the line-of-duty.

But I gotta take the chance. So I hitch up my pants and pull on the fancy brass door handle.

As I walk through the carved wooden doors, I think of that first plate of pasta. The old decor's gone now: no more hand-painted

scenes of Napoli, no more red napkins on starched white table-
cloths, no more red carnations. The place has real class: peach-
colored napkins folded into goblets like Chinese fans. More forks
than a guy could use in three dinners.

I liked it better before, but I'd never tell Mr. C. I wouldn't want
to hurt his feelings.

There's a new maître d'. I tell him I want to see the boss, but
then I start feeling ashamed. What if Mr. C thinks I'm there just
to cadge a free meal? I start to mumble something about coming
back another time.

Before I can turn my stupid leg around to walk out the door,
he's there. Mr. Carlucci in person, his hair just as white and his
eyes just as blue and sharp as they ever were. He puts out his hand;
I shake it. It feels good when he says, "Officer Sweeney. It's been
too long, my friend."

Just like he done that first time, Mr. C ushers me over to his
private table. There are peach-colored flowers, real exotic-looking,
in the cut-glass vase that used to hold carnations. Like always, his
bouquet is bigger and fuller than the ones on the other tables. And
none of his flowers are brown at the edges neither.

I sit. It takes a minute to get the freakin knee under the table.
Mr. C looks the other way, like the gentleman he is, and then sits
down next to me. He waves a waiter over and orders for both of
us.

I'm no Italian, but I know better than to talk business right away.
So I tell Mr. C how I busted up my knee, and he shakes his head
and says it's a shame. We talk about the old days, what happened
to Klinger, the deli owner, how the blind newsie on the corner got
robbed again. How nothing's the same since Kennedy was shot.

When the food comes, we stop talking. Fettucine alfredo, veal
piccata, and escarole sautéed in garlic butter. Dessert is espresso
coffee with a jolt of anisette. Mr. C takes the tiny slice of lemon
peel and rubs it around the rim of his cup. He takes a sip, then
leans back in his chair with a sigh of contentment.

That's my signal. Business can now be mentioned.

I come into the restaurant a defrocked cop. I leave a bagman.

I coulda kidded myself. I coulda bought Mr. Carlucci's kind words as he walked me to the door. I can always use a good man, he says, in my business. His business. He don't mean the restaurant, and we both know it. We both know what I am, but he's too much the gentleman to say the word.

He proves it when I go out the first time. He pours me a glass of red wine and gives me my instructions in person. I know for a fact he never done that with the other guys who collected for him. They take orders from Vinnie the Fish.

When I leave the restaurant and start walkin up the street, it's like I'm breathing brand-new air. It's like spring came overnight, even though I still see patches of dirty snow in the gutter. I belong again. I own the streets; I have my blocks and my people.

First thing I do, I buy a new suit. Like I was starting a new job, only I never had to buy a suit for a job before. I always had the uniform. Funny thing is, I buy a blue suit. Some things never change.

My first collection is from a skinny little Greek who sells fruit and vegetables. He tries to offer me some avocados, free, but I shake my head. Taking them would break both my rules.

Next stop: a Puerto Rican social club. Only thing he offers me is a hard-eyed stare, but it don't make no nevermind to me. I get the bag.

Same result at the Jewish dairy restaurant and the jazz joint with a soul food smell so good I almost break the rule. The black mama in the kitchen gives me a big Aunt Jemima smile and says she loves to see a man enjoy his food. I smile back, but I know better than to trust her. The minute my back is turned, I'll find her kitchen knife between my ribs, the lard not even washed off. So no smothered pork chops. Just the bag.

Sometimes I feel bad. But hey, if it's not me, it'll be somebody else, just like if it's not Mr. C, it'll be somebody else. They probably had bagmen in the Old Testament. It's keeping me off the park bench is all I know. All I want to know.

It starts to go wrong about the time the trees in the park behind the courthouse start blooming. All these little pink buds, real nice, like looking through rose-colored glasses. Then the rain comes and the buds fall off and stick to your shoes and who needs it?

It starts with little things but hey, I'm a cop, or I was before I got the line-of-duty, and I know how little things can add up until finally you're up crap creek and somebody stole your paddle.

So even the first time I don't see Mr. Carlucci before I go out to collect I get a funny feeling. Vinnie the Fish tells me Mr. C's home with the flu, and maybe he is. So okay, I take my orders, but I let him know I don't like it, and the next week there's Mr. C and no sign of the Fish.

It was the Fish gave me the new stop on my route. It's a fag bar at the ass end of Christopher Street, which is in the Village, which figures. I start to object; I don't want to go to no fag bar, but Mr. C says these fruits are givin him a hard time, refusing to pay up, and the place needs special handling.

I walk down Christopher as fast as I can, cursing the limp for slowing me down. There's fag bars all over the place; I can tell even though they gotta be careful. I pass one called Stonewall that I know is run by the mob so there's no trouble about them paying up.

I'm practically in the Hudson River before I reach the joint I'm supposed to collect. It's called Christopher's End, and it's next to the West Side Highway; there are trucks parked on the cobblestones under the road. Skinny guys in black leather jackets and Greek sailor caps lounge around by the trucks. I get the shivers just looking at them, knowing what they're waiting for.

Inside, I expect wall-to-wall fruits. But it's afternoon, and there's only a couple guys sitting at the bar and a foursome playing pool. None of them look faggy; if I hadn't of known, I might not have guessed. The bartender's got muscles like Gorgeous George and a USMC tattoo on his right arm. Hired muscle. No wonder the fags think they can defy Mr. C.

I walk up to the bar. Real quick, before the bartender starts to think I'm there for the wrong reason, I mention Mr. C and say I'm here for the pickup.

The bartender fixes me with the kind of hard blue eyes only an Irishman can have and says, "We're not paying."

Cold, flat. Just like that. I get my Irish up and say, "Who do you think you are, you don't have to pay? Just because the fruits that run this place hire some muscle means they're different from every other fag bar on this street?"

"Hell, yes, we're different," the bartender says. Leans over the bar and gives me an evil grin. "See, I'm not hired muscle. This is *my* bar for *my* friends, and I'm not paying anybody to stay in business. Got that?"

I sit there stunned, like I been hit with a ball-peen hammer. The man was a marine! A United States marine turned fruit. I can't hardly take it in.

He talks about how hard it is to be a fag, what with cops keeping tabs on who comes into the bars, writing down license plate numbers of cars parked nearby, then running a make. He says why should guys get a jacket just for going into a bar? He also says why should they have to pay Mr. C to stay in business?

I turn my head away, thinking what to say next. I look at the guys playing pool. There's this one kid, well built, with dark hair. Never take him for a nelly, the way he eyes the ball, places his cue. Shoots like a master, makes his shot, then grins into the glare of the green-shaded light over the table. White teeth in a tanned face. An actor's face. He catches my eye and gives me a victory salute. Like he wants me to applaud or something.

I turn back to the bartender. "Bad things happen to guys who cross Mr. C," I remind him.

"We'll take our chances," he says. He turns his back on me. I want to say more; hell, I want to rush the bar and beat the shit out of the bastard. The queer punk bastard. Only he ain't no pansy; he's got ten years and twenty pounds on me, and his is muscle, not flab.

So there's nothing to do but go. For now. I turn and hoist my leg off the barstool. As I slide off the leather seat, the kid with the actor's face is standing next to me. I get a noseful of Brut as he whispers, "Can I buy you a drink?"

I run out of the place as fast as my gimpy leg will let me.

As I walk back down Christopher, I look for the cops the bartender talked about. Sure enough, hidden around the corner on Washington there's a beat-up '59 Chevy the department thinks nobody knows is an unmarked. There's one guy behind the wheel, another with a notebook in his hand. Prominent, like they want people to see they're there.

I can't have them gettin' the wrong idea. What if it came back to Chick Dunahee that Biff Sweeney was seen comin out of a fag bar? I walk over to the unmarked and start thinking fast.

By the time I get the recorder's attention, I got a story all ready. About how I do a little private investigation now I'm retired, about how this father came to me real upset, said his son was hangin around with queers and he wanted it stopped. About how I only went into the bar to see if the bartender knew the kid.

Nothing about collecting for Mr. Carlucci.

They stare at me with blank cop eyes. I got no idea whether or not they believe me. I open my mouth to add to the story, then realize that would really make me sound like a mutt tryin to talk himself out of a jam. So I shrug and walk away.

When I get back to the restaurant, the Fish is not happy. Mr. C is not happy. How can a man with Mr. C's rep let a bunch of fairies push him around?

He can't. I have to go back, make noises about how places without insurance have been known to burn to the ground. With people inside. Owner-type people.

But one thing I make clear: Any damage to the bar has to be done by somebody other than me. I may be a bagman, but I'm no hit man. I'm still too much cop for that.

The Fish starts to say I'll do what I'm told, but Mr. C cuts him off. "I understand," he says. Always the gent.

This time I learn the bartender's name is Mick Hennessey. Not just a marine but an Irishman. Go figure. He feeds me a drink. I take it; hell, I need a drink to sit in a place like this, the way I feel about fags.

We talk about fire. I talk about fire. About how dangerous it is, how it can trap people inside and burn them to bacon before they knew what hit them.

Mick talks about sports, about how someday the football leagues are gonna get together and have a big playoff game. Which'll never happen, you ask me. Why should the NFL bother with a bunch of farm teams like they got in the AFL? You think a team calls itself Dolphins can take on the Green Bay Packers?

I don't say none of that; I keep talking about fire. I keep drinking. Things are getting blurry when I smell Brut and turn to see the kid from the pool table sitting next to me. He says his name's Darius. Darius Kroeger. Only he uses the name Cooper when he goes for auditions.

"I knew you was an actor," I tell him. "You got the face for it."

He smiles. That's all, just a smile. But his eyes reach into mine the way no guy's eyes are supposed to reach into another guy's.

I'm drunk. I mean I'm as plastered as I ever been in my life. That's the only way it could've happened. I had to be drunk outa my face. I hadda be.

I wake up the next morning with a large furry animal in my mouth. I think it's my tongue. My head feels like—ah, hell, you ever had a hangover, you know how my head feels.

But that's not the bad part. The bad part is what I think happened between me and Darius.

I lay in bed with the cold sweats, with shakes so bad I can't lift a glass of water to my mouth to pop an aspirin. But it's not the booze; it's the memory.

I never felt like that before. I never knew I could feel like that. Even Monica O'Shea, who gave the best hand job in Hell's Kitchen, never made me feel like that, and every guy at Sacred Heart knew what she could do with those long white fingers of hers.

Oh, I used to brag, just like the other guys. How horny I was, how much I needed a woman. Then I'd go to Monica, get what I came for, and tell my buddies it was great. But I was just blowing smoke; it was okay, but that was all. Just okay.

Same thing with the Times Square hookers we used to bust. They'd offer freebies to stay on the street. You hadda take it once in a while. The other cops would talk about how Crystal or Bobbie Jo, how they did stuff the cops' wives never even *heard* of and wouldn't do for a million bucks. Me, I figured they was okay, but nothing special.

Darius was more than okay. Much more.

I was drunk. I was drunk, I lost my head, and it'll never happen again.

Once doesn't mean you're a faggot.

Does it?

The phone rings. It's as loud as the last trump, and it scares me as much.

I'm right to be scared. It's Mick Hennessey; he asks me how Darius and I got along last night.

He knows. He fucking knows. I didn't think I had any more sweat left in my body, but there's a cold stream trickling down my back.

He knows.

He also knows there will be no fire at Christopher's End.

I put the phone back in the cradle and try to stop shaking.

It rings a second time. I pick it up. What could be worse than what I just heard?

The Fish, that's what.

"So, you're too high-and-mighty to torch a place for the boss," he says, his voice slimy with self-satisfaction. "The truth is you don't want to hurt your fag buddies, do you, *faggot?*"

He spits the last word; it practically jumps through the phone and wets my face.

"You think Mr. C's dumb or something, *faggot?* You think he doesn't watch his back at all times? Well, there better be a nice big bonfire at that fag bar or everyone in the NYPD's going to know you like it with boys. Got that, *faggot?*"

I lean over the bed and throw up on the floor, with Vinnie the Fish on the other end of the line listening to every retch.

I can't believe Mr. C will let this happen. He's too much the gent. But when I ask to talk to the boss, the Fish says, "He's taking a shave. Besides, he's got no use for faggots. Except to collect from fag bars, which is all you're gonna be doing from now on. *After* you light that fire."

"I won't—" I croak, but the Fish chops me off.

"You *won't?* You forget, we own your ass. At least"—he sniggers—"we own whatever's left over after your pretty boyfriend gets through with it. So you *will* light that fire and it will cause great damage to life and property. Won't it, faggot?"

The fire. The fire that will cook Christopher's End and Mick Hennessey and Darius Kroeger-Cooper and burn the memory of last night to the ground. To the ground.

Darius. I think about last night, about how he made me feel, and I realize I been under cover my whole life. Thinking it was like this for all guys: that they bragged about women but didn't really like it all that much. But it wasn't them; it was me. It was me that was missing something, and now I found it and I gotta burn it up. I gotta burn it up or be called a faggot the rest of my life.

I seen plenty of fairies on the job. Guys in skirts beat up when the john getting the blow job realized what they had between their legs. Guys caught in men's rooms copping some boy's joint, begging the cops not to book them or the wife'll find out.

I never in my life thought that I—

Once! Once doesn't make you a faggot. Anybody can make one mistake.

I clean up the mess on the floor and start thinking about the fire. How I have to plan. How it has to go smooth as silk, nothing coming back to me.

I think about Mick Hennessey, how talking to him was no different from talking to Chick Dunahee or any other ex-cop. I think about Darius, his white smile, his smooth dark face. I remember the way his hands caressed my .38; he said he used to go target shooting with his dad. He liked guns; he liked that I was a cop.

I think about burning him to bacon.

It takes me a week to set things up right. To get my alibi in place. To case the joint, working out where the fire should start. How I can get to the site without being seen hefting a can of gasoline through the streets. How I can get away without being spotted.

Every night I dream of Darius, waking with an ache in my groin.

There's only one way I can do this. I gotta become a cop again in my head. I gotta think about it like I was writing up a 61 on a torch job some mope already done. In my mind I start dictating a police report.

At 1500 hours the perpetrator approached the location. Male White, 6', 185 pounds, no limp or other identifying characteristics. Carrying a duffel bag.

It's a half hour after closing. I've got the gasoline can in the duffel bag. My leg's wrapped tighter than hell in an Ace bandage so's I can keep from limping. One less thing to be identified by.

I peer through the windows, just to make sure. There they are, taking a drink together. The two guys I need to eliminate if I'm going to have peace in my life.

The fire originated at the rear exit. Source of the fire was garbage bags ignited by means of an accelerant later identified as gasoline.

I stop a minute before lighting the matches. This is wrong. Everything in my life tells me how wrong. It's like all the priests and nuns I ever knew, all the sergeants I answered to, even my dead mother are standing over me, telling me they're ashamed they ever knew me.

But I have to do it. I have to.

After four tries I get a match lit and toss it onto the garbage bags. Flames jump at me right away; the gasoline is that ready to burn.

Perpetrator ignited a second fire at the front entrance to the location by dousing the wooden door with accelerant.

I slip around the corner and duck into an alley. It's back streets all the way and a quick subway ride. The duffel bag's ash now, along with the garbage. So's the watch cap. I leave the pea jacket in the subway; it'll be gone by morning.

I can't believe I did it.

I need a drink to steady my hands, settle my stomach.

I walk out of the subway. The Ace bandage is killing me; my leg feels like a blimp. But I force myself to walk straight, no limp, past my own car, toward the light pouring onto the pavement from the window of my destination.

I have a report to make.

I open the door and walk in.

"Is it done?"

I nod.

"To a crisp," another voice says. Darius slides off the barstool and walks over to me. Embraces me in a cloud of Brut, his lips brushing my cheek. Mick Hennessey pours me a drink.

We toast Darius for his acting job. Thanks to him, the cops watching Christopher's End have my license plate number and a description of a man in a trench coat and fedora limping into a fag bar at the same time Carlucci's Ristorante went up in flames.

Who's going to believe a cop set up a phony alibi in a fag bar? Nobody, that's who.

I lock eyes with Darius; we both know how the night will end.

Like I said, you can get away with murder if you don't mind copping to something worse.

I don't mind. I'm with my own now, and I don't mind at all.

ANGEL FACE

DANIEL HELPINGSTINE

Alex had forgotten he had her picture in his wallet. It was clipped from a newspaper over a year before. He always kept his wallet with him so the picture was dirty and the creases divided her face into quarters. Alex was enamored by the red hair and the freckles on the face to match. Lucy Summerfield was his age, thirty-three, but she looked so much younger. He first saw her on TV when her husband was murdered in one of the three fancy restaurants he owned. The camera caught her as she walked into the restaurant, staring straight ahead, the look of shock all over her. She looked helpless, afraid, alone, and Alex wished he could hold her and tell her everything was all right.

Sam Summerfield had been shot by another husband, a jealous husband. It was after hours when the husband came in. Sam was sitting at the bar. The man walked up to him and, without a word, fired two shots.

Alex felt that he knew what Lucy was going through. He knew what it was like to be lied to and deceived.

But then the other side of the story came out. Lucy was accused of paying the killer. With this Alex's sympathy was gone. She was nothing but an opportunist, a gold digger, and a conspirator. Lucy said she didn't do it, but Alex didn't believe her. He believed that when someone was arrested, that person usually did it.

Alex followed the trial closely and wasn't surprised when the prosecuting attorney noticed the Lucy Summerfield face. "Don't be fooled by that angel face," he told the jury in his closing remarks. "Remember, some of the prettiest roses have thorns."

The jury said there wasn't enough evidence, and Alex couldn't believe it. Rich people got all the breaks even when they didn't deserve them. He wanted to tear up Lucy's picture but couldn't find it. It wasn't until Lucy called his shop that he finally realized where it was.

Alex had been under a hood when the call came. He was irritated by the interruption and was going to let it ring even if it meant turning away business. But things weren't as they used to be, and he had to answer it. He recognized her voice immediately. There was nothing special about it, but he had heard it over and over on TV and radio. He couldn't believe *the* Lucy Summerfield was on the other end of the line.

"Do you charge a lot for your work?" she asked.

Alex had the impulse to scream at her, "Did that killer charge a lot for his work?" He controlled his temper, however, and simply said, "That all depends. What do you need done?"

"I really don't know. My car won't start. The guy who towed it thought it was the timing chain."

"It's possible, but I won't know until I get a look at it. Have it towed to my place and I'll see what I can do."

"Wait a minute. If it is the timing chain, how much is that going to cost?"

"Oh, I don't know. Probably around three hundred dollars."

"I was afraid of that," she said. "I don't know if I can afford it."

"Look, lady, either you can afford it or not. I can't make that choice for you."

"Your price is a little high. Couldn't you come down some?"

"No, I don't make bargains like that. I have to make a living."

"I need that car, but I can't afford that."

Alex almost laughed. Twice she admitted she couldn't afford a simple repair. She had fallen hard, and she deserved it.

"You're wasting my time," he said. "I don't do charity work."

He started to hang up, but she called after him. She was yelling, and he heard her clearly even though he had the earpiece away from his face. Alex was growing tired of her, but he was curious. He had never given anyone else so much time.

"What is it?" he asked.

"I don't have any money to speak of," she said, "but I'm not bad-looking, and well, maybe we could work something out."

"What are you saying?"

"Do I have to spell it out for you? I've made you an offer. Take it or leave it."

"Um, this is interesting. I'd like to think about this."

"No way. This is a one-time shot. If you say no, I'll find someone else."

"Hold on, I didn't say no."

"You didn't say yes either. Are you interested or not?"

"I'm very interested. I can do this kind of repair right at your house."

"I'll be in touch."

After she hung up, Alex stared at the receiver and smiled. She thought she was being so secretive. He had heard that she was forced to move out of that big house she had shared with her unfortunate husband. Alex could find out where she lived if he really wanted, but he decided to wait for her to call. He found it amusing that she at one time could buy just about anything but now had to sell herself and sell at a very cheap price.

Lucy did call, and Alex went to her on a Saturday afternoon. When Alex saw her house, he couldn't believe Lucy Summerfield could be happy there. Like the house Alex lived in as a boy, it had an enclosed front porch, a front porch not made anymore. There were no signs of peeling paint. A smooth cement driveway led to the back of the lot, where an old-fashioned brick garage stood.

Actually it was a nice house, but he didn't think she would like it after living in one of the largest houses in town.

He knocked on the front door, and Lucy answered from a window above him and to the right. Walking over, Alex looked up at the screen and heard a voice but didn't see a face.

"You're Alex Gibson, I take it," she said.

"That's right."

"I'll be right out."

Alex wandered toward the back until he heard the front door slam behind him. He turned around and stared. It was a hot day, and she wore shorts and a sleeveless top. Alex didn't look at her body, though. It was that face, the face the district attorney had called an angel face.

Lucy walked toward him slowly and held out her hand. "Lucy Summerfield," she said.

"*The* Lucy Summerfield?" Alex said as he shook her hand and stared.

"Is there any other?"

"I guess not."

"The car is in the garage," she said, and started to walk.

"Why did that guy think it was the timing chain?" he asked as he began to match her strides.

"I don't know. He said a lot of things I didn't understand. Do you think it could be something else?"

"Maybe. Let's just hope it's nothing too complicated."

She opened the door. Inside was a year-old white Oldsmobile. Alex thought it was bought around the time Lucy went on trial. It shouldn't have had such problems. He would have felt sorry for anyone else.

"I'll need the keys," he said.

"Okay," she replied.

"And another thing, I don't want you hanging around when I'm doing my work. I don't like an audience."

"Then how am I going to know if you do the work or not?"

"Believe me, you'll know when you see this car running again. Now get me those keys." She stood there numbly as if she did not understand him. "Now, Lucy," he said.

Two hours later Alex finished his work. After collecting his tools, he backed the car out of the garage and let it idle in the driveway. Lucy came with a beer in her hand. She had not come around asking him questions as he worked. He thought she would at least do that much and was surprised she obeyed his command to stay away.

"I thought you might like this," she said, and handed him the beer. She went over to the car. Circling it, she ran her fingers along the edges as if it had just been waxed. Alex recognized that look, a look he had seen from many customers who came into his shop. Can it be fixed? they'd say, and he'd tell them yes, and there was that expression of relief.

Alex got in and sat behind the wheel. "Hop in," he said. "Let's take it for a test ride."

She got in slowly, as if she didn't trust his driving. He said nothing, did nothing to reassure her. Lucy leaned back in her seat and glanced at him as if to say, "I'm ready," and he backed the car into the street.

Alex thought of how he had dreamed of driving her in his car. He had wanted everyone to see her and know she was with him. Of course, that had changed now. As he drove through town, he hoped no one would recognize her and then him.

After he parked the car in her driveway, he handed her the keys, and they both got out.

"Thank you," she said, "I see you are a man of your word."

"I always mean what I say. How about you?"

"I'm going to hold up my end of the deal. You come back to-night, and you'll see."

Alex finished the rest of what was now warm beer and said noth-ing. In a grudging way he admired her. She did what she had to do to survive. This, however, didn't change his opinion of her.

He walked up to her and dropped the beer bottle at her feet. "I'll be back at eight," he said, "and I'm going to want my money's worth."

Alex arrived at eight as promised. She was wearing, in what he thought was fitting, a bloodred dress. Alex recalled what a reporter had written a week before the trial. It was a story that probably led to the district attorney's "angel face" remark, Alex thought. "She doesn't look like a killer," the reporter wrote. "She looks like someone you'd like to take to the prom."

Alex couldn't remember anybody at the prom who looked like this. He had to admit, when he looked in her face, in her eyes, something was behind the freckles and under the red hair. It was something he had not seen before.

After taking her by the shoulders, Alex kissed her. She was tense at first, but her body slowly relaxed, and she began to respond. Alex pressed down on her mouth harder, and she pushed him away.

"Hey," he said, "what is this?"

"You were getting a little rough, Alex," she replied.

"Okay," he said, stepping back toward her, "I'll go easy."

"Wouldn't you like a drink?"

"No."

"Well, I would."

"You're stalling."

"No, I'm not. I never done anything like this before, and I'm nervous. You can understand that, can't you?"

"Get your drink," he said, and turned away.

"Don't you want one?"

"No."

Lucy left, and Alex took time to look around. The house, on the inside, was smaller than it appeared from the outside. A couch and two firm chairs sat in the living room. The kitchen was on the other side of the wall. Off to the left, he guessed, was Lucy's bedroom. Although the door was closed almost all the way, he could still see the reflection of a streetlight in the corner of her mirror.

Alex was sitting in one of the chairs when Lucy returned with a beer. He was surprised because he expected her to have some kind of mixed drink.

"So, how did you get to be a mechanic?" she asked, taking a seat on the couch.

"There's not much to my story," Alex replied. "Let's talk about you."

"Okay, let's talk about me."

"How do you like living here?"

"You mean, how do I like living here compared to the big house I was used to?"

"I didn't say that."

"You were thinking it."

"Look, I don't like it when people try to put words in my mouth."

"Or thoughts in your head. Don't get so touchy. To answer your question, I like it here fine."

"It's an awful old house."

"It was my mother's. Sam tried to get me to sell it after she died. I couldn't bring myself to do it. Turned out to be a good thing."

"How did you go through all that money?"

"There was never as much as everybody thought. Sam was good for appearances. The truth was his restaurants were starting to lose money and he left me with a lot of bills. And there was my lawyer. He didn't take my case for nothing."

"I still don't see how you went through all that money."

"I told you there wasn't all that much money. And try to find a job when people think you killed your husband."

"Am I supposed to feel sorry for you now?"

"I wasn't asking for any sympathy. I'm only telling you like it is."

"Yes, but you're not telling the most important part."

Lucy said nothing. Absentmindedly she sipped on her beer, one short drink after another. It was up to Alex to start the conversation again.

"Why don't you want to tell me?" he asked.

"It's not part of the deal."

"They say confession is good for the soul."

"Sure, if you have something to feel guilty about."

"Then you're saying you didn't do it."

"I didn't say that."

"Then you did it."

"Nope, I didn't say that either."

Frustrated, Alex shifted in his chair and shook his head. He knew she did it, but he needed to hear her say it. He had cared about her, and she had thrown that away.

"So you won't tell me," Alex said again.

"I'll make you a deal," Lucy replied. "I'll tell you, but that's all you get."

"That doesn't sound fair."

"Maybe it is and maybe it isn't, but it's the only choice you've got."

Even Alex couldn't believe the words that came from his mouth. Not after he had dreamed of her, of being with her.

"Okay," he said, "you tell me everything and we're even."

"That's fine by me," she said, "but I'm holding you to this. I'll be right back."

"Where are you going?"

"To my bedroom. But you have to stay here."

Alex leaned back in his chair. Although he didn't know why, he felt uneasy. He could hear her rummaging through a drawer and decided to see what she was doing. However, by the time he stood up, she had returned with a gun in her hand.

The gun had a long barrel. Alex didn't know anything about guns, but it appeared Lucy knew how to handle one. Her hand was not shaking, and the barrel was pointed right at his chest.

"Stay right where you are," she said, and he did.

"Is this some kind of joke?" he asked as he took a step toward her.

"Stop right there," she shouted, and he again obeyed. "I assure you," she said softly, "this is no joke."

"What are you going to do?"

"You wanted to know what really happened. I'm giving you the chance to find out. You should be flattered. I haven't done this for anyone else."

"I still don't understand."

"You want to know if I did it or not. Now, I want you to stand still for a minute. If you step toward me and I don't shoot, you'll know the jury made the right choice. If I shoot, well, you will have made a bad choice of your own."

"You're bluffing," Alex said, but he didn't make a move.

"You have about a half minute to make up your mind, or I'll make it up for you."

Alex didn't think she had the guts to shoot. After all, she had paid that guy to do her dirty work. He again remembered what the district attorney said about her. "Don't be fooled by that angel face," the DA said. Alex wasn't fooled, or at least he didn't think he was fooled. The truth was he hoped that she hadn't done it and that she'd put the gun down and tell him everything and he would make things all right. He took a step forward, and Lucy pulled the trigger.

His body lurched as if he had been shot, but there was nothing except the sound of an empty chamber. Lucy brought the barrel to her lips and blew away imaginary smoke.

"It's not loaded," she said.

Alex was on her in a second. Grabbing her shoulders, he threw her against the wall and pinned her there. Her eyes closed, and her face winced with pain for a moment.

"Just what in the hell do you think you were doing?" Alex said.

"And what are you going to do? Kill me?"

Alex looked into her eyes. They were smiling at him. It scared him because it was a devilish kind of grin.

He let go and stood in the middle of the room. He didn't know what to do. Lucy took a few steps toward him. She spread her arms out as if to invite him to hold her, but he knew that wasn't what she wanted.

"Go ahead," she told him, "I won't stop you. Kill me. When it comes right down to it, you can't do anything that hasn't been done to me already."

"I don't—I don't want to."

"You don't want to? Did anyone tell you how kind you are?"

Alex said nothing. Lucy was right. He couldn't do anything to her. After all this time there wasn't anything he could do after what she had done to him. He looked at her. She seemed indestructible, and he felt small.

"We had a deal," he said weakly. "I still don't know."

"What's the matter? Don't think you got your money's worth?"

Alex didn't respond. He wasn't going to admit it, but he'd got more than his money's worth. At that click, things passed before him. The loneliness, the emptiness, the not wanting to go home because nothing was there. And now Lucy rejecting him after he thought he had rejected her a long time ago.

"I'm going in there," Lucy said as she pointed to the bedroom. She picked up the gun. "When I come back out, you better be gone."

She went into the room and slammed the door. Alex knew he would never get past that door and would never know the truth about Lucy.

IMPROVIDENT EXCESS

BARRY N. MALZBERG

Harmless tracked the candidate from motel to grange hall, from civic auditorium to the review stand in front of City Hall, from Des Moines to St. Pete to North Platte, finally catching up to him in the parking lot of Toys "R" Us in Newton, leveled the rifle for the killing shot, blew off the candidate's head at thirty feet downrange in a crowd, a spectacular shot for an amateur but the same old stuff for Gerald Harmless, skilled assassin and political consultant for hire. He disassembled the Mauser quickly, slipped it under the floorboards of the Blazer wagon they had shipped him, scooted the hell out of there before the ordnance around the candidate had even reacted to the impact. Harmless had great reflexes. Reflexes, of course, were all that you had to count on in this business; everything else was ideology and excuses—crap, that was to say. At the big traffic circle which spun him off to the south Harmless found a covey of police cars spinning out the other way, timed his release carefully, then opened the Blazer to full throttle and barreled off behind a huge truck. A quarter mile down the road he pulled into a diner, locked and abandoned the car, not worrying about the floorboards, and went inside to phone for a cab. Thirty-five minutes later he was at the airport, and the rest of the stuff was easy. The candidate's head, exploded, had been huge, had blown into the air like someone's air ball on a gymnasium floor, had hit the platform with a rotten bump before Harmless had pulled his glance away and had worked on getting out of there. Watching the consequences of his work was along with the money the only compensation he got from his work, reading about this stuff in the newspaper only depressed him, but there was no way that he could hang around and follow through on any of this stuff. You could watch or you could fire, he liked to tell his contracts, and they had nodded understandingly enough at that. Thorough and careful were best every time. There was no substitute for forethought.

On the plane, Gerald Harmless, thirty-eight years old, college dropout (accounting major), man of affairs and projects, hummed an odd little victory tune to himself, a song of accomplishment, of toneless satisfaction while businessmen on the commuter special made a little time with the stewardesses and complained about expense allowances. It all went past Harmless; it represented a view of life which he had put out of his head many, many years ago. Now he was a political consultant, public affairs division, deeply involved in the displacement and management of potential governments. He had a stack of business cards which said that. Left to his own, Harmless would as soon have taken his losses, cashed it in now, spent the remainder of his life considering the rich and mottled past and the consternation which he had so often left behind, but this would have been unwise. Ceaseless motion was the only way to address the current situation, and there were also powerful expenses to meet. Isn't that so? he said to the blond stewardess when she told him to secure his tray, please, and put the notebook underneath the seat. You have to control your situation at all costs. I suppose that's exactly right, sir, the stewardess said. Somewhere back of her blond, vacant eyes shone—Harmless speculated—the pure and awful fear of the disaster which awaited them all underneath, but he would not probe for it. The time for casual relationships had come and gone in his life without ever being exploited; he was a political consultant, not a casual pursuer of stewardesses. Fucking was only a metaphor for purer, deadlier stuff anyway, Harmless speculated. The plane bounced slightly on the landing, and Harmless thought of the scandal which might have ensued if there had been a fatal crash but somehow his diary had been saved. He kept a careful record of his accomplishments; the accounting mentality and need for ledgers persisted. He had had more to do with political life in America, he supposed, than any consultant, newspaper publisher, or ideologue, he supposed. Not that he had gotten into this to effect great changes. He had gotten into this to make a living, no meglomaniac he, and that rather than fantasies of influence was what had kept him in the trade.

Debarking casually at La Guardia, just another squat, slightly defeated thirty-eight-year-old guy among hundreds of voyagers, Harmless enjoyed the somnolent breezes of the city, conveyed his valise to the rental counter, asked for a compact with air-conditioning and signed the necessary pages, drove cautiously into New York, parked freely on West Forty-eighth Street at this late and safe hour, and went directly to the room which he had booked two days earlier at the Hilton, opened it, found his contact sitting in the armchair, waiting for him. It no longer concerned Harmless that these people had no respect for his privacy, that, too, was part of the trade-off, and as they had warned him from the beginning, they got in anywhere. A little late, his contact, a bearded man named Brown said. He looked a little bit like Tchaikovsky, a Slavic-looking fellow with hot eyes and a huge gray beard, a haunted expression in those eyes which might have come from too much *Pathètique* but most likely from the strains of being a political mover and shaker, a whole directorate on his own. You had any trouble?

Harmless shrugged, put down the valise, closed the door quietly. No trouble, he said. Delay on takeoff, a little bit of a rough landing. Traffic might have been a little tricky over the Willets Point Bridge, but nothing spectacular.

It went all right, Brown said. You looked at the papers, listened to the radio?

I never read the papers or listen to the radio, Harmless said. I drive with the windows up and the radio off. I figure if there's any real news, it will get to me, and otherwise it breaks my concentration. There was no trouble, was there?

Well, no, Brown said. Not that kind of trouble. You took his head off. He was dead before he moved, he probably thought that he was having a sudden bad dream, and then he stopped noticing anything. I don't think that there's going to be too much of a vote for him in the primary; of course, you can never tell about protest votes. His handlers seem pretty broken up about it.

That's a shame, Harmless said. What I try to do, I try to keep the handlers happy. I wouldn't want to displease them in any way. Did they really make you drink poison? Harmless said. That's the story I hear, that they made you drink up the poison because you were supposed to be a fag.

What the hell are you talking about?

Tchaikovsky, Harmless said. Don't you know anything about serious music? You look just like Tchaikovsky, a top Russian composer. He died at fifty-three, supposed to be poisoned water in an epidemic, but the word now is that the czar didn't like a fag being his court composer so he got the nobles together and they advised him he'd better check out. That's a kind of humiliating way to go, you know? Socrates this guy wasn't. He should have defied them, made an issue of it. But I guess that they were rough on you if you weren't straight in old Russia. Of course, I don't know anything about it, either straight or bent. I am truly sublimated in my craft.

You talk crazy, Brown said. You always talk crazy. I don't know why they put up with this. He touched his beard. You say I look like this guy Tchaikovsky?

He's dead. You look like pictures of him. I can get you some, you want to look.

I don't think I need to look, Brown said. Now there's another assignment here, and it's a little bit of a tricky one, so I want to put it to you fast and get your reaction if you'll sit down.

Harmless sat on the couch, looked at the floor, then slyly at Brown. There's a matter of five grand on delivery, he said. You got the delivery, the papers make that clear, right? So how about the five grand?

That's coming, Brown said. That's no problem. Now this assignment, we want you to off Curley. We want you to call him and tell him you got to report directly on some business we had down here and you got to meet him someplace private. You take him to the Inn, he won't give you any trouble, he's been taken out there before. Then you do him in close range. Some stuff came up, and we can't carry him no more. Curley is going to have to go.

That's ridiculous, Harmless said. Curley's my contact; he's my setup guy, just like you're my reporting-in guy. I can't kill him. I never heard of anything like that. Who do you think I am?

Well, that's the deal, Brown said. He looked uncomfortable for a moment; then it passed, and he was his bearded, imposing, death-haunted Tchaikovskyan self again. This concerns stuff you don't need to know about anyway, but Curley has got to go. He's made a lot of trouble, never mind what, and it's going to be bad news until we clear the way.

That's crazy, Harmless said. Curley sends me out on these jobs. How do I know this isn't all a trick, a test? You and Curley want to find out if I'm loyal to him, if I can be trusted. If I say no, I won't take him out, then I get good marks, but if I go along with the deal, I get offed. Hey, Harmless said, I got cable and a videotape recorder, I watch the same stuff everybody does in my time off. I've seen the movies; this is a loyalty test. No, I won't play; I can't go along with any of this stuff. Staring at Brown, Harmless succumbed to an old intimation, one that he had recently felt on the plane: He had been in the business too long; it was time to get out. He was being edged that way; there were things about it which more and more were pushing him out of any sense of choice. There were no old hit men and no old political consultants either, and that was a clear truism in the trade, along with the need to clear your path of exit every time, before you got started. I think I'll just be on my way, Harmless said. I'll just go out into the night. I got the car on a week's rental. Maybe I'll go to the mountains or something. I could use some recuperative time. I recuperate, I turn the car in, that's the end of it. There are no hard feelings, you understand? I guess I'm saying that this is my career and retirement plan which is going into effect, my personal pension and higher horizons program, you know what I'm saying? I appreciate the opportunity, but this isn't a career tenure track position, you get the drift. He pulled up his socks, made scrambling motions with his feet, looked poised.

Sit down, Brown said loudly. This is no test, and I'm afraid that your options aren't so good. In fact, they're quite limited. You want to get out, that's your decision, sometimes a guy can't hack it no more, and we don't want to stand in anyone's way. But before that you're going to take care of Curley.

Look here, Brown said, putting a huge, cautionary hand on Harmless's shoulder, his piercing eyes seeming to radiate the same pain and intensity that Tchaikovsky's might have registered as he leaned forward to smell the cholera-loaded water. Maybe this seems a little tough for you, but I'm afraid we've got no alternatives here. Curley has to go, and you're the only guy we know who can get close to him no questions asked, you been carrying his water for quite a while now. So you go into Bensonhurst, you take care of this business, and we're quits, that's all. Later on you can go any-where you want; we got a nice locker at Grand Central full of stuff you can use, take you on your way. Brown reached into his pocket, extended a key as if it were a baton. It's all yours in locker twenty sixty-five after you take care of this one piece of business. I would suggest that you make this as easy for us as possible, Harmless, because one way or the other you're going to have to do it.

I never wanted to get into intrigue, Harmless said. That was never the deal. Political consultancy, outside work, that was why I hired on. Curley said that I'd never get tied into the inside stuff, and I trusted him.

Well, Brown said, well, yes, that's true. A lot of us trusted him. A lot of us trusted him and found that was a pretty big mistake. He took Harmless's wrist, pulled him near, put the key in the palm, and closed Harmless's fingers one by one around them. Trust me, Brown said. The checkout guy's word is gold even if the check-in guy turned out to be a louse and a double-crosser. You tell Curley you got to give him some important inside information, and then you give him the information deep inside, you know? And that will be the end of it. I know for a fact, Harmless, that you got a very poor personal life, almost no personal life at all, what you find in locker twenty sixty-five could change all of that around. You do us this assignment, then we're quits. Otherwise we're quits in a different way. That's all I have to say, Brown said, towering over the confused and unsettled Harmless with a truly czarist elegance even though the height difference could only have been a couple of inches. The phone is here, the key is there, the ordnance I assume is in the valise, Brown said, so you're all set. You sure don't need any more instructions, do you? So that's it, Brown said. I don't mean to be terse or inconsiderate or anything, really, but that's all I have to say. Brown was at the door, then out of the door quickly, the vastly discombobulated Harmless feeling the heat of the key slowly coiling through his palm, reaching with its tendrils toward that heart of purpose which previously only politics had inflamed.

Harmless thought of the ramifications of American politics, the marvelous possibilities of government by accident or assassination as he rode on the subway into Bensonhurst. The arranged meeting with Curley could not have gone easier: Just meet me at the usual place, the back room, Curley had said when Harmless had said he needed to talk. You did good today, Curley said, I seen all the papers, I read the reports, you cleaned him out of the race. That's one goddamned less problem we got to face in these times. Harmless wondered if the people at the St. Petersburg Conservatory had talked this way when they squeezed the poison into Tchaikovsky: one less fag for whom to apologize, one less set of scandals. Squeezing the pistol in his inner coat pocket, Harmless considered not only government by accident or assassination but his own role in the vast convulsions and eddies of history. Also, the roles of all these people in the subway with him, New Yorkers and urban denizens of various ages, colors, and backgrounds, each of them scrambling around trying to assert some control but knowing at the center that there was no control at all. Everything was beyond them. Find someone who made a little bit too much trouble, and the shot would come from the roof or maybe there would be the sudden revelation from the secret woman, and that would be the end of him. Everything was in the grip of larger forces, not necessarily sinister but certainly insistent, Harmless thought, and that includes me, too. Except that I decided to go to work for them at an earlier age and express political consultancy in a little more direct manner. Also, I have no opinions and get paid for having no opinions; that puts me on the opposite end of almost everyone these days.

Harmless considered the forces and vast convulsions, disguised as accidents, in contemporary America all the way to the Atlantic Avenue stop, made it out into the air, then in the quick, stinking dark of the abandoned railroad yards, took a cab to the bar, no worry about leaving witnesses or identification, no one gave a damn in Brooklyn or anywhere else, and walked through the bar, past the video games and the football replay on the back wall and into the anteroom, where Curley sat alone, a gin in front of him, smoking a cigar and looking at him incuriously. Boy, oh, boy, Gerry, Curley said, you're sure looking terrible for a guy who changed the face of history today. You ought to take a little pleasure in what you're doing; you made a real contribution. Curley shook his head, laughed, banged the seat next to him. So sit down, he said, tell me what you got in mind? What's the problem, Gerry? I hear *agita* on the phone, and *agita* is not my thing. You made a botch? Everything seemed all right on TV; they're already changing the subject back to football. You want more work? We got to wait a little while until this cools. There may be something else later on this year, it's hard to tell. What do you have to say, Gerry? I'm patient, I been waiting, but I got my own exposure on this deal, too.

Feeling the weight of the gun, of all history on him, Harmless felt something else as well; it might have been a disdain so profound that it leached into all the crevices of activity and possibility. I don't want to do this, he said, and Curley stared at him, his brown eyes bright with consternation, a twinkle shading a little toward consternation but ready at any time to go back to merriment. I don't get it, Curley said, what's the deal here now, Gerry? I got no time to play twenty questions with you, and Harmless could feel the disdain emerging, driving him toward a shrug, a shrug of marvelous callousness and ease as he withdrew the gun. I got orders, he said pointlessly. I mean, I got pretty strong orders; I wouldn't do this on my own. He pulled the trigger. Curley's head, Harmless noted, did not explode like the candidate's, but rather it *cracked*, split into uneven parts like a rotten cantaloupe, and from the crack at the center the lymph sprang, settling into a thick ooze. Disgusting. That was political consultancy for you. Harmless put the second slug into his contact man's throat and watched the consequences come out, pus and pulp, the American condition itself scrambling its way from the man's head. The enraged heart, still astonished by this immediacy, raced frantically: Curley spewed the colors of the flag into the air. Had to do it, Harmless said, not quite sure whom he was addressing, and backed the chair from the table, stood, held the gun, turned toward the door.

They would be coming in soon; he knew this with that utter precision for which he had already through his deeds become famous. They would be coming in soon, cleaning out the issue, settling things cold. It was like Tchaikovsky, get the situation settled, the embarrassment pushed away with the least amount of trouble. But in that slow and burning instant before Brown and his pals came in to even off the job and close down the curtains, in that uneven and attenuated instant, Harmless said, Let's hear it for the red, white, and blue, three cheers for the grand old flag we all love, and aimed the gun not at his head but at the aperture, waiting for the czar and his minions to come through the door then, waiting in that certainty that no Tchaikovsky he, he would shoot to kill, and they would have to take him down screaming. We live here; it's our country, he said to the vomitous, stinking, headless thing spread on the table; we made it, and we can break it. They would have to put the poison in, Harmless thought. He would not do it to himself. He waited in pallid and perfect attention, hearing at last the thunder of the Cossacks.

THE KING OF HORROR

STEPHEN MERTZ

I'm the greatest horror writer who ever lived.

The tragedy—for me as a professional writer, for you as a reader—is that, more than likely, you've never heard of me.

You've heard of Stephen King. You've heard of Clive Barker. You've heard of Dean R. Koontz. Pretenders to the throne, every one of them, and there are too many others like them. Talentless pygmies in a land once ruled by giants like Poe, Lovecraft, Derleth, Bloch.

And yours truly, Rigley Balbo. A prophet without honor in his own country. A man who was cheated and pushed aside by these grubby, johnny-come-lately punks and their million-dollar contracts and their *New York Times* best-sellers.

They went to school reading my stuff. *The Cemetery People. The Goblins Are Hungry. Blood on My Hatchet.*

And what did I get out of it? Lousy advances, no reviews, crummy distribution, and even that was years ago. In other words, I got nothing out of it. Nada. Zip. Not a damn thing. Not money. Not fame. Hell, my last book was published nine years ago in England only. The bastards paid me four hundred frigging dollars for it, and it's never been reprinted since, in England or anywhere else.

Pardon me for sounding more than a little bitter, folks, but I'm talking hunger here, and pain, and the indescribable ache of seeing men and women not fit to kiss my platen roller going after big bucks time after time after time.

The only horror about their writing is that they can get away with recycling the same third-rate crap—lifted from old movies, old pulps, old comics, and the work of their betters—and foisting it off on a semiliterate public that doesn't know any better.

But have any of these jerks ever said a nice word about me in public after they became famous? Have they ever cited me as one of the founding fathers of this genre they've coasted on to the bank? Have they ever helped a tired old pro out by maybe slipping him a few bucks when it could have helped? No, no, and no. Scum, talentless scum, every one of them.

Well, there was one who was different. His name was Mark Darby, and his is the last story I want to tell. Or maybe it's my story, I'm not sure. I'm not sure of anything anymore.

I'll just tell the story.

You decide.

He chose a restaurant we'd been to a couple of times before when he'd been to New York, one of those places just off Broadway, midtown, that has still managed to hold off against the closing-in sleaze that's rotted most of that part of Manhattan into something unrecognizable since the days when I and the city were a whole lot younger.

Writers rarely run with the pack. We'd set a lunch date for after the noon rush, but a good restaurant in that part of town is rarely empty, even at midafternoon.

He was waiting for me at a corner table when I walked in. The murmur of conversation, the clink of silverware from nearby tables, and the Muzak the place piped in did nothing to ease the tension that had wrapped my gut into a knot and strangely juxtaposed the ringing in my ears that began when I approached the table.

He rose to greet me with that fresh-faced grin of his that the world knew from his book jacket photograph. He must have been about forty by now, but he could have passed for ten or fifteen years younger than that with no problem, damn him. There were no stress lines at the corners of his eyes or mouth, no gray in his beard or longish hair. Why should there be? He had the world by the tail. He was dressed casually, but the clothes were expensive, I could tell.

I wondered if he noticed how out of style, how threadbare my own jacket, slacks, and shirt were.

His handshake was firm and friendly, like his voice.

"Rig. Damn, it's good to see you again. How the hell have you been?"

"Getting by."

We ordered. A beer for him, scotch on the rocks for me. Then we ordered lunch. He ordered the hamburger steak. I ordered salad. Lunch is usually my main meal of the day, but the knot in my stomach had taken away my appetite.

We touched glasses in a silent toast.

"Jeez, Rig, I'm glad you were able to make it. What's it been, four or five years?"

Glad I could make it. You sniveling little shit. It's not like I've been balancing an overloaded social calendar, exactly. More like sitting around waiting for the goddamn phone to ring.

I sipped my drink and was surprised to see that my hand was trembling. Just a tremor, not enough to spill more than a drop. He probably noticed, but he didn't say anything.

"I've been wondering how you were doing, kid." I tried to make my voice sound cordial. "I saw your book all over the best-seller lists. What was it—three years ago?—then nothing."

"I had to cut the world loose for a while."

"Still, I didn't figure you'd cut me loose. No one seemed to know what happened to you. I figured you'd stay in touch with me at least. Ever since you wrote me that fan letter twenty years ago, I guess I always thought of us as friends more than just teacher and student. I've got to say, kid, I didn't know what to make of it. It sort of hurt my feelings."

"I'm sorry," he said, and he sounded sincere. "My brain blocked after that first book went through the ceiling like it did."

"So where have you been?"

"Bummed around Europe some. Lived on Majorca for a while. Fell in and out of love in Paris. I finally hammered another book into shape. I'm in town to deliver it to my agent."

"Big bucks, I'll bet, huh?"

"Uh, let's not get into that, Rig."

"Hey, it's okay. I heard about it at a fan convention I went to a couple months back. I still attend the damn things even if I haven't written in the field in twenty years. Anyway, I heard. You pulled down half a mil for an advance. How does it feel?"

"Every page is still a battle. My back still goes out on me. Hemorrhoids still give me hell. Not that much has changed."

"Yeah, right."

"How about you? What are you working on these days?"

I shrugged. I polished off my drink.

"I'm not working. Why bother? It wouldn't sell." I set the glass back down on the table, maybe a little too hard. "I'm washed up, or haven't you heard? My career was in the toilet before you left. I can't get work. No agent will handle me. Ten years ago I made a stink about how they were screwing me on royalty payments and the bastards blacklisted me. You know that. I need another drink."

I ordered another, a double this time. He was still working on his beer. He waited until the waitress had come and gone before he spoke.

"You did piss off and alienate a hell of a lot of people," he agreed, "but that was a long time ago. Editors come and go. Writers write until they die, and then their work lives forever. You taught me that, remember?"

"Yeah, but the blacklist stayed around forever, too. The last ten years have been tough, Mark. Real tough. I can't get arrested on publishers' row."

"Rig, every writing career has its ups and downs, its lean stretches. Look at so-called bad boys like Harlan Ellison. He's made a second career out of bad-mouthing crooked publishers, but other houses still publish his stuff. Editors will buy books if they think the books will sell."

"Listen, kid, every writer in the world is getting screwed by every publisher in the world." I made an effort to sip my drink, not toss it back the way I wanted to. The tremors had stopped, but not the knot in my stomach or the ringing in my ears. I set the glass down easy this time. "So what is it, Mark? Now that you've got a best-seller under your belt and some oversize advances, you're not going to go condescending on me, are you? You're not going to forget where you came from?"

"Don't be mean, Rig. I thought we were friends."

"I guess I've just about had it up to here with this current crop of so-called brand-name authors. A bunch of what's-in-it-for-me thieves, that's all they are. You'd think I had leprosy at the cons I go to. You can see it in their eyes from across the room."

"I hope you don't think I feel that way."

I couldn't stop the words from spilling out. I was getting drunk. Whiskey on an empty stomach. But I didn't give a shit.

"They're just showing their true colors," I said. "One oversize paycheck, and the little buggers actually start to believe that they're better writers. All of a sudden they're not available when the big issues come up, like getting shafted over royalties or fighting for fair play. Buck the establishment? All of a sudden they can't be bothered. They can't afford to choose sides or do the right thing. Damn them for the hypocrites they are."

"I'm sorry to see you like this, man."

"What the hell did you expect? You know what that blacklist did to my career."

An uncomfortable silence. Then the food came. We both ate for a few minutes without saying anything.

Then he said, quietly, "Are you sure there was a blacklist, Rig, or were you just making yourself too difficult to do business with?"

I'd been forcing myself to eat. I couldn't take another bite. I swallowed and set my fork down next to the half-finished salad.

"Who have you been talking to? Of course, there was a blacklist. I fought city hall, and I lost. They ran me out on a rail, and they never let me back in. Okay, if there wasn't a blacklist, what the hell happened to my career?"

Another stretch of silence. He pushed his plate away with most of his hamburger still on it.

"This is a hell of a get-together after all these years."

"Tell me. If it wasn't them, who the hell did this to me?"

"It was you, Rig."

That caught me off guard. I blinked.

"Me?"

There was hurt in his eyes. He spoke softly, for no other ears but mine.

He said, "You allowed your ego and laziness to grind your talent into dust."

"Laziness? After my first few books I wrote ten books a year for ten years!"

"Those were gothic novels, Rig. Your first four horror books were terrific, but when the gothic boom hit in the sixties and early seventies, you wrote one and it sold better than your horror stuff, so you took on a pen name and cranked out nothing but from then on."

"Writers have to eat. And they were good gothics, heavy on atmosphere with a lot of horror elements."

"Maybe, but you weren't writing ten books a year. You were writing the same book ten times a year for ten years. Your editors wouldn't have bought that type of book if you'd tried to break the formula."

"And I suppose you're not lazy, mister four-years-to-write-a-book?"

"Maybe a creative block is laziness," he conceded. "I've done formula work for hire when I had to, to pay the rent. But I know it's a hell of a lot harder to take the time and the patience to dig down inside and try to do something different each time out, to try to make yourself a better writer with each book, than just to work the treadmill." He looked across the table, looked me straight in the eye then. "That's the kind of writer you were in the beginning, Rig, and it's the kind of writer you could still be unless your ego precludes you from learning, from creative growth."

I wanted to lean across the table and strangle the life out of him right then, but of course, that wouldn't do, and I was aware that a few heads had already turned from nearby tables at my last outburst, although they had since returned to minding their own business.

Stay cool, I told myself. It won't be long now.

"Writing is everything to me," I told him.

He shook his head.

"Don't give me that," he said, not unkindly. His tone was friendly, in fact. "Your ego is everything to you. You wrote for as long as it came easy, and it came easy because you never struggled to better yourself, only to write faster. When it no longer came easily, you blew up at everyone in sight, the good and the bad, and you threw in the towel."

"What the hell do you know about it?" I snapped. "I have a closetful of unpublished manuscripts that I can't give away, and you tell me there was no blacklist."

"You're forgetting that you let me read some of those manuscripts. The ones I read were sabotaged by every bad habit you'd picked up over ten years of writing those trash books: uncertain point of view, authorial intrusion, ungrammatical as hell."

"Well, aren't you the authority all of a sudden?"

"Not all of a sudden. It took me a long time to learn what good writing is. Dammit, Rig, you spent years turning out faddish, ephemeral junk, and now you're bitter because you're not regarded as a major talent. You want to be a major writer? Write a major book."

"Like you did, I suppose."

"No, like *you* did in the beginning. Do what you can already do. Write a page turner that sends shivers up the spine. That's what your best stuff always did to me. That's why I wrote you that first fan letter all those years ago. Write a book for today's market, and instead of focusing your considerable energies and talent on volume, focus on improving for a change."

"Listen to you." I tried to keep the snarl out of my voice and failed. "Today's market! What you mean is, I should turn myself into one of those derivative, bloodless hacks with no sound of their own. Listen, I'm going to outlive and outclass nine tenths of these flash-in-the-pan scribblers."

"Maybe so, but in the meantime, they're going to the bank and you're in the poorhouse."

I felt wash through me the brooding blackness of despair that always alternated with the rage.

"Don't remind me. I'm almost glad Ginny isn't alive to see what became of me. She used to share my dreams, crazy lady. I'm glad we didn't have kids. I'm a rotten goddamn failure. It's hard to believe that once upon a time I was so full of dreams and ambition. Oh, I was going to set the world on fire with my typewriter. I was going to be a great entertainer. But after all those books, after all those millions of words, you want to know how I feel now? If you ever wake up surrounded by books and typewriters, you've died and gone to hell."

I heard my words taper off, heard the sentence dwindle away, and I didn't want to see the look on Mark Darby's face because I knew I'd see pity and nothing else. I waved down the waitress and ordered another double.

The kid passed. He still hadn't finished his beer.

The distraction gave me some time to rein in my emotions. Slow down, Rig, I told myself. Slow down. Don't lose it. What's going to happen will happen any minute now.

I glanced over Darby's shoulder at the glass doors behind him that led to the street.

Still no sign of Lester. But he'd be putting in an appearance soon enough. Lester wasn't the type to pull a no-show, not on something like this.

Mark Darby may have been my biggest fan once upon a time, and maybe he thought he was my friend, but he didn't know everything about me. Not by a long shot.

For starters, he didn't know that I actually had been writing some over the past few years, some hard-core porn work I'd managed to scare up and, almost as bad, one entry in an action adventure paperback series before the editor found out who I was. I'd approached the series editor using a pen name for cover, not giving my own name. They paid me a kill fee on that one and never published it, said it wasn't up to snuff—too purple, they called it; overwritten—but I knew better. The blacklist was still in effect.

The kill fee was peanuts, but I got something worth a whole lot more out of the experience besides humiliation and rejection.

I got Lester.

Maybe you know a guy like Lester. They sent him to Vietnam a lifetime ago and part of him never came back. I met him at my favorite neighborhood tavern about the time I was writing that action adventure book.

You know the kind of book I mean: Big, tough macho hero saves the world from foreign bad guys and annihilation, book after book, month after month, all in 192 pages. Real juvenile crap.

Anyway, Lester reads that stuff. He's collected all of the different series, and we got to be regular drinking buddies after he found out I was working on one. He'd been trained in the Special Forces but been bounced even before the war was over. My guess would be he started liking it too much, but that was one thing he never spoke about.

What he did talk about was his guns. He had a regular arsenal in his basement. I saw it once. He talked about all the ways he knew of killing a man, of the satisfaction he had always gotten when he'd take someone out and it had gone like clockwork. He told me that he missed those days.

Of course, I talked some, too. I told him about the fair-haired boys who had stolen my place in the sun, had stolen my markets, my readers, my livelihood. I told him about my hatred for the ones who were selling the books that I should have sold instead of getting blacklisted and living off my Social Security and getting drunk on cheap booze and my festering hatred.

One thing led to another.

"You'd like to see them dead, wouldn't you, Rig?" he said late one night after last call, just before the bartender threw us out.

I didn't even have to think about it.

"Yeah, I'd like to see them dead, Lester. In the worst way. I dream about it. After what they did to me, I'd love to see them get theirs, every last one of them. I'd do it myself except I don't have the guts."

"Well, I do," he'd said quietly.

At first I thought he was kidding, egging me on, just having fun with the demons and misery of a broken-down old drunk.

But he wasn't kidding.

He had demons, too, and they needed to be satisfied, it turned out, as much as mine did. It was as if Fate had brought us together. One of those coincidences you're not supposed to use in fiction, but it happens all the time in what we call real life.

That was the beginning. We started getting together more regularly. We'd fire our demons with alcohol at the tavern, and then we'd adjourn to his place or mine, where I'd supply the names and the cities where they lived and he would take considerable time between our meetings to draw up extensive plans for the elimination of each one of them. Contracts, he called them, and none of them would look like murder, he said. One could be a suicide; another would be an accident; another would be made to look like the victim of a burglary. That one would look like murder, of course, but he would ensure that there would be no way either of us could be tied into any of the deaths.

The best thing was, it wouldn't cost me a cent. Lester looked healthier every time I saw him. He even gave up drinking after the first few planning sessions. It was as if he were born again or something. I guess his reward would be in knowing that he could still perform at what had once given his life its meaning and purpose.

Me? I just fell asleep smiling, thinking about it every night. I couldn't stop drinking, and it didn't make me want to write, but revenge would be its own sweet reward. The ones who had stolen from me and built careers on it would be as dead as my career was, and anticipation of that was all I needed. Hell, it was better than writing. It was better than sex.

Lester had been a week away from implementing the first "contract" when I'd gotten the unexpected call last night from Darby.

I'd lost touch with Mark, but what I felt for the others was even stronger for him because he had written me those glowing fan letters all those years ago. He'd almost literally learned at my knee, and so the hatred I felt for him was a more personal thing. The others had learned from reading my books; that's how they'd stolen from me. Mark Darby had been much more personal about it. Over the years he'd stolen from my brain, and so his end would be more personal, too. I wanted to see him die, unlike with the others. Lester had explained that it would be much better if I were nowhere nearby, if I had myself a strong alibi, when those contracts were carried out. But this . . . payback, let's call it, would have to be different, I knew.

I'd called Lester and explained all of this to him as soon as I'd hung up after getting Darby's call.

Lester hadn't skipped a beat. "Shouldn't be a problem. They taught us in the Berets to adapt and improvise. When do you want me to do it?"

I guess I was taken aback a little at his readiness and his willingness.

"How about while he and I are having lunch together?" I suggested. "But will that work? I mean, it'll be broad daylight. There'll be witnesses. That will be good for me, they'll know I didn't do it, but what about you?"

"No problem." Lester always spoke briskly when he talked about killing people. "A hit in public can be the easiest. A man walks up to the table in a restaurant and blows some guy away. Crazy shit like that happens in New York all the time."

"But the witnesses—"

"In a situation like that people are in shock from what they've seen. That's all they see. I come in, I execute this Darby guy, and I run out. No one will try to stop me. Shock, like I said. As many people who witness it, that's how many descriptions the police will get of the killer, and not one of them will be worth a damn."

"So how will you do it? A gun? A knife?"

"Don't worry about it. Maybe a gun, maybe a knife, maybe something else. The more spectacular, the less anyone will see of me. They'll see the blood and a dead man and that's all. But there is one thing."

"What's that?"

"Like you said, Rig, this one will be different from the others because you'll be there."

"So?"

"Ever see a man killed before?"

"Uh, not really."

"It won't be pretty. Just don't get cold feet on me, okay? Once I commit myself to taking someone out, I do it, and nothing stops me, understand?"

"I understand."

"Good. You just meet the guy for lunch, and I'll take care of the rest. But if you want to back out, now's the time. Nothing gets in my way, and that includes you. From the minute I walk into that restaurant tomorrow, this guy is dead meat. You try to stop it, and I'll take you out, too. I just want that clear between us."

"Don't worry about it. Nothing will change my mind. In fact, I'm looking forward to it."

Not only had nothing changed my mind, but the more time I spent over lunch with Mark Darby, the more I wanted to see the disrespectful creep get his.

I had to work to keep my eyes from wandering to the street entrance. It would be better if it came as a surprise to me when it did happen, I told myself. It would look better that way.

I sipped my drink and watched him over the rim of the glass. I realized he was saying something, that my attention had drifted. He didn't have a clue to what my thoughts had been. How could he? The smug bastard would never guess in a million years, and all he had left was a few more minutes at most.

"You're right, Rig," he was saying in a gentler tone than before. "I did learn from reading you when I was a kid, and so did a lot of other writers who are hot today."

"Well, there you are," I managed to say. "Filthy thieves."

"But learning isn't stealing," he said, "and we learned from reading hundreds of other writers, too, and if some of the writers in my age group do appear to be condescending toward you at times, it may be because we've continued to learn and grow as writers over the years and you haven't."

"Bullshit."

"Not bullshit, Rig. You do need to improve your work. You should want to, every writer needs to, and for you a big start would be just to go back to being as good as you were in the beginning. You can do that. You can become a modern stylist. Those first novels of yours are exactly what editors are looking for today. But it was as if, at some point early on, you decided you'd learned enough."

I couldn't help myself. My eyes shifted over his shoulder again to the door. Come on, Lester, I thought. Come on. The ringing in my ears was growing louder.

"So thanks for the postmortem," I said. "So why are you wasting your time? What is this, talented student gives mentor a pep talk? So you are like all the others after all."

"Rig, you have got to stop blaming everyone else. You're deluding yourself. Why don't you fix the blame where it belongs and everything else could fall into place? God knows the world is a far from perfect place, and that sure does include the writing profession and the publishing industry. You're right, they are shark-infested waters."

"So I'm right."

"Only about that, but that can't be an excuse for everything you've let happen to yourself. Your biggest enemies are your ego and your inability to adapt."

"Adapt and improvise, eh?"

"Exactly. Cut through that, and you can be three times the writer you ever were. No one can make a page sing the way you do when you're in top form. Get your act together, and we'll do business."

That threw me for a loop.

"Business?"

"I haven't been hammering at you like this for fun. See, Rig, I'm not 'like the others,' and you're wrong about most of them. I'm taking a big chunk of that last advance I was paid, and I'm going into the publishing business myself."

"You're what?"

"I dunno, it's just something I've always wanted to do, maybe for some of the reasons you've just stated about what's wrong with the industry. I want to do it right. I've hired one of the best editors in town." He was talking faster now, bubbling, in rising spirits. "I control the purse strings, and I want to give you your chance. Just this week I reread *The Cemetery People*. Hadn't read that one since I was a kid, and you know what? It absolutely bowled me over."

"That was one of my masterpieces," I admitted.

I'd forgotten all about watching the glass doors.

"I do owe you for what you've given me, Rig," he said. "When I was a kid, your writing helped make me want to be a writer. When I started writing and I contacted you, you encouraged me, and your books have entertained me through the years. I even read those lame gothics you wrote. I'm still a fan. I've reread some of your old books several times. I want to pay some of that back if I can. You'd do the same for me."

"What are you saying, kid?"

"I'm saying that if you'll get your act together, I mean really together, if you'll write a book for today's market, free of cliché and the other problems we've discussed, if you'll really go back to being the king of horror, then I'll see to it that my editor buys that book from you and that it's published. All I'm asking for is the blockbuster I know you've got in you. I'll see to it that you get a top dollar advance on acceptance with a major promo budget, and I'll want to reprint some of that great old stuff, too."

"I . . . don't know what to say," was all I could manage.

"Please say yes, Rig, and please don't screw up this chance I'm giving you."

I didn't have time to reply to that.

I saw Lester come in from the street, looking straight ahead. His face was like I'd never seen it before, like a mask carved in granite.

He saw us and started straight for the table. His eyes were on the back of Mark's head, and he was reaching for something in his pocket.

A NICE SAVE

EDWARD WELLEN

Mal spotted Woolf in the darkness beyond the glassed-in section of the promenade. Mal followed him out onto the deserted after-deck, into the gale-force wind that made the sensible and the queasy take cover.

The deck shoved up and then dropped away underfoot. Woolf was butting through wind buffets right up to the bulwark rail. Mal had to smile; looked as if the guy were going to feed his dinner to the fish.

With alarm, Mal caught on to the stupid bastard's real intent.

Woolf started to climb over the rail, the wind fluffing the surround of his tonsure and flapping his sport shirt.

Mal could reach him in time only with a shout. "Hey! You're forgetting something!"

Woolf's head jerked around. "Who the hell said that?"

Mal, holding the rail along the superstructure, leaned out of shadow. "Me."

"Who the hell are you?"

"A guy who can tell you why you don't want to do it."

"What makes it your business?"

"Look, the wind is tearing our words. Climb back down, and I'll tell you. Don't worry, I won't make a grab."

Mal could almost feel the guy's stare. A toss-up for a long minute, to jump or not to jump.

Then Woolf climbed down off the rail. But he held it, ready to hurdle. "Shit. It would've been all over by now." He sounded somewhere between sore and sullen. "Okay. So tell me why not."

"Because there has to be a body."

He said it so seriously that—after initial surprise—the other laughed.

The laugh died into a thoughtful grunt. "You got something there. If I vanish into salt air, it could take my ever-loving heirs seven years to settle my estate. Not that I couldn't care less. But shit, man, you know how long it took me to nerve myself to the jumping point? I'd have to work up the nerve all over again." He shivered all at once. "Goddammit, let me buy you a drink. I know I sure could use one."

"Likewise."

Woolf let go the rail and skidded downhill to Mal and caught hold beside him. He stuck out his free hand. "The name's . . . Max Schaf." The voice strained but with a politician's rote frank heartiness, the flesh clammy but with a politician's preemptive grip.

"Harry Pace." The name *he* was traveling under.

"Great, Harry."

Mal saw that Woolf failed to make him from the lifeboat drill the *Queen Mab*'s first day out. They had the same boat station, and Mal had certainly sized up Woolf at the time, but Woolf's obvious preoccupation had kept Woolf from registering Mal. And in between Woolf had holed up in his cabin, living on room service while he thrashed out whether to stonewall the federal investigation or to spill his guts. Some vacation, the Caribbean cruise his doctor had ordered to avert breakdown and elude the media. Some vacationer, Borough President Al Woolf traveling sans mustache and sans toupee as "Max Schaf."

Woolf looked around. "I guess we go back through the glass section to the stairs."

"Never mind those stairs." Mal steered him to another door. "I found a shortcut. It's a way just the crew uses. It goes straight down all the way to the engine room."

Actually, it didn't go straight down; it corkscrewed. But you could see the shaft had doors so you could get off at the decks along the way.

He ushered Woolf in. "Hold tight and watch your step."

Woolf started down the twisting stairs. "You know, I feel born again." He sounded manic. "I'm glad you happened along when you did."

Mal was busy taking plastic gloves from his pocket and pulling them on. "I'm glad you're glad."

The guy started to look around with a big smile. Mal gave him a hard neck chop and then a shove. Woolf ended in a heap a dozen steps below. Mal swung swiftly down to make sure the guy was dead. The guy was dead.

He had *told* the guy there had to be a body. Mal's client needed to know that Woolf hadn't faked a suicide, needed to know that Woolf wasn't still around in some new identity, needed to be sure that Woolf couldn't still bleat if the feds caught up with him.

Mal's client needed to *know* Woolf was dead.

WITHOUT A TRACE

WARREN MURPHY

There are days when you're just not safe anywhere because the crazies will find you.

This one day, for instance. I was drinking coffee, turned the television on, and there was some nutcase on the tube asking for money to save dolphins. Her final, grand reason? Because we've all heard of how dolphins save shipwrecked people by pushing them into shore to safety. So send her money.

Come on now. Doesn't anybody out there think anymore? Sure, we've all heard how dolphins save people. But we don't get a chance to hear about all the people in shipwrecks that dolphins bump out to sea until they drown. Dolphins don't have any sense. They think people floating around in the water are big beach balls to play with. Some they push in; some they push out. It's beach ball bingo, and for this I'm supposed to send money?

This lunacy so unnerved me that I decided it was safer to go to the office where at least I didn't have a television to intrude on my reveries.

But that dolphin lady stayed on my mind. Some people will say anything for money. Some people will *do* anything for money: lie, cheat, steal, even kill. I know this is a fact because occasionally people go so far as to marry for money.

Anything for money. You'll just have to faith it out on this one and trust me, as well you should. I am a private detective, and I know all about anything for money, and on this awful day I also knew that we didn't have any and that if some didn't come in pretty soon, I might have to start turning tricks in Washington Square Park. *Who's the cheap bastard who gave you the dime? All of them.*

I was sitting inside our office on Twenty-sixth Street, behind the neatly lettered door sign which read TRACY AND MANGINI, CONFIDENTIAL INVESTIGATIONS.

First of all, Tracy and Mangini. See, there are two Tracys. There is Patrick Tracy, the founder of this vast detection empire. He is my father and a retired New York City police sergeant, and one of the two marks him as almost sane.

The other Tracy is me, Devlin Tracy. I am, on my best days, considered a ne'er-do-well. Some people call me Trace. Mangini is Michiko Mangini, also known as Chico, also known as my significant other, who is an Italian-Japanese–American homicidal maniac who has just gotten her private detective's license, can now carry a gun, and is just waiting for someone to play touchy-feely with her on the subway so she has a chance to use it. And she'd walk. Chico is so knockout that no jury could find her guilty of anything, including hot-blooded Sicilian murder.

So Sarge, my father, was down in Florida, doing penance for his sins by taking my mother on vacation, and Chico was over in Jersey, trying to scout up some business, and I was sitting in the office, alone, thinking the big thoughts that go with being one of the last of the urban knights who would bring order to this disorderly world.

We private eyes talk like that, you know. That and clever little wines and imported Polish beers and the best place in America to get an authentic chimichanga . . . all that kind of stuff that we operatives know and average Americans are just dying to find out about, and when I wasn't thinking big thoughts about chimichangas and Polack beer and valor and stuff, I was wondering how we were going to pay the rent on this sinkhole.

Sarge always says that I should stop worrying and that God will provide, but I don't know about that because the last time I counted on God to provide, he provided me with a wife and two kids—what's his name and the girl—and I don't know that I'm yet ready to trust God again. Chico, meanwhile, says that *she* will provide, but I don't know. She doesn't seem to be exactly overwhelmed with paying cases that require our special blend of ratiocination, logic, differential calculus, and degenerate drinking. So it's really left to me to worry, and I'm not so good at it because I've always thought that if we lose this office and get thrown out into the street, we could all go back to doing what we do better. Sarge to being harassed at home by my mother, God love her sainted spoon rests, I can go back to being a sort of a bum, and Chico can get a real job and support us both in a somewhat better fashion than she's been doing for the past couple of years.

Do you begin to suspect that I do not have a calling for this sort of work?

So anyway, there I am sitting in the office, alone, pretending to worry about the rent, when there is a knock on the door. Now I was hoping it would be a lady client with money to burn and legs from here to here, but instead it was a guy wearing mirrored sunglasses and a yachtsman's outfit with a gold-buttoned blue blazer and white pants and a hat with more scrambled eggs on it than my pajama tops. He is clearly not impressed by the office decor—Early Landfill—but nevertheless he lays a business card on the desk in front of me.

It's a silly-looking thing with a black border, like an undertaker's card, but it tells me that he is Jeff Padderson, a private investigator with offices in Beverly Hills, California—address given, no phone number—but he didn't have to tell me about California because he's just so damned tan and lean and lovely and big that he looks like George Hamilton on steroids. The boy from Ipanema. I knew he was from California.

I waved him to a chair, and he sits and smiles expectantly at me. I don't like this guy. I can tell that already. He is very smiley and I don't like that and I just bet that he would give money for dolphins if asked. And he leaves his sunglasses on the whole time. And they are cheap plastic sunglasses, too. I don't like people who keep their sunglasses on indoors. Although that is better than wearing them on top of your head, as if you had eyes under your hair.

Another thing I don't like is people who start conversations by asking a question. Chico says I'm only interested in schmooze, booze, and cooze, but I've never really liked schmooze. Still I do think a little personal comment is the best way to start a conversation. Instead this Jeff Padderson went right for my throat.

"Do you know who Old Brown Eyes is?"

"Elsie the Cow?"

He starts in with the loud laughing, another thing I'm not crazy about.

"Ha-ha-ha, very good, Tracy," he said. "No. Old Brown Eyes. Albie Newmeyer himself."

"Yeah," I said. "I know who he is."

Come on, I'm not stupid. Everybody knows who Albie Newmeyer is. After Crosby and Sinatra, just the world's greatest singer. And Crosby's gone to the nineteenth hole in the sky and Sinatra is so old that he's keeping it zipped these days and Elvis is doing supermarkets in Arkansas, so I guess Old Brown Eyes must be just about the biggest entertainer in the whole civilized world. And Nashville.

"So what about Old Brown Eyes?" I asked.

Padderson took a deep breath. "Before I say any more, I just want to be clear about something. Out in California, we PIs, well, we're like doctors or priests. Anything you tell us is in absolute confidence." He looked at me hopefully.

"I'm exactly like a doctor or a priest," I said. "Some of my friends even think I should wear a clerical collar."

"Yeah, yeah, but I've got to ask. I'm going to give you some confidential stuff. Anything I tell you stays in this room?"

"Wild horses wouldn't drag it out of me." About now I reached under my jacket and turned on the small hidden tape recorder I always wear as the only tool of my trade.

"Okay," he said. "I work for Albie pretty much full-time. Checking people out. Watching over his security when he goes on a nightclub tour. Stuff like that. I don't really work as a PI for him, more like a personal assistant. You know how it is. Busy men need assistants who can get the trucks out of the garage in the morning."

"*If* they own a garage," I said.

He ignored that and waited until I nodded. So I nodded.

"We want you to find someone."

"Anyone in particular?"

"You've got a sense of humor, Tracy. I like that. In our business you've got to have that or else go crazy."

"I agree."

"We want you to find Muffy Maguire. Think you could handle that?"

Who Muffy Maguire is is this writer. I guess they call her a tell-all biographer, which means she prints dirt about celebrities that no one else would print. Anyway, she's done a half dozen books or so on the rich and famous and it's all very sleazy and she's very rich and they're always talking about her on television, like she is this kind of bitch big time that everybody hates. But since I don't care what the rich and famous are doing, I don't read her junk, and I only know enough about her to know that I don't like her either.

"Why do you need somebody to find her? Is she missing?"

"No such luck," he said. "She's hiding out somewhere working on her next book. We want to talk to her."

Dawn started to break. "And her next book is about Old Brown Eyes, right?"

"You're a quick study, Tracy. I like that in a person."

I hate people who tell me I'm a quick study. I'm not a study at all. I'm more like a laundry room. With an open box of powdered Oxydol and a dripping faucet and a lightbulb that burned out eleven years ago.

On the other hand, the rent was due, so I didn't say anything, and Padderson did ha-ha-ha for a while and then nodded and said, "Yeah, she's doing a real ax murder job on Albie Newmeyer."

"So why do you want me to find her?"

"So we can talk to her about her book. A couple of years ago we thought we had her talked out of writing it, but we were wrong, and she's doing it yet. So we want to get her to soften some of the cheap shots we know she's going to take. Try to set the record straight, if you would." He paused. "Get her to go easy."

"What about her First Amendment rights?"

"We'll pay you a thousand dollars to find her," he said.

"Screw the First Amendment," I said.

"I like the cut of your jib, Tracy. Shall we say five hundred now, five hundred when you find her?"

"I like the cut of my jib, too. Shall we say let's wait until I know what the hell we're talking about?"

"What do you mean?" He sounded annoyed as if he had just reexamined my jib and found it wanting. A lot of people feel that way about my jib.

"What I mean is you're a private detective yourself. Why not find her yourself? You could probably do it in the morning, when you're not busy getting the trucks out of the garage."

"Reasonable question. A couple of answers. One. In the field of entertainment I'm pretty well known as being associated with Old Brown Eyes. I wouldn't want it to get around that we're worried about her book or we're looking for her or anything like that. She'd turn that into bad publicity for us, more hype for her book. That's why I swore you to secrecy. Two. I don't know anything about New York. I know L.A. I know Hollywood. But in this city I couldn't tell a shoeshine parlor from a strip joint. And I thought we should have a man who knows his way around. And that's where you come in."

"I can live with that. Any idea where the woman is?"

"We know she lives on"—he fished a piece of paper out of his pocket and read from it—"East Sixty-ninth Street, and she's got an office on West Fifty-seventh, where she works with her assistant. His name is Bruce Stillwell."

"Does he know where she is?"

Padderson scratched his head for a moment. "Of course he does, and I'll tell you the truth, Tracy, I called him. I used a phony name, of course, and tried to find out her whereabouts, but he wouldn't say anything. He's one of those loyal types."

"I hate loyalty," I said.

"Exactly." Did you ever notice how often Californians say "exactly" when they don't have a clue about what you're really saying?

Anyway, he went on. "This was going to be my suggestion. From what we gather, this Maguire broad is holed up in an apartment somewhere, working on the final draft of her book. Stillwell's running her office or whatever it is writers do. But he's got to be able to reach her. I figured you put a tail on this Stillwell and he's got to lead you to her. You find out, then tell me. Actually, it seems pretty cut-and-dried for a thousand dollars."

He had me there, so I admitted it. "It is, so I'll do it."

"Good. And the next time Albie is playing in New York, I'll get you and your lady some front-row seats. You'll love it."

"Very nice of you. Now look. A thousand dollars buys you where Maguire is or three days of my time. If I don't find her by then, my other five hundred's due and payable anyway. And I do the job my way."

That doesn't really mean anything, but I always say it. I just don't like to be pestered on a case by some client who thinks I should leave the tavern right now and go tracking somebody into the Everglades or some other stupid place.

Padderson was agreeable, so we shook hands and he gave me five hundred-dollar bills and the phone number of his hotel over on the West Side.

"Oh. And here's a picture of that Stillwell so you can recognize him." He reached into his jacket pocket and came out with a handkerchief, and inside was a small snapshot which he dropped onto the desk. I glanced at it. It was a thirty-something with funny hair. I nodded, and Padderson left. I resisted the urge to salute. So that was that, but I barely had a chance to congratulate myself on my good fortune when Chico came prancing back into the office.

Actually Chico doesn't prance. She sort of saunters, and when she saunters, everyone stares. Including me.

"What a day," she said. She wiped her brow and smiled at me. I took a deep breath. Her smile has that effect on me. I cheat on her, too. I think I am a jerk. She thinks I am just a drunk who will sober up someday. I hope she's right.

"I just saw Commander Schweppes leaving the building. Was he here for us?"

"For me, dear heart. A personal emissary from Old Brown himself. Sent to give us the rent money."

I held up the five hundreds.

"Old Brown? Who the hell is Old Brown?"

"Well, to you people who aren't on the inside, you might know him as Old Brown Eyes. Those of us in the inner circle just call him Old Brown. For short."

"Albie Newmeyer?"

"None other."

"What's he want with you? And don't tell me you're going to be a backup singer or anything."

"Of course not. He wants me to find somebody. Muffy Maguire, to be exact."

"That sleazeball? Is she missing?"

"No. She's holed up somewhere, finishing up a poison-pen letter to Old Brown. The guy in the sailor suit is his personal private detective. He hit a dead end and wants me to find Muffy for them."

"What do they want her for?"

"They want to talk to her and get her to soften her exposé. My guess is that they've got dirt on her and want to blackmail her, but naturally, that's none of my business. All I have to do is find her and we're a thousand dollars richer."

"Is that his business card?" When I nodded, she picked up the card, read it, and then went inside the small bathroom in our office and I heard the water running.

She came back, drying her hands on one of the clean cloth towels she brings each week to the office.

"Why you, Trace? Why do you get all the good ones? I'm out pounding the pavement with some awful nickel-and-dime cheating husband junk that won't be enough to keep us in Cream of Wheat and you get a primo, number one job. Why you? Why not me?"

"Because while you were out gallivanting with lowlifes, I was here, manning the barricades, ready and willing to spring into action at the drop of a hundred-dollar bill. Chance, my dear, favors the prepared mind."

"And good luck favors whatever drunk happens to stagger in its way," she grumbled. She is not a very good loser. "I'll trade you," she said.

"I'm sorry. Under most circumstances, I would, but Old Brown asked for me personally. I feel I would be cheating him if I had a young assistant handle the case."

"Stop with the Old Brown, please. You're making me crazy. Jeff Padderson, huh?"

"His given name is Jeff Padderson from Beverly Hills. But I regard him as Old Money Bags. Or Old Bags. That's what us people close to the scene call him. Old Bags."

"Did you notice what color his eyes were?"

"No. He had on those cheap sunglasses the whole time he was here. Why?" I said.

"No reason. A private detective, you said."

"Yes. Old Bags. Works for Old Brown."

"I think we should trade jobs," she said.

"I think you have been licking peyote weed."

"No. Seriously."

"Very seriously. Why would you make such a laughable suggestion?"

"Because the job I have . . . this cheating husband . . . involves sneaking around into sordid, slimy places. You were obviously born for that task. On the other hand, looking for Muffy Maguire is liable to involve me with the Beautiful People, around whom you may be sure I will not burp, pass wind, scratch myself, or get into a vodka-drinking contest."

"Good try, Chico. But Old Brown wants me. Burping and all."

"I hate you," she said.

I wasn't worried, though. Everybody hates me. So I decided that it was time to take a look at Muffy Maguire's assistant, Bruce Stillwell.

Padderson had given me an address on Fifty-seventh Street for the office where Maguire and Stillwell usually worked. I expected an office building, but instead it was a simple four-story brownstone, divided by rent control and liberal politicians into four units, one to a floor.

There was no doorman, and there were four intercoms-cum-mailboxes in the foyer. One had the name Maguire hand-lettered in the name slot. I rang the bell.

A male voice answered cautiously. "Yes?"

I'm not one of those people who can tell a lot about other people by hearing them speak one word. All I could tell about Bruce Stillwell by hearing him say yes was that he was still alive. *And* still in his office, which was what I really wanted to know.

"Jawda beetsa?" I said into the intercom.

"Excuse me?"

"Beetsa. Beetsa. Jawda beetsa?"

"Oh. No. I didn't order pizza."

"Aaaah, for Christ's sake."

He clicked off, and I waited in the foyer for a while in case he was looking out the window to see the pizza man. Then I left, and as luck would have it found a tavern across the street where the bar commanded a good view of Stillwell's front door, and I ordered a vodka and sat down to wait.

I was prepared to tough it out as long as I had to. Let no man call me frivolous.

> They reckon ill who leave me out.
> When me they fly, I am the wings.

I pitied poor Bruce Stillwell. Because I was on the job.

Devlin Tracy, private eye. We never sleep. Down these mean streets I go, a man who is himself neither mean nor tarnished nor afraid. I . . . the private eye.

The bartender asked me if I wanted another one.

"Damned tooting," I said.

"You waiting for somebody?"

"Nope."

"You look like you were waiting for somebody 'cause you keep looking out the window."

"You got me. I'm a private eye, and I'm on a stakeout. My man will never escape me. Because that's the kind of guy I am."

"Who you staking out? Maybe I know him."

"A dangerous man. By the name of Bruce. If that's even his real name."

"You don't mean Bruce Stillwell, do you?"

"Shhhh," I said, looking around furtively. "He has eyes and ears everywhere."

"Come on, gimme a break. Bruce Stillwell's a lollipop."

"The streets of old Budapest are filled with the bodies of people who thought that way."

He rolled his eyes. Acting like a madman is, most times, a wonderfully effective way to get people to leave you alone.

"There he is now."

The bartender was looking past me and pointing, and I turned and saw Bruce Stillwell, a vision in lavender and cerise, hopping down the front steps of the brownstone and strolling off up the block. Padderson's snapshot of him had not done him justice. Stillwell had bleached hair, the color of delicatessen sliced cheese, and it was glued in such a way that it stood straight up in spikes. He wore red-framed John Lennon glasses that even at this distance I could tell had no lenses in them. He had a big bag of patchwork leather hanging from one shoulder. And while it was too far away to hear him, he was whistling. Or else he was saying "kitchee kitchee koo." I couldn't tell.

"You'd better get after him before he kills again," the bartender said.

I left my change on the bar as a tip, gulped down the dregs of my drink, and went out and fell in behind Bruce, close enough to confirm that he was indeed whistling.

He kept whistling over and over again the only phrase from *Evita* that anybody remembers:

Don't cry for me, Argentina.
Don't cry for me, Argentina.
Don't cry for me, Argentina.

This was just going to be an awful day.

I kept my eyes on the violet shorts and the cerise top as Bruce ambled slowly westward, toward some depraved cesspool, I was sure, but near Tenth Avenue he walked into a street-level gymnasium.

It had big plate glass windows, and I was able to see inside a lot of bodybuilder types pushing around vast amounts of refined iron ore in the vain hope that it would make them as smart as Arnold Schwarzenegger.

I saw Bruce go into a back room, obviously a locker room, for he came out a few minutes later wearing bikini briefs and a fishnet shirt and matching head and wristbands and he started to hop around like a Canadian jackrabbit and it was all so disgusting that I found another bar across the street that commanded a view of the front door and figured I would wait him out.

But a little later I got an even better idea and walked across to the gym myself.

There is a rule in New York that any establishment that deals with the public, no matter how swish or chichi it might be, must have at its front door a Lebanese malcontent with an attitude.

The health club had one, too.

"Whaddya want?"

"I want to work out."

"Twenty dollars. Two hours."

"What do I get for twenty dollars?"

He waved his arm around the vast room of sweating gorillas. Bruce Stillwell was not among them.

"You got anything else?" I asked. "A pool? Racquetball? Steam rooms?"

"I got what I got, ha? Gimme your twenty dollars. Change back there."

He jerked a thumb over his shoulder to the locker room. I gave him twenty; he gave me a locker key.

Bruce had just finished dressing when I went into the locker room and sat in front of the locker. When Bruce looked at me, I turned on my tape recorder and said aloud, "I am *such* a fool."

"Oh?" he said.

"I came here to work out, and I left all my gear in my office. I don't know *what* I was thinking of. Dash it. Dash it. Dash it."

"I've been coming here for five years, and I forget yet," Bruce said agreeably.

"Well, catpoop," I said. "Maybe the fates don't want me to exercise today. Maybe they just want me to drink white zinfandel instead."

"One should always do what the fates want him to do."

"Then it's settled." I stood up from the locker. "And no more guilt about it. Thank you for your help."

"My pleasure. Would you like company for that glass of wine?"

"I hate to drink alone," I said.

So that was how Bruce and I wound up a block away in a place that was filled with so many potted plants and hanging ferns that I felt like the Littlest Mermaid. He put his patchwork leather bag on the barstool next to me. I could see it was filled with typed sheets of paper.

He was Bruce. I was Devlin. I was an accountant in a *so-boring* job with an insurance company. He was a writer who worked for "one of the nicest people in the world, and you would know who she is, but I can't tell you her name."

"Is she a writer, too?"

"Yes," Bruce said. He ordered red wine. I sucked up my courage and ordered white zinfandel and hoped nobody I knew saw me.

"What can one writer do working for another writer?" I asked. "Isn't one writer enough?"

"Well, we tell everyone that I'm just a researcher, but in reality I do a lot of the writing, too."

"And your boss gets the credit for it?"

"Yes, but that's all right. I only want my name on books that represent totally me. These collaborative things are her work, not mine, and I gladly let her have all the credit. And she deserves it. She's a nice lady who works hard." He paused. "Just as long as I get paid on time. And I always do."

We clinked glasses and sipped, and I asked him, "Are you working on anything interesting now?"

"Just another sordid and tawdry little exposé of some no-account's life. It's really not worth discussing."

"I don't know. Sordid and tawdry are my favorite discussion topics," I said.

"Well, maybe some other time, Devvie."

Devvie? This petunia calls me Devvie? Oh, the things we put up with to pay the rent.

Bruce stood up from the bar. "I have some things to do," he said. "Perhaps we'll meet again?"

"That would be nice. Do you come to the gym often?"

"Monday, Wednesday, and Friday. Next time bring your shorts."

"If I have to," I said with a pout, and he giggled as we shook hands and he left. Outside he waved good-bye to me through the picture window. I finished my wine, waited a few seconds, and walked outside.

He was as easy to spot as Lowell Weicker in a punchbowl. He was pacing it off on the far side of the street, and I took off my jacket and carried it in my arm, just to change my silhouette in case he looked behind him.

But he didn't. He walked three blocks down the avenue, then up a side street. I hustled along after him and saw him going into a small apartment building. He paused outside the front door, apparently checking the papers in his ditty bag, before going inside.

I started to count to twenty but lost the count at eleven, so I walked into the foyer of the building. It was a building without a doorman, and I could see the elevator at the end of the front hall. The dial above it showed it had stopped at the third floor. I looked at the intercoms alongside the door. "Apartment 317. M. Maguire."

Bingo. Time to go home.

Good-bye, Bruce. See you at the gymnasium sometime. Hold your breath.

"What's his sexual orientation?" Chico wanted to know.

"Sort of north and south vertical, I think. I'm east and west horizontal. It never would have worked out. But he liked me a lot."

"Trace, I don't trust this guy," she said.

"Why not?"

"Nobody likes you a lot."

"You're forgetting Old Brown. He likes me."

"Arrggggh," she hinted. "Are you going to call Captain Queeg?"

"Maybe tomorrow," I said. "This was all too easy, and if I call him right away, he's going to try to beat us out of our fee. Let him sweat it and think I'm working around the clock."

"Hey, you already got five hundred dollars for two hours' work, most of it spent in a bar. We've got no complaints."

"It was only easy because I am so good at this work. Hire Tracy and Mangini, and you get the best. That's what people pay for. You notice that this Padderson guy couldn't do it himself."

"Yeah, I've been thinking about that," she said darkly, and when it seemed she was going to talk some more about it, I asked her what she'd like to eat for dinner.

The thought of food—her nightly ingestion of ten thousand calories of fat and protein—instantly pushed all other thoughts from her mind. So she dropped the subject, and we went to dinner (she ate both of ours) and then back to our apartment, which is in Manhattan, as far from my parents' house in Queens as you can get without falling off the island.

All throughout dinner she wanted to talk about my case, but I kept deflecting her, and then we got home and so to bed.

Except I woke up and saw on the bedside clock that it was 2:00 A.M. and Chico wasn't there. From the living room I heard my own voice. Chico was playing the tapes I had made that day of my conversations with Jeff Padderson and Bruce Stillwell.

I smirked. The woman couldn't get enough of me.

Or something.

I rolled over and went back to sleep.

The next morning I struggled up, and after my regular routine —shower, shave, and vomit—I found a note from Chico on the kitchen table: "Trace. I've gone to the airport to pick up Sarge and her. Do nothing about Old Brown until we talk. Chico."

The nerve of the woman. Old Brown indeed. Albie Newmeyer was my friend, not hers, and it was cutting in on my action for her to call him Old Brown. As Durante said, everybody wants to get into the act.

"Her" by the way is the loving diminutive way Chico refers to my mother. The feeling is mutual. My mother regards Chico as personally responsible for Pearl Harbor, World War II, the Holocaust, the AIDS virus, and the election of any Republican anywhere.

Chico, on the other hand, regards my mother as the primary source for the breakdown in American standards, her belief being that any Jewish matron who would knowingly buy a Jesus statue made of plaster would be appreciated more in some alternate universe.

Me? I butt out.

So I got dressed and went to the office, and as I let myself in, the telephone started ringing.

And there was Jeff Padderson. "Hello, Tracy, how are you doing for me?"

"Fine. I've got that address for you."

"Hey, that's great. You work fast. What is it?"

"I don't work *that* fast. Come on up to the office with some money, and I'll give it to you."

"Ha-ha-ha, a man after my own heart. I'll be right there."

"Ha-ha-ha. I'll wait."

Not ten minutes later Padderson was in my office, looking all shiny and new in another sailor suit and the same sunglasses, and he laid five new hundred-dollar bills across my palm and I wrote out the address of Muffy Maguire's private little workshop. He also wanted back the small photo of Bruce Stillwell. I didn't dare ask why, so I just gave it to him and he left.

Then, tired out by the morning's activities, I leaned back in my chair and put my feet up and rested. Being the breadwinner for this firm was exhausting.

There's one thing I know about this world. Whenever you want to nap, really nap, somebody's always pestering you. If it's not the telephone, it's the mailman. And if it's not the mailman or Federal Express, which is usually a wrong address and they're looking for somebody in Minnesota, it's your partners. And there they were, just a couple of minutes later, Chico and Sarge blasting into the office, Chico looking beautiful, Sarge looking harassed but tan.

"You look great, Sarge. Did you learn the tango?"

"Cut the chatter," Chico said. She really talks like that. "Has Padderson contacted you yet?"

"Yup." I smirked. "Old Bags was here and just left." I waved toward the five hundreds on the desk. "I got paid, too. We've got rent money, Sarge."

"And you gave him Muffy Maguire's address?" Chico asked.

"Of course, I gave him the address. You think I got paid for not giving him the address?"

"You idiot," she said. "I left you a note to do nothing."

I looked at her, then at my father. He said, "You idiot."

Chico said, "Come on, dork," and turned toward the door. Sarge followed after her, and because I thought my presence might be required, I did, too.

But I'm getting tired of being called a dork. I hate this kind of work.

The knock on the door of Muffy Maguire's apartment came less than an hour later.

"Come in. It's unlocked," a woman's musical voice called out.

The door pushed open, and Jeff Padderson stepped inside. He looked across the room at the blond-haired woman who sat at a word processor with her back to him. She was busy typing and did not even turn toward him.

Padderson smiled and took a long pistol, with a silencer screwed onto the end of it, from under his yachtsman's blazer. He lifted it toward the woman and—

Then Sarge came out of the closet behind the door and clubbed him upside the head with his old .38 police special.

Padderson dropped like a lump of wet bread. He didn't even squirm as I came out of the closet, too, and cuffed his hands behind his back.

I looked across the room, and Chico swung around from the desk, a big grin on her face, as she peeled off the blond wig she had borrowed from Muffy Maguire.

"Hot damn," she said. "We did it."

Then Muffy Maguire, puffy and potato-faced, came out of the bedroom and came over to look at Jeff Padderson.

"Never saw him before in my life," she said.

"It'll all get sorted out," Sarge said, and nodded to Chico. "Call the police."

"Not until I call my press agent," Maguire said. "This is going to make my Newmeyer book go ballistic."

"Lady, if you reach for that phone, I'll twist your head off your neck," Sarge told her, and Muffy decided her press agent could wait.

Chico called the police, and then Maguire said sullenly, "Do you mind if I use the phone *now*?"

Chico said, "For your press agent?"

"Actually, for my assistant, Bruce Stillwell. He can get everybody else involved."

She reached for the telephone, but Chico put her hand over Muffy's on the phone. "I don't think you ought to call Stillwell just yet," she said.

Muffy looked at me. I shrugged.

"Hey, I got my own problems, lady," I said. "I just blew a pair of front-row seats for Old Brown's next concert."

Well, by now, of course, everyone's heard about what happened. How Jeff Padderson wasn't a private eye at all but a hired killer. And he didn't have anything to do with Albie Newmeyer at all. It turned out he'd been hired by Bruce Stillwell to do the dirty deed.

Later I brought sandwiches back to the office. Chico was pretty smug, explaining the whole thing to me.

"It was all too easy," she said.

"What was?"

"The whole thing. It took you exactly two hours to find where Muffy Maguire was holed up. All you had to do was walk down the street and follow Stillwell to her private apartment."

"Yeah?"

"Now why should anybody pay you a thousand dollars to do something so simple that he could do it himself in two hours? Especially a guy who said he was a private detective. Especially a guy who had a snapshot of Stillwell that he obviously took on the street. It just wouldn't occur to him to follow the man himself?"

"I thought he liked me. Him and Old Brown. I thought I was one of their favorites."

"Afraid not, Trace. He told the cops he picked our names out of the phone book."

"Then why'd he get Albie Newmeyer involved? I don't understand this whole thing."

"Look. If somebody pulls the plug on Muffy Maguire, Bruce Stillwell's going to be one of the first people they suspect. So this guy comes along with his razzle-dazzle story about Albie Newmeyer, and what he does is guarantee that Stillwell's going to have an alibi. You're going to come along later and say that Stillwell was loyal and wouldn't reveal Maguire's whereabouts and that the killer said he was from Newmeyer and that you only found out where Maguire was by following Stillwell. You were Stillwell's alibi."

"All right, all right, all right. So how'd you get on to them?"

"First there was Padderson's business card. The ink was still wet on it. And I remembered the design. Out at the airport they have a machine that makes business cards while you wait. This was the same design, that boxy black border." She twitched her nose, like a mouse smelling cheese.

"So that kind of smelled. And Padderson's sunglasses. Here he comes, into your office, dressed like an Armani display window, and you yourself said he was wearing those cheap mirrored sunglasses and never took them off. And I thought maybe he just bought them and he was only wearing them so you'd have trouble giving a description of him later on.

"So then I listened to the tapes, and the more I listened, the more the Newmeyer story sounded like a phony. And then there was Bruce, talking about how nice his boss was. Well, the one thing Muffy Maguire is not is nice. Everybody knows she's a bitch. So that sounded like a guy who was helping to build himself an alibi, too. I think it's pretty clear that Bruce felt he did all the work and Muffy got all the credit. With her out of the picture, he'd just step in and start doing these exposé books himself. And the fame and the money would be his."

I had to grumble about something, so I said, "It's still all a lot of supposition and maybes and perhapses."

Chico shrugged. "You've got to listen to your tapes more often. When you were talking with Padderson, he said 'she's doing it yet' and what he really meant was she's 'still' doing it. And then Stillwell said the same kind of thing . . . about his gym shorts . . . 'I forget yet' . . . and he meant 'still.' Trace, that's Pennsylvania Dutch dialect, and I just thought it was too much of a coincidence for you to meet two PA Dutchmen in one day. Mark my words . . . the cops will find out these guys were boys in Pennsylvania together."

All I could do with that was grunt.

"So when I went to the airport to pick up Sarge, I had him call one of his old cop friends in California. That nailed it down. There's no private detective named Jeff Padderson licensed in California. That's when I knew you were dealing with a fake, so we hustled back to the office, but you'd already told him where Muffy was hiding out. We were lucky we got there in time."

"You seem to have thought of almost everything." I sniffed.

"Everything," she corrected.

"Not quite," I said. "The rent money, for instance."

"What about the rent money?"

"Padderson, or whatever his name is, gave me a thousand dollars in hundreds. When the cops wake up, they're going to want that for evidence."

"Oh, balls," Chico said in exasperation. "Trace, that's stinking unfair."

"Not to worry, old girl. I've taken care of it."

"How'd you do that?" she asked.

"When I went out before for sandwiches, I went to the off-track betting parlor on the corner. That's why I was late."

"You didn't bet our rent money?"

"No, no, no. But I picked up a lot of losing tickets off the floor. When the cops ask for the thousand, I'm going to tell them I gambled it all away. Screw 'em. I worked hard for that money."

"Trace, I knew there was something I liked about you."

"Tell me about it. I love it."

"You're a sneak."

"Yeah, but I'm your sneak."

"For now," she said.

RUNNER AND
THE DEATHBRINGER
··

TERI WHITE

Fat Jack was buying gold again.

The word spread hyperfast through the park, and all the gangers cheered the news. Fat Jack always paid out top chit for the contra he bought, and it wasn't like the yellow stuff was hard to get ahold of, like some of the shit the merchants wanted.

Gold was easy pickings, if you knew which streets to do your prospecting on.

As soon as he heard the news, Runner shanked it over to the lagoon to see if any of his Tontos were there. Maybe somebody would want to hit the avenue with him, rip some shiny, and then split the grab. Two was sometimes better than one, especially if the citizen you were trying to rip turned out to be bearing. Runner would never forget the time a fat West Side bitch pulled out an old mag .44 and shoved it in his face. He was only ripping her chit pouch, fer chrissake, not trying to off her. Or even put it to her, as if he would, somebody that old and fat. But she was ready to do him, just for that damned pouch. People were crazy, sometimes, and it didn't hurt to have a Tonto scoping your ass, just in case.

But nobody was around this particular night except WillyBoy, and he was completely blown on ganja, as usual, and talking about leaving the city, also as usual. Willyboy had this dream about moving out to Angeltown, where, according to his sources, you could microwave your brain on drugs real cheap and get humped or blown anytime you liked, cause the whole place was filled with street sexers, girls or boys or whatever, and they were all pretty, not like the slags on this isle.

Runner crouched in the bushes and listened to WillyBoy talk for a while, mostly so he could cop a few drags on the ganj. But WillyBoy was not the kind of a guy you'd take out on a ripping, cause he was totally unreliable. Runner personally thought that was due to the fact that WillyBoy's whole entire brain was like nuked. WillyBoy was a good role model, because Runner absolutely did not want to end up like him, drooling at the mouth and talking dumb.

So, anyway, it looked like he'd have to hit the avenue all by himself.

Before leaving the park, he checked to be sure that his blade was within easy reach, just in case. Okay, Runner, he told himself, no shit now. Hit the pavement. Rip some shiny. Earn some chits.

This job should have been a walk-through.

Sagan always surveilled a commission thoroughly beforehand, figuring it all down to the smallest detail, and that was why he was the best in the game. Nobody could outplay the Deathbringer.

Well, no one ever had. Until now.

At first there had been no reason to think that this commission was going to be any different. His plan was simplicity itself: to hit the isle, do the job first thing in the morning, and then catch the jet train back to Chitown in plenty of time for lunch. Easy, fast, and netting him mucho, mucho chits. That was the plan, and it should have worked. After all, he had been a pro for twenty years. Deathbringer *knew* how to do his job.

Nowhere had there been a thought that he could or would find himself in this position.

Unfortunately, it turned out that the damned bull's-eye had a fucking guard with him, and that guard was bearing full heat. That one little fact had not been in the specs.

Sagan was alive only because he could move faster than the other guy.

And that condition—being alive—was quite probably only temporary.

He looked down again at the wound in his side. The blood had soaked through his undershirt, his polo, and was now drenching the silk lining of his black leather jacket. He was a little surprised that there wasn't more pain involved in this business of dying.

It wasn't supposed to end like this.

Here he was, quietly bleeding to death all by himself in some squatter's paradise. The Deathbringer deserved better. In truth, he had always rather imagined that his own dying would be somewhat more . . . romantic than was turning out to be the case.

Sagan sighed.

Some time passed.

He was almost asleep, in fact, or slipped into unconsciousness anyway, when the sound of shattering glass somewhere in the building brought him wide-awake again. Automatically his hands scrabbled across the old wooden floor, toward where his gun lay. He clutched it to his chest, pointing the deadly barrel toward where he thought the doorway was.

They shouldn't have been able to find me this quickly, he thought, mild panic making his finger twitch on the trigger. Not this quickly.

He could hear the footsteps approaching, the unmistakable sounds made by someone trying to walk silently and failing.

Sagan moistened his lips with the tip of his tongue, staring at the doorway, his vision blurring.

A figure appeared, and he tried to fire, but without warning, his finger would not work as he wanted it to. As it had always worked before. His vision fuzzed even more, partly from hot tears of frustration.

His last thought, before he pitched forward onto the floor, was the surprised realization that the figure in the doorway was not that of the very tall, very black man with the unerring aim who had been guarding the senator earlier.

It's just a kid, he thought, and then the floor hit him in the face.

Runner was scared.

He had supposed this building to be empty, just like all the others along this stretch of Madison. It had certainly seemed so when he smashed a window and crawled in, trying to escape his pursuers. There had been no noise as he crept along the corridor and up the shaky stairs to the third floor.

It wasn't until he stepped in through the doorway and entered the room bathed in moonlight that he saw the man. Actually he saw the gun first.

Dios, que noche bruta, he thought helplessly.

First, he almost gets himself good and truly offed by the guy with the shiny, who, it turned out, seemed not to want to lose the fancy watch. It took a couple of good swipes from Runner's blade to discourage him. But at least the watch changed hands during the whole fuckup.

Well, that was enough hassle for one night, so Runner decided to hit Fat Jack's, collect on the watch, and then just head back for the park.

He never even made it to Fifth, however, before the gutter rats hit.

Runner had always hated them, the rats. Too damned lazy to get out and hustle up a living like everybody else, they just stole from the gangers, who had already done the real work. Well, after everything he had gone through to get the damned watch, Runner wasn't about to give it up without a helluva fight.

So he fought the rats, all five of them.

And he won, sort of. At least he managed to escape with both his life and the watch. That could be called a victory, he supposed.

But the bad news was, he had hurt one of them with his blade. In fact, he sort of thought the girl was dead. And that was too bad because it meant the rats would call out a bounty on him.

Runner didn't know a single living being who wouldn't turn him over, without even thinking twice, if the bounty was right.

He ran and ran until he couldn't run anymore, and then he came into this building, which was supposed to be empty.

Only to find some big muthafucka gun pointed at him.

What a bitchin' night, for sure.

When Runner finally realized that the man holding the gun was actually unconscious and not just pulling some scam, his legs stopped shaking a little. He crept further into the room, crouched beside the man, and then turned him over for a better look.

He admired the man's boots: They were made of real leather, black with silver studs, and reached nearly to his knees. Runner envied him the jacket, too. It was also leather.

The man himself looked ancient, maybe forty. His dark hair was starting to turn gray. There was an old scar across his cheek, running from the corner of one eye nearly to his mouth. He didn't stir, even when Runner reached out to finger the leather jacket carefully. Underneath the black polo he wore a thin gold chain, which Runner managed to remove.

It was only then that he realized the guy was bleeding.

Well, shit. This dude was dying.

Runner eyed the boots again. They just might fit him, if he could stuff some paper or something inside. After all, it wasn't like this guy was going to need them much longer.

He edged around the still figure and started to tug at one of the boots.

It was a moment before he realized that the man's eyes were now open. He leaned back quickly, dropping his hold on the smooth leather.

"You might wait until the body is cold," the stranger said in a hoarse whisper, sounding more amused than angry.

"Thought you was dying," Runner offered. "Dead man don't need no boots."

"Well, I am dying, that's true enough. But I'd prefer to go out with a little dignity if you don't mind."

Runner shrugged. "I can wait."

"Thank you."

They sat in near silence for several moments, the only sound that of the man's strained, raspy breaths.

Finally he turned his head to look at Runner. "I don't suppose you have anything to drink, do you?"

"Nope."

The man coughed, then sighed, still looking at him.

Runner shifted a little, suddenly uncomfortable under the steady dark gaze. "I could maybe go find something," he offered at last. "If you want me to."

"I wouldn't mind." A faint smile seemed to flicker across the man's face. "We could consider it payment for the chain you took off my neck."

For the first time in his life Runner felt ashamed of ripping something. "I'm sorry," he said. "I thought . . ."

"I know. And a dead man doesn't need a gold chain either, does he?"

Runner stood. "I'll go get some water."

"Thank you," the man said again.

Runner left the room.

Alone again, Sagan rested back against the floor with a sigh. The wound in his side was starting to hurt now, so he figured it wouldn't take much longer for the whole thing to be over.

He hoped the boy would hurry with the water; he hated to die with this terrible thirst still seizing him. Of course, there was no way of knowing that the boy would even come back at all. Except that he sure wanted the boots. Well, it seemed an equitable trade.

He did hope the kid would wait until he was actually dead before he started stripping the corpse. Sagan hated to think of himself dying without a shred of dignity left.

The Deathbringer never robbed his targets of that particular commodity, only of their lives. He never once ripped a corpse for gold or chits, never mutilated them, nothing like that. Not like some of the hired assassins he knew of. Men who did things like that were more like animals than skilled craftsmen.

Sagan did not put himself in their company.

It seemed a very long time before he heard the sound of some-one coming along the corridor again. He tried to lift the gun once more but could barely manage to do it this time.

"It's only me," the boy said, appearing in the doorway.

"Finally," Sagan muttered.

"Sorry it took so long. I got some fix-up stuff." The boy crouched beside him. "And this." He held out a bottle of cheap whiskey.

"Ahh," Sagan said. "Thank you."

The boy unscrewed the cap and handed him the whiskey.

Sagan took one long swallow, then lowered the bottle and looked at the boy. "What's your name?"

"Runner."

"Well, Runner, I am in your debt." He surveyed the other items that had been dumped on the floor. "You ripped a clinic, did you?"

"Yeah." Runner had come back with a bottle of antiseptic, a roll of gauze, and some pain pills.

Sagan smiled faintly. "Well, I appreciate the effort, but I don't think it'll do much good."

Runner shrugged. "Can't hurt to try."

"Whatever." Sagan lay back and watched with only mild interest as Runner used a wicked-looking blade to slice open the bloody polo and undershirt, laying bare the wound.

The boy gasped.

"It actually looks worse than it feels," Sagan said.

Runner sloshed antiseptic over the area. "What's your name?" he mumbled, trying to clean away the blood.

"Sagan. Except most people don't call me that."

"What do they call you?"

He took another small swallow of the dreadful whiskey. "Death-bringer."

Runner straightened abruptly and stared at him. "You're Death-bringer? For real?"

"You've heard of me?" Sagan felt a faint and, he knew, entirely ridiculous glow of pride.

"Oh, sure. Everybody knows about you." He was trying to wrap the wound in the gauze, but every time Sagan had to move, his face reflected the pain it caused. Runner finally gave up and just wadded the gauze over the wound.

His hands were bloody. He wiped them uselessly on the front of his tattered, filthy jeans. "What happened to you anyway?" he asked.

Sagan shrugged and drank again. "Somebody else shot first."

"I'm sorry."

"So am I." A stabbing pain made him close his eyes briefly. Then he looked at Runner again. "So tell me about you."

He shrugged. "Nothing to tell."

"How old are you?"

"Fifteen."

"You a ganger?"

"Yeah." Runner settled down, resting his back against the wall next to him. "I was out ripping tonight, cause Fat Jack is buying gold. Then the rats got me." He wiped a hand across his mouth, oblivious of the blood it left there. "I killed one of them, I think."

Sagan gave a soft whistle. "Too bad. They'll be after you."

He nodded glumly.

"Well," Sagan said. "A dead man doesn't need a gun either. Take mine. It might give you an edge."

"Maybe you won't die," Runner said. "Then you could off the rats for me."

"Oh, I think I'm probably going to die," Sagan replied.

"I saw a guy once," Runner said. "He was shot up worse than you, and he didn't die."

"Uh-huh."

"If you don't die," Runner went on, "will you off the rats for me?"

"Sure. Least I can do."

There was a pause as Runner stared at the bloody gauze. "I oughta tell you—they'll have a big bounty out. Maybe you'd want to collect that instead." He glanced at Sagan's face and then away again. "I mean, anybody would."

Sagan shook his head. "Not me. Can't betray a man who helped me. Otherwise I'd be no better than the rest of them."

There was no conversation for a time.

It was actually Runner who heard the noise first. He lifted his head. "What's that?" he whispered into Sagan's ear. "Think it's the rats come for me?"

Sagan listened, then shook his head. "More likely it's the shooter coming for me," he said softly. "You better vanish." He tried to pick up the gun again, but his hands were shaking and so weak that he couldn't hold on to it. "Damn," he muttered.

"Want me to do it?" Runner said suddenly.

"You ever use a gun?"

He shook his head. "But I seen them used plenty a times."

"Take it then," Sagan said. "Stand back over there. Soon as he walks in, you blast, got it?"

"Got it." He hoisted the gun and went to hide in the dark corner.

They waited in silence, listening to the soft footfalls coming closer.

Sagan stared at the doorway.

If it was him, see, he wouldn't even come all the way into the room. He'd just stand in the hall and blast. But maybe the senator's stooge wasn't that smart. Maybe he'd step in just far enough to give Runner a chance.

If Runner could do it.

Then there was no more time to think. There was only a massive shape filling the doorway. "Well, Deathbringer," a deep and pleasant voice said, "you've had a nice long stretch of luck. And nobody lives forever."

Shoot, dammit, Sagan ordered silently.

And Runner shot. He just put his finger on the trigger and held it there as the big man's body was ripped apart.

The assassin hesitated, started to turn toward the corner, and then pitched over, dead.

It was a moment before Runner came over and knelt beside Sagan again. "How'd I do, Deathbringer?" he asked eagerly.

Sagan gave his arm a pat. "You did fine," he said. "Only wish I could help you out with the rats."

"You will. I don't think you're going to die, Deathbringer."

Sagan looked at him for a moment. "Do me a favor?" he said then.

"Sure."

"Call me Sagan."

Runner looked puzzled. "Why?"

He had no logical answer for that, so he only shrugged. "I'm so tired," he said. "Think I'll sleep for a while."

Runner checked the gauze. "That's a good idea. You sleep." Very carefully he pulled the jacket closed over the wound. "I'll watch out for the bad guys." He took the gun and went to crouch by the window.

"Thanks." Sagan watched him for a long time, until he couldn't fight off the wave of blackness any longer.

Runner could see the first light of dawn touching the sky. He was glad to see the night end. There was a lot to be done today. First of all, he had to get some food and stuff, for Death—for Sagan. Maybe he could even find a medic.

People got shot all the time, and they didn't necessarily die. Sagan would be fine.

As Runner watched the lightening of the sky, he had an idea. Maybe . . . maybe they could leave the isle. He wondered if Sagan had ever been to Angeltown. That would be the place for them.

He glanced back to where Sagan lay. The sound of the injured man's breathing was much fainter now. It was scary.

Runner yanked his gaze back to the window. His fingers tightened on the gun.

Everything would be fine as soon as the sun was up. Sagan would open his eyes then. They could talk about going to Angeltown.

Runner rested his chin on the windowsill and watched the sunrise as he waited for Sagan to wake up.

THE OPERATION

HENRY SLESAR

Just his luck. When he turned the corner of Bushwick, the first person he saw was Bomba, his foot on a hydrant, tying a crepe-soled shoe. The last three years had given Bomba more forehead and an overhanging paunch, but he had the same dumb, hostile look, a face like a fist. Mikey, grateful for the loose shoelace that prevented Bomba from spotting him, ducked back out of sight to think things over.

It was Mikey who had given Bomba his nickname. They had been friends then, neighborhood punks who still hadn't made their bones with the local wise guys. Bomba liked jewelry, and one day he found a shark-tooth necklace in a church bazaar sale. He wore it all the time, and one night, hanging out on the corner with Barney Lopes and Savario and some of the other guys, Mikey saw him approach and said, "Hey, here comes Jungle Boy." He got his laugh, and Bomba got his hated new name, and it stuck even after he threw away the shark-tooth necklace.

Mikey looked at the rented compact parked on the side street and almost jumped back inside. He had felt secure in the tight fit of that front seat, the wheel so close he could steer with his ribs. He had learned to like small spaces; that was the gist of his three-year curriculum in the joint. He got used to the walls, the narrow bunks, the constricted corridors. In the yard he picked himself a sunless spot in a corner that nobody else coveted. He began to feel his body shrinking, and it didn't bother him, it made him feel secure. His brother, Paulie, visiting him one Sunday, gave him a worried look and asked if he was losing weight. Paulie was a sick kid; he needed a healthy older brother. But Mikey wasn't losing weight. He was just making himself smaller; his goal was invisibility.

Paulie. The name itself was an ache. Paulie's face on that hospital pillow, the skull coming through. He tried to turn the ache into a resolve, but it didn't work. He was afraid to round that corner again. Afraid of Bomba, afraid of keeping his appointment with Barney, sorry now he had placed the call from St. Luke's. He thought guts would earn him respect. He wanted to believe he heard grudging admiration in Bernie's voice when Barney asked him to come down to the old clubhouse, to "work things out." There had been a smile in Bernie's voice, but Mikey knew that smiles and silky voices and friendly words didn't mean much here, not in this neighborhood. It was a dumb idea, sticking his head right in the mouth of the lion, a dumb idea! He grabbed the door handle of the Ford and jumped into the driver's seat.

He was two seconds too late. Savario was rapping on the window before he could start the engine. He had a wild notion to turn the key anyway, gun the engine, burn rubber, drive straight to the airport, the Bahamas, sunshine, women in bikinis, Paulie's face on the pillow: It was amazing how many images can flash through a panicky mind. Then he saw Bomba himself, pushing his paunch against the hood of the car, Bomba's fistlike face bunched up in a mocking grin. Bomba had seen him; his peripheral vision was better than Mikey thought.

He pulled the key out of the ignition, took a deep breath, and opened the door. There was only one way to play this game now: like he was holding good cards. He looked at Savario, skinny, dark as an Arab, and said, "Hey, Savvy, how's it going?"

"Welcome back," Savario said. "You shoulda let us know you were coming out, we woulda had a party."

Bomba's paunch bumped him. "You're looking good, Mikey." He dropped a beefy hand on his shoulder, hard enough to hurt. "Barney was real happy to hear from you, it was a nice surprise."

"So was Joey D," Savario said, beginning a little dance of excitement on the sidewalk. "Joey D said you'd never show your face around here again; he said you'd head straight for Hawaii or someplace." He giggled. "And here you are! In the flesh!" He pinched half an inch of it on Mikey's arm, and Mikey yelped.

"Cut it out," he said. "Just let me go see Barney, okay?"

"Sure, sure." Savario laughed and coughed, his skin turning even darker as he choked and ejected brown spittle into the gutter. Three years ago they said Savario would be dead in six months, and here he was, dancing and coughing.

They flanked Mikey, and for a moment he thought he was going to be frog-marched down the street to the clubhouse, but their grip on his elbow was easy, amiable; it didn't make Mikey feel any more comfortable.

The clubhouse had gone through still another metamorphosis in the time he was away. It had been a cafeteria before it became the home of the Four Aces SAC. Now it was called the Four Aces Diner, closing the circle. The fluorescents were dark, and the tables were empty. There was an old man behind the counter, pushing a dishcloth into a thick white mug. No sign of Barney, no Joey D. He looked at Bomba, who said, "Relax, have some coffee, have a piece of cake. Hey, Arnie! What's the special today?"

The old man grumbled something that made both Bomba and Savario laugh hysterically. These guys are up, Mikey thought, they're high, and he knew the narcotic was his own surprise appearance. He asked about Barney, and Bomba said: "Barney had to see a guy, on business. He said you should wait for him."

"How long you been out, Mikey?" Savario was kneading his shoulders. "We was all surprised, Barney getting out of the joint before you did."

"Barney's got a better lawyer," Mikey said, attempting a smile that twisted unwillingly into a sneer. "Four, five weeks ago. I would have come around sooner only they handed me this nosy parole officer, the guy was breathing down my neck all the time."

"So what are you doing with yourself?"

"I'm working," Mikey said. "Like I had a choice? They found a job for me on Seventh Avenue, I'm pushing a hand truck." The lips twisted again, only this time on purpose.

"Hey, what's so bad about that?" Bomba said. "You can pick up a lot of good stuff down the garment district. Remember Johnny the Nose? He used to snatch two, three shipments a week for that discount guy in Jersey. You talk to Barney about it."

"That's not what I came to talk to Barney about."

"No." Savario grinned. "You got other things, huh, Mikey? Like Turkeyman?"

The word shot out of his mouth like the brown glob he had left in the gutter. The old man behind the counter stopped wiping, and Bomba looked embarrassed. It was obviously a subject they weren't allowed to discuss. That was Barney's prerogative. Barney had taken the five-year rap for Turkeyman's death, the charge Sharp Sherman Barry had managed to reduce to "negligent homicide." Mikey had been the codefendant, the judge had decided to give him only three, but Barney was on the outside six months before Mikey. Funny how things worked out.

Turkeyman was Kenny Turo. They called him Turkeyman because he kept one in his backyard, a big live bird he won in a Thanksgiving raffle and didn't have the heart to slaughter. That was funny, too, because Turkey was a bad man with a knife. He had slit the throats of at least three guys Mikey knew about, all for personal grudges. For a while he was almost as notorious for whacking people as Barney himself.

Barney had the record, of course. Barney was famous for his body count even before Mikey became part of his circle. But Barney wasn't crazy like Turkeyman. Barney considered murder a business tactic, like selling off inventory or underpricing competitors. He did such neat, quick work that he started getting independent assignments. Whacking became more profitable than the three dry cleaning stores he operated, the pizza parlor, the diner he owned, with his brother, Vinnie. He was a professional, and he was good, and the proof was his yellow sheet. Barney had three arrests on his record and only one conviction. He wouldn't have had that one if it wasn't for Turkeyman. And Mikey.

It hadn't been the first time Barney had taken Mikey along on a hit. The first time had been two years before. Mikey hadn't known why Barney asked him to meet him at Moochy's chop shop in Bay Ridge. Mikey worked a summer for Moochy; he was strong as an ox and maybe as dumb. It never occurred to him that someone would want a big dumb ox dead.

Barney had pushed Mikey ahead of him into the garage. Moochy was yanking a tire off a rim. He smiled when he saw Mikey. Mikey still wished he could forget that smile. Then Barney pushed him aside and took a gun out of his pocket. He didn't say anything, didn't make any movie wisecracks, just the gun, the squeeze, the deafening noise, and there was Moochy on the floor, blood mixing in with the oil stains. Then they left. Barney drove him to the VinBar Diner and gave him a free meal. Mikey had a pasta he couldn't finish, but Barney ate a steak like a natural hungry man.

Mikey was shook, no doubt about it. He'd seen plenty of blood before; he knew muscle was the ground floor of his business. He had been one of the four street corner guys who had kicked Sammy Crown to death, but that had been an accident, it was supposed to have been a lesson in manners. Moochy was the first guy he'd seen whacked in cold blood, and it made him afraid of Barney Lopes.

Uncle Barney. That's what Paulie called him. Good old Uncle Barney, who bought Paulie his first bike, who took him out to Far Rockaway and taught him how to fish for snapper, who always asked about Paulie whenever he saw Mikey.

It was because of Paulie, his hospital bills, that Barney offered Mikey the job of taking care of Turkeyman. He even took the time to tell Mikey why the guy needed whacking. Turkeyman was driving a rig for a shipping company. It gave him good contacts for the hijacking operation run by the Queens family to whom Turkeyman swore allegiance. Only Turkeyman wasn't keeping his vows; he was booking jobs on the side, making deals without head office approval, stuffing his own pockets without giving the capos a taste. The deals were small; Turkeyman didn't think they'd mind. He was wrong; they minded.

Mikey wasn't happy about the job, but he needed the money, and he was afraid to say no. They drove to Turkeyman's house in Red Hook, first making sure he wasn't home. The turkey was scratching at the earth in his backyard, a string tying it to a picket fence. Barney busted the screen door lock with one contemptuous kick, and they were inside. The place was a mess. Turkeyman's wife had left him five years ago. He lived on pizza. There were empty grease-spotted boxes all over the living room. The kitchen was pristine. Turkeyman never used it.

Barney used it now. He pulled open drawers until he found a serrated knife. He handed it to Mikey.

"Kill the bird," he said. Mikey blinked at him stupidly, but Barney was patient. "Go on," he said. "They want the son of a bitch's bird whacked, too."

"Jeez," Mikey said. "What for, Barney? The turkey wasn't making deals!"

"Kill the turkey! What do you want, it should starve?"

Mikey wanted to argue some more, but there was something in Barney's eyes that changed his mind. He took the knife and went outside, wishing he'd never taken the job. The fat, ungainly fowl started to flap its tattered wings when he approached. Mikey's heart pounded. He was afraid of the damned bird. The bird was afraid of him, too, and its frantic fluttering prevented its capture. Mikey chased after it, feeling like a circus clown. The bird started a high-pitched gobble, and Barney came thundering out of the house, his face plum dark with anger. He cursed both Mikey and the bird, said something about the neighbors, and then with a lightning motion seized the turkey's neck and grabbed the kitchen knife out of Mikey's hand.

Neither one of them had heard the semitrailer pulling up at the front of the house, so they weren't prepared for the roaring express that was Turkeyman's 260-pound body. Bellowing with rage at the assassination in progress, he threw himself at Barney, and Barney did what he had come to do anyway: He swept the kitchen knife in an underhand arc and buried it deep in the Turkeyman's chest.

But this time there wasn't any cool professional exit. Turkeyman had too many neighbors. The squawking bird, Turkeyman's bellows drew an audience like Saturday night at the Meadowlands. There must have been half a dozen eyewitnesses, but by the time the cops got around to question-and-answer time, there wasn't one who was "sure" of what he saw, not one who wasn't willing to nod his head, the head he wanted to keep on his shoulders, to the defense suggestion that it was an accidental thrust, that only the turkey was the target, the intended victim, Sharp Sherman said, of a not-so-harmless prank. . . .

But the DA hunkered down on this one. They knew what Barney Lopes did for a living; there were grim-faced people in the office who had been waiting years to slam iron on Barney. They became bulldogs, and they sank their teeth into the most vulnerable leg they had, the one belonging to Mikey.

Mikey had never had a homicide rap against him, but he had enough lesser convictions to convince a judge that a ten to twenty stretch would serve the community interest. And then they found the most convincing argument of all. An assistant DA, a pert young woman with Big Politics in her future, sniffed around Mikey's private life and came up with Paulie. His sick kid brother, Paulie. In and out of the hospital Paulie. Nobody-to-take-care-of-him Paulie . . .

"How's Paulie?"

Mikey looked up and saw Barney Lopes breathing down on him. Barney had soft feet, you never heard him coming. Joey D was at the door, shutting it carefully. Then Mikey realized that the old man was gone from behind the counter, that Bomba and Savario were no longer in sight. Minutes before he had wished for their disappearance, but now their absence worried him.

"Hey, I asked you a question," Barney said. His gravelly voice was harsh, but he had a little lopsided smile on his face. He twirled a cane chair around and sat on it backward, one of Barney's shticks.

"Paulie's sick," Mikey said. "He's back in the hospital."

"You don't look so hot yourself," Barney said. "You got no

color, Mikey. Hey, Joey, go get Mikey a tomato juice; maybe that'll put some roses in his cheeks."

Joey D grunted, but he didn't move. "I ain't getting him nothing," he said. He fixed his small dark eyes on Mikey's face, his foxy nose twitching in disapproval.

"Joey's sore at you." Barney grinned. "I'm the one who did the time, and Joey's got the grudge. The hospital again, huh? What is it this time?"

"It's the same thing," Mikey said. "I mean, not the same, it's worse. They say cirrhosis, can you figure that? Paulie never had more than a few beers all his life, and he gets this. . . . That's why I come to see you, Barney."

"Hey, what is this?" Joey D said. "What are we, a free clinic?"

"Shut up, Joey."

"What are we listening to this guy for? This little rat?"

Mikey was sweating now; he could feel his underarms getting sticky. He looked at Barney's round, placid face and tried to read what he was thinking, but it didn't help.

"This ain't about me," Mikey said. "This is about my kid brother. You always liked Paulie, Barney, he used to call you Uncle, remember, when he was a kid? Jeez, he's still a kid; he's not even twenty-four years old. And they say he's going to die."

"Die? From this liver thing?"

"He's had problems since he was little, jaundice, hepatitis, all that kind of stuff. Now it's really bad; now he doesn't have a chance unless he gets this operation—"

"So that's it!" Joey exploded. "He come here to ask for *money*, can you believe the nerve of this guy?"

"It's not the money! He's got insurance. He was working for the city; they gave him Blue Cross or something. . . . The money's no problem!"

"So what is?"

"It's the kind of operation," Mikey said. "They got to replace the liver, Barney; they got to do a transplant. There's a surgeon in Pittsburgh who'll do it for him; they got a special hospital for this kind of thing out there."

"So what do you need, plane fare?"

"No," Mikey said. "I need a liver."

Barney scraped back the cane chair. "Are you shitting me?"

"They need a liver, from a dead guy, a cadaver they call it. Only they can't get one. Only Paulie ain't the only patient. There's thousands of these cases waiting around for some organ donor to kick off! He's way down on the list, Barney; I mean, right at the bottom. And there's no time left!"

Now Barney's face had a frozen look. Mikey still couldn't read his thoughts, but he knew he had his attention. He knew Barney was a sentimental slob: The guy would cry at phone company commercials; he sent Valentines to his own mother. That was what he was counting on, that small soft center in Barney's brute body, even if Mikey was the last guy in the world who deserved a favor.

"It's not for me," Mikey said. "It's for Paulie. It's Paulie you got to help, Barney; you're the only guy I know who could do it."

"Do what?"

Mikey took a deep breath, a man on a high springboard.

"I thought maybe you had some work coming up," he said. "I mean, you're always working, Barney. I thought maybe you could add a little extra, for Paulie."

"What the fuck's he talking about?" Joey said.

"It won't make any difference to the guy," Mikey said. "And it'll save Paulie's life. . . . I talked to his doctor. They don't think he'll make it through another month, six weeks at the most—"

"Hey!" Barney bellowed suddenly. He bounced forward and shoved his unshaven jaw close to Mikey's face. "Say what you mean, asshole! What do you want me to do?"

"The next guy you whack," Mikey said, his throat tightening so fast it was painful to talk, "you get him to sign something, you know? A donor card. You get him to sign like a will, saying if anything happens to him, he wants Paulie to have his organs. . . ."

Joey D sat down quietly. Barney slid back his chair a few inches and began to shake his head slowly. After a moment he stood up and went to the counter. There was a cake stand with a plastic bowl covering some kind of thick-crusted pie. He helped himself to a slab, took an oversize bite, and chewed on it noisily. Then he came back to the table and sat down.

"For Paulie," he said.

From the notebook of Richard W. Fleischman, M.D.

Patient's name: Paul C. Slavin
History: Postnecrotic cirrhosis
Surgery: Liver transplantation
Result: Patient has made a rapid recovery from surgery.
Since there is no sign of tissue rejection, use of FK-506 has been postponed. Latest tests show liver chemistry normal. Patient is ambulatory and taking nourishment by mouth. Transplantation appears to be entirely successful and may be partially credited to the fact that the donor was a sibling.
Prognosis: Excellent

SURROGATE

....

ED GORMAN

That spring I began following fourteen-year-old David Mallory
home from school.

I always borrowed a car from one of the other lawyers in the
firm, and I always wore a hat with the brim low over my face.

With all the talk of child molesters in the news, I knew what
people would think if I ever got caught trailing him. To make
things worse, his father, Stephen, was my racquetball partner three
days a week. We lived on the same upwardly mobile street, attended
the same upwardly mobile church, and drove the same kind of upwardly mobile car. Their family BMW was blue; ours was red.

Most days David went straight home from school, a ten-block
walk that skirted a shaggy wooded area where the neighborhood
kids liked to play.

After a week of tailing him, I was about to give up. Then came
the rainy day when he met the tall boy at the south end of the
woods and handed him what appeared to be a white number ten
business envelope.

I used my binoculars so I could get a better look at the other
boy. He was blond, freckled, and thin, though it was a sinewy thin-
ness that suggested both strength and speed. He looked to be about

fourteen, but there was an anger and cunning in his face that you don't often see in kids, not in our kind of neighborhood anyway.

He opened the envelope, peeked inside, and gave David an angry shove. I couldn't hear their words, but I didn't need to. The tall boy was disappointed by what he'd found inside and was obviously making this clear to David.

He lashed out and grabbed David by the jacket and hoisted him half a foot off the ground. He flung the envelope to the ground and then slapped David twice hard across the mouth.

Then he let David fall in a heap to the ground.

The only sounds were the light rain thrumming on my borrowed car and the faint irregular pulse of an engine badly in need of a tune-up. In the rain and the faint fog, the tall boy stood over fallen David, still cursing him.

He brought a leg up and kicked David in the stomach.

David went backward, splayed faceup on the winter brown grass.

The other boy bent over him, shaking the white envelope in David's face.

The tall boy left abruptly, with no further words, with no warning of any sort. He turned and ran at a trot into the woods and then vanished, seeming to be as much a creature of the forest as a fox.

David lay in the rain for a long time. I doubted he was badly hurt. Even the kick couldn't have done all that much damage. But he was probably embarrassed and afraid, the way I'd always been at his age when bullies had taken their turn with me. Even with nobody around to witness your beating, you still felt humiliated.

Eventually he struggled to his feet. He was soaked. He took a few tentative steps and then fell into his regular pace. He was all right.

He reached the sidewalk and then finished the rest of the walk home.

In the next three weeks he met the blond boy three more times. Always on Wednesdays. All three times David handed over a white number ten business envelope, and all three times the blond boy quickly peered inside. David had obviously done what the other boy had demanded. The boy accepted the envelope, said a few words I couldn't hear, of course, and then went back into the same dark woods he'd come from.

Who was he? Where did he live? What was in the envelopes David was giving him?

A week later I got to the site where they met and hid myself in the woods, far to the right of the narrow dirt path the blond boy always used. I got there half an hour early.

He came up from the wide creek that wound through the center of the woods. He moved as usual at a trot, showing no signs of exertion at all. On a sunny spring day like this one he wore only a T-shirt and a pair of jeans.

He reached the mouth of the woods, stopped, and within a minute or so David was there, looking nervous as usual, handing over the white envelope as if in appeasement to a dark god who might smite him dead at any moment.

As I hunched down behind the low-hanging branches of a jack pine, I saw an American copper butterfly light on a green bush, and I felt a terrible and sudden melancholy, thinking of what had happened in the past and how my wife still woke up sobbing at night and what surely lay before us in the days ahead. I wanted the peace and wisdom of the butterfly for my own, to know the succor of sunlight and release from my rage.

But all I could do was follow the boy back into the woods, into the shifting shadows and ripe spring scents in which squirrels and stray kittens and birds slept and romped and luxuriated.

The boy went back into his trot, indifferent to the branches slapping him on face and arms. He came to a fork and went west, toward the wide muddy creek.

After a few more minutes I lost him completely. I couldn't even hear him disturb the undergrowth.

I was just inching my way to the clearing on the bank above the creek when he reappeared.

He climbed without pause to the very top of the railroad trestle bridge that lay across the fast-moving creek. He scurried up to the top, which rose twenty feet above the tracks below, and stood there gaping at the countryside.

He was king of the hill up there, taking a package of cigarettes from his jeans pocket and lighting up, looking over the world below with his customary sneer.

A train came soon enough, twenty-six swaying rattling boxcars pulled by an engine running hard and fast and invincible.

This was the nightmare shared by every parent in our neighborhood: that one of our children (even though strictly forbidden to play anywhere near the bridge) would fall into the path of the pitiless engine and be killed instantly.

The train roared through.

The entire bridge swayed.

But the boy, still enjoying his cigarette, stood upright, swaying with the power beneath him, becoming one with its rhythm, as if he were riding a wild animal.

And then the train was gone, taking its furious sounds with it, till all you could hear in the silence after was the incomprehensible chitter and chatter of birds.

From my hiding place I watched the boy a few more minutes, trying to make some sense of that sullen, angry face and insolent stance. But I could make no sense of him at all.

Soon after I left.

Next afternoon it rained again. I parked two blocks down from school.

When I saw David, I honked my horn. Today I was in my own car, and without hat, so he recognized me right away.

He came over and opened the door.

"Hi, Mr. Rhodes."

"Hi, David. Get in, and I'll give you a ride home."

He looked confused for a moment. What was I doing parked along the street this way? he had to be wondering.

"Really, Mr. Rhodes, I can walk."

"C'mon, David, get in. It's going to start raining again anytime now."

He still seemed apprehensive, but he reluctantly got in and closed the door.

I pulled away from the curb, out into traffic.

"So how've you been, David?"

"Oh, you know, fine, I guess."

"Your dad tells me you're getting good grades."

"Yeah, well, you know." He half smiled, embarrassed.

"Makes me think about Jeff. You know, how he'd be doing in these days."

I looked over at David. I knew he'd get uncomfortable and start squirming. That is just what he did.

"He'd be doing just great, Jeff would," David said. "He really would," he added, as if he needed to convince me of it.

"You ever think about him?"

"Sure. He was my best friend."

"He felt the same way about you."

David was getting uncomfortable again. Staring out the window. His house was approaching. I sped up.

"Hey, Mr. Rhodes, we're goin' right past my house."

"Yeah, I guess we are."

"Mr. Rhodes, I'm gettin' kind of nervous. I mean, I wish you'd just let me out right here."

I stared at him a long moment and said, "David, you're going to tell me what happened to Jeff or I'm going to hurt you. Hurt you very badly. Do you understand?"

He got pale. He was just a kid.

I said, "I want to know what's in that envelope you're giving that blond kid every Wednesday, and I want to know who the blond kid is. Though I think I've got a pretty good idea."

I made it as pleasant as possible. I took him to a Pizza Hut in a nearby mall. We had a double cheese and two large Cokes, and eventually he told me all about it.

He didn't show up Sunday, Monday, or Tuesday, the blond kid, but Wednesday, just as I reached my hiding place back of the clearing, I saw him climb the bridge and stand on top in that swaggering way of his.

I watched him for a few moments, and then I walked into the clearing and through the buffalo grass to the bridge.

I wasn't nearly as good at it as the kid, of course. He was younger; the monkey in him hadn't yet fled.

He watched me. He watched me very carefully and very curiously.

He wasn't afraid. If he had been, he'd have walked down the other side and run into the woods.

No. He just stood there smoking his cigarette, watching me, as I finally reached the top and started across to him.

For the first time he showed some anxiety as to who I might be. "Nice up here, ain't it?" he said.

But I didn't hear him. I heard only the approaching train.

"Don't usually see guys your age up here," he said, smirking a little about my thirty-eight years.

The train was right on time according to what I'd been able to observe over the past week, shuddering through the iron span of bridge.

The blond kid looked behind him. At the other end of the bridge. The free end. He looked as if he wanted to turn and run now.

The big bass horn of the train set the forest animals to scurrying. And then the engine came hurtling around the bend into the straightaway toward the bridge.

The kid finally figured out what I was going to do, but he was too late.

I grabbed him by the hair, jerked him to me, and then held him till the train was twenty yards from crossing the bridge. We were up too high for anybody in the train to see us. He smelled of sweat and heat and dirt and cigarette smoke.

His mouth swore at me, but I couldn't hear in all the noise. He fought, but he was no match for me, not at all.

I shoved him downward just at the right moment.

I suppose I should have looked away, but I didn't. I watched every moment of it.

How he hit the tracks on his back, legs flung across one track, head and arms across the opposite track.

He screamed, but he was in pantomime. He tried to scramble to his feet, but it was too late.

The train lifted him and punted him into the side of the bridge. When his body collided with the iron, he splattered. That's the only way to describe it. Splattered.

Then the train was gone, receding, receding, and there was just birdsong and sunlight and the fast muddy movement of the creek far below, and the ragged bloody remains of what had once been a human boy. The animals would come soon and feast on it.

Just as I was getting in bed that night, my wife came in and said, "My God, Charlie, on the news."

She was ashen.

"What about the news?" I said, sliding between the covers.

"A boy. Fourteen years old. Playing on that railroad bridge. He—was killed just the way Jeff was."

She started sobbing, so I held her. She was a good true woman and good true mother and good true wife. Nothing bad should happen to her. Not ever.

I suppose that was why I never quit looking into our son's "accidental" death. Going through his things one day up in the attic, I'd come across a note he'd written to David Mallory, saying that even though David was mad at Jeff because Jeff kissed his girlfriend, Jeff didn't think it was fair that David would hire Lon McKenzie to beat him up.

David had finally told me all about it that afternoon at the Pizza Hut. The blond kid was Lon McKenzie from the steeltown section of the city, a bully who not only took pride in his work but charged for it. If you wanted somebody taken care of, you hired Lon to do it, and if the price was right, your enemy would receive a beating that he would remember for a long, long time.

A hitman for the junior high set.

Lon had probably followed Jeff to the bridge, where Jeff—despite our constant complaints—frequently played. Jeff loved to sit up on the top span and look out at the woods.

Afterward McKenzie had bragged to David that he'd killed Jeff on purpose. He'd never seen anybody die before and he was curious. Then he'd started blackmailing David. Twenty-five dollars a week—or McKenzie would go to the police and implicate David in Jeff's death. David had been scared and guilty enough to go along, saving every bit of his allowance to pay McKenzie.

Now it was all done. I suppose I should have hated David, but I couldn't quite. Foolish as he'd been, he hadn't wanted to see Jeff die.

My wife turned off the light and got in next to me and clung to me in the darkness the way she would cling to a life preserver.

"I just keep thinking of that boy's poor parents," she said, starting to cry again. "It must be terrible for them."

"Yeah," I said there in the darkness, seeing again the train lift Lon McKenzie's body and smash it against the bridge, "yeah, it must be awful for them."

KELLER ON HORSEBACK

LAWRENCE BLOCK

At the airport newsstand Keller picked up a paperback western. The cover was pretty much generic, showing a standard-issue Marlboro man, long and lean, walking down the dusty streets of a western town with a gun riding his hip. Neither the title nor the author's name meant anything to Keller. What drew him was a line that seemed to leap out from the cover.

"He rode a thousand miles," Keller read, "to kill a man he never met."

Keller paid for the book and tucked it into his carry-on bag. When the plane was in the air, he dug it out and looked at the cover, wondering why he'd bought it. He didn't read much, and when he did, he never chose westerns.

Maybe he wasn't supposed to read this book. Maybe he was supposed to keep it for a talisman.

All for that one sentence. Imagine riding a thousand miles on a horse for any purpose, let alone the killing of a stranger. How long would it take, a thousand-mile journey on horseback? A thoroughbred got around a racecourse in something like two minutes, but it couldn't go all day at that pace any more than a human being could string together twenty-six four-minute miles and call it a marathon.

What could you manage on a horse, fifty miles a day? A hundred miles in two days, a thousand miles in twenty? Three weeks, say, at the conclusion of which a man would probably be eager to kill anybody, stranger or blood kin.

Was Ol' Sweat 'n' Leather getting paid for his thousand miles? Was he in the trade? Keller turned the book over in his hands, read the paragraph on the back cover. It did not sound promising. Something about a drifter in the Arizona Territory, a saddle tramp, looking to avenge an old Civil War grievance.

Forgive and forget, Keller advised him.

Keller, riding substantially more than a thousand miles, albeit on a plane instead of a horse, was similarly charged with killing a man as yet unmet. And he was drifting into the Old West to do it, first to Denver, then to Casper, Wyoming, and finally to a town called Martingale. That had been reason enough to pick up the book, but was it reason enough to read it?

He gave it a try. He read a few pages before they came down the aisle with the drinks cart, read a couple more while he sipped his V-8 and ate the salted nuts. Then he evidently dozed off because the next thing he knew the stewardess was waking him to apologize for not having the fruit plate he'd ordered. He told her it didn't matter, he'd have the regular dinner.

"Or there's a Hindu meal that's going begging," she said.

His mind filled with a vision of an airline tray wrapped in one of those saffron-colored robes, extending itself beseechingly and demanding alms. He had the regular dinner instead and ate most of it, except for the mystery meat. He dozed off afterward and didn't wake up until they were making their descent into Stapleton Airport.

Earlier he'd tucked the book into the seat pocket in front of him, and he'd intended to let it ride off into the sunset wedged between the airsickness bag and the plastic card with the emergency exit diagrams. At the last minute he changed his mind and brought the book along.

He spent an hour on the ground in Denver, another hour in the air flying to Casper. The cheerful young man at the Avis counter had a car reserved for Dale Whitlock. Keller showed him a Connecticut driver's license and an American Express card, and the young man gave him a set of keys and told him to have a nice day.

The keys fitted a white Chevy Caprice. Cruising north on the interstate, Keller decided he liked everything about the car but its name. There was nothing capricious about his mission. Riding a thousand miles to kill a man you hadn't met was not something one undertook on a whim.

Ideally, he thought, he'd be bouncing along on a rutted two-lane blacktop in a Mustang, say, or maybe a Bronco. Even a Pinto sounded like a better match for a rawboned, leathery desperado like Dale Whitlock than a Caprice.

It was comfortable, though, and he liked the way it handled. And the color was okay. But forget white. As far as he was concerned, the car was a palomino.

It took about an hour to drive to Martingale, a town of around ten thousand midway between Casper and Sheridan on I-25. Just looking around, you knew right away that you'd left the East Coast far behind. Mountains in the distance, a great expanse of sky overhead. And, right in front of you, frame buildings that could have been false fronts in a Randolph Scott film. A feedstore, a western wear emporium, a run-down hotel where you'd expect to find Wild Bill Hickok holding aces and eights at a table in the saloon, or Doc Holliday coughing his lungs out in a bedroom on the second floor.

Of course, there were also a couple of supermarkets and gas stations, a two-screen movie house and a Toyota dealership, a Pizza Hut and a Taco John's, so it wasn't too hard to keep track of what century you were in. He saw a man walk out of the Taco John's looking a lot like the young Randolph Scott, from his boots to his Stetson, but he spoiled the illusion by climbing into a pickup truck.

The hotel that inspired Hickok-Holliday fantasies was the Martingale, located right in the center of things on the wide main street. Keller imagined himself walking in, slapping a credit card on the counter. Then the desk clerk—Henry Jones always played him in the movie—would say that they didn't take plastic. "Or p-p-paper either," he'd say, eyes darting, looking for a place to duck when the shooting started.

And Keller would set a silver dollar spinning on the counter. "I'll be here a few days," he'd announce. "If I have any change coming, buy yourself a new pair of suspenders."

And Henry Jones would glance down at his suspenders, to see what was wrong with them.

He sighed, shook his head, and drove to the Holiday Inn near the interstate exit. It had plenty of rooms and gave him what he asked for, a nonsmoking room on the third floor in the rear. The desk clerk was a woman, very young, very blond, very perky, with nothing about her to remind you of Henry Jones. She said, "Enjoy your stay with us, Mr. Whitlock." Not stammering, eyes steady.

He unpacked, showered, and went to the window to look at the sunset. It was the sort of sunset a hero would ride off into, leaving a slender blonde to bite back tears while calling after him, "I hope you enjoyed your stay with us, Mr. Whitlock."

Stop it, he told himself. Stay with reality. You've flown a couple of thousand miles to kill a man you never met. Just get it done. The sunset can wait.

He hadn't met the man, but he knew his name. Even if he wasn't sure how to pronounce it.

The man in White Plains had handed Keller an index card with two lines of block capitals hand-printed.

"Lyman Crowder," he read, as if it rhymed with louder. "Or should that be Crowder?"—as if it rhymed with loader.

A shrug in response.

"Martingale, WY," Keller went on. "Why indeed? And where, besides Wyoming? Is Martingale near anything?"

Another shrug, accompanied by a photograph. Or a part of one; it had apparently been cropped from a larger photo and showed the upper half of a middle-aged man who looked to have spent a lot of time outdoors. A big man, too. Keller wasn't sure how he knew that. You couldn't see the man's legs, and there was nothing else in the photo to give you an idea of scale. But somehow he could tell.

"What did he do?"

Again a shrug, but one that conveyed information to Keller. If the other man didn't know what Crowder had done, he had evidently done it to somebody else. That meant the man in White Plains had no personal interest in the matter. It was strictly business.

"So who's the client?"

A shake of the head. Meaning that he didn't know who was picking up the tab or that he knew but wasn't saying? Hard to tell. The man in White Plains was a man of few words and master of none.

"What's the time frame?"

"The time frame," the man said, evidently enjoying the phrase. "No big hurry. One week, two weeks." He leaned forward, patted Keller on the knee. "Take your time," he said. "Enjoy yourself."

On the way out he'd shown the index card to Dot. He said, "How would you pronounce this? As in 'crow' or as in 'crowd'?"

Dot shrugged.

"Jesus," he said, "you're as bad as he is."

"Nobody's as bad as he is," Dot said. "Keller, what difference does it make how Lyman pronounces his last name?"

"I just wondered."

"Well, stick around for the funeral," she suggested. "See what the minister says."

"You're a big help," Keller said.

There was only one Crowder listed in the Martingale phone book. Lyman Crowder, with a telephone number but no address. About a third of the book's listings were like that. Keller wondered why. Did these people assume everybody knew where they lived in a town this size? Or were they saddle tramps with cellular phones and no fixed abode?

Probably rural, he decided. Lived out of town on some unnamed road, picked up their mail at the post office, so why list an address in the phone book?

Great. His quarry lived in the boondocks outside a town that wasn't big enough to have boondocks, and Keller didn't even have an address for him. He had a phone number, but what good was that? What was he supposed to do, call him up and ask directions? "Hi, this here's Dale Whitlock, we haven't met, but I just rode a thousand miles and—"

Scratch that.

He drove around and ate at a downtown café called the Singletree. It was housed in a weathered frame building just down the street from the Martingale Hotel. The café's name was spelled out in rope nailed to the vertical clapboards. For Keller the name brought a vision of a solitary pine or oak set out in the middle of vast grasslands, a landmark for herdsmen, a rare bit of shade from the relentless sun.

From the menu he learned that a singletree was some kind of apparatus used in hitching up a horse, or a team of horses. It was a little unclear to him just what it was or how it functioned, but it certainly didn't spread its branches in the middle of the prairie.

Keller had the special, a chicken-fried steak and some french fries that came smothered in gravy. He was hungry enough to eat everything in spite of the way it tasted.

You don't want to live here, he told himself.

It was a relief to know this. Driving around Martingale, Keller had found himself reminded of Roseburg, Oregon. Roseburg was larger, with none of the Old West feel of Martingale, but they both were small western towns of a sort Keller rarely got to. In Roseburg Keller had allowed his imagination to get away from him for a little while, and he wouldn't want to let that happen again.

Still, crossing the threshold of the Singletree, he had been unable to avoid remembering the little Mexican place in Roseburg. If the food and service here turned out to be on that level—

Forget it. He was safe.

After his meal Keller strode out through the bat-wing doors and walked up one side of the street and down the other. It seemed to him that there was something unusual about the way he was walking, that his gait was that of a man who had just climbed down from a horse.

Keller had been on a horse once in his life, and he couldn't remember how he'd walked after he got off it. So this walk he was doing now wasn't coming from his own past. It must have been something he'd learned unconsciously from movies and TV, a synthesis of all those riders of the purple sage and the silver screen.

No need to worry about yearning to settle here, he knew now. Because his fantasy now was not of someone settling in but passing through, the saddle tramp, the shootist, the flint-eyed loner who does his business and moves on.

That was a good fantasy, he decided. You wouldn't get into any trouble with a fantasy like that.

Back in his room Keller tried the book again but couldn't keep his mind on what he was reading. He turned on the TV and worked his way through the channels, using the remote control bolted to the nightstand. Westerns, he decided, were like cops and cabs, never around when you wanted them. It seemed to him that he never made a trip around the cable circuit without running into John Wayne or Randolph Scott or Joel McCrea or a rerun of *Gunsmoke* or *Rawhide* or one of those spaghetti westerns with Eastwood or Lee Van Cleef. Or the great villains—Jack Elam, Strother Martin, the young Lee Marvin in *The Man Who Shot Liberty Valance*.

It probably said something about you, Keller thought, when your favorite actor was Jack Elam.

He switched off the set and looked up Lyman Crowder's phone number. He could dial it, and when someone picked up and said, "Crowder residence," he'd know how the name was pronounced. "Just checking," he could say, cradling the phone and giving them something to think about.

Of course, he wouldn't say that; he'd mutter something harmless about a wrong number, but was even that much contact a good idea? Maybe it would put Crowder on his guard. Maybe Crowder was already on his guard, as far as that went. That was the trouble with going in blind like this, knowing nothing about either the target or the client.

If he called Crowder's house from the motel, there might be a record of the call, a link between Lyman Crowder and Dale Whitlock. That wouldn't matter much to Keller, who would shed the Whitlock identity on his way out of town, but there was no reason to create more grief for the real Dale Whitlock.

Because there *was* a real Dale Whitlock, and Keller was giving him grief enough without making him a murder suspect.

It was pretty slick the way the man in White Plains worked it. He knew a man who had a machine with which he could make flawless American Express cards. He knew someone else who could obtain the names and account numbers of bona fide American Express cardholders. Then he had cards made which were essentially duplicates of existing cards. You didn't have to worry that the cardholder had reported his card stolen because it hadn't been stolen; it was still sitting in his wallet. You were off somewhere charging the earth, and he didn't have a clue until the charges turned up on his monthly statement.

The driver's license was real, too. Well, technically, it was a counterfeit, of course, and the photograph on it showed Keller, not Whitlock. But someone had managed to access the Connecticut Bureau of Motor Vehicles' computer, and thus the counterfeit license showed the same number as Whitlock's, and gave the same address.

In the old days, Keller thought, it had been a lot more straightforward. You didn't need a license to ride a horse or a credit card to rent one. You bought or stole one, and when you rode into town on it, nobody asked to see your ID. They might not even come right out and ask your name, and if they did, they wouldn't expect a detailed reply. "Call me Tex," you'd say, and that's what they'd call you as you rode off into the sunset.

"Good-bye, Tex," the blonde would call out. "I hope you enjoyed your stay with us."

The lounge downstairs turned out to be the hot spot in Martingale. Restless, Keller had gone downstairs to have a quiet drink. He walked into a thickly carpeted room with soft lighting and a good sound system. There were fifteen or twenty people in the place, all of them either having a good time or looking for one.

Keller ordered a Coors at the bar. On the jukebox Barbara Mandrell sang a song about cheating. When she was done, a duo he didn't recognize sang a song about cheating. Then came Hank Williams's oldie, "Your Cheating Heart."

A subtle pattern was beginning to emerge.

"I love this song," the blonde said.

A different blonde, not the perky young thing from the front desk. This woman was taller, older, and fuller-figured. She wore a skirt and a sort of cowgirl blouse with piping and embroidery on it.

"Old Hank," Keller said, to say something.

"I'm June."

"Call me Tex."

"Tex!" Her laughter came in a sort of yelp. "When did anybody ever call you Tex, tell me that?"

"Well, nobody has," he admitted, "but that's not to say they never will."

"Where are you from, Tex? No, I'm sorry, I can't call you that; it sticks in my throat. If you want me to call you Tex, you're going to have to start wearing boots."

"You see by my outfit that I'm not a cowboy."

"Your outfit, your accent, your haircut. If you're not an easterner, then I'm a virgin."

"I'm from Connecticut."

"I knew it."

"My name's Dale."

"Well, you could keep that. If you were fixing to be a cowboy, I mean. You'd have to change the way you dress and talk and comb your hair, but you could hang on to Dale. There another name that goes with it?"

In for a penny, in for a pound. "Whitlock," he said.

"Dale Whitlock. Shoot, that's pretty close to perfect. You tell 'em a name like that, you got credit down at the Agway in a New York minute. Wouldn't even have to fill out a form. You married, Dale?"

What was the right answer? She was wearing a ring herself, and the jukebox was now playing yet another cheating song.

"Not in Martingale," he said.

"Oh, I like that," she said, eyes sparkling. "I like the whole idea of regional marriage. I *am* married in Martingale, but we're not *in* Martingale. The town line's Front Street."

"In that case," he said, "maybe I could buy you a drink."

"You easterners," she said. "You're just so damn fast."

There had to be a catch.

Keller didn't do too badly with women. He got lucky once in a while. But he didn't have the sort of looks that made heads turn, nor had he made seduction his life's work. Some years ago he'd read a book called *How to Pick Up Girls*, filled with opening lines that were guaranteed to work. Keller thought they were silly. He was willing to believe they would work, but he was not able to believe they would work for him.

This woman, though, had hit on him before he'd had time to become aware of her presence. This sort of thing happened, especially when you were dealing with a married woman in a bar where all they played was cheating songs. Everybody knew what everybody else was there for, and nobody had time to dawdle. So this sort of thing happened, but it never seemed to happen to him, and he didn't trust it.

Something would go wrong. She'd call home and find out her kid was running a fever. Her husband would walk in the door just as the jukebox gave out with "You Picked a Fine Time to Leave Me, Lucille." She'd be overcome by conscience or rendered unconscious by the drink Keller had just bought her.

"I'd say my place or yours," she said, "but we both know the answer to that one. What's your room number?" Keller told her. "You go on up," she said. "I won't be a minute. Don't start without me."

He brushed his teeth, splashed on a little aftershave. She wouldn't show, he told himself. Or she'd expect to be paid, which would take a little of the frost off the pumpkin. Or her husband would turn up and they'd try to work some variation of the badger game.

Or she'd be sloppy drunk, or he'd be impotent. Or something.

"Whew," she said. "I don't guess you need boots after all. I'll call you Tex or Slim or any damn thing you want me to, just so you come when you're called. How long are you in town for, Dale?"

"I'm not sure. A few days."

"Business, I suppose. What sort of business are you in?"

"I work for a big corporation," he said. "They fly me over to look into situations."

"Sounds like you can't talk about it."

"Well, we do a lot of government work," he said. "So I'm really not supposed to."

"Say no more," she said. "Oh, Lord, look at the time!"

While she showered, he picked up the paperback and rewrote the blurb. He killed a thousand miles, he thought, to ride a woman he never met. Well, sometimes you got lucky. The stars were in the right place; the forces that ruled the universe decided you deserved a present. There didn't always have to be a catch to it, did there?

She turned off the shower, and he heard the last line of the song she'd been singing. " 'And Margie's at the Lincoln Park Inn,' " she sang, and moments later she emerged from the bathroom and began dressing.

"What's this?" she said. " 'He rode a thousand miles to kill a man he never met.' You know, that's funny, because I just had the darnedest thought while I was runnin' the soap over my pink and tender flesh."

"Oh?"

"I just said that last to remind you what's under this here skirt and blouse. Oh, the thought I had? Well, something you said, government work. I thought maybe this man's CIA, maybe he's some old soldier of fortune, maybe he's the answer to this maiden's prayer."

"What do you mean?"

"Just that it was already a real fine evening, Dale, but it would be heaven on earth if what you came to Martingale for was to kill my damn husband."

Christ. Was *she* the client? Was the pickup downstairs a cute way for them to meet? Could she actually be that stupid, coming on in a public place to a man she was hiring to kill her husband?

For that matter, how had she recognized him? Only Dot and the man in White Plains had known the name he was using. They'd have kept it to themselves. And she'd made her move before she knew his name. Had she been able to recognize him? I see by your outfit that you are a hit man? Something along those lines?

"Yarnell," she was saying. "Hobart Lee Yarnell, and what he'd like is for people to call him Bart, and what everybody calls him is Hobie. Now what does that tell you about the man?"

That he's not the man I came here to kill, Keller thought. This was comforting to realize but left her waiting for an answer to her question. "That he's not used to getting his own way," Keller said.

She laughed. "He's not," she said, "but it's not for lack of trying. You know, I like you, Dale. You're a nice fellow. But if it wasn't you tonight, it would have been somebody else."

"And here I thought it was my aftershave."

"I'll just bet you did. No, the kind of marriage I got, I come around here a lot. I've put a lot of quarters in that jukebox the last year or so."

"And played a lot of cheating songs?"

"And done a fair amount of cheating. But it doesn't really work. I still wake up the next day married to that bastard."

"Why don't you divorce him?"

"I've thought about it."

"And?"

"I was brought up not to believe in it," she said. "But I don't guess that's it. I wasn't raised to believe in cheating either." She frowned. "Money's part of it," she admitted. "I won't bore you with the details, but I'd get gored pretty bad in a divorce."

"That's a problem."

"I guess, except what do I care about money anyway? Enough's as much as a person needs, and my daddy's got pots of money. He's not about to let me starve."

"Well, then—"

"But he thinks the world of Hobie," she said, glaring at Keller as if it were his fault. "Hunts elk with him, goes after trout and salmon with him, thinks he's just the best thing ever came over the pass. And he doesn't even want to hear the word 'divorce.' You know that Tammy Wynette song where she spells it out a letter at a time? I swear he'd leave the room before you got past *R*. I say it'd about break Lyman Crowder's heart if his little girl ever got herself divorced."

Well, it was true. If you kept your mouth shut and your ears open, you learned things. What he had learned was that "Crowder" rhymed with "powder."

Now what?

After her departure, after his own shower, he paced back and forth, trying to sort it all out. In the few hours since his arrival in Martingale, he'd slept with a woman who turned out to be the loving daughter of the target and, in all likelihood, the unloving wife of the client.

Well, maybe not. Lyman Crowder was a rich man, lived north of town on a good-size ranch that he ran pretty much as a hobby. He'd made his real money in oil, and nobody ever made a small amount of money that way. You either went broke or got rich. Rich men had enemies: people they'd crossed in business, people who stood to profit from their death.

But it figured that Yarnell was the client. There was a kind of poetic inevitability about it. She picks him up in the lounge, it's not enough that she's the target's daughter. She also ought to be the client's wife. Round things out, tie up all the loose ends.

The thing to do . . . well, he knew the thing to do. The thing to do was get a few hours' sleep and then, bright and early, reverse the usual order of affairs by riding off into the sunrise. Get on a plane, get off in New York, and write off Martingale as a happy little romantic adventure. Men, after all, had been known to travel farther than that in the hope of getting laid.

He'd tell the man in White Plains to find somebody else. Sometimes you had to do that. No blame attached, as long as you didn't make a habit of it. He'd say he was blown.

As, come to think of it, he was. Quite expertly, as a matter of fact.

In the morning he got up and packed his carry-on. He'd call White Plains from the airport or wait until he was back in New York. He didn't want to phone from the room. When the real Dale Whitlock had a fit and called American Express, they'd look over things like the Holiday Inn statement. No sense leaving anything that led anywhere.

He thought about June, and the memory made him playful. He checked the time. Eight o'clock, two hours later in the East, not an uncivil time to call.

He called Whitlock's home in Rowayton, Connecticut. A woman answered. He identified himself as a representative of a political polling organization, using a name she would recognize. By asking questions that encouraged lengthy responses, he had no trouble keeping her on the phone. "Well, thank you very much," he said at length. "And have a nice day."

Now let Whitlock explain that one to American Express.

He finished packing and was almost out the door when his eye caught the paperback western. Take it along? Leave it for the maid? What?

He picked it up, read the cover line, sighed. Was this what Randolph Scott would do? Or John Wayne, or Clint Eastwood? How about Jack Elam?

No, of course not.

Because then there'd be no movie. A man rides into town, starts to have a look at the situation, meets a woman, gets it on with her, then just backs out and rides off? You put something like that on the screen, it wouldn't even play in the art houses.

Still, this wasn't a movie.

Still . . .

He looked at the book and wanted to heave it across the room. But all he heaved was a sigh. Then he unpacked.

He was having a cup of coffee in town when a pickup pulled up across the street and two men got out of it. One of them was Lyman Crowder. The other, not quite as tall, was twenty pounds lighter and twenty years younger. Crowder's son, by the looks of him.

His son-in-law, as it turned out. Keller followed the two men into a store where the fellow behind the counter greeted them as Lyman and Hobie. Crowder had a lengthy shopping list composed largely of items Keller would have been hard put to find a use for.

While the owner filled the order, Keller had a look at the display of hand-tooled boots. The pointed toes would be handy in New York, he thought, for killing cockroaches in corners. The heels would add better than an inch to his height. He wondered if he'd feel awkward in the boots, like a teenager in her first pair of high heels. Lyman and Hobie looked comfortable enough in their boots, as pointy in the toes and as elevated in the heels as any on display, but they also looked comfortable in their string ties and ten-gallon hats, and Keller was sure he'd feel ridiculous dressed like that.

They were a pair, he thought. They looked alike, they talked alike, they dressed alike, and they seemed uncommonly fond of each other.

Back in his room Keller stood at the window and looked down at the parking lot, then across the way at a pair of mountains. A few years ago his work had taken him to Miami, where he'd met a Cuban who'd cautioned him against ever taking a hotel room above the second floor. "Suppose you got to leave in a hurry?" the man said. "Ground floor, no problem. Second floor, no problem. Third floor, break your fockeen leg."

The logic of this had impressed Keller, and for a while he had made a point of taking the man's advice. Then he happened to learn that the Cuban not only shunned the higher floors of hotels but also refused to enter an elevator or fly on an airplane. What had looked like tradecraft now appeared to be nothing more than phobia.

It struck Keller that he had never in his life had to leave a hotel room, or any other sort of room, by the window. This was not to say that it would never happen, but he'd decided it was a risk he was prepared to run. He liked high floors. Maybe he even liked running risks.

He picked up the phone, made a call. When she answered, he said, "This is Tex. Would you believe my business appointment canceled? Left me with the whole afternoon to myself."

"Are you where I left you?"

"I've barely moved since then."

"Well, don't move now," she said. "I'll be right on over."

Around nine that night Keller wanted a drink, but he didn't want to have it in the company of adulterers and their favorite music. He drove around in his palomino Caprice until he found a place on the edge of town that looked promising. It called itself Joe's Bar. Outside, it was nondescript. Inside, it smelled of stale beer and casual plumbing. The lights were low. There was sawdust on the floor and the heads of dead animals on the walls. The clientele was exclusively male, and for a moment this gave Keller pause. There were gay bars in New York that tried hard to look like this place, though it was hard for Keller to imagine why. But Joe's, he realized, was not a gay bar, not in any sense of the word.

He sat on a wobbly stool and ordered a beer. The other drinkers left him alone, even as they left one another alone. The jukebox played intermittently, with men dropping in quarters when they could no longer bear the silence.

The songs, Keller noted, ran to type. There were the tryin'-to-drink-that-woman-off-of-my-mind songs and the if-it-wasn't-for-bad-luck-I-wouldn't-have-no-luck-at-all songs. Nothing about Margie in the Lincoln Park Inn, nothing about heaven being just a sin away. These songs were for drinking and feeling really rotten about it.

" 'Nother damn day," said a voice at Keller's elbow.

He knew who it was without turning. He supposed he might have recognized the voice, but he didn't think that was it. No, it was more a recognition of the inevitability of it all. Of course it would be Yarnell, making conversation with him in this bar where no one made conversation with anyone. Who else could it be?

" 'Nother damn day," Keller agreed.

"Don't believe I've seen you around."

"I'm just passing through."

"Well, you got the right idea," Yarnell said. "Name's Bart."

In for a pound, in for a ton. "Dale," Keller said.

"Good to know you, Dale."

"Same here, Bart."

The bartender loomed before them. "Hey, Hobie," he said. "The usual?"

Yarnell nodded. "And another of those for Dale here." The bartender poured Yarnell's usual, which turned out to be bourbon with water back, and uncapped another beer for Keller. Somebody broke down and fed the jukebox a quarter and played "There Stands the Glass."

Yarnell said, "You hear what he called me?"

"I wasn't paying attention."

"Called me Hobie," Yarnell said. "Everybody does. You'll be doing the same, won't be able to help yourself."

"The world is a terrible place," Keller said.

"By God, you got that right," Yarnell said. "No one ever said it better. You a married man, Dale?"

"Not at the moment."

" 'Not at the moment.' I swear I'd give a lot if I could say the same."

"Troubles?"

"Married to one woman and in love with another one. I guess you could call that trouble."

"I guess you could."

"Sweetest, gentlest, darlingest, lovingest creature God ever made," Yarnell said. "When she whispers 'Bart,' it don't matter if the whole rest of the world shouts 'Hobie.' "

"This isn't your wife you're talking about," Keller guessed.

"God, no! My wife's a round-heeled meanspirited hardhearted tramp. I hate my damn wife. I love my girlfriend."

They were silent for a moment, and so was the whole room. Then someone played "The Last Word in Lonesome Is Me."

"They don't write songs like that anymore," Yarnell said.

The hell they didn't. "I'm sure I'm not the first person to suggest this," Keller said, "but have you thought about—"

"Leaving June," Yarnell said. "Running off with Edith. Getting a divorce."

"Something like that."

"Never an hour that I don't think about it, Dale. Night and goddamn day I think about it. I think about it, and I drink about it, but the one thing I can't do is do it."

"Why's that?"

"There is a man," Yarnell said, "who is a father and a best friend to me all rolled into one. Finest man I ever met in my life, and the only wrong thing he ever did in his life was have a daughter, and the biggest mistake I ever made was marrying her. And if there's one thing that man believes in, it's the sanctity of marriage. Why, he thinks 'divorce' is the dirtiest word in the language."

So Yarnell couldn't even let on to his father-in-law that his marriage was hell on earth, let alone take steps to end it. He had to keep his affair with Edith very much backstreet. The only person he could talk to was Edith, and she was out of town for the next week or so, leaving him dying of loneliness and ready to pour out his heart to the first stranger he could find. For which he apologized, but—

"Hey, that's all right, Bart," Keller said. "A man can't keep it all locked up inside."

"Calling me Bart, I appreciate that, I truly do. Even Lyman calls me Hobie, and he's the best friend any man ever had. Hell, he can't help it. Everybody calls me Hobie sooner or later."

"Well," Keller said, "I'll hold out as long as I can."

Alone, Keller reviewed his options.

He could kill Lyman Crowder. He'd be keeping it simple, carrying out the mission as it had been given to him. And it would solve everybody's problems. June and Hobie could get the divorce they both so desperately wanted.

On the downside, they'd both be losing the man each regarded as the greatest thing since microwave popcorn.

He could toss a coin and take out either June or her husband, thus serving as a sort of divorce court of last resort. If it came up heads, June could spend the rest of her life cheating on a ghost. If it was tails, Yarnell could have his cake and Edith, too. Only a question of time until she stopped calling him Bart and took to calling him Hobie, of course, and next thing you knew she would turn up at the Holiday Inn, dropping her quarter in the slot to play "Third-Rate Romance, Low-Rent Rendezvous."

It struck Keller that there ought to be some sort of solution that didn't involve lowering the population. But he knew he was the person least likely to come up with it.

If you had a medical problem, the treatment you got depended on the sort of person you went to. You didn't expect a surgeon to manipulate your spine, or prescribe herbs and enemas, or kneel down and pray with you. Whatever the problem was, the first thing the surgeon would do was look around for something to cut. That's how he'd been trained; that's how he saw the world; that's what he did.

Keller, too, was predisposed to a surgical approach. While others might push counseling or twelve-step programs, Keller reached for a scalpel. But sometimes it was difficult to tell where to make the incision.

Kill 'em all, he thought savagely, and let God sort 'em out. Or ride off into the sunset with your tail between your legs.

First thing in the morning Keller drove to Sheridan and caught a plane to Salt Lake City. He paid cash for his ticket and used the name John Richards. At the TWA counter in Salt Lake City he bought a one-way ticket to Las Vegas and again paid cash, this time using the name Alan Johnson.

At the Las Vegas airport he walked around the long-term parking lot as if looking for his car. He'd been doing this for five minutes or so when a balding man wearing a glen plaid sport coat parked a two-year-old Plymouth and removed several large suitcases from its trunk, affixing them to one of those aluminum luggage carriers. Wherever he was headed, he'd packed enough to stay there for a while.

As soon as he was out of sight, Keller dropped to a knee and groped the undercarriage until he found the magnetized hide-a-key. He always looked before breaking into a car, and he got lucky about one time in five. As usual, he was elated. Finding a key was a good omen. It boded well.

Keller had been to Vegas frequently over the years. He didn't like the place, but he knew his way around. He drove to Caesars Palace and left his borrowed Plymouth for the attendant to park. He knocked on the door of an eighth-floor room until its occupant protested that she was trying to sleep.

He said, "It's news from Martingale, Miss Bodine. For Christ's sake, open the door."

She opened the door a crack but kept the chain fastened. She was about the same age as June but looked older, her black hair a mess, her eyes bleary, her face still bearing traces of yesterday's makeup.

"Crowder's dead," he said.

Keller could think of any number of things she might have said, ranging from "What happened?" to "Who cares?" This woman cut to the chase. "You idiot," she said. "What are you doing here?"

Mistake.

"Let me in," he said, and she did.

Another mistake.

The attendant brought Keller's Plymouth and seemed happy with the tip Keller gave him. At the airport someone else had left a Toyota Camry in the spot where the balding man had originally parked the Plymouth, and the best Keller could do was wedge it into a spot one aisle over and a dozen spaces off to the side. He figured the owner would find it and hoped he wouldn't worry that he was in the early stages of Alzheimer's.

Keller flew to Denver as Richard Hill, to Sheridan as David

Edwards. En route he thought about Edith Bodine, who'd evidently slipped on a wet tile in the bathroom of her room at Caesars, cracking her skull on the side of the big tub. With the Do Not Disturb sign hanging from the doorknob and the air conditioner at its highest setting, there was no telling how long she might remain undisturbed.

He'd figured she had to be the client. It wasn't June or Hobie, both of whom thought the world revolved around Lyman Crowder, so whom did that leave? Crowder himself, turned sneakily suicidal? Some old enemy, some business rival?

No, Edith was the best prospect. A client would either want to meet Keller—not obliquely, as both Yarnells had done, but by arrangement—or would contrive to be demonstrably off the scene when it all happened. Thus the trip to Las Vegas.

Why? The Crowder fortune, of course. She had Hobie Yarnell crazy about her, but he wouldn't leave June for fear of breaking Crowder's heart, and even if he did, he'd go empty-handed. Having June killed wouldn't work, either, because she didn't have any real money of her own. But June would inherit if the old man died, and later on something could always happen to June.

Anyway, that was how he figured it. If he'd wanted to know Edith's exact reasoning, he'd have had to ask her, and that had struck him as a waste of time. More to the point, the last thing he'd wanted was a chance to get to know her. That just screwed everything up when you got to know these people.

If you were going to ride a thousand miles to kill a man you'd never met, you were really well advised to be the tight-lipped stranger every step of the way. No point in talking to anybody, not the target, not the client, and not anybody else either. If you had anything to say, you could whisper it to your horse.

He got off the fourth plane of the day at Sheridan, picked up his Caprice—the name was seeming more appropriate with every passing hour—and drove back to Martingale. He kept it right around the speed limit, then slowed down along with everyone else five miles outside Martingale. They were clearing a wreck out of the northbound lane. That shouldn't have slowed things down in the southbound lane, but of course it did; everybody had to slow down to see what everyone else was slowing down to look at.

Back in his room he had his bag packed before he realized that he couldn't go anywhere. The client was dead, but that didn't change anything; since he had no way of knowing that she was the client or that she was dead, his mission remained unchanged. He could go home and admit an inability to get the job done, waiting for the news to seep through that there was no longer any job to be done. That would get him off the hook after the fact, but he wouldn't have covered himself with glory, nor would he get paid. The client had almost certainly paid in advance, and if there'd been a middleman between the client and the man in White Plains, he had almost certainly passed the money on, and there was very little likelihood that the man in White Plains would even consider the notion of refunding a fee to a dead client, not that anyone would raise the subject. But neither would the man in White Plains pay Keller for work he'd failed to perform. The man in White Plains would just keep everything.

Keller thought about it. It looked to him as though his best course lay in playing a waiting game. How long could it take before a sneak thief or a chambermaid walked in on Edith Bodine? How long before news of her death found its way to White Plains?

The more he thought about it, the longer it seemed likely to take. If there were, as sometimes happened, a whole string of intermediaries involved, the message might very well never get to García.

Maybe the simplest thing was to kill Crowder and be done with it.

No, he thought. He'd just made a side trip of, yes, more than a thousand miles—and at his own expense yet—solely to keep from having to kill this legendary Man He Never Met. Damned if he was going to kill him now, after all that.

He'd wait a while anyway. He didn't want to drive anywhere

now, and he couldn't bear to look at another airplane, let alone get on board.

He stretched out on the bed, closed his eyes.

He had a frightful dream. In it he was walking at night out in the middle of the desert, lost, chilled, desperately alone. Then a horse came galloping out of nowhere, and on his back was a magnificent woman with a great mane of hair and eyes that flashed in the moonlight. She extended a hand, and Keller leaped up on the horse and rode behind her. She was naked. So was Keller, although he had somehow failed to notice this before.

They fell in love. Wordless, they told each other everything, knew each other like twin souls. And then, gazing into her eyes, Keller realized who she was. She was Edith Bodine, and she was dead; he'd killed her earlier without knowing she'd turn out to be the girl of his dreams. It was done, it could never be undone, and his heart was broken for eternity.

Keller woke up shaking. For five minutes he paced the room, struggling to sort out what was a dream and what was real. He hadn't been sleeping long. The sun was setting; it was still the same endless day.

God, what a hellish dream.

He couldn't get caught up in TV, and he had no luck at all with the book. He put it down, picked up the phone, and dialed June's number.

"It's Dale," he said. "I was sitting here and—"

"Oh, Dale," she cut in, "you're so thoughtful to call. Isn't it terrible? Isn't it the most awful thing?"

"Uh," he said.

"I can't talk now," she said. "I can't even think straight. I've never been so upset in my life. Thank you, Dale, for being so thoughtful."

She hung up and left him staring at the phone. Unless she was a better actress than he would have guessed, she sounded absolutely overcome. He was surprised that news of Edith Bodine's death could have reached her so soon, but far more surprised that she could be taking it so hard. Was there more to all this than met the eye? Were Hobie's wife and mistress actually close friends? Or were they—Jesus—*more* than just good friends?

Things were certainly a lot simpler for Randolph Scott.

The same bartender was on duty at Joe's. "I don't guess your friend Hobie'll be coming around tonight," he said. "I suppose you heard the news."

"Uh," Keller said. Some backstreet affair, he thought, if the whole town was ready to comfort Hobie before the body was cold.

"Hell of a thing," the man went on. "Terrible loss for this town. Martingale won't be the same without him."

"This news," Keller said carefully. "I think maybe I missed it. What happened anyway?"

He called the airlines from his motel room. The next flight out of Casper wasn't until morning. Of course, if he wanted to drive to Denver—

He didn't want to drive to Denver. He booked the first flight out in the morning, using the Whitlock name and the Whitlock credit card.

No need to stick around, not with Lyman Crowder stretched out somewhere getting pumped full of embalming fluid. Dead in a car crash on I-25 North, the very accident that had slowed Keller down on his way back from Sheridan.

He wouldn't be around for the funeral, but should he send flowers? It was quite clear that he shouldn't. Still, the impulse was there.

He dialed 1-800-FLOWERS and sent a dozen roses to Mrs. Dale Whitlock in Rowayton, charging them to Whitlock's American Express account. He asked them to enclose a card reading, "Just because I love you—Dale."

He felt it was the least he could do.

Two days later he was on Taunton Place in White Plains, making his report. Accidents were always good, the man told him. Accidents and natural causes, always the best. Oh, sometimes you needed a noisy hit to send a message, but the rest of the time you couldn't beat an accident.

"Good you could arrange it," the man said.

Would have taken a hell of an arranger, Keller thought. First you'd have had to arrange for Lyman Crowder to be speeding north in his pickup. Then you'd have had to get an unemployed sheepherder named Danny Vasco good and drunk and sent him hurtling toward Martingale, racing his own pickup—Jesus, didn't they drive anything but pickups?—racing it at ninety-plus miles an hour, and proceeding southbound in the northbound lane. Arrange for a few near misses. Arrange for Vasco to brush a school bus and sideswipe a minivan, and then let him ram Crowder head-on.

Some arrangement.

If the man in White Plains had any idea that the client was dead as well or even who the client was, he gave no sign to Keller. On the way out Dot asked him how Crowder pronounced his name.

"Rhymes with 'chowder,' " he said.

"I knew you'd find out," she said. "Keller, are you all right? You seem different."

"Just awed by the workings of fate," he said.

"Well," she said, "that'll do it."

On the train back to the city he thought about the workings of fate. Earlier he'd tried to tell himself that his side trip to Las Vegas had been a waste of time and money and human life. All he'd had to do was wait a day for Danny Vasco to take the game off the boards.

Never would have happened.

Without his trip to Vegas, there would have been no wreck on the highway. One event had opened some channel that allowed the other to happen. He couldn't explain this, couldn't make sense out of it, but somehow he knew it was true.

Everything had happened exactly the way it had had to happen. Encountering June in the Meet 'n' Cheat, running into Hobie at the Burnout Bar. He could no more have avoided those meetings than he could have kept himself from buying the paperback western novel that had set the tone for everything that followed.

He hoped Mrs. Whitlock liked the flowers.

EVERYBODY'S WATCHING ME

MICKEY SPILLANE

I handed the guy the note and shivered a little bit because the guy was as big as they come, and even though he had a belly you couldn't get your arms around, you wouldn't want to be the one who figured you could sink your fist in it. The belly was as hard as the rest of him, but not quite as hard as his face.

Then I knew how hard the back of his hand was because he smashed it across my jaw and I could taste the blood where my teeth bit into my cheek.

Maybe the guy holding my arm knew I couldn't talk because he said, "A guy give him a fin to bring it, boss. He said that."

"Who, kid?"

I spit the blood out easy so it dribbled down my chin instead of going on the floor. "Gee, Mr. Renzo . . ."

His hand made a dull, soggy crack on my skin. The buzz got louder in my ears and there was a jagged, pounding pain in my skull.

"Maybe you didn't hear me the first time, kid. I said who."

The hand let go my arm and I slumped to the floor. I didn't want to, but I had to. There were no legs under me anymore. My eyes were open, conscious of only the movement of ponderous things that got closer. Things that moved quickly and seemed to dent my side without causing any feeling at all.

That other voice said, "He's out, boss. He ain't saying a thing."

"I'll make him talk."

"Won't help none. So a guy gives him a fin to bring the note. He's not going into a song and dance with it. To the kid a fin's a lot of dough. He watches the fin, not the guy."

"You're getting too damn bright," Renzo said.

"That's what you pay me for being, boss."

"Then act bright. You think a guy hands a note like this to some kid? Any kid at all? You think a kid's gonna bull in here to deliver it when he can chuck it down a drain and take off with the fin?"

"So the kid's got morals."

"So the kid knows the guy or the guy knows him. He ain't letting no kid get away with his fin." The feet moved away from me, propped themselves against the dark blur of the desk. "You read this thing?" Renzo asked.

"No."

"Listen then. 'Cooley is dead. Now my fine fat louse, I'm going to spill your guts all over your own floor.'" Renzo's voice droned to a stop. He sucked hard on the cigar and said, "It's signed, *Vetter.*"

You could hear the unspoken words in the silence. That hush that comes when the name was mentioned and the other's half-whispered "Son of a bitch, they were buddies, boss?"

"Who cares? If that crumb shows his face around here, I'll break his lousy back. Vetter, Vetter, Vetter. Everyplace you go that crumb's name you hear."

"Boss, look. You don't want to tangle with that guy. He's killed plenty of guys. He's . . ."

"He's different from me? You think he's a hard guy?"

"You ask around, boss. They'll tell you. That guy don't give a damn for nobody. He'll kill you for looking at him."

"Maybe in his own back yard he will. Not here, Johnny, not here. This is my city and my back yard. Here things go my way and Vetter'll get what Cooley got." He sucked on the cigar again and I began to smell the smoke. "Guys what pull a fastie on me get killed. Now Cooley don't work on my tables for no more smart plays. Pretty soon the cops can take Vetter off their list because he won't be around no more either."

"You going to take him, boss?" Johnny said.

"What do you think?"

"Anything you say, boss. I'll pass the word around. Somebody'll know what he looks like and'll finger him." He paused, then, "What about the kid?"

"He's our finger, Johnny."

"Him?"

"You ain't so bright as I thought. You should get your ears to the ground more. You should hear things about Vetter. He pays off for favors. The errand was worth a fin, but he's gonna look in to make sure the letter got here. Then he spots the kid for his busted up face. First time he makes contact we got him. You know what, Johnnie? To Vetter I'm going to do things slow. When they find him the cops get all excited but they don't do nothing. They're glad to see Vetter dead. But other places the word gets around, see? Anybody can bump Vetter gets to be pretty big and nobody pulls any more smart ones. You understand, Johnny?"

"Sure, boss. I get it. You're going to do it yourself?"

"Just me, kid, just me. Like Helen says, I got a passion to do something myself and I just got to do it. Vetter's for me. He better be plenty big, plenty fast and ready to start shooting the second we meet up."

It was like when Pop used to say he'd do something and we knew he'd do it sure. You look at him with your face showing the awe a kid gets when he knows fear and respect at the same time and that's how Johnny must have been looking at Renzo. I knew it because it was in his voice when he said, "You'll do it, boss. You'll own this town, lock, stock and gun butt yet."

"I own it now, Johnny. Never forget it. Now wake that kid up."

This time I had feeling and it hurt. The hand that slapped the full vision back to my eyes started the blood running in my mouth again and I could feel my lungs choking on a sob.

"What was he like, kid?" The hand came down again and this

time Renzo took a step forward. His fingers grabbed my coat and jerked me to the floor.

"You got asked a question. What was he like?"

"He was . . . big," I said. The damn slob choked me again and I wanted to break something over his head.

"How big?"

"Like you. Bigger'n six. Heavy."

Renzo's mouth twisted into a sneer and he grinned at me. "More. What was his face like?"

"I don't know. It was dark. I couldn't see him good."

He threw me. Right across the room he threw me and my back smashed the wall and twisted and I could feel the tears rolling down my face from the pain.

"You don't lie to Renzo, kid. If you was older and bigger I'd break you up into little pieces until you talked. It ain't worth a fin. Now you start telling me what I want to hear and maybe I'll slip you something."

"I . . . I don't know. Honest, I . . . if I saw him again it'd be different." The pain caught me again and I had to gag back my voice.

"You'd know him again?"

"Yes."

Johnny said, "What's your name, kid?"

"Joe . . . Boyle."

"Where do you live?" It was Renzo this time.

"Gidney Street," I told him. "Number three."

"You work?"

"Gordon's. I . . . push."

"What'd he say?" Renzo's voice had a nasty tone to it.

"Gordon's a junkie," Johnny said for me. "Has a place on River Street. The kid pushes a cart for him collecting metal scraps."

"Check on it," Renzo said, "then stick with him. You know what to do."

"He won't get away, boss. He'll be around whenever we want him. You think Vetter will do what you say?"

"Don't things always happen like I say? Now get him out of

here. Go over him again so he'll know we mean what we say. That was a lousy fin he worked for."

After things hurt so much they begin to stop hurting completely. I could feel the way I went through the air, knew my foot hit the railing and could taste the cinders that ground in my mouth. I lay there like I was passing out, waiting for the pain to come swelling back, making sounds I didn't want to make. My stomach wanted to break loose but couldn't find the strength and I just lay there cursing guys like Renzo who could do anything they wanted and get away with it.

Then the darkness came, went away briefly and came back again. When it lost itself in the dawn of agony there were hands brushing the dirt from my face and the smell of flowers from the softness that was a woman who held me and said, "You poor kid, you poor kid."

My eyes opened and looked at her. It was like something you dream about because she was the kind of woman you always stare at, knowing you can't have. She was beautiful, with yellow hair that tumbled down her neck like a torch that lit up her whole body. Her name was Helen Troy and I wanted to say, "Hello, Helen," but couldn't get the words out of my mouth.

Know her? Sure, everybody knew her. She was Renzo's feature attraction at his Hideaway Club. But I never thought I'd live to have my head in her lap.

There were feet coming up the path that turned into one of the men from the stop at the gate and Helen said, "Give me a hand, Finney. Something happened to the kid."

The guy she called Finney stood there with his hands on his hips shaking his head. "Something'll happen to you if you don't leave him be. The boss gives orders."

She tightened up all over, her fingers biting into my shoulder. It hurt but I didn't care a bit. "Renzo? The pig!" She spat it out with a hiss. She turned her head slowly and looked at me. "Did he do this, kid?"

I nodded. It was all I could do.

"Finney," she said, "go get my car. I'm taking the kid to a doctor."

"Helen, I'm telling you . . ."

"Suppose I told the cops . . . no, not the cops, the feds in this town that you have holes in your arms?"

I thought Finney was going to smack her. He reached down with his hand back but he stopped. When a dame looks at you that way you don't do anything except what she tells you to.

"I'll get the car," he said.

She got me on my feet and I had to lean on her to stay there. She was just as big as I was. Stronger at the moment. Faces as bad off as mine weren't new to her, so she smiled and I tried to smile back and we started off down the path.

We said it was a fight and the doctor did what he had to do. He laid on the tape and told me to rest a week then come back. I saw my face in his mirror, shuddered and turned away. No matter what I did I hurt all over and when I thought of Renzo all I could think of was that I hoped somebody would kill him. I hoped they'd kill him while I watched and I hoped it would take a long, long time for him to die.

Helen got me out to the car, closed the door after me and slid in behind the wheel. I told her where I lived and she drove up to the house. The garbage cans had been spilled all over the sidewalk and it stank.

She looked at me curiously. "Here?"

"That's right," I told her. "Thanks for everything."

Then she saw the sign on the door. It read, "rooms." "Your family live here too?"

"I don't have a family. It's a rooming house."

For a second I saw her teeth, white and even, as she pulled her mouth tight. "I can't leave you here. Somebody has to look after you."

"Lady, if . . ."

"Ease off, kid. What did you say your name was?"

"Joe."

"Okay, Joe. Let me do things my way. I'm not much good for anything but every once in awhile I come in handy for something decent."

"Gee, lady . . ."

"Helen."

"Well, you're the nicest person I've ever known."

I said she was beautiful. She had the beauty of the flashiest tramp you could find. That kind of beauty. She was like the dames in the big shows who are always tall and sleepy looking and who you'd always look at but wouldn't marry or take home to your folks. That's the kind of beauty she had. But for a long couple of seconds she seemed to grow a new kind of beauty that was entirely different and she smiled at me.

"Joe . . ." and her voice was warm and husky, "that's the nicest thing said in the nicest way I've heard in a very long time."

My mouth still hurt too much to smile back so I did it with my eyes. Then something happened to her face. It got all strange and curious, a little bit puzzled and she leaned forward and I could smell the flowers again as that impossible something happened when she barely touched her mouth to mine before drawing back with that searching movement of her eyes.

"You're a funny kid, Joe."

She shoved the car into gear and let it roll away from the curb. I tried to sit upright, my hand on the door latch. "Look, I got to get out."

"I can't leave you here."

"Then where . . ."

"You're going back to my place. Damn it, Renzo did this to you and I feel partly responsible."

"That's all right. You only work for him."

"It doesn't matter. You can't stay there."

"You're going to get in trouble, Helen."

She turned and flashed me a smile. "I'm always in trouble."

"Not with him."

"I can handle that guy."

She must have felt the shudder that went through me.

"You'd be surprised how I can handle that fat slob," she said. Then added in an undertone I wasn't supposed to hear, "Sometimes."

It was a place that belonged to her like flowers belong in a rock garden. It was the top floor of an apartment hotel where the wheels all stayed in the best part of town with a private lawn twelve stories up where you could look out over the city and watch the lights wink back at you.

She made me take all my clothes off and while I soaked in a warm bath full of suds she scrounged up a decent suit that was a size too big, but still the cleanest thing I had worn in a long while. I put it on and came out in the living room feeling good and sat down in the big chair while she brought in tea.

Helen of Troy, I thought. So this is what she looked like. Somebody it would take a million bucks and a million years to get close to . . . and here I was with nothing in no time at all.

"Feel better, Joe?"

"A little."

"Want to talk? You don't have to if you don't want to."

"There's not much to say. He worked me over."

"How old are you, Joe?"

I didn't want to go too high. "Twenty-one," I said.

There it was again, that same curious expression. I was glad of the bandages across my face so she couldn't be sure if I was lying or not.

I said, "How old are you?" and grinned at her.

"Almost thirty, Joe. That's pretty old, isn't it?"

"Not so old."

She sipped at the tea in her hand. "How did you happen to cross Renzo?"

It hurt to think about it. "Tonight," I said, "it had just gotten dark. A guy asked me if I'd run a message to somebody for five bucks and I said I would. It was for Mr. Renzo and he told me to take it to the Hideaway Club. At first the guy at the gate wouldn't let me in, then he called down that other one, Johnny. He took me in, all right."

"Yes?"

"Renzo started giving it to me."

"Remember what the message said?"

Remember? I'd never forget it. I'd hope from now until I died that the guy who wrote it did everything he said he'd do.

"Somebody called Vetter said he'd kill Renzo," I told her.

Her smile was distant, hard. "He'll have to be a pretty tough guy," she said. What she said next was almost under her breath and she was staring into the night when she said it. "A guy like that I could go for."

"What?"

"Nothing, Joe." The hardness left her smile until she was a soft thing. "What else happened?"

Inside my chest my heart beat so fast it felt like it was going to smash my ribs loose. "I . . . heard them say . . . I would have to finger the man for them."

"You?"

I nodded, my hand feeling the soreness across my jaw.

She stood up slowly, the way a cat would. She was all mad and tense but you couldn't tell unless you saw her eyes. They were the same eyes that made the Finney guy jump. "Vetter," she said. "I've heard the name before."

"The note said something about a guy named Cooley who's dead."

I was watching her back and I saw the shock of the name make the muscles across her shoulders dance in the light. The tightness went down her body until she stood there stiff-legged, the flowing curves of her chest the only things that moved at all.

"Vetter," she said. "He was Cooley's friend."

"You knew Cooley?"

Her shoulders relaxed and she picked a cigarette out of a box and lit it. She turned around, smiling, the beauty I had seen in the car there again.

"Yes," Helen said softly, "I knew Cooley."

"Gee."

She wasn't talking to me anymore. She was speaking to somebody who wasn't there and each word stabbed her deeper until her eyes were wet. "I knew Cooley very well. He was . . . nice. He was a big man, broad in the shoulders with hands that could squeeze a woman . . ." She paused and took a slow pull on the cigarette. "His voice could make you laugh or cry. Sometimes both. He was an engineer with a quick mind. He figured how he could make money from Renzo's tables and did it. He even laughed at Renzo and told him crooked wheels could be taken by anybody who knew how."

The tears started in the corners of her eyes but didn't fall. They stayed there, held back by pride maybe.

"We met one night. I had never met anyone like him before. It was wonderful, but we were never meant for each other. It was one of those things. Cooley was engaged to a girl in town, a very prominent girl."

The smoke of the cigarette in her hand swirled up and blurred her face.

"But I loved him," she said. With a sudden flick of her fingers she snapped the butt on the rug and ground it out with her shoe. "I hope he kills him! I hope he kills him!"

Her eyes drew a line up the floor until they were on mine. They were clear again, steady, curious for another moment, then steady again. I said, "You don't . . . like Renzo very much?"

"How well do you know people, Joe?"

I didn't say anything.

"You know them too, don't you? You don't live in the nice section of town. You know the dirt and how people are underneath. In a way you're lucky. You know it now, not when you're too old. Look at me, Joe. You've seen women like me before? I'm not much good. I look like a million but I'm not worth a cent. A lot of names fit me and they belong. I didn't get that way because I wanted to. He did it, Renzo. I was doing fine until I met him.

"Sure, some young kids might think I'm on top, but they never get to peek behind the curtain. They never see what I'm forced into and the kind of people I have to know because others don't want to know me. If they do they don't want anybody to know about it."

"Don't say those things, Helen."

"Kid, in ten years I've met two decent people. Cooley was the first." She grinned and the hate left her face. "You're the other one. You don't give a hang what I'm like, do you?"

"I never met anybody like you before."

"Tell me more." Her grin got bigger.

"Well, you're beautiful. I mean real beautiful. And nice. You sure are built . . ."

"Good enough," she said and let the laugh come out. It was a deep, happy laugh and sounded just right for her. "Finish your tea."

I had almost forgotten about it. I drained it down, the heat of it biting into the cuts along my cheek. "Helen . . . I ought to go home. If Mr. Renzo finds out about this, he's going to burn up."

"He won't touch me, Joe."

I let out a grunt.

"You either. There's a bed in there. Crawl into it. You've had enough talk for the night."

I woke up before she did. My back hurt too much to sleep and the blood pounded in my head too hard to keep it on the pillow. The clock beside the bed said it was seven-twenty and I kicked off the covers and dragged my clothes on.

The telephone was in the living room and I took it off the cradle quietly. When I dialed the number I waited, said hello as softly as I could and asked for Nick.

He came on in a minute with a coarse, "Yeah?"

"This is Joe, Nick."

"Hey, where are you, boy? I been scrounging all over the dump for you. Gordon'll kick your tail if you don't get down here. Two other guys didn't show . . ."

"Shut up and listen. I'm in a spot."

"You ain't kidding. Gordon said . . ."

"Not that, jerk. You see anybody around the house this morning?"

I could almost hear him think. Finally he said, "Car parked across the street. Think there was a guy in it." Then, "Yeah, yeah, wait up. Somebody was giving the old lady some lip this morning. Guess I was still half asleep. Heard your name mentioned."

"Brother!"

"What's up, pal?"

"I can't tell you now. You tell Gordon I'm sick or something, okay?"

"Nuts. I'll tell him you're in the clink. He's tired of that sick business. You ain't been there long enough to get sick yet."

"Tell him what you please. Just tell him. I'll call you tonight." I slipped the phone back and turned around. I hadn't been as quiet as I thought I'd been. Helen was standing there in the doorway of her bedroom, a lovely golden girl, a bright morning flower wrapped in a black stem like a bud ready to pop.

"What is it, Joe?"

There wasn't any use hiding things from her. "Somebody's watching the house. They were looking for me this morning."

"Scared, Joe?"

"Darn right I'm scared! I don't want to get laid out in some swamp with my neck broken. That guy Renzo is nuts. He'll do anything when he gets mad."

"I know," Helen said quietly. Her hand made an unconscious movement across her mouth. "Come on, let's get some breakfast."

We found out who Vetter was that morning. At least Helen found out. She didn't cut corners or make sly inquiries. She did an impossible thing and drove me into town, parked the car and took a cab to a big brownstone building that didn't look a bit different from any other building like it in the country. Across the door it said "PRECINCT NO. 4" and the cop at the desk said the captain would be more than pleased to see us.

The captain was more than pleased, all right. It started his day off right when she came in and he almost offered me a cigar. The nameplate said his name was Gerot and if I had to pick a cop out to talk to, I'd pick him. He was in his late thirties with a build like a wrestler and I'd hate to be in the guy's shoes who tried to bribe him.

It took him a minute to settle down. A gorgeous blonde in a dark green gabardine suit blossoming with curves didn't walk in every day. And when he did settle down, it was to look at me and say, "What can I do for you?" but looking like he already knew what happened.

Helen surprised him. "I'd like to know something about a man," she said. "His name is Vetter."

The scowl started in the middle of his forehead and spread to his hairline.

"Why?"

She surprised him again. "Because he promised to kill Mark Renzo."

You could watch his face change, see it grow intense, sharpen, notice the beginning of a caustic smile twitch at his lips. "Lady, do you know what you're talking about?"

"I think so."

"You think?"

"Look at me," she said. Captain Gerot's eyes met hers, narrowed and stayed that way. "What do you see, Captain?"

"Somebody who's been around. You know all the answers, don't you?"

"All of them, Captain. The questions, too."

I was forgotten. I was something that didn't matter and I was happy about it.

Helen said, "What do you think about Renzo, Captain?"

"He stinks. He operates outside city limits where the police have no jurisdiction and he has the county police sewed up. I think he has some of my men sewed up too. I can't be sure but I wish I were. He's got a record in two states, he's clean here. I'd like to pin a few jobs on that guy. There's no evidence, yet he pulled them. I know this . . . if I start investigating I'm going to have some wheels on my neck."

Helen nodded. "I could add more. It really doesn't matter. You know what happened to Jack Cooley?"

Gerot's face looked mean. "I know I've had the papers and the state attorney climb me for it."

"I don't mean that."

The captain dropped his face in his hands resignedly, wiped his eyes and looked up again. "His car was found with bullet holes in it. The quantity of blood in the car indicated that nobody could have spilled that much and kept on living. We never found the body."

"You know why he died?"

"Who knows? I can guess from what I heard. He crossed Renzo, some said. I even picked up some info that said he was in the narcotics racket. He had plenty of cash and no place to show where it came from."

"Even so, Captain, if it was murder, and Renzo's behind it, you'd like it to be paid for."

The light blue of Gerot's eyes softened dangerously. "One way or another . . . if you must know."

"It could happen. Who is Vetter?"

He leaned back in his chair and folded his hands behind his neck. "I could show you reams of copy written about this guy. I could show you transcripts of statements we've taken down and copies that the police in other cities have sent out. I could show you all that but I can't pull out a picture and I can't drop in a print number on the guy. The people who got to know him and who finally saw him, all seem to be dead."

My voice didn't sound right. "Dead?"

Gerot's hands came down and flattened on the desk. "The guy's a killer. He's wanted every place I could think of. Word has it that he's the one who bumped Tony Briggs in Chicago. When Birdie Cullen was going to sing to the grand jury, somebody was paid fifty thousand to cool him off and Vetter collected from the syndicate. Vetter was paid another ten to knock off the guy who paid him the first time so somebody could move into his spot."

"So far he's only a name, Captain?"

"Not quite. We have a few details on him but we can't give them out. That much you understand, of course."

"Of course. But I'm still interested."

"He's tough. He seems to know things and do things nobody else would touch. He's a professional gunman in the worst sense of the word and he'll sell that gun as long as the price is right."

Helen crossed her legs with a motion that brought her whole

body into play. "Supposing, Captain, that this Vetter was a friend of Jack Cooley? Supposing he got mad at the thought of his friend being killed and wanted to do something about it?"

Gerot said, "Go on."

"What would you do, Captain?"

The smile went up one side of his face. "Most likely nothing." He sat back again. "Nothing at all . . . until it happened."

"Two birds with one stone, Captain? Let Vetter get Renzo . . . and you get Vetter?"

"The papers would like that," he mused.

"No doubt." Helen seemed to uncoil from the chair. I stood up too and that's when I found out just how shrewd the captain was. He didn't bother to look at Helen at all. His blue eyes were all on me and being very, very sleepy.

"Where do you come in, kid?" he asked me.

Helen said it for me. "Vetter gave him a warning note to hand to Renzo."

Gerot smiled silently and you could see that he had the whole picture in his mind. He had our faces, he knew who she was and all about her, he was thinking of me and wanted to know all about me. He would. He was that kind of cop. You could tell.

We stood on the steps of the building and the cops coming in gave her the kind of look every man on the street gave her. Appreciative. It made me feel good just to be with her. I said, "He's a smart cop."

"They're all smart. Some are just smarter than others." A look of impatience crossed her face. "He said something . . ."

"Reams of copy?" I suggested.

I was easy for her to smile at. She didn't have to look up or down. Just a turn of her head. "Bright boy."

She took my hand and this time I led the way. I took her to the street I knew. It was off the main drag and the people on it had a look in their eyes you don't see uptown. It was a place where the dames walked at night and followed you into bars if they thought you had an extra buck to pass out.

They're little joints, most of them. They don't have neon lights and padded stools, but when a guy talks he says something and doesn't play games. There's excitement there and always that feeling that something is going to happen.

One of those places was called The Clipper and the boys from the *News* made it their hangout. Cagey boys with the big think under their hats. Fast boys with a buck and always ready to pay off on something hot. Guys who took you like you were and didn't ask too many questions.

My kind of people.

Bucky Edwards was at his usual stool getting a little bit potted because it was his day off. I got the big stare and the exaggerated wink when he saw the blonde which meant I'd finally made good about dragging one in with me. I didn't feel like bragging, though. I brought Helen over, went to introduce her, but Bucky said, "Hi, Helen. Never thought I'd see you out in the daylight," before I could pass on her name.

"Okay, so you caught a show at the Hideaway," I said. "We have something to ask you."

"Come on, Joe. Let the lady ask me alone."

"Lay off. We want to know about Vetter."

The long eyebrows settled down low. He looked at me, then Helen, then back at me again. "You're making big sounds, boy."

I didn't want anyone else in on it. I leaned forward and said, "He's in town, Bucky. He's after Renzo."

He let out a long whistle. "Who else knows about it?"

"Gerot. Renzo. Us."

"There's going to be trouble, sure."

Helen said, "Only for Renzo."

Bucky's head made a slow negative. "You don't know. The rackets boys'll flip their lids at this. If Vetter moves in here there's going to be some mighty big trouble."

My face started working under the bandages. "Renzo's top dog, isn't he?"

Bucky's tongue made a swipe at his lips. "One of 'em. There's a few more. They're not going to like Renzo pulling in trouble like Vetter." For the first time Bucky seemed to really look at us hard.

"Vetter is poison. He'll cut into everything and they'll pay off. Sure as shooting, if he sticks around they'll be piling the cabbage in his lap."

"Then everybody'll be after Vetter," I said.

Bucky's face furrowed in a frown. "Uh-uh. I wasn't thinking that." He polished off his drink and set the empty on the bar. "If Vetter's here after Renzo they'll do better nailing Renzo's hide to the wall. Maybe they can stop it before it starts."

It was trouble, all right. The kind I wasn't feeling too bad about.

Bucky stared into his empty glass and said, "They'll bury Renzo or he'll come out of it bigger than ever."

The bartender came down and filled his glass again. I shook my head when he wanted to know what we'd have. "Good story," Bucky said, "if it happens." Then he threw the drink down and Bucky was all finished. His eyes got frosty and he sat there grinning at himself in the mirror with his mind saying things to itself. I knew him too well to say anything else so I nudged Helen and we walked out.

Some days go fast and this was one of them. She was nice to be with and nice to talk to. I wasn't important enough to hide anything from so for one day she opened her life up and fed me pieces of it. She seemed to grow younger as the day wore on and when we reached her apartment the sun was gilding her hair with golden reddish streaks and I was gone, all gone. For one day I was king and there wasn't any trouble. The laughter poured out of us and people stopped to look and laugh back. It was a day to remember when all the days are done with and you're on your last.

I was tired, dead tired. I didn't try to refuse when she told me to come up and I didn't want to. She let me open the door for her and I followed her inside. She had almost started for the kitchen to cook up the bacon and eggs we had talked about when she stopped by the arch leading to the living room.

The voice from the chair said, "Come on in, sugar pie. You too, kid."

And there was Johnny, a nasty smile on his mouth, leering at us.

"How did you get in here?"

He laughed at her. "I do tricks with locks, remember?" His head moved with a short jerk. "Get in here!" There was a flat, nasal tone in his voice.

I moved in beside Helen. My hands kept opening and closing at my side and my breath was coming a little fast in my throat.

"You like kids now, Helen?"

"Shut up, you louse," she said.

His lips peeled back showing his teeth. "The mother type. Old fashioned type, you know." He leered again like it was funny. My chest started to hurt from the breathing. "Too big for a bottle, so . . ."

I grabbed the lamp and let it fly and if the cord hadn't caught in the wall it would have taken his head off. I was all set to go into him but all he had to do to stop me was bring his hand up. The rod was one of those Banker's Specials that were deadly as hell at close range and Johnny looked too much like he wanted to use it for me to move.

He said, "The boss don't like your little arrangement, Helen. It didn't take him long to catch on. Come over here, kid."

I took a half step.

"Closer.

"Now listen carefully, kid. You go home, see. Go home and do what you feel like doing, but stay home and away from this place. You do that and you'll pick up a few bucks from Mr. Renzo. Now after you had it so nice here, you might not want to go home, so just in case you don't, I'm going to show you what's going to happen to you."

I heard Helen's breath suck in with a harsh gasp and my own sounded the same way. You could see what Johnny was setting himself to do and he was letting me know all about it and there wasn't a thing I could do. The gun was pointing right at my belly even while he jammed his elbows into the arms of the chair to get the leverage for the kick that was going to maim me for the rest of my life. His shoe was hard and pointed, a deadly weight that swung like a gentle pendulum.

I saw it coming and thought there might be a chance even yet but I didn't have to take it. From the side of the room Helen said, "Don't move, Johnny. I've got a gun in my hand."

And she had.

The ugly grimace on Johnny's face turned into a snarl when he knew how stupid he'd been in taking his eyes off her to enjoy what he was doing to me.

"Make him drop it, Helen."

"You heard the kid, Johnny."

Johnny dropped the gun. It lay there on the floor and I hooked it with my toe. I picked it up, punched the shells out of the chambers and tossed them under the sofa. The gun followed them.

"Come here, Helen," I said.

I felt her come up behind me and reached around for the .25 automatic in her hand. For a second Johnny's face turned pale and when it did I grinned at him.

Then I threw the .25 under the sofa too.

They look funny when you do things like that. Their little brains don't get it right away and it stuns them or something. I let him get right in the middle of that surprised look before I slammed my fist into his face and felt his teeth rip loose under my knuckles.

Helen went down on her knees for the gun and I yelled for her to let it alone, then Johnny was on me. He thought he was on me. I had his arm over my shoulder, laid him into a hip roll and tumbled him easy.

I walked up. I took my time. He started to get up and I chopped down on his neck and watched his head bob. I got him twice more in the same place and Johnny simply fell back. His eyes were seeing, his brain thinking and feeling but he couldn't move. While he lay there, I chopped twice again and Johnny's face became blotched and swollen while his eyes screamed in agony.

I put him in a cab downstairs. I told the driver he was drunk and fell and gave him a ten spot from Johnny's own wallet with instructions to take him out to the Hideaway and deliver same to Mr. Renzo. The driver was very sympathetic and took him away.

Then I went back for Helen. She was sitting on the couch wait-

ing for me, the strangeness back in her eyes. She said, "When he
finished with you, he would have started on me."

"I know."

"Joe, you did pretty good for a kid."

"I was brought up tough."

"I've seen Johnny take some pretty big guys. He's awfully
strong."

"You know what I do for a living, Helen? I push a junk cart,
loaded with iron. There's competition and pretty soon you learn
things. Those iron loaders are strong guys too. If they can tumble
you, they lift your pay."

"You had a gun, Joe," she reminded me.

And her eyes mellowed into a strange softness that sent chills
right through me. They were eyes that called me closer and I
couldn't say no to them. I stood there looking at her, wondering
what she saw under the bandages.

"Renzo's going after us for that," I said.

"That's right, Joe."

"We'll have to get out of here. You, anyway."

"Later we'll think about it."

"Now, damn it."

Her face seemed to laugh at me. A curious laugh. A strange
laugh. A bewildered laugh. There was a sparkling dance to her eyes
she kept half veiled and her mouth parted just a little bit. Her
tongue touched the tip of her teeth, withdrew and she said, "Now
is for something else, Joe. Now is for a woman going back a long
time who sees somebody she could have loved then."

I looked at her and held my breath. She was so completely beautiful I ached and I didn't want to make a fool of myself. Not yet.

"Now is for you to kiss me, Joe," she said.

I tasted her.

I waited until midnight before I left. I looked in her room and
saw her bathed in moonlight, her features softly relaxed into the
faintest trace of a smile, a soft, golden halo around her head.

*They should take your picture like you are now, Helen. It wouldn't
need a retoucher and there would never be a man who saw it who would*

forget it. You're beautiful, baby. You're lovely as a woman could ever be and you don't know it. You've had it so rough you can't think of anything else and thinking of it puts the lines in your face and that chiseled granite in your eyes. But you've been around and so have I. There have been dozens of dames I've thought things about but not things like I'm thinking now. You don't care what or who a guy is; you just give him part of yourself as a favor and ask for nothing back.

Sorry, Helen, you have to take something back. Or at least keep what you have. For you I'll let Renzo push me around. For you I'll let him make me finger a guy. Maybe at the end I'll have a chance to make a break. Maybe not. At least it's for you and you'll know that much. If I stay around, Renzo'll squeeze you and do it so hard you'll never be the same. I'll leave, beautiful. I'm not much. You're not much either. It was a wonderful day.

I lay the note by the lamp on the night table where she couldn't miss it. I leaned over and blew a kiss into her hair, then turned and got out of there.

Nobody had to tell me to be careful. I made sure nobody saw me leave the building and double-checked on it when I got to the corner. The trip over the back fences wasn't easy, but it was quiet and dark and if anybody so much as breathed near me I would have heard it. Then when I stood in the shadows of the store at the intersection I was glad I had made the trip the hard way. Buried between the parked cars along the curb was a police cruiser. There were no markings. Just a trunk aerial and the red glow of a cigarette behind the wheel.

Captain Gerot wasn't taking any chances. It made me feel a little better. Upstairs there Helen could go on sleeping and always be sure of waking up. I waited a few minutes longer then drifted back into the shadows toward the rooming house.

That's where they were waiting for me. I knew it a long time before I got there because I had seen them wait for other guys before. Things like that you don't miss when you live around the factories and near the waterfronts. Things like that you watch and remember so that when it happens to you, it's no surprise and you figure things out beforehand.

They saw me and as long as I kept on going in the right direction they didn't say anything. I knew they were where I couldn't see them and even if I made a break for it, it wouldn't do me any good at all.

You get a funny feeling after a while. Like a rabbit walking between rows of guns wondering which one is going to go off. Hoping that if it does you don't get to see it or feel it. Your stomach seems to get all loose inside you and your heart makes too much noise against your ribs. You try not to, but you sweat and the little muscles in your hands and thighs start to jump and twitch and all the while there's no sound at all, just a deep, startling silence with a voice that's there just the same. A statue, laughing with its mouth open. No sound, but you can hear the voice. You keep walking, and the breathing keeps time with your footsteps, sometimes trying to get ahead of them. You find yourself chewing on your lips because you already know the horrible impact of a fist against your flesh and the uncontrollable spasms that come after a pointed shoe bites into the muscle and bone of your side.

So much so that when you're almost there and a hand grabs your arm you don't do anything except look at the face above it and wait until it says, "Where you been, kid?"

I felt the hand tighten with a gentle pressure, pulling me in close. "Lay off me, I'm minding my own . . ."

"I said something, sonny."

"So I was out. What's it to you?"

His expression said he didn't give a hang at all. "Somebody wants to know. Feel like taking a little ride?"

"You asking?"

"I'm telling." The hand tightened again. "The car's over there, bud. Let's go get in it, huh?"

For a second I wondered if I could take him or not and I knew I couldn't. He was too big and too relaxed. He'd known trouble all his life, from little guys to big guys and he didn't fool easily. You can tell after you've seen a lot of them. They knew that some day they'd wind up holding their hands over a bullet hole or screaming through the bars of a cell, but until then they were trouble and too big to buck.

I got in the car and sat next to the guy in the back seat. I kept my mouth shut and my eyes open and when we started to head the wrong way, I looked at the guy next to me. "Where we going?"

He grinned on one side of his face and looked out the window again.

"Come on, come on, quit messing around! Where we going?"

"Shut up."

"Nuts, brother. If I'm getting knocked off I'm doing a lot of yelling first, starting right now. Where . . ."

"Shut up. You ain't getting knocked off." He rolled the window down, flipped the dead cigar butt out and cranked it back up again. He said it too easily not to mean it and the jumps in my hands quieted down a little.

No, they weren't going to bump me. Not with all the trouble they went to in finding me. You don't put a couple dozen men on a mug like me if all you wanted was a simple kill. One hopped up punk would do that for a week's supply of snow . . .

We went back through town, turned west into the suburbs and kept right on going to where the suburbs turned into estates and when we came to the right one the car turned into a surfaced driveway that wound past a dozen flashy heaps parked bumper to bumper and stopped in front of the fieldstone mansion.

The guy beside me got out first. He jerked his head at me and stayed at my back when I got out too. The driver grinned, but it was the kind of face a dog makes when he sees you with a chunk of meat in your fist.

A flunky met us at the door. He didn't look comfortable in his monkey suit and his face had scar tissue it took a lot of leather-covered punches to produce. He waved us in, shut the door and led the way down the hall to a room cloudy with smoke, rumbling with the voices of a dozen men.

When we came in the rumble stopped and I could feel the eyes crawl over me. The guy who drove the car looked across the room at the one in the tux, said, "Here he is, boss," and gave me a gentle push into the middle of the room.

"Hi, kid." He finished pouring out of the decanter, stopped it and picked up his glass. He wasn't an inch bigger than me, but he had the walk of a cat and the eyes of something dead. He got up close to me, faked a smile and held out the glass. "In case the boys had you worried."

"I'm not worried."

He shrugged and sipped the top off the drink himself. "Sit down, kid. You're among friends here." He looked over my shoulder. "Haul a chair up, Rocco."

All over the room the others settled down and shifted into position. A chair seat hit the back of my legs and I sat. When I looked around everybody was sitting, which was the way the little guy wanted it. He didn't like to have to look up to anybody.

He made it real casual. He introduced the boys when they didn't have to be introduced because they were always in the papers and the kind of guys people point out when they go by in their cars. You heard their names mentioned even in the junk business and among the punks in the streets. These were the big boys. Top dogs. Fat fingers. Big rings. The little guy was biggest of all. He was Phil Carboy and he ran the West Side the way he wanted it run.

When everything quieted down just right, Carboy leaned on the back of a chair and said, "In case you're wondering why you're here, kid, I'm going to tell you."

"I got my own ideas," I said.

"Fine. That's just fine. Let's check your ideas with mine, okay? Now we hear a lot of things around here. Things like that note you delivered to Renzo and who gave it to you and what Renzo did to you." He finished his drink and smiled. "Like what you did to Johnny, too. That's all straight now, isn't it?"

"So far."

"Swell. Tell you what I want now. I want to give you a job. How'd you like to make a cool hundred a week, kid?"

"Peanuts."

Somebody grunted. Carboy smiled again, a little thinner. "The kid's in the know," he said. "That's what I like. Okay, kid. We'll make it five hundred per for a month. If it don't run a month you get it anyway. That's better than having Renzo slap you around, right?"

"Anything's better than that." My voice started getting chalky.

Carboy held out his hand and said, "Rocco . . ." Another hand slid a sheaf of bills into his. He counted it out, reached two thousand and tossed it into my lap. "Yours, kid."

"For what?"

His lips were a narrow gash between his cheekbones. "For a guy named Vetter. The guy who gave you a note. Describe him."

"Tall," I said. "Big shoulders. I didn't see his face. Deep voice that sounded tough. He had on a trench coat and a hat."

"That's not enough."

"A funny way of standing," I told him. "I saw Sling Herman when I was a kid before the cops got him. He stood like that. Always ready to go for something in his pocket the cops said."

"You saw more than that, kid."

The room was too quiet now. They were all hanging on, waiting for the word. They were sitting there without smoking, beady little eyes waiting for the finger to swing until it stopped and I was the one who could stop it.

My throat squeezed out the words. I went back into the night to remember a guy and drag up the little things that would bring him into the light. I said, "I'd know him again. He was a guy to be scared of. When he talks you get a cold feeling and you know what he's like." My tongue ran over my lips and I lifted my eyes up to Carboy. "I wouldn't want to mess with a guy like that. Nobody's ever going to be tougher."

"You'll know him again. You're sure?"

"I'm sure." I looked around the room at the faces. Any one of them a guy who could say a word and have me dead the next day. "He's tougher than any of you."

Carboy grinned and let his tiny white teeth show through. "Nobody's that tough, kid."

"He'll kill me," I said. "Maybe you too. I don't like this."

"You don't have to like it. You just do it. In a way you're lucky. I'm paying you cash. If I wanted I could just tell you and you'd do it. You know that?"

I nodded.

"Tonight starts it. From now on you'll have somebody close by, see? In one pocket you'll carry a white handkerchief. If you gotta blow, use it. In the other one there'll be a red wiper. When you see him blow into that."

"That's all?"

"Just duck about then, kid," Phil Carboy said softly, "and maybe you'll get to spend that two grand. Try to use it for run-out money and you won't get past the bus station." He stared into his glass, looked up at Rocco expectantly and held it out for a refill. "Kid, let me tell you something. I'm an old hand in this racket. I can tell what a guy or a dame is like from a block away. You've been around. I can tell that. I'm giving you a break because you're the type who knows the score and will play on the right side. I don't have to warn you about anything, do I?"

"No. I got the pitch."

"Any questions?"

"Just one," I said. "Renzo wants me to finger Vetter too. He isn't putting out any two grand for it. He just wants it, see? Suppose he catches up with me? What then?"

Carboy shouldn't've hesitated. He shouldn't have let that momentary look come into his eyes because it told me everything I wanted to know. Renzo was higher than the whole pack of them and they got the jumps just thinking about it. All by himself he held a fifty-one percent interest and they were moving slowly when they bucked him. The little guy threw down the fresh drink with a quick motion of his hand and brought the smile back again. *In that second he had done a lot of thinking and spilled the answer straight out.* "We'll take care of Mark Renzo," he said. "Rocco, you and Lou take the kid home."

So I went out to the car and we drove back to the slums again. In the rear the reflections from the headlights of another car showed and the killers in it would be waiting for me to show the red handkerchief Carboy had handed me. I didn't know them and unless I was on the ball every minute I'd never get to know them. But they'd always be there, shadows that had no substance until the red showed, then the ground would get sticky with an even brighter red and maybe some of it would be mine.

They let me out two blocks away. The other car didn't show at all and I didn't look for it. My feet made hollow sounds on the sidewalk, going faster and faster until I was running up the steps of the house and when I was inside I slammed the door and leaned against it, trying hard to stop the pain in my chest.

Three-fifteen, the clock said. It ticked monotonously in the stillness, trailing me upstairs to my room. I eased inside, shut the door and locked it, standing there in the darkness until my eyes could see things. Outside a truck clashed its gears as it pulled up the hill and off in the distance a horn sounded.

I listened to them; familiar sounds, my face tightening as a not-so-familiar sound echoed behind them. It was a soft thing, a whisper that came at regular intervals in a choked-up way. Then I knew it was a sob coming from the other room and I went back to the hall and knocked on Nick's door.

His feet hit the floor, stayed there and I could hear his breathing coming hard. "It's Joe—open up."

I heard the wheeze his breath made as he let it out. The bedsprings creaked, he fell once getting to the door and the bolt snapped back. I looked at the purple blotches on his face and the open cuts over his eyes and grabbed him before he fell again. "Nick! What happened to you?"

"I'm . . . okay." He steadied himself on me and I led him back to the bed. "You got . . . some friends, pal."

"Cut it out. What happened? Who ran you through? Damn it, who did it?"

Nick managed to show a smile. It wasn't much and it hurt, but he made it. "You . . . in pretty big trouble, Joe."

"Pretty big."

"I didn't say nothing. They were here . . . asking questions. They didn't . . . believe what I told them, I guess. They sure laced me."

"The miserable slobs! You recognized them?"

His smile got sort of twisted and he nodded his head. "Sure, Joe . . . I know 'em. The fat one sat in . . . the car while they did it." His mouth clamped together hard. "It hurt . . . brother, it hurt!"

"Look," I said. "We're . . ."

"Nothing doing. I got enough. I don't want no more. Maybe they figured it's enough. That Renzo feller . . . he got hard boys around. See what they did, Joe? One . . . used a gun on me. You shoulda stood with Gordon, Joe. What the hell got into you to mess with them guys?"

"It wasn't me, Nick. Something came up. We can square it. I'll nail that fat slob if it's the last thing I do."

"It'll be the last thing. They gimme a message for you, pal. You're to stick around, see? You get seen with any other big boys in this town . . . and that's all. You know?"

"I know. Renzo told me that himself. He didn't have to go through you."

"Joe . . ."

"Yeah?"

"He said for you to take a good look . . . at me. I'm an example. A little one. He says to do what he told you."

"He knows what he can do."

"Joe . . . for me. Lay off, huh? I don't feel so good. Now I can't work for awhile."

I patted his arm, fished a hundred-buck bill out of my pocket and squeezed it into his hand. "Don't worry about it," I told him.

He looked at the bill unbelievingly, then at me.

"Dough can't pay for . . . this, Joe. Kind of . . . stay away from me . . . for awhile anyway, okay?" He smiled again, lamely this time. "Thanks for the C anyway. We been pretty good buddies, huh?"

"Sure, Nick."

"Later we'll be again. Lemme knock off now. You take it easy." His hands came up to his face and covered it. I could hear the sobs starting again and cursed the whole damn system up and down and Renzo in particular. I swore at the filth men like to wade in and the things they do to other men. When I was done I got up off the bed and walked to the door.

Behind me Nick said, "Joey . . ."

"Right here."

"Something's crazy in this town. Stories are going around . . .

there's gonna be a lot of trouble. Everybody is after . . . you. You'll . . . be careful?"

"Sure." I opened the door, shut it softly and went back to my room. I stripped off my clothes and lay down in the bed, my mind turning over fast until I had it straightened out, then I closed my eyes and fell asleep.

My landlady waited until a quarter to twelve before she gave it the business on my door. She didn't do it like she usually did it. No jarring smashes against the panels, just a light tapping that grew louder until I said, "Yeah?"

"Mrs. Stacey, Joe. You think you should get up? A man is downstairs to see you."

"What kind of a man?"

This time the knob twisted slowly and the door opened a crack. Her voice was a harsh whisper that sounded nervous. "He's got on old clothes and a city water truck is parked outside. He didn't come to look at my water."

I grinned at that one. "I'll be right down," I said. I splashed water over my face, shaved it close and worked the adhesive off the bridge of my nose. It was swollen on one side, the blue running down to my mouth. One eye was smudged with purple.

Before I pulled on my jacket I stuffed the wad of dough into the lining through the tear in the sleeve, then I took a look in Nick's room. There were traces of blood on his pillow and the place was pretty upset, but Nick had managed to get out somehow for a day's work.

The guy in the chair sitting by the window was short and wiry looking. There was dirt under his fingernails and a stubble on his chin. He had a couple of small wrenches in a leather holster on his belt that bulged his coat out but the stuff was pure camouflage. There was a gun further back and I saw the same thing Mrs. Stacey saw. The guy was pure copper with badges for eyes.

He looked at me, nodded and said, "Joe Boyle?"

"Suppose I said no?" I sat down opposite him with a grin that said I knew all about it and though I knew he got it nothing registered at all.

"Captain Gerot tells me you'll cooperate. That true?"

There was a laugh in his eyes, an attitude of being deliberately polite when he didn't have to be. "Why?" I asked him. "Everybody seems to think I'm pretty hot stuff all of a sudden."

"You are, junior, you are. You're the only guy who can put his finger on a million dollar baby that we want bad. So you'll cooperate."

"Like a good citizen?" I made it sound the same as he did. "How much rides on Vetter and how much do I get?"

The sarcasm in his eyes turned to a nasty sneer. "Thousands ride, junior . . . and you don't get any. You just cooperate. Too many cops have worked too damn long on Vetter to let a crummy kid cut into the cake. *Now I'll tell you why you'll cooperate. There's a dame, see? Helen Troy. There's ways of slapping that tomato with a fat conviction for various reasons and unless you want to see her slapped, you'll cooperate. Catch now?*"

I called him something that fitted him right down to his shoes. He didn't lose a bit of that grin at all. "Catch something else," he said. "Get smart and I'll make your other playmates look like school kids. I like tough guys. I have fun working 'em over because that's what they understand. What there is to know I know. Take last night for instance. The boys paid you off for a finger job. Mark Renzo pays but in his own way. Now I'm setting up a deal. Hell, you don't have to take it . . . you can do what you please. Three people are dickering for what you know. I'm the only one who can hit where it really hurts.

"Think it over, Joey boy. Think hard but do it fast. I'll be waiting for a call from you and wherever you are, I'll know about it. I get impatient sometimes, so let's hear from you soon. Maybe if you take too long I'll prod you a little bit." He got up, stretched and wiped his eyes like he was tired. "Just ask for Detective Sergeant Gonzales," he said. "That's me."

The cop patted the tools on his belt and stood by the door. I said, "It's stinking to be a little man, isn't it? You got to keep making up for it."

There was pure hate in his eyes for an answer. He gave me a

long look that a snake would give a rabbit when he isn't too hungry yet. A look that said wait a little while, feller. Wait until I'm real hungry.

I watched the truck pull away, then sat there at the window looking at the street. I had to wait almost an hour before I spotted the first, then picked up the second one ten minutes later. If there were more I didn't see them. I went back to the kitchen and took a look through the curtains at the blank behinds of the warehouses across the alley. Mrs. Stacey didn't say anything. She sat there with her coffee, making clicking noises with her false teeth.

I said, "Somebody washed the windows upstairs in the wholesale house."

"A man. Early this morning."

"They haven't been washed since I've been here."

"Not for two years."

I turned around and she was looking at me as if something had scared her to death. "*How much are they paying you?*" I said.

She couldn't keep that greedy look out of her face even with all the phony indignation she tried to put on. Her mouth opened to say something when the phone rang and gave her the chance to cover up. She came back a few seconds later and said, "It's for you. Some man."

Then she stood there by the door where she always stood whenever somebody was on the phone. I said, "Joe Boyle speaking," and that was all. I let the other one speak his few words and when he was done I hung up.

I felt it starting to burn me. A nasty feeling that makes you want to slam something. Nobody asked me . . . they just told and I was supposed to jump. I was the low man on the totem pole, a lousy kid who happened to fit into things . . . just the right size to get pushed around.

Vetter, I kept saying to myself. They were all scared to death of Vetter. The guy had something they couldn't touch. He was tough. He was smart. He was moving in for a kill and if ever one was needed it was needed now. They were all after him and no matter how many people who didn't belong there stood in the way their bullets would go right through them to reach Vetter. Yeah, they wanted him bad. So bad they'd kill each other to make sure he died too.

Well, the whole pack of 'em knew what they could do.

I pulled my jacket on and got outside. I went up the corner, grabbed a downtown bus and sat there without bothering to look around. At Third and Main I hopped off, ducked into a cafeteria and had a combination lunch. I let Mrs. Stacey get her calls in, gave them time to keep me well under cover, then flagged down a roving cab and gave the driver Helen's address. On the way over I looked out the back window for the second time and the light blue Chevy was still in place, two cars behind and trailing steadily. In a way it didn't bother me if the boys inside were smart enough to check the black Caddie that rode behind it again.

I tapped the cabbie a block away, told him to let me out on the corner and paid him off. There wasn't a parking place along the street so the laddies in the cars were either going to cruise or double park, but it would keep them moving around so I could see what they were like anyway.

When I punched the bell I had to wait a full minute before the lobby door clicked open. I went up the stairs, jolted the apartment door a few times and walked right into those beautiful eyes that were even prettier than the last time because they were worried first, then relieved when they saw me. She grabbed my arm and gave me that quick grin then pulled me inside and stood with her back to the door.

"Joe, Joe, you little jughead," she laughed. "You had me scared silly. Don't do anything like that again."

"Had to, Helen. I wasn't going to come back but I had to do that too."

Maybe it was the way I said it that made her frown. "You're a funny kid."

"Don't say that."

Something changed in her eyes. "No. Maybe I shouldn't, should I?" She looked at me hard, her eyes soft, but piercing. "I feel funny when I look at you. I don't know why. Sometimes I've thought it was because I had a brother who was always in trouble. Always getting hurt. I used to worry about him too."

"What happened to him?"

"He was killed on the Anzio beachhead."

"Sorry."

She shook her head. "He didn't join the army because he was patriotic. He and another kid held up a joint. The owner was shot. He was dead by the time they found out who did it."

"You've been running all your life too, haven't you?"

The eyes dropped a second. "You could put it that way."

"What ties you here?"

"Guess."

"If you had the dough you'd beat it? Some place where nobody knew you?"

She laughed, a short jerky laugh. It was answer enough. I reached in the jacket, got out the pack of bills and flipped off a couple for myself. I shoved the rest in her hand before she knew what it was. "Get going. Don't even bother to pack. Just move out of here and keep moving."

Her eyes were big and wide with an incredulous sort of wonder, then slightly misty when they came back to mine and she shook her head a little bit and said, "Joe . . . why? Why?"

"It would sound silly if I said it."

"Say it."

"When I'm all grown up I'll tell you maybe."

"Now."

I could feel the ache starting in me and my tongue didn't want to move, but I said, "Sometimes even a kid can feel pretty hard about a woman. Sad, isn't it?"

Helen said, "Joe," softly and had my face in her hands and her mouth was a hot torch that played against mine with a crazy kind of fierceness and it was all I could do to keep from grabbing her instead of pushing her away. My hands squeezed her hard, then I yanked the door open and got out of there. Behind me there was a sob and I heard my name said again, softly.

I ran the rest of the way down with my face all screwed up tight.

The blue Chevy was down the street on the other side. It seemed to be empty and I didn't bother to poke around it. All I wanted was for whoever followed me to follow me away from there. So I gave it the full treatment. I made it look great. To them I must have seemed pretty jumpy and on the way to see somebody important. It took a full hour to reach The Clipper that way and the only important one around was Bucky Edwards and he wasn't drunk this time.

He nodded, said, "Beer?" and when I shook my head, called down the bar for a tall orange. "Figured you'd be in sooner or later."

"Yeah?"

That wise old face wrinkled a little. "How does it feel to be live bait, kiddo?"

"You got big ears, grandma."

"I get around." He toasted his beer against my orange, put it down and said, "You're in pretty big trouble, Joe. Maybe you don't know it."

"I know it."

"You don't know how big. You haven't been here that long. Those boys put on the big squeeze."

It was my turn to squint. His face was set as if he smelled something he didn't like and there was ice in his eyes. "How much do you know, Bucky?"

His shoulders made a quick shrug. "Phil Carboy didn't post the depot and the bus station for nothing. He's got cars cruising the highways too. Making sure, isn't he?"

He looked at me and I nodded.

"Renzo is kicking loose too. He's pulling the strings tight. The guys on his payroll are getting nervous but they can't do a thing. No, sir, not a thing. Like a war. Everybody's just waiting." The set mouth flashed me a quick grin. "You're the key, boy. *If there was a way out I'd tell you to take it.*"

"Suppose I went to the cops?"

"Gerot?" Bucky shook his head. "You'd get help as long as he could keep you in a cell. People'd like to see him dead too. He's got an awfully bad habit of being honest. Ask him to show you his scars someday. It wouldn't be so bad if he was just honest, but he's smart and mean as hell too."

I drank half the orange and set it down in the wet circle on the bar. "Funny how things work out. All because of Vetter. And he's here because of Jack Cooley."

"I was wondering when you were gonna get around to it, kid," Bucky said.

"What?"

He didn't look at me. "Who *are* you working for?"

I waited a pretty long time before he turned his head around. I let him look at my face another long time before I said anything. Then: "I was pushing a junk cart, friend. I was doing okay, too. I wasn't working for trouble. Now I'm getting pretty curious. In my own way I'm not so stupid, but now I want to find out the score. One way or another I'm finding out. So they paid me off but they aren't figuring on me spending much of that cabbage. After it's over I get chopped down and it starts all over again, whatever it is. That's what I'm finding out. Why I'm bait for whatever it is. Who do I see, Bucky? You're in the know. Where do I go to find out?"

"Cooley could have told you," he said quietly.

"Nuts. He's dead."

"Maybe he can still tell you."

My fingers were tight around the glass now. "The business about Cooley getting it because of the deal on Renzo's tables is out?"

"Might be."

"Talk straight unless you're scared silly of those punks too. Don't give me any puzzles if you know something."

Bucky's eyebrows went up, then down slowly over the grin in his eyes. "Talk may be cheap, son," he said, "but life comes pretty expensively." He nodded sagely and said, "I met Cooley in lotsa places. Places he shouldn't have been. He was a man looking around. He could have found something."

"Like why we have gangs in this formerly peaceful city of ours. Why we have paid-for politicians and clambakes with some big faces showing. They're not eating clams . . . they're talking."

"These places where you kept seeing Cooley . . ."

"River joints. Maybe he liked fish."

You could tell when Bucky was done talking. I went down to Main, found a show I hadn't seen and went in. There were a lot of things I wanted to think about.

At eleven-fifteen the feature wound up and I started back outside. In the glass reflection of the lobby door I saw somebody behind me but I didn't look back. There could have been one more in the crowd that was around the entrance outside. Maybe two. Nobody seemed to pay any attention to me and I didn't care if they did or not.

I waited for a Main Street bus, took it down about a half mile, got off at the darkened supermarket and started up the road. You get the creeps in places like that. It was an area where some optimist had started a factory and ran it until the swamp crept in. When the footings gave and the walls cracked, they moved out, and now the black skeletons of the buildings were all that were left, with gaping holes for eyes and a mouth that seemed to breathe out a fetid swamp odor. But there were still people there. The dozen or so company houses that were propped against the invading swamp showed dull yellow lights, and the garbage smell of unwanted humanity fought the swamp odor. You could hear them, too, knowing that they watched you from the shadows of their porches. You could feel them stirring in their jungle shacks and catch the pungency of the alcohol they brewed out of anything they could find.

There was a low moan of a train from the south side and its single eye picked out the trestle across the bay and followed it. The freight lumbered up, slowed for the curve that ran through the swamps and I heard the bindle stiffs yelling as they hopped off, looking for the single hard topped road that took them to their quarters for the night.

The circus sign was on the board fence. In the darkness it was nothing but a bleached white square, but when I lit a cigarette I could see the faint orange impressions that used to be supposedly wild animals. The match went out and I lit another, got the smoke fired up and stood there a minute in the dark.

The voice was low. A soft, quiet voice more inaudible than a whisper.
"One is back at the corner. There's another a hundred feet down."

"I know," I said.

"You got nerve."

"Let's not kid me. I got your message. Sorry I had to cut it short, but a pair of paid-for ears were listening in."

"Sorry Renzo gave you a hard time."

"So am I. The others did better by me."

Somebody coughed down the road and I flattened against the boards away from the white sign. It came again, farther away this time and I felt better. I said, "What gives?"

"You had a cop at your place this morning."

"I spotted him."

"There's a regular parade behind you." *A pause, then,* "What did you tell them?"

I dragged in on the smoke, watched it curl. "I told them he was big. Tough. I didn't see his face too well. What did you expect me to tell them?"

I had a feeling like he smiled.

"They aren't happy," *he said.*

I grinned too. "Vetter. They hate the name. It scares them." *I pulled on the butt again.* "It scares me too when I think of it too much."

"You don't have anything to worry about."

"Thanks."

"Keep playing it smart. You know what they're after?"

I nodded, even though he couldn't see me. "Cooley comes into it someplace. It was something he knew."

"Smart lad. I knew you were a smart lad the first time I saw you. Yes, it was Cooley."

"Who was he?" *I asked.*

Nothing for a moment. I could hear him breathing and his feet moved but that was all. The red light on the tail of the caboose winked at me and I knew it would have to be short.

"An adventurer, son. A romantic adventurer who went where the hunting was profitable and the odds long. He liked long odds. He found how they were slipping narcotics in through a new door and tapped them *for a sweet haul. They say four million. It was a paid-for shipment and he got away with it. Now the boys have to make good."*

The caboose was almost past now. He said, "I'll call you if I want you."

I flipped the butt away, watching it bounce sparks across the dirt. I went on a little bit farther where I could watch the fires from the jungles and when I had enough of it I started back.

At the tree the guy who had been waiting there said, "You weren't thinking of hopping that freight, were you kid?"

I didn't jump like I was supposed to. I said, "When I want to leave, I'll leave."

"Be sure to tell Mr. Carboy first, huh?"

"I'll tell him," I said.

He stayed there, not following me. I passed the buildings again, then felt better when I saw the single street light on the corner of Main. There was nobody there that I could see, but that didn't count. He was around someplace.

I had to wait ten minutes for a bus. It seemed longer than it was. I stayed drenched in the yellow light and thought of the voice behind the fence and what it had to say. When the bus pulled up I got on, stayed there until I reached the lights again and got off. By that time a lot of things were making sense, falling into a recognizable pattern. I walked down the street to an all-night drug store, had a drink at the counter then went back to the phone booth.

I dialed the police number and asked for Gonzales, Sergeant Gonzales. There was a series of clicks as the call was switched and the cop said, "Gonzales speaking."

"This is Joe, copper. Remember me?"

"Don't get too fresh, sonny," he said. His voice had a knife in it.

"Phil Carboy paid me some big money to finger Vetter. He's got men tailing me."

His pencil kept up a steady tapping against the side of the phone. Finally he said, "I was wondering when you'd call in. You were real lucky, Joe. For a while I thought I was going to have to persuade you a little to cooperate. You were real lucky. Keep me posted."

I heard the click in my ear as he hung up and I spat out the things into the dead phone I felt like telling him to his face. Then I fished out another coin, dropped it in and dialed the same number. This time I asked for Captain Gerot. The guy at the switchboard said he had left about six but that he could probably be reached at his club. He gave me the number and I checked it through. The attendant who answered said he had left about an hour ago but would probably call back to see if there were any messages for him and were there? I told him to get the number so I could put the call through myself and hung up.

It took me a little longer to find Bucky Edwards. He had stewed in his own juices too long and he was almost all gone. I said, "Bucky, I need something bad. I want Jack Cooley's last address. You remember that much?"

He hummed a little bit. "Rooming house. Between Wells and Capitol. It's all white, Joe. Only white house."

"Thanks, Bucky."

"You in trouble, Joe?"

"Not yet."

"You will be. Now you will be."

That was all. He put the phone back so easily I didn't hear it go. Damn, I thought, he knows the score but he won't talk. He's got all the scoop and he clams up.

I had another drink at the counter, picked up a deck of smokes and stood outside while I lit one. The street was quieting down. Both curbs were lined with parked heaps, dead things that rested until morning when they'd be whipped alive again.

Not all of them though. I was sure of that. I thought I caught a movement across the street in a doorway. It was hard to tell. I turned north and walked fast until I reached Benson Road, then cut down it to the used car lot.

Now was when they'd have a hard time. Now was when they were playing games in my back yard and if they didn't know every inch of the way somebody was going to get hurt. They weren't kids, these guys. They had played the game themselves and they'd know all the angles. Almost all, anyway. They'd know when I tried to get out of the noose and as soon as they did, they'd quit playing and start working. They wouldn't break their necks sticking to a trail when they could bottle me up.

All I had to do was keep them from knowing for a while.

I crossed the lot, cutting through the parked cars, picked up the alley going back of the houses and stuck to the hedgerows until I was well down it. By that time I had a lead. If I looked back I'd spoil it so I didn't look back. I picked up another block at the fork in the alley, standing deliberately under the lone light at the end, not hurrying, so they could see me. I made it seem as though I were trying to pick out one of the houses in the darkness, and when I made up my mind, went through the gate in the fence.

After that I hurried. I picked up the short-cuts, made the street and crossed it between lights. I reached Main again, grabbed a cruising cab in the middle of the block, had him haul me across town to the docks and got out. It took fifteen minutes longer to reach the white house Bucky told me about. I grinned to myself and wondered if the boys were still watching the place they thought I went into. Maybe it would be a little while before they figured the thing out.

It would be time enough.

The guy who answered the door was all wrapped up in a bathrobe, his hair stringing down his face. He squinted at me, reluctant to be polite, but not naturally tough enough to be anything else but. He said, "If you're looking for a room you'll have to come around in the morning. I'm sorry."

I showed him a bill with two numbers on it.

"Well . . ."

"I don't want a room."

He looked at the bill again, then a quick flash of terror crossed his face. His eyes rounded open, looked at me hard, then dissolved into curiosity. "Come . . . in."

The door closed and he stepped around me into a small sitting room and snapped on a shaded desk lamp. His eyes went back down to the bill. I handed it over and watched it disappear into the bathrobe. "Yes?"

"Jack Cooley."

The words did something to his face. It showed terror again, but not as much as before.

"I really don't . . ."

"Forget the act. I'm not working for anybody in town. I was a friend of his."

This time he scowled, not believing me.

I said, "Maybe I don't look it, but I was."

"So? What is it you want?" He licked his lips, seemed to tune his ears for some sound from upstairs. "Everybody's been here. Police, newspapers. Those . . . men from town. They all want something."

"Did Jack leave anything behind?"

"Sure. Clothes, letters, the usual junk. The police have all that."

"Did you get to see any of it?"

"Well . . . the letters were from dames. Nothing important."

I nodded, fished around for a question a second before I found one. "How about his habits?"

The guy shrugged. "He paid on time. Usually came in late and slept late. No dames in his room."

"That's all?"

He was getting edgy. "What else is there? I didn't go out with the guy. So now I know he spent plenty of nights in Renzo's joint. I hear talk. You want to know what kind of butts he smoked? Hobbies, maybe? Hell, what is there to tell? He goes out at night. Sometimes he goes fishing. Sometimes . . ."

"Where?" I interrupted.

"Where what?"

"Fishing."

"On one of his boats. He borrowed my stuff. He was fishing the day before he got bumped. Sometimes he'd slip me a ticket and I'd get away from the old lady."

"How do the boats operate?"

He shrugged again, pursing his mouth. "They go down the bay to the tip of the inlet, gas up, pick up beer at Gulley's and go about ten miles out. Coming back they stop at Gulley's for more beer and for the guys to dump the fish they don't want. Gulley sells it in town. Everybody is usually drunk and happy." He gave me another thoughtful look. "You writing a book about your friend?" he said sarcastically.

"Could be. Could be. I hate to see him dead."

"If you ask me, he never should've fooled around Renzo. You better go home and save your money from now on, sonny."

"I'll take your advice," I said, "and be handyman around a rooming house."

He gave me a dull stare as I stood up and didn't bother to go to the door with me. He still had his hand in his pocket wrapped around the bill I gave him.

The street was empty and dark enough to keep me wrapped in a blanket of shadows. I stayed close to the houses, stopping now and then to listen. When I was sure I was by myself I felt better and followed the water smell of the bay.

At River Road a single-pump gas station showed lights and the guy inside sat with his feet propped up on the desk. He opened one eye when I walked in, gave me the change I wanted for the phone, then went back to sleep again. I dialed the number of Gerot's club, got the attendant and told him what I wanted. He gave me another number and I punched it out on the dial. Two persons answered before a voice said, "Gerot speaking."

"Hello, Captain. This is Joe. I was . . ."

"I remember," he said.

"I called Sergeant Gonzales tonight. Phil Carboy paid me off to finger Vetter. Now I got two parties pushing me."

"Three. Don't forget us."

"I'm not forgetting."

"I hear those parties are excited. Where are you?"

I didn't think he'd bother to trace the call, so I said, "Some joint in town."

His voice sounded light this time. "About Vetter. Tell me."

"Nothing to tell."

"You had a call this morning." I felt the chills starting to run up my back. They had a tap on my line already. "The voice wasn't familiar and it said some peculiar things."

"I know. I didn't get it. I thought it was part of Renzo's outfit getting wise. They beat up a buddy of mine so I'd know what a real beat-up guy looks like. It was all double talk to me."

He was thinking it over. When he was ready he said, "Maybe so, kid. You hear about that dame you were with?"

I could hardly get the words out of my mouth. "Helen? No . . . What?"

"Somebody shot at her. Twice."

"Did . . ."

"Not this time. She was able to walk away from it this time."

"Who was it? Who shot at her?"

"That, little chum, is something we'd like to know too. She was waiting for a train out of town. The next time maybe we'll have better luck. There'll be a next time, in case you're interested."

"Yeah, I'm interested . . . and thanks. You know where she is now?"

"No, but we're looking around. *I hope we can find her first.*"

I put the phone back and tried to get the dry taste out of my mouth. When I thought I could talk again I dialed Helen's apartment, hung on while the phone rang endlessly, then held the receiver fork down until I got my coin back. I had to get Renzo's club number from the book and the gravelly voice that answered rasped that the feature attraction hadn't put in an appearance that night and for something's sake to cut off the chatter and wait until tomorrow because the club was closed.

So I stood there and said things to myself until I was all balled up into a knot. I could see the parade of faces I hated drifting past my mind and all I could think of was how bad I wanted to smash every one of them as they came by. Helen had tried to run for it. She didn't get far. Now where could she be? Where does a beautiful blonde go who is trying to hide? Who would take her in if they knew the score?

I could feel the sweat starting on my neck, soaking the back of my shirt. All of a sudden I felt washed out and wrung dry. Gone. All the way gone. Like there wasn't anything left of me anymore except a big hate for a whole damn city, the mugs who ran it and the people who were afraid of the mugs. And it wasn't just one city either. There would be more of them scattered all over the states. For the people, by the people, Lincoln had said. Yeah. Great.

I turned around and walked out. I didn't even bother to look back and if they were there, let them come. I walked for a half hour, found a cab parked at a corner with the driver sacking it behind the wheel and woke him up. I gave him the boarding house address and climbed in the back.

He let me off at the corner, collected his dough and turned around.

Then I heard that voice again and I froze the butt halfway to my mouth and squashed the matches in the palm of my hand.

It said, "Go ahead and light it."

I breathed that first drag out with the words, "You nuts? They're all around this place."

"I know. Now be still and listen. The dame knows the score. They tried for her . . ."

We heard the feet at the same time. They were light as a cat, fast. Then he came out of the darkness and all I could see was the glint of the knife in his hand and the yell that was in my throat choked off when his fingers bit into my flesh. I had time to see that same hardened face that had looked into mine not so long ago, catch an expressionless grin from the hard boy, then the other shadows opened and the side of a palm smashed down against his neck. He pitched forward with his head at a queer, stiff angle, his mouth wrenched open and I knew it was only a reflex that kept it that way because the hard boy was dead. You could hear the knife chatter across the sidewalk and the sound of the body hitting, a sound that really wasn't much yet was a thunderous crash that split the night wide open.

The shadows the hand had reached out from seemed to open and close again, and for a short second I was alone. Just a short second. I heard the whisper that was said too loud. The snick of a gun somewhere, then I closed in against the building and ran for it.

At the third house I faded into the alley and listened. Back there I could hear them talking, then a car started up down the street. I cut around behind the houses, found the fences and stuck with them until I was at my place, then snaked into the cellar door.

When I got upstairs I slipped into the hall and reached for the phone. I asked for the police and got them. All I said was that somebody was being killed and gave the address. Then I grinned at the darkness, hung up without giving my name and went upstairs to my room. From way across town a siren wailed a lonely note, coming closer little by little. It was a pleasant sound at that. It would give my friend from the shadows plenty of warning too. He was quite a guy. Strong. Whoever owned the dead man was going to walk easy with Vetter after this.

I walked into my room, closed the door and was reaching for the bolt when the chair moved in the corner. Then she said, "Hello, Joe," and the air in my lungs hissed out slowly between my teeth.

I said, "Helen." I don't know which of us moved. I like to think it was her. But suddenly she was there in my arms with her face buried in my shoulder, stifled sobs pouring out of her body while I tried to tell her that it was all right. Her body was pressed against me, a fire that seemed to dance as she trembled, fighting to stay close.

"Helen, Helen, take it easy. Nothing will hurt you now. You're okay." I lifted her head away and smoothed back her hair. "Listen, you're all right here."

Her mouth was too close. Her eyes too wet and my mind was thinking things that didn't belong there. My arms closed tighter and I found her mouth, warm and soft, a salty sweetness that clung desperately and talked to me soundlessly. But it stopped the trembling and when she pulled away she smiled and said my name softly.

"How'd you get here, Helen?"

Her smile tightened. "I was brought up in a place like this a long time ago. There are always ways. I found one."

"I heard what happened. Who was it?"

She tightened under my hands. "I don't know. I was waiting for a train when it happened. I just ran after that. When I got out on the street, it happened again."

"No cops?"

She shook her head. "Too fast. I kept running."

"They know it was you?"

"I was recognized in the station. Two men there had caught my

show and said hello. You know how. They could have said something."

I could feel my eyes starting to squint. "Don't be so damn calm
about it."

The tight smile twisted up at the corner. It was like she was
reading my mind. She seemed to soften a moment and I felt her
fingers brush my face. "I told you I wasn't like other girls, Joe. Not
like the kind of girl you should know. Let's say it's all something
I've seen before. After a bit you get used to it."

"Helen . . ."

"I'm sorry, Joe."

I shook my head slowly. "No . . . I'm the one who's sorry.
People like you should never get like that. Not you."

"Thanks." She looked at me, something strange in her eyes that
I could see even in the half light of the room. And this time it
happened slowly, the way it should be. The fire was close again,
and real this time, very real. Fire that could have burned deeply if
the siren hadn't closed in and stopped outside.

I pushed her away and went to the window. The beams of the
flashlights traced paths up the sidewalk. The two cops were cursing
the cranks in the neighborhood until one stopped, grunted something and picked up a sliver of steel that lay by the curb. But there
was nothing else. Then they got back in the cruiser and drove off.

Helen said, "What was it?"

"There was a dead man out there. Tomorrow there'll be some
fun."

"Joe!"

"Don't worry about it. At least we know how we stand. It was
one of their boys. He made a pass at me on the street and got
taken."

"You do it?"

I shook my head. "Not me. A guy. A real big guy with hands
that can kill."

"*Vetter.*" She said it breathlessly.

I shrugged.

Her voice was a whisper. "I hope he kills them all. Every one."

Her hand touched my arm. "Somebody tried to kill Renzo earlier. They got one of his boys." Her teeth bit into her lip. "There were two of them so it wasn't Vetter. You know what that means?"

I nodded. "War. They want Renzo dead to get Vetter out of town. They don't want him around or he'll move into their racket sure."

"He already has." I looked at her sharply and she nodded. "I saw one of the boys in the band. Renzo's special car was hijacked as it was leaving the city. Renzo claimed they got nothing but he's pretty upset. I heard other things too. The whole town's tight."

"Where do you come in, Helen?"

"What?" Her voice seemed taut.

"You. Let's say you and Cooley. What string are you pulling?" Her hand left my arm and hung down at her side. If I'd slapped her she would have had the same expression on her face. I said, "I'm sorry. I didn't mean it like that. You liked Jack Cooley, didn't you?"

"Yes." She said it quietly.

"You told me what he was like once. What was he really like?"

The hurt flashed in her face again. "Like them," she said. "Gay, charming, but like them. He wanted the same things. He just went after them differently, that's all."

"The guy I saw tonight said you know things."

Her breath caught a little bit. "I didn't know before, Joe."

"Tell me."

"When I packed to leave . . . then I found out. Jack . . . left certain things with me. One was an envelope. There were cancelled checks in it for thousands of dollars made out to Renzo. The one who wrote the checks is a racketeer in New York. There was a note pad too with dates and amounts that Renzo paid Cooley."

"Blackmail."

"I think so. What was more important was what was in the box he left with me. *Heroin.*"

I swung around slowly. "Where is it?"

"Down a sewer. I've seen what the stuff can do to a person."

"Much of it?"

"Maybe a quarter pound."

"We could have had him," I said. "We could have had him and you dumped the stuff!"

Her hand touched me again. "No . . . there wasn't that much of it. Don't you see, it's bigger than that. What Jack had was only a sample. Some place there's more of it, much more."

"Yeah," I said. I was beginning to see things now. They were starting to straighten themselves out and it made a pattern. The only trouble was that the pattern was so simple it didn't begin to look real.

"Tomorrow we start," I said. "We work by night. Roll into the sack and get some sleep. If I can keep the landlady out of here we'll be okay. You sure nobody saw you come in?"

"Nobody saw me."

"Good. Then they'll only be looking for me."

"Where will you sleep?"

I grinned at her. "In the chair."

I heard the bed creak as she eased back on it, then I slid into the chair. After a long time she said, "Who are you, Joe?"

I grunted something and closed my eyes. I wished I knew myself sometimes.

I woke up just past noon. Helen was still asleep, restlessly tossing in some dream. The sheet had slipped down to her waist, and everytime she moved, her body rippled with sinuous grace. I stood looking at her for a long time, my eyes devouring her, every muscle in my body wanting her. There were other things to do, and I cursed those other things and set out to do them.

When I knew the landlady was gone I made a trip downstairs to her ice box and lifted enough for a quick meal. I had to wake Helen up to eat, then sat back with an old magazine to let the rest of the day pass by. At seven we made the first move. It was a nice simple little thing that put the whole neighborhood in an uproar for a half hour but gave us a chance to get out without being spotted.

All I did was call the fire department and tell them there was a gas leak in one of the tenements. They did the rest. Besides holding everybody back from the area they evacuated a whole row of houses, including us and while they were trying to run down the false alarm we grabbed a cab and got out.

Helen asked, "Where to?"

"A place called Gulley's. It's a stop for the fishing boats. You know it?"

"I know it." She leaned back against the cushions. "It's a tough place to be. Jack took me out there a couple of times."

"He did? Why?"

"Oh, we ate, then he met some friends of his. We were there when the place was raided. Gulley was selling liquor after closing hours. Good thing Jack had a friend on the force."

"Who was that?"

"Some detective with a Mexican name."

"Gonzales," I said.

She looked at me. "That's right." She frowned. "I didn't like him."

That was a new angle. One that didn't fit in. Jack with a friend on the force. I handed Helen a cigarette, lit it and sat back with mine.

It took a good hour to reach the place and at first glance it didn't seem worth the ride. From the highway the road weaved out onto a sand spit and in the shadows you could see the parked cars and occasionally couples in them. Here and there along the road the lights of the car picked up the glint of beer cans and empty bottles. I gave the cabbie an extra five and told him to wait and when we went down the gravel path, he pulled it under the trees and switched off his lights. Gulley's was a huge shack built on the sand with a porch extending out over the water. There wasn't a speck of paint on the weather-racked framework and over the whole place the smell of fish hung like a blanket. It looked like a creep joint until you turned the corner and got a peek at the nice modern dock setup he had and the new addition on the side that probably made the place the yacht club's slumming section. If it didn't have anything else it had atmosphere. We were right on the tip of the peninsula that jutted out from the mainland and like the sign said, it was the last chance for the boats to fill up with the bottled stuff before heading out to deep water.

I told Helen to stick in the shadows of the hedge row that ran around the place while I took a look around, and though she didn't like it, she melted back into the brush. I could see a couple of figures on the porch, but they were talking too low for me to hear what was going on. Behind the bar that ran across the main room inside, a flat-faced guy leaned over reading the paper with his ears pinned inside a headset. Twice he reached back, frowning and fiddled with a radio under the counter. When the phone rang he scowled again, slipped off the headset and said, "Gulley speaking. Yeah. Okay. So long."

When he went back to his paper I crouched down under the rows of windows and eased around the side. The sand was a thick carpet that silenced all noise and the gentle lapping of the water against the docks covered any other racket I could make. I was glad to have it that way too. There were guys spotted around the place that you couldn't see until you looked hard and they were just lounging. Two were by the building and the other two at the foot of the docks, edgy birds who lit occasional cigarettes and shifted around as they smoked them. One of them said something and a pair of them swung around to watch the twin beams of a car coming up the highway. I looked too, saw them turn in a long arc then cut straight for the shack.

One of the boys started walking my way, his feet squeaking in the dry sand. I dropped back around the corner of the building, watched while he pulled a bottle out from under the brush, then started back the way I had come.

The car door slammed. A pair of voices mixed in an argument and another one cut them off. When I heard it I could feel my lips peel back and I knew that if I had a knife in my fist and Mark Renzo passed by me in the dark, whatever he had for supper would spill all over the ground. There was another voice swearing at something. Johnny. Nice, gentle Johnny who was going to cripple me for life.

I wasn't worrying about Helen because she wouldn't be sticking her neck out. I was hoping hard that my cabbie wasn't reading any paper by his dome light and when I heard the boys reach the porch and go in, I let my breath out hardly realizing that my chest hurt from holding it in so long.

You could hear their hellos from inside, muffled sounds that were barely audible. I had maybe a minute to do what I had to do and didn't waste any time doing it. I scuttled back under the window that was at one end of the bar, had time to see Gulley shaking hands with Renzo over by the door, watched him close and lock it and while they were still far enough away not to notice the movement, slid the window up an inch and flattened against the wall.

They did what I expected they'd do. I heard Gulley invite them to the bar for a drink and set out the glasses. Renzo said, "Good stuff."

"Only the best. You know that."

Johnny said, "Sure. You treat your best customers right."

Bottle and glasses clinked again for another round. Then the headset that was under the bar started clicking. I took a quick look, watched Gulley pick it up, slap one earpiece against his head and jot something down on a pad.

Renzo said, "She getting in without trouble?"

Gulley set the headset down and leaned across the bar. He looked soft, but he'd been around a long time and not even Renzo was playing any games with him. "Look," he said, "you got your end of the racket. Keep out of mine. You know?"

"Getting tough, Gulley?"

I could almost hear Gulley smile. "Yeah. Yeah, in case you want to know. You damn well better blow off to them city lads, not me."

"Ease off," Renzo told him. He didn't sound rough anymore. "Heard a load was due in tonight."

"You hear too damn much."

"It didn't come easy. I put out a bundle for the information. You know why?" Gulley didn't say anything. Renzo said, "I'll tell you why. I need that stuff. You know why?"

"Tough. Too bad. You know. What you want is already paid

for and is being delivered. You ought to get your head out of your whoosis."

"Gulley . . ." Johnny said really quiet. "We ain't kidding. We need that stuff. The big boys are getting jumpy. They think we pulled a fast one. They don't like it. They don't like it so bad maybe they'll send a crew down here to straighten everything out and you may get straightened too."

Inside Gulley's feet were nervous on the floorboards. He passed in front of me once, his hands busy wiping glasses. "You guys are nuts. Carboy paid for this load. So I should stand in the middle?"

"Maybe it's better than standing in front of us," Johnny said.

"You got rocks. Phil's out of the local stuff now. He's got a pretty big outfit."

"Just peanuts, Gulley, just peanuts."

"Not anymore. He's moving in since you dumped the big deal."

Gulley's feet stopped moving. His voice had a whisper in it. "So you were big once. Now I see you sliding. The big boys are going for bargains and they don't like who can't deliver, especially when it's been paid for. That was one big load. It was special. So you dumped it. Phil's smart enough to pick it up from there and now he may be top dog. I'm not in the middle. Not without an answer to Phil and he'll need a good one."

"*Vetter's in town, Gulley!*" Renzo almost spat the words out. "You know how he is? He ain't a gang you bust up. He's got a nasty habit of killing people. Like always, he's moving in. So we pay you for the stuff and deliver what we lost. We make it look good and you tell Phil it was Vetter. He'll believe that."

I could hear Gulley breathing hard. "Jerks, you guys," he said. There was a hiss in his words. "I should string it on Vetter. Man, you're plain nuts. I seen that guy operate before. Who the hell you think edged into that Frisco deal? Who got Morgan in El Paso while he was packing a half million in cash and another half in powder? So a chowderhead hauls him in to cream some local fish and the guy walks away with the town. *Who the hell is that guy?*"

Johnny's laugh was bitter. Sharp. Gulley had said it all and it was like a knife sticking in and being twisted. "I'd like to meet him. Seems like he was a buddy of Jack Cooley. You remember Jack

Cooley, Gulley? You were in on that. Cooley got off with your kick too. Maybe Vetter would like to know about that."

"Shut up."

"Not yet. We got business to talk about."

Gulley seemed out of breath. "Business be damned. I ain't tangling with Vetter."

"Scared?"

"Damn right, and so are you. So's everybody else."

"Okay," Johnny said. "So for one guy or a couple he's trouble. In a big town he can make his play and move fast. Thing is with enough guys in a burg like this he can get nailed."

"And how many guys get nailed with him? He's no dope. Who you trying to smoke?"

"Nuts, who cares who gets nailed as long as it ain't your own bunch? You think Phil Carboy'll go easy if he thinks Vetter jacked a load out from under him? Like you told us, Phil's an up and coming guy. He's growing. He figures on being the top kick around here and let Vetter give him the business and he goes all out to get the guy. So two birds are killed. Vetter and Carboy. Even if Carboy gets him, his load's gone. He's small peanuts again."

"Where does that get me?" Gulley asked.

"I was coming to that. You make yours. The percentage goes up ten. Good?"

Gulley must have been thinking greedy. He started moving again, his feet coming closer. He said, "Big talk. Where's the cabbage?"

"I got it on me," Renzo said.

"You know what Phil was paying for the junk?"

"The word said two million."

"It's gonna cost to take care of the boys on the boat."

"Not so much." Renzo's laugh had no humor in it. "They talk and either Carboy'll finish 'em or Vetter will. They stay shut up for free."

"How much for me?" Gulley asked.

"One hundred thousand for swinging the deal, plus the extra percentage. You think it's worth it?"

"I'll go it," Gulley said.

Nobody spoke for a second, then Gulley said, "I'll phone the boat to pull into the slipside docks. They can unload there. The stuff is packed in beer cans. It won't make a big package so look around for it. They'll probably shove it under one of the benches."

"Who gets the dough?"

"You row out to the last boat mooring. The thing is red with a white stripe around it. Unscrew the top and drop it in."

"Same as the way we used to work it?"

"Right. The boys on the boat won't like going in the harbor and they'll be plenty careful, so don't stick around to lift the dough and the stuff too. That 'breed on the ship got a lockerful of chatter guns he likes to hand out to his crew."

"It'll get played straight."

"I'm just telling you."

Renzo said, "What do you tell Phil?"

"You kidding? I don't say nothing. All I know is I lose contact with the boat. Next the word goes that Vetter is mixed up in it. I don't say nothing." He paused for a few seconds, his breath whistling in his throat, then, "But don't forget something . . . You take Carboy for a sucker and maybe even Vetter. Lay off me. I keep myself covered. Anything happens to me and the next day the cops get a letter naming names. Don't ever forget that."

Renzo must have wanted to say something. He didn't. Instead he rasped, "Go get the cash for this guy."

Somebody said, "Sure, boss," and walked across the room. I heard the lock snick open, then the door.

"This better work," Renzo said. He fiddled with his glass a while. "I'd sure like to know what that punk did with the other stuff."

"He ain't gonna sell it, that's for sure," Johnny told him. "You think maybe Cooley and Vetter were in business together?"

"I'm thinking maybe Cooley was in business with a lot of people. That lousy blonde. When I get her she'll talk plenty. I should've kept my damn eyes open."

"I tried to tell you, boss."

"Shut up," Renzo said. "You just see that she gets found."

I didn't wait to hear any more. I got down in the darkness and headed back to the path. Overhead the sky was starting to lighten as the moon came up, a red circle that did funny things to the night and started the long fingers of shadows drifting out from the scraggly brush. The trees seemed to be ponderous things that reached down with sharp claws, feeling around in the breeze for something to grab. I found the place where I had left Helen, found a couple of pebbles and tossed them back into the brush. I heard her gasp.

She came forward silently, said, "Joe?" in a hushed tone.

"Yeah. *Let's get out of here.*"

"What happened?"

"Later. I'll start back to the cab to make sure it's clear. If you don't hear anything, follow me. Got it?"

". . . Yes." She was hesitant and I couldn't blame her. I got off the gravel path into the sand, took it easy and tried to search out the shadows. I reached the clearing, stood there until I was sure the place was empty then hopped over to the cab.

I had to shake the driver awake and he came out of it stupidly. "Look, keep your lights off going back until you're on the highway, then keep 'em on low. There's enough moon to see by."

"Hey . . . I don't want trouble."

"You'll get it unless you do what I tell you."

"Well . . . okay."

"A dame's coming out in a minute. Soon as she comes start it up and try to keep it quiet."

I didn't have long to wait. I heard her feet on the gravel, walking fast but not hurrying. Then I heard something else that froze me a second. A long, low whistle of appreciation like the kind any blonde'll get from the pool hall boys. I hopped in the cab, held the door open. "Let's go feller," I said.

As soon as the engine ticked over Helen started to run. I yanked her inside as the car started moving and kept down under the windows. She said, "Somebody . . ."

"I heard it."

"I didn't see who it was."

"Maybe it'll pass. Enough cars came out here to park."

Her hand was tight in mine, the nails biting into my palm. She was half-turned on the seat, her dress pulled back over the glossy knees of her nylons, her breasts pressed against my arm. She stayed that way until we reached the highway then little by little eased up until she was sitting back against the cushions. I tapped my forefinger against my lips then pointed to the driver. Helen nodded, smiled, then squeezed my hand again. This time it was different. The squeeze went with the smile.

I paid off the driver at the edge of town. He got more than the meter said, a lot more. It was big enough to keep a man's mouth shut long enough to get him in trouble when he opened it too late. When he was out of sight we walked until we found another cab, told the driver to get us to a small hotel someplace. He gave the usual leer and blonde inspection, muttered the name of a joint and pulled away from the curb.

It was the kind of place where they don't ask questions and don't believe what you write in the register anyway. I signed *Mr. and Mrs. Valiscivitch*, paid the bill in advance for a week and when the clerk read the name I got a screwy look because the name was too screwballed to be anything but real to him. Maybe he figured his clientele was changing. When we got to the room I said, "You park here for a few days."

"Are you going to tell me anything?"

"Should I?"

"You're strange, Joe. A very strange boy."

"Stop calling me a boy."

Her face got all beautiful again and when she smiled there was a real grin in it. She stood there with her hands on her hips and her feet apart like she was going into some part of her routine and I could feel my body starting to burn at the sight of her. She could do things with herself by just breathing and she did them, the smile and her eyes getting deeper all the time. She saw what was happening to me and said, "You're not such a boy after all." She held out her hand and I took it, pulling her in close. "The first time you were a boy. All bloody, dirt ground into your face. When Renzo tore you apart I could have killed him. Nobody should do that to another one, especially a boy. But then there was Johnny and you seemed to grow up. I'll never forget what you did to him."

"He would have hurt you."

"You're even older now. Or should I say matured? I think you finished growing up last night, Joe, last night . . . with me. I saw you grow up, and *I* only hope I haven't hurt you in the process. I never was much good for anybody. That's why I left home, I guess. Everyone I was near seemed to get hurt. Even me."

"You're better than they are, Helen. The breaks were against you, that's all."

"Joe . . . do you know you're the first one who did anything nice for me without wanting . . . something?"

"Helen . . ."

"No, don't say anything. Just take a good look at me. See everything that I am? It shows. I know it shows. I was a lot of things that weren't nice. I'm the kind men want but who won't introduce to their families. I'm a beautiful piece of dirt, Joe." Her eyes were wet. I wanted to brush away the wetness but she wouldn't let my hands go. "You see what I'm telling you? You're young . . . don't brush up against me too close. You'll get dirty and you'll get hurt."

She tried to hide the sob in her throat but couldn't. It came up anyway and I made her let my hands go and when she did I wrapped them around her and held her tight against me. "Helen," I said. "Helen . . ."

She looked at me, grinned weakly. "We must make a funny pair," she said. "Run for it, Joe. Don't stay around any longer."

When I didn't answer right away her eyes looked at mine. I could see her starting to frown a little bit and the curious bewilderment crept across her face. Her mouth was red and moist, poised as if she were going to ask a question, but had forgotten what it was she wanted to say. I let her look and look and look and when she shook her head in a minute gesture of puzzlement I said, "Helen . . . I've rubbed against you. No dirt came off. Maybe it's because I'm no better than you think you are."

"Joe . . ."

"It never happened to me before, kid. When it happens I sure pick a good one for it to happen with." I ran my fingers through her hair. It was nice looking at her like that. Not down, not up, but right into her eyes. "I don't have any family to introduce you to, but if I had I would. Yellow head, don't worry about me getting hurt."

Her eyes were wide now as if she had the answer. She wasn't believing what she saw.

"I love you, Helen. It's not the way a boy would love anybody. It's a peculiar kind of thing I never want to change."

"Joe . . ."

"But it's yours now. You have to decide. Look at me, kid. Then say it."

Those lovely wide eyes grew misty again and the smile came back slowly. It was a warm, radiant smile that told me more than her words. "It can happen to us, can't it? Perhaps it's happened before to somebody else, but it can happen to *us*, can't it? Joe . . . It seems so . . . I can't describe it. There's something . . ."

"Say it out."

"I love you, Joe. Maybe it's better that I should love a little boy. Twenty . . . twenty-one you said? Oh, please, please don't let it be wrong, please . . ." She pressed herself to me with a deep-throated sob and clung there. My fingers rubbed her neck, ran across the width of her shoulders then I pushed her away. I was grinning a little bit now.

"In eighty years it won't make much difference," I said. Then what else I had to say her mouth cut off like a burning torch that tried to seek out the answer and when it was over it didn't seem important enough to mention anyway.

I pushed her away gently, "Now, listen, there isn't much time. I want you to stay here. Don't go out at all and if you want anything, have it sent up. When I come back, I'll knock once. Just once. Keep that door locked and stay out of sight. You got that?"

"Yes, but . . ."

"Don't worry about me. I won't be long. Just remember to make sure it's me and nobody else." I grinned at her. "You aren't getting away from me anymore, blondie. Now it's us for keeps, together."

"All right, Joe."

I nudged her chin with my fist, held her face up and kissed it. That curious look was back and she was trying to think of something again. I grinned, winked at her and got out before she could keep me. I even grinned at the clerk downstairs, but he didn't grin back. He probably thought anybody who'd leave a blonde like that alone was nuts or married and he wasn't used to it.

But it sure felt good. You know how. You feel so good you want to tear something apart or laugh and it may be a little crazy, but that's all part of it. That's how I was feeling until I remembered the other things and knew what I had to do.

I found a gin mill down the street and changed a buck into a handful of coins. Three of them got my party and I said, "Mr. Carboy?"

"That's right. Who is this?"

"Joe Boyle."

Carboy told somebody to be quiet then, "What do you want, kid?"

I got the pitch as soon as I caught the tone in his voice. "Your boys haven't got me, if that's what you're thinking," I told him.

"Yeah?"

"I didn't take a powder. I was trying to get something done. For once figure somebody else got brains too."

"You weren't supposed to do any thinking, kid."

"Well, if I don't, you lose a boatload of merchandise, friend."

"What?" It was a whisper that barely came through.

"Renzo's ticking you off. He and Gulley are pulling a switch. Your stuff gets delivered to him."

"Knock it off, kid. What do you know?"

"*I know the boat's coming into the slipside docks with the load and Renzo will be picking it up. You hold the bag, brother.*"

"Joe," he said. "You know what happens if you're queering me."

"I know."

"Where'd you pick it up?"

"Let's say I sat in on Renzo's conference with Gulley."

"Okay, boy. I'll stick with it. You better be right. Hold on." He

turned away from the phone and shouted muffled orders at someone. There were more muffled shouts in the background then he
got back on the line again. "Just one thing more. What about
Vetter?"

"Not yet, Mr. Carboy. Not yet."

"You get some of my boys to stick with you. I don't like my
plans interfered with. Where are you?"

"In a place called Patty's. A gin mill."

"I know it. Stay there ten minutes. I'll shoot a couple guys down.
You got that handkerchief yet?"

"Still in my pocket."

"Good. Keep your eyes open."

He slapped the phone back and left me there. I checked the
clock on the wall, went to the bar and had an orange, then when
the ten minutes were up, drifted outside. I was half a block away
when a car door slapped shut and I heard the steady tread of footsteps across the street.

Now it was set. Now the big blow. The show ought to be good
when it happened and I wanted to see it happen. There was a cab
stand at the end of the block and I hopped in the one on the end.
He nodded when I gave him the address, looked at the bill in my
hand and took off. In back of us the lights of another car prowled
through the night, but always looking our way.

You smelt the place before you reached it. On one side the
darkened store fronts were like sleeping drunks, little ones and big
ones in a jumbled mass, but all smelling the same. There was the
fish smell and on top that of wood the salt spray had started to rot.
The bay stretched out endlessly on the other side, a few boats here
and there marked with running lights, the rest just vague silhouettes
against the sky. In the distance the moon turned the train trestle
into a giant spidery hand. The white sign, "SLIPSIDE," pointed on
the dock area and I told the driver to turn up the street and keep
right on going. He picked the bill from my fingers, slowed around
the turn, then picked it up when I hopped out. In a few seconds
the other car came by, made the turn and lost itself further up the
street. When it was gone I stepped out of the shadows and crossed

over. Maybe thirty seconds later the car came tearing back up the street again and I ducked back into a doorway. Phil Carboy was going to be pretty sore at those boys of his.

I stood still when I reached the corner again and listened. It was too quiet. You could hear the things that scurried around on the dock. The things were even bold enough to cross the street and one was dragging something in its mouth. Another, a curious elongated creature whose fur shone silvery in the street light pounced on it and the two fought and squealed until the raider had what it went after.

It happens even with rats, I thought. Who learns from who? Do the rats watch the men or the men watch the rats?

Another one of them ran into the gutter. It was going to cross, then stood on its hind legs in an attitude of attention, its face pointing toward the dock. I never saw it move, but it disappeared, then I heard what it had heard, carefully muffled sounds, then a curse.

It came too quick to say it had a starting point. First the quick stab of orange and the sharp thunder of the gun, then the others following and the screams of the slugs whining off across the water. They didn't try to be quiet now. There was a startled shout, a hoarse scream and the yell of somebody who was hit.

Somebody put out the street light and the darkness was a blanket that slid in. I could hear them running across the street, then the moon reached down before sliding behind a cloud again and I saw them, a dozen or so closing in on the dock from both sides.

Out on the water an engine barked into life, was gunned and a boat wheeled away down the channel. The car that had been cruising around suddenly dimmed its lights, turned off the street and stopped. I was right there with no place to duck into and feet started running my way. I couldn't go back and there was trouble ahead. The only other thing was to make a break for it across the street and hope nobody spotted me.

I'd pushed it too far. I was being a dope again. One of them yelled and started behind me at a long angle. I didn't stop at the rail. I went over the side into the water, kicked away from the concrete abutment and hoped I'd come up under the pier. I almost made it. I was a foot away from the piling but it wasn't enough. When I looked back the guy was there at the rail with a gun bucking in his hand and the bullets were walking up the water toward me. He must have still had half a load left and only a foot to go when another shot blasted out over my head and the guy grabbed at his face with a scream and fell back to the street. The guy up above said, "Get the son . . ." and the last word had a whistle to it as something caught him in the belly. He was all doubled up when he hit the water and his tombstone was a tiny trail of bubbles that broke the surface a few seconds before stopping altogether.

I pulled myself further under the dock. From where I was I could hear the voices and now they had quieted down. Out on the street somebody yelled to stand back and before the words were out cut loose with a sharp blast of an automatic rifle. It gave the bunch on the street time to close in and those on the dock scurried back farther.

Right over my head the planks were warped away and when a voice said, "I found it," I could pick Johnny's voice out of the racket.

"Where?"

"Back ten feet on the pole. Better hop to it before they get wise and cut the wires."

Johnny moved fast and I tried to move with him. By the time I reached the next piling I could hear him dialing the phone. He talked fast, but kept his voice down. *"Renzo? Yeah, they bottled us. Somebody pulled the cork out of the deal. Yeah. The hell with that, you call the cops. Let them break it up.* Sure, sure. Move it. We can make it to one of the boats. They got Tommy and Balco. Two of the others were hit but not bad. Yeah, it's Carboy all right. He ain't here himself, but they're his guys. Yeah, I got the stuff. Shake it."

His feet pounded on the planking overhead and I could hear his voice without making out what he said. The next minute the blasting picked up and I knew they were trying for a standoff. Whatever they had for cover up there must have been pretty good because the guys on the street were swearing at it and yelling for somebody to spread out and get them from the sides. The only trouble was that there was no protection on the street and if the moon came out again they'd be nice easy targets.

It was the moan of the siren that stopped it. First one, then another joined in and I heard them running for their cars. A man screamed and yelled for them to take it easy. Something rattled over my head and when I looked up, a frame of black marred the flooring. Something was rolled to the edge, then crammed over. Another followed it. Men. Dead. They bobbed for a minute, then sank slowly. Somebody said, "Damn, I hate to do that. He was okay."

"Shut up and get out there." It was Johnny.

The voice said, "Yeah, come on, you," then they went over the side. I stayed back of the piling and watched them swim for the boats. The sirens were coming closer now. One had a lead as if it knew the way and the others didn't. Johnny didn't come down. I grinned to myself, reached for a cross-brace and swung up on it. From there it was easy to make the trapdoor.

And there was Johnny by the end of the pier squatting down behind a packing case that seemed to be built around some machinery, squatting with that tenseness of a guy about to run. He had a box in his arms about two feet square and when I said, "Hello, chum," he stood up so fast he dropped it, but he would have had to do that anyway the way he was reaching for his rod.

He almost had it when I belted him across the nose. I got him with another sharp hook and heard the breath hiss out of him. It spun him around until the packing case caught him and when I was coming in he let me have it with his foot. I skidded sidewise, took the toe of his shoe on my hip then had his arm in a lock that brought a scream tearing out of his throat. He was going for the rod again when the arm broke and in a crazy surge of pain he jerked loose, tripped me, and got the gun out with his good hand. I rolled into his feet as it coughed over my head, grabbed his wrist and turned it into his neck and he pulled the trigger for the last time in trying to get his hand loose. There was just one last, brief, horrified expression in his eyes as he looked at me, then they filmed over to start rotting away.

The siren that was screaming turned the corner with its wail dying out. Brakes squealed against the pavement and the car stopped, the red light on its hood snapping shut. The door opened opposite the driver, stayed open as if the one inside was listening. Then a guy crawled out, a little guy with a big gun in his hand. He said, "Johnny?"

Then he ran. Silently, like an Indian, I almost had Johnny's gun back in my hand when he reached me.

"You," Sergeant Gonzales said. He saw the package there, twisted his mouth into a smile and let me see the hole in the end of his gun. I still made one last try for Johnny's gun when the blast went off. I half expected the sickening smash of a bullet, but none came. When I looked up, Gonzales was still there. Something on the packing crate had hooked his coat and held him up.

I couldn't see into the shadows where the voice came from. But it was a familiar voice. It said, "You ought to be more careful, son."

The gun the voice held slithered back into the leather.

"Thirty seconds. No more. You might even do the job right and beat it in his car. He was in on it. The cop . . . he was working with Cooley. Then Cooley ran out on him too so he played along with Renzo. Better move, kid."

The other sirens were almost there. I said, "Watch yourself. And thanks."

"Sure, kid. I hate crooked cops worse than crooks."

I ran for the car, hopped in and pulled the door shut. Behind me something splashed and a two foot square package floated on the water a moment, then turned over and sunk out of sight. I left the lights off, turned down the first street I reached and headed across town. At the main drag I pulled up, wiped the wheel and gearshift free of prints and got out.

There was dawn showing in the sky. It would be another hour yet before it was morning. I walked until I reached the junkyard in back of Gordon's office, found the wreck of a car that still had cushions in it, climbed in and went to sleep.

Morning, afternoon, then evening. I slept through the first two. The last one was harder. I sat there thinking things, keeping out of sight. My clothes were dry now, but the cigarettes had a lousy taste. There was a twinge in my stomach and my mouth was dry. I gave it another hour before I moved, then went back over the fence and down the street to a dirty little diner that everybody avoided except the boys who rode the rods into town. I knocked off a plate of bacon and eggs, paid for it with some of the change I had left, picked up a pack of butts and started out. That was when I saw the paper on the table.

It made quite a story. GANG WAR FLARES ON WATERFRONT, and under it a subhead that said, *Cop, Hoodlum, Slain in Gun Duel.* It was a masterpiece of writing that said nothing, intimated much and brought out the fact that though the place was bullet sprayed and though evidence of other wounded was found, there were no bodies to account for what had happened. One sentence mentioned the fact that Johnny was connected with Mark Renzo. The press hinted at police inefficiency. There was the usual statement from Captain Gerot.

The thing stunk. Even the press was afraid to talk out. How long would it take to find out Gonzales didn't die by a shot from Johnny's gun? Not very long. And Johnny . . . a cute little twist like that would usually get a big splash. There wasn't even any curiosity shown about Johnny. I let out a short laugh and threw the paper back again.

They were like rats, all right. They just went the rats one better. They dragged their bodies away with them so there wouldn't be any ties. Nice. Now find the doctor who patched them up. Find what they were after on the docks. Maybe they figured to heist ten tons or so of machinery. Yeah, try and find it.

No, they wouldn't say anything. Maybe they'd have to hit it a little harder when the big one broke. When the boys came in who paid a few million out for a package that was never delivered. Maybe when the big trouble came and the blood ran again somebody would crawl back out of his hole long enough to put it into print. Or it could be that Bucky Edwards was right. Life was too precious a thing to sell cheaply.

I thought about it, remembering everything he had told me.

When I had it all back in my head again I turned toward the place where I knew Bucky would be and walked faster. Halfway there it started to drizzle. I turned up the collar of my coat.

It was a soft rain, one of those things that comes down at the end of a summer, making its own music like a dull concert you think will have no end. It drove people indoors until even the cabs didn't bother to cruise. The cars that went by had their windows steamed into opaque squares, the drivers peering through the hand-wiped panes.

I jumped a streetcar when one came along, took it downtown and got off again. And I was back with the people I knew and the places made for them. Bucky was on his usual stool and I wondered if it was a little too late. He had that all gone look in his face and his fingers were caressing a tall amber-colored glass.

When I sat down next to him his eyes moved, giving me a glassy stare. It was like the cars on the street, they were cloudy with mist, then a hand seemed to reach out and rub them clear. They weren't glass anymore. I could see the white in his fingers as they tightened around the glass and he said, "You did it fancy, kiddo. Get out of here."

"Scared, Bucky?"

His eyes went past me to the door, then came back again. "Yes. You said it right. I'm scared. Get out. I don't want to be around when they find you."

"For a guy who's crocked most of the time you seem to know a lot about what happens."

"I think a lot. I figure it out. There's only one answer."

"If you know it why don't you write it?"

"Living's not much fun anymore, but what there is of it, I like. Beat it, kid."

This time I grinned at him, a big fat grin and told the bartender to get me an orange. Large. He shoved it down, picked up my dime and went back to his paper.

I said, "Let's hear about it, Bucky." I could feel my mouth changing the grin into something else. "I don't like to be a target either. I want to know the score."

Bucky's tongue made a pass over dry lips. He seemed to look back inside himself to something he had been a long time ago, dredging the memory up. He found himself in the mirror behind the back bar, twisted his mouth at it and looked back at me again.

"This used to be a good town."

"Not that," I said.

He didn't hear me. "Now anybody who knows anything is scared to death. To death, I said. Let them talk and that's what they get. Death. From one side or another. It was bad enough when Renzo took over, worse when Carboy came in. It's not over yet." His shoulders made an involuntary shudder and he pulled the drink halfway down the glass. "Friend Gulley had an accident this afternoon. He was leaving town and was run off the road. He's dead."

I whistled softly. "Who?"

For the first time a trace of humor put lines at the corner of his lips. "It wasn't Renzo. It wasn't Phil Carboy. They were all accounted for. The tire marks are very interesting. It looks like the guy wanted to stop friend Gulley for a chat but Gulley hit the ditch. You could call it a real accident without lying." He finished the rest of the drink, put it down and said, "The boys are scared stiff." He looked at me closely then. "Vetter," he said.

"He's getting close."

Bucky didn't hear me. "I'm getting to like the guy. He does what should have been done a long time ago. By himself he does it. They know who killed Gonzales. One of Phil's boys saw it happen before he ran for it. There's a guy with a broken neck who was found out on the highway and they know who did that and how." He swirled the ice around in his glass. "He's taking good care of you, kiddo."

I didn't say anything.

"There's just one little catch to it, Joe. One little catch."

"What?"

"That boy who saw Gonzales get it saw something else. He saw you and Johnny tangle over the package. He figures you got it. Everybody knows and now they want you. It can't happen twice. Renzo wants it and Carboy wants it. You know who gets it?"

I shook my head.

"You get it. In the belly or in the head. Even the cops want you that bad. Captain Gerot even thinks that way. You better get out of here, Joe. Keep away from me. There's something about you that spooks me. Something in the way your eyes look. Something about your face. I wish I could see into that mind of yours. I always thought I knew people, but I don't know you at all. You spook me. You should see your own eyes. I've seen eyes like yours before but I can't remember where. They're familiar as hell, but I can't place them. They don't belong in a kid's face at all. Go on, Joe, beat it. The boys are all over town. They got orders to do just one thing. Find you. When they do I don't want you sitting next to me."

"When do you write the big story, Bucky?"

"You tell me."

My teeth were tight together with the smile moving around them. "It won't be long."

"No . . . maybe just a short obit. They're tracking you fast. That hotel was no cover at all. Do it smarter the next time."

The ice seemed to pour down all over me. It went down over my shoulders, ate through my skin until it was in the blood that pounded through my body. I grabbed his arm and damn near jerked him off the stool. "What about the hotel?"

All he did was shrug. Bucky was gone again.

I cursed silently, ran back into the rain again and down the block to the cab stand.

The clerk said he was sorry, he didn't know anything about room 612. The night man had taken a week off. I grabbed the key from his hand and pounded up the stairs. All I could feel was that mad frenzy of hate swelling in me and I kept saying her name over and over to myself. I threw the door open, stood there breathing fast while I called myself a dozen different kinds of fool.

She wasn't there. It was empty.

A note lay beside the telephone. All it said was, *"Bring it where you brought the first one."*

I laid the note down again and stared out the window into the night. There was sweat on the backs of my hands. Bucky had called it. They thought I had the package and they were forcing a trade. Then Mark Renzo would kill us both. He thought.

I brought the laugh up from way down in my throat. It didn't sound much like me at all. I looked at my hands and watched them open and close into fists. There were callouses across the palms, huge things that came from Gordon's junk carts. A year and a half of it, I thought. Eighteen months of pushing loads of scrap iron for pennies then all of a sudden I was part of a multi-million dollar operation. The critical part of it. I was the enigma. Me, Joey the junk pusher. Not even Vetter now. Just me. Vetter would come after me.

For a while I stared at the street. That tiny piece of luck that chased me caught up again and I saw the car stop and the men jump out. One was Phil Carboy's right hand man. In a way it was funny. Renzo was always a step ahead of the challenger, but Phil was coming up fast. He'd caught on too and was ready to pull the same deal. He didn't know it had already been pulled.

But that was all right too.

I reached for the pen on the desk, lifted a sheet of cheap stationery out of the drawer and scrawled across it, "*Joe . . . be back in a few hours. Stay here with the package until I return. I'll have the car ready.*" I signed it, *Helen*, put it by the phone and picked up the receiver.

The clerk said, "Yes?"

I said, "In a minute some men will come in looking for the blonde and me. You think the room is empty, but let them come up. You haven't seen me at all yet. Understand?"

"Say . . ."

"Mister, if you want to walk out of here tonight you'll do what you're told. You're liable to get killed otherwise. Understand that?"

I hung up and let him think about it. I'd seen his type before and I wasn't worried a bit. I got out, locked the door and started up the stairs to the roof. It didn't take me longer than five minutes to reach the street and when I turned the corner the light was back on in the room I had just left. I gave it another five minutes and the tall guy came out again, spoke to the driver of the car and the fellow reached in and shut off the engine. It had worked. The light in the window went out. The vigil had started and the boys could afford to be pretty patient. They thought.

The rain was a steady thing coming down just a little bit harder than it had. It was cool and fresh with the slightest nip in it. I walked, putting the pieces together in my head. I did it slowly, replacing the fury that had been there, deliberately wiping out the gnawing worry that tried to grow. I reached the deserted square of the park and picked out a bench under a tree and sat there letting the rain drip down around me. When I looked at my hands they were shaking.

I was thinking wrong. I should have been thinking about fat, ugly faces; rat faces with deep voices and whining faces. I should have been thinking about the splashes of orange a rod makes when it cuts a man down and blood on the street. Cops who want the big payoff. Thinking of a town where even the press was cut off and the big boys came from the city to pick up the stuff that started more people on the long slide down to the grave.

Those were the things I should have thought of.

All I could think of was Helen. Lovely Helen who had been all things to many men and hated it. Beautiful Helen who didn't want me to be hurt, who was afraid the dirt would rub off. Helen who found love for the first time . . . and me. The beauty in her face when I told her. Beauty that waited to be kicked and wasn't because I loved her too much and didn't give a damn what she had been. She was different now. Maybe I was too. She didn't know it, but she was the good one, not me. She was the child that needed taking care of, not me. Now she was hours away from being dead and so was I. The thing they wanted, the thing that could buy her life I saw floating in the water beside the dock. It was like having a yacht with no fuel aboard.

The police? No, not them. They'd want me. They'd think it was a phony. That wasn't the answer. Not Phil Carboy either. He was after the same thing Renzo was.

I started to laugh, it was so damn, pathetically funny. I had it all in my hand and couldn't turn it around. What the devil does a guy have to do? How many times does he have to kill himself? The answer. It was right there but wouldn't come through. It wasn't the same answer I had started with, but a better one.

So I said it all out to myself. Out loud, with words. I started with the night I brought the note to Renzo, the one that promised him Vetter would cut his guts out. I even described their faces to myself when Vetter's name was mentioned. One name, that's all it took, and you could see the fear creep in because Vetter was deadly and unknown. He was the shadow that stood there, the one they couldn't trust, the one they all knew in the society that stayed outside the law. He was a high-priced killer who never missed and always got more than he was paid to take. So deadly they'd give anything to keep him out of town, even to doing the job he was there for. So deadly they could throw me or anybody else to the wolves just to finger him. So damn deadly they put an army on him, yet so deadly he could move behind their lines without any trouble at all.

Vetter.

I cursed the name. I said Helen's. Vetter wasn't important anymore.

The rain lashed at my face as I looked up into it. The things I knew fell into place and I knew what the answer was. I remembered something I didn't know was there, a sign on the docks by the fishing fleet that said "SEASON LOCKERS."

Jack Cooley had been smart by playing it simple. He even left me the ransom.

I got up, walked to the corner and waited until a cab came by. I flagged him down, got it and gave the address of the white house where Cooley had lived.

The same guy answered the door. He took the bill from my hand and nodded me in. I said, "Did he leave any old clothes behind at all?"

"Some fishing stuff downstairs. It's behind the coal bin. You want that?"

"I want that," I said.

He got up and I followed him. He switched on the cellar light, took me downstairs and across the littered pile of refuse a cellar can collect. When he pointed to the old set of dungarees on the nail in the wall, I went over and felt through the pockets. The key was in the jacket. I said thanks and went back upstairs. The taxi was still waiting. He flipped his butt away when I got in, threw the heap into gear and headed toward the smell of the water.

I had to climb the fence to get on the pier. There wasn't much to it. The lockers were tall steel affairs, each with somebody's name scrawled across it in chalk. The number that matched the key didn't say Cooley, but it didn't matter anymore either. I opened it up and saw the cardboard box that had been jammed in there so hard it had snapped one of the rods in the corner. Just to be sure I pulled one end open, tore through the other box inside and tasted the white powder.

Heroin.

They never expected Cooley to do it so simply. He had found a way to grab their load and stashed it without any trouble at all. Friend Jack was good at that sort of thing. Real clever. Walked away with a couple million bucks' worth of stuff and never lived to convert it. He wasn't quite smart enough. Not quite as smart as Carboy, Gerot, Renzo . . . or even a kid who pushed a junk cart. Smart enough to grab the load, but not smart enough to keep on living.

I closed the locker and went back over the fence with the box in my arms. The cabbie found me a phone in a gin mill and waited while I made my calls. The first one got me Gerot's home number. The second got me Captain Gerot himself, a very annoyed Gerot who had been pulled out of bed.

I said, "Captain, this is Joe Boyle and if you trace this call you're going to scramble the whole deal."

So the captain played it smart. "Go ahead," was all he told me.

"You can have them all. Every one on a platter. You know what I'm talking about?"

"I know."

"You want it that way?"

"I want you, Joe. Just you."

"I'll give you that chance. First you have to take the rest. There won't be any doubt this time. They won't be big enough to crawl out of it. There isn't enough money to buy them out either. You'll have every one of them cold."

"I'll still want you."

I laughed at him. "I said you'll get your chance. All you have to do is play it my way. You don't mind that, do you?"

"Not if I get you, Joe."

I laughed again. "You'll need a dozen men. Ones you can trust. Ones who can shoot straight and aren't afraid of what might come later."

"I can get them."

"Have them stand by. It won't be long. I'll call again."

I hung up, stared at the phone a second, then went back outside. The cabbie was working his way through another cigarette. I said, "I need a fast car. Where do I get one?"

"How fast for how much?"

"The limit."

"I got a friend with a souped-up Ford. Nothing can touch it. It'll cost you."

I showed him the thing in my hand. His eyes narrowed at the edges. "Maybe it won't cost you at that," he said. He looked at me the same way Helen had, then waved me in.

We made a stop at an out of the way rooming house. I kicked my clothes off and climbed into some fresh stuff, then tossed everything else into a bag and woke up the landlady of the place. I told her to mail it to the post office address on the label and gave her a few bucks for her trouble. She promised me she would, took the bag into her room and I went outside. I felt better in the suit. I patted it down to make sure everything was set. The cabbie shot me a half smile when he saw me and held the door open.

I got the Ford and it didn't cost me a thing unless I piled it up. The guy grinned when he handed me the keys and made a familiar gesture with his hand. I grinned back. I gave the cabbie his fare with a little extra and got in the Ford with my box. It was almost over.

A mile outside Mark Renzo's roadhouse I stopped at a gas station and while the attendant filled me up all around, I used his phone. I got Renzo on the first try and said, "This is Joe, fat boy."

His breath in the phone came louder than the words. "Where are you?"

"Never mind. I'll be there. Let me talk to Helen."

I heard him call and then there was Helen. Her voice was tired and all the hope was gone from it. She said, "Joe . . ."

It was enough. I'd know her voice any time. I said, "Honey . . . don't worry about it. You'll be okay."

She started to say something else, but Renzo must have grabbed the phone from her. "You got the stuff, kid?"

"I got it."

"Let's go, sonny. You know what happens if you don't."

"I know," I said. "You better do something first. I want to see the place of yours empty in a hurry. I don't feel like being stopped going in. Tell them to drive out and keep on going. I'll deliver the stuff to you, that's all."

"Sure, kid, sure. You'll see the boys leave."

"I'll be watching," I said.

Joke.

I made the other call then. It went back to my hotel room and I did it smart. I heard the phone ring when the clerk hit the room number, heard the phone get picked up and said as though I were in one big hurry, "*Look, Helen, I'm hopping the stuff out to Renzo's. He's waiting for it. As soon as he pays off we'll blow. See you later.*"

When I slapped the phone back I laughed again then got Gerot again. This time he was waiting. I said, "Captain . . . they'll all be at Renzo's place. There'll be plenty of fun for everybody. You'll even find a fortune in heroin."

"You're the one I want, Joe."

"Not even Vetter?"

"No, he comes next. First you." This time he hung up on me. So I laughed again as the joke got funnier and made my last call.

The next voice was the one I had come to know so well. I said, "Joe Boyle. I'm heading for Renzo's. Cooley had cached the stuff in a locker and I need it for a trade. I have a light blue Ford and need a quick way out. The trouble is going to start."

"There's a side entrance," the voice said. "They don't use it anymore. If you're careful you can come in that way and if you stay careful you can make it to the big town without getting spotted."

"I heard about Gulley," I said.

"Saddening. He was a wealthy man."

"You'll be here?"

"Give me five minutes," the voice told me. "I'll be at the side entrance. I'll make sure nobody stops you."

"There'll be police. They won't be asking questions."

"Let me take care of that."

"Everybody wants Vetter," I said.

"Naturally. Do you think they'll find him?"

I grinned. "I doubt it."

The other voice chuckled as it hung up.

I saw them come out from where I stood in the bushes. They got into cars, eight of them and drove down the drive slowly. They turned back toward town and I waited until their lights were a mile away before I went up the steps of the club.

At that hour it was an eerie place, a dimly lit ghost house showing the signs of people that had been there earlier. I stood inside the door, stopped and listened. Up the stairs I heard a cough. It was like that first night, only this time I didn't have somebody dragging me. I could remember the stairs and the long, narrow corridor at the top, and the oak-panelled door at the end of it. Even the thin line of light that came from under the door. I snuggled the box under my arm and walked in.

Renzo was smiling from his chair behind the desk. It was a funny kind of smile like I was a sucker. Helen was huddled on the floor in a corner holding a hand to the side of her cheek. Her dress had been shredded down to the waist, and tendrils of tattered cloth clung to the high swell of her breasts, followed the smooth flow of her body. Her other hand tried desperately to hide her nakedness from Renzo's leer. She was trembling, and the terror in her eyes was an ungodly thing.

And Renzo grinned. Big, fat Renzo. Renzo the louse whose eyes were now on the package under my arm, with the grin turning to a slow sneer. Renzo the killer who found a lot of ways to get away with murder and was looking at me as if he were seeing me for the first time.

He said, "You got your going away clothes on, kid."

"Yeah."

"You won't be needing them." He made the sneer bigger, but I wasn't watching him. I was watching Helen, seeing the incredible thing that crossed her face.

"I'm different, Helen?"

She couldn't speak. All she could do was nod.

"I told you I wasn't such a kid. I just look that way. Twenty . . . twenty-one you thought?" I laughed and it had a funny sound. Renzo stopped sneering. "I got ten years on that, honey. Don't worry about being in love with a kid."

Renzo started to get up then. Slowly, a ponderous monster with hands spread apart to kill something. "You two did it. You damn near ruined me. You know what happens now?" He licked his lips and the muscles rolled under his shirt.

My face was changing shape and I nodded. Renzo never noticed. Helen saw it. I said, "A lot happens now, fat boy." I dropped the package on the floor and kicked it to one side. Renzo moved out from behind the desk. He wasn't thinking anymore. He was just seeing me and thinking of his empire that had almost toppled. The package could set it up again. I said, "Listen, you can hear it happen."

Then he stopped to think. He turned his head and you could hear the whine of engines and the shots coming clear across the night through the rain. There was a frenzy about the way it was happening, the frenzy and madness that goes into a *banzai* charge and above it the moan of sirens that seemed to go ignored.

It was happening to Renzo too, the kill hate in his eyes, the saliva that made wet paths from the corners of his tight mouth. His whole body heaved and when his head turned back to me again, the eyes were bright with the lust of murder.

I said, "Come here, Helen," and she came to me. I took the envelope out of my pocket and gave it to her, and then I took off my jacket, slipping it over her shoulders. She pulled it closed over her breasts, the terror in her eyes fading. "Go out the side . . . the old road. The car is waiting there. You'll see a tall guy beside it, a big guy all around and if you happen to see his face, forget it. Tell him this. Tell him I said to give the report to the Chief. Tell him to wait until I contact him for the next assignment then start the car and wait for me. I'll be in a hurry. You got that?"

"Yes, Joe." The disbelief was still in her eyes.

Renzo moved slowly, the purpose plain in his face. His hands were out and he circled between me and the door. There was something fiendish about his face.

The sirens and the shooting were getting closer.

He said, "Vetter won't get you out of this, kid. I'm going to kill you and it'll be the best thing I ever did. Then the dame. The blonde. Weber told me he saw a blonde at Gulley's and I knew who did this to me. The both of you are going to die, kid. There ain't no Vetter here now."

I let him have a long look at me. I grinned. I said, "Remember what that note said? It said Vetter was going to spill your guts all over the floor. You remember that, Renzo?"

"Yeah," he said. "Now tell me you got a gun, kid. Tell me that and I'll tell you you're a liar. I can smell a rod a mile away. You had it, kid. There ain't no Vetter here now."

Maybe it was the way I let myself go. I could feel the loosening in my shoulders and my face was a picture only Renzo could see. "You killed too many men, Renzo, one too many. The ones you peddle the dope to die slowly, the ones who take it away die quick. It's still a lot of men. You killed them, Renzo, a whole lot of them. You know what happens to killers in this country? It's a funny law, but it works. Sometimes to get what it wants, it works in peculiar fashion. But it works.

"Remember the note. Remember hard what it said." I grinned and what was in it stopped him five feet away. What was in it made him frown, then his eyes opened wide, almost too wide and he had the expression Helen had the first time.

I said to her, "Don't wait, Helen," and heard the door open and close. Renzo was backing away, his feet shuffling on the carpet.

Two minutes at the most.

"I'm Vetter," I said. "Didn't you know? Couldn't you tell? Me . . . Vetter. The one everybody wonders about, even the cops. Vetter the puzzle. Vetter the one who's there but isn't there." The air was cold against my teeth. "Remember the note, Renzo. No, you can't smell a gun because I haven't got one. But look at my hand. You're big and strong . . . you're a killer, but look at my hand and find out who the specialist really is and you'll know that there was no lie in that note."

Renzo tried to scream, stumbled and fell. I laughed again and moved in on him. He was reaching for something in the desk drawer, knowing all the time that he wasn't going to make it and the knife in my hand made a nasty little snick and he screamed again so high it almost blended with the sirens.

Maybe one minute left, but it would be enough and the puzzle would always be there and the name when mentioned would start another ball rolling and the country would be a little cleaner and the report when the Chief read it would mean one more done with . . . done differently, but done.